Praise for *Impaired Judgment*

"MOVE OVER, JOHN GRISHAM AND SCOTT TUROW, and make room for David Compton among the master weavers of legal suspense/political-intrigue tapestries.... Compton spins a web of mob brutality, extortion, malignant loyalties, judicial integrity, and political ambition that ensnares the First Family in its sticky mesh.... [He] pulls the reader to frightening heights of suspense and plunges them into the lowest of troughs, where the righteously uncompromisable are forced to compromise and the question of just who the good guys are hangs in the balance." —*The Tennessean*

"CONSPIRACY IN HIGH PLACES.... As Christie made her formula work brilliantly [in *And Then There Were None*], so too does Compton. This is the ultimate end-of-summer book."—*The Boston Globe*

"A TENSE PLOT whose twists and turns include corrupt courts, a mob ring, blackmail, and a political scandal or two ... fast-paced suspense and political intrigue." —*Publishers Weekly*

continued ...

IMPAIRED JUDGMENT

David Compton

A SIGNET BOOK

SIGNET
Published by New American Library, a division of
Penguin Putnam Inc., 375 Hudson Street,
New York, New York 10014, U.S.A.
Penguin Books Ltd, 80 Strand,
London WC2R ORL, England
Penguin Books Australia Ltd, Ringwood,
Victoria, Australia
Penguin Books Canada Ltd, 10 Alcorn Avenue,
Toronto, Ontario, Canada M4V 3B2
Penguin Books (N.Z.) Ltd, 182–190 Wairau Road,
Auckland 10, New Zealand

Penguin Books Ltd, Registered Offices:
Harmondsworth, Middlesex, England

Published by Signet, an imprint of New American Library,
a division of Penguin Putnam Inc. Previously published in a Dutton hardcover
edition.

First Signet Printing, December 2001
10 9 8 7 6 5 4 3 2 1

PUBLISHER'S NOTE
This is a work of fiction. Names, characters, places, and incidents either are the
products of the author's imagination or are used fictitiously, and any
resemblance to actual persons, living or dead, business establishments, events, or
locales is entirely coincidental.

For Mary Katherine

ACKNOWLEDGMENTS

Many people generously contributed background information.

U.S. District Court Chief Judge Julia Gibbons and U.S. Magistrate Judges Dan Breen and Diane Vescovo all provided important insights from the judicial point of view. U.S. Clerk of Court Norman Meyer provided background on the court system, as did Linda Booker and Mark Dodson. I am particularly grateful to Sean Saxon for his patience with my many questions and his eagerness to help.

Federal prosecutors Joe Murphy and Delk Kennedy provided much stimulating advice, as did John Bobo. Ed Trosper and John Clark helped me better understand the role of the U.S. marshals. I am grateful to John Ryder for opening many doors and to Greg Pavlovitz for his knowledge of the law. Jack Corn provided a tutorial in professional photography. Deserving special praise for his many hours of reviewing the manuscript is Ken Melson, a federal prosecutor in Alexandria, Virginia.

Thanks also to Joe Pittman and Carolyn Nichols for their editorial advice, and to Sloan Harris, who makes it all possible.

Prologue

It is prematurely dark on a blustery, bone-chilling Friday evening in late October. The thunderstorms that have swept the hilly wooded landscape have only in the past half hour ceased, but the skies are still filled with heavy low clouds, tinted orange with the lights of a nearby city.

Municipal street lamps do not extend this far out along the narrow, winding road. The only evidence of human life is the glint of distant windows occasionally viewed through the forest.

The twin beams of a single, slow-moving vehicle shine on the tree trunks as a car negotiates a tricky hairpin turn. A late-model Taurus pulls to the side of the road. The headlamps are left on, directed through dense brush.

With the car engine left running and windshield wipers still engaged, a man emerges swiftly and stands silhouetted in front of the car. He holds a flashlight in one hand, a rolled-up umbrella in the other. He looks up and down the length of the road, searching for a landmark. He eventually finds what he is seeking, a rotting fence post.

He quickly returns to the car, cuts the engine, and turns off all the lights. At the fence post he heads up an embankment away from the road. He emerges from the heavy growth into a clearing. He sweeps the area on his left with his flashlight and sees only a bit of overgrazed pasture. He swings the beam to the other side of the field, where he finds nothing. Just an ancient hickory tree, its open limbs backlit by the roiling clouds. He is about to turn and leave when his light strikes a patch of sodden ground.

He runs in that direction into a slight depression. His light falls upon a bright strip of silver in the mud. He takes two more steps forward, but stumbles over something in the dark and drops his flashlight. He rights himself, then sees that the beam from his flashlight illuminates the cover of a book: *First-Year Algebra*. He discovers more books scattered about. An empty potato chip bag and a sandwich spill out of a small brown sack, remnants of a half-eaten lunch.

He picks up the flashlight and immediately recognizes the bright strip of reflective material on a backpack. He splashes through water collected in the thick exposed roots of the great tree. And it is there that he catches sight of a portion of a bare white limb—scraped raw and muddy, but unmistakably human.

A boy is lying on his side in almost a half foot of water at the base of the tree. He wears dark trousers and a gray pullover sweater.

The man kneels in the cold water, takes a glove off, and searches for a pulse at the side of the boy's neck. He feels nothing.

The boy lies motionless, although steam rises off his still warm body. The temperature of the child's skin is only slightly cooler than his own. The man realizes from the awkward position of the boy's limbs that his legs are broken.

He studies the boy's face and guesses he is about fourteen years old. He notices something odd on the chin: a curious sheen of metallic gold.

A thought flashes through the man's mind: is it too late to call for help?

Suddenly the boy lurches to the side, startling the man. The child begins vomiting, coughing, wheezing, trying to suck life back in through his lungs. The boy's lips quiver. In the weakest of voices he says, "Help me."

The man says nothing for a moment, his mind racing. He squints through the dark. There is no one anywhere close by to help.

"What happened?" the man says.

Through labored breathing the boy answers. "A car . . . hit me."

The man gently pats the boy's head. "You're going to be all right. Does your neck or back hurt?"

He slowly shakes his head from side to side. "My legs . . ."

"Let's get you turned back over on your side in the recovery position. You remember anything about the car?" the man asks as he carefully helps the boy roll back onto his side in the water.

"I saw it," he pants. "I saw them in the car. I saw her face." He groans with the pain of the grating broken bones in his legs as he turns.

"Okay, you can tell the police all about it later. I've got to go for help."

"Hurry," the boy says, shivering. "It hurts . . . and I'm so cold."

"Just close your eyes. Everything will be fine."

The man stands upright. He gazes down at the boy and clenches his eyes shut.

Then, as he knows he has to do, the man places his foot on the boy's head and pushes it down hard into the water.

The boy begins thrashing, flailing his arms. Trying to upright himself with his useless, broken legs. But the more he struggles to free himself, the more the man leans onto him with his body weight.

The boy fights for another half-minute, then he is still.

The man remains with his foot on the boy's head, watches the body spasm and twitch for a few more seconds, then all motion ceases.

He steps back to the base of the tree, watching just to make sure, until the ripples on the water's surface have completely ceased. All is calm. Nothing but the distant rumble of thunder.

The man—now a murderer—looks back at the road to gauge the distance. It is easily thirty feet from where cars pass, he reckons, and infrequently at that. No one would ever think to look up here tonight.

He retraces his steps to the roadside. The man pauses before emerging from the cover of the brush, making sure no one is approaching. Then he sprints to his car.

It has begun to rain hard again. That is good, he thinks, because the rain will wash away most—if any—evidence of his being anywhere near the scene. He drives off and mentally plots the long journey ahead of him later that night. Behind him, rain dripping from the bare tree limbs collects in puddles in the badly rutted pavement.

Chapter 1

The Marine VH-3 helicopter banked slowly to the west. Judge Paula Candler, dressed down in an oversized Aran-knit sweater and slacks, looked up from the stack of lawyers' briefs in her lap. Out the window, the heavy clouds were parting as a fat red sun set on the horizon. Below, she could see they were just crossing the Washington beltway. A thick layer of snow dumped on the city the previous night, still covered the landscape.

Seated beside her, Paula's husband, President James Madison Candler, tensely worked the zipper of his leather bomber jacket, a gift from the Marines of the unit that flew *Marine One*, the commander-in-chief's helicopter.

"Fountain *hates* you," the wiry man across from them was saying in a thick Appalachian drawl, even though he had left behind the hollows of western Virginia twenty years earlier. "More than anyone else in this town. That's what this is all about now. It's personal."

Del Owens—the man who had successfully managed every one of Jim's political campaigns, from student body president at the University of Virginia to the governor's mansion in Richmond and finally to the White House—sank low in his seat and stretched his legs in front of him. "You gutted him," Del continued, "smoked him, hung him up like a ham in the Southern primaries, and made a damned fool out of him in his own state. This is payback."

"Barely halfway through your first hundred days in office and I'm afraid the honeymoon with Congress is over," Paula said, stuffing her paperwork into a folder. "When Fountain went on the talk shows this morning and publicly said your budget wasn't going to make it out of his committee, the line was drawn."

"So what about everything we talked about at our strategy session at Camp David this weekend?" Jim said irritably. "I'm supposed to trash our agenda—the platform I was elected on—just to appease one man?"

"This is Washington, Mr. President." Del rubbed a hand over his prematurely bald head. A pair of glassy black eyes—set a bit too close together—and a blunt nose sometimes gave him the unnerving appearance of a snake, a copperhead about to strike. "Those codgers up on Capitol Hill are used to being stroked. They survive here by accommodation. Compromise. They expect it."

"Damn it!" Jim thumped the arm of his seat for emphasis. "Don't tell me what I already know."

Jefferson, the family's well-fed yellow Labrador, sitting at the President's feet, lifted his head at Jim's rising voice and barked.

Paula reminded her husband with a nod of the head that Chip, aged twelve, and Missy, fourteen, strapped into the seats behind them, were within earshot.

But Jim Candler was thinking of only one thing. He grabbed the phone receiver beside his seat. "Get me Senator Fountain," he ordered.

Paula studied her husband's face. Up close she saw what the cameras on the evening news did not. The endless hours of campaigning in the open sun and the million smiles it had taken to win the election had deepened the wrinkles on his otherwise youthful face.

There were a few more strands of gray in his thick black hair. His eyes seemed darker, harder. The run for the White House was different from any of the other races he had won. It had changed him.

The President took a deep breath and answered the buzzing phone.

"Senator," he said smoothly. "How the hell are you?"

Del Owens sat back in his seat, hands clasped behind his head, and smiled. He and Paula both knew this was Jim Candler at his best. Satisfied that his boss had the situation under control, Del leaned in and motioned to Paula so they could talk without anyone else hearing.

"Look," he said in a lowered voice, "I had a couple of people come up to me this weekend. . . ."

All of the key staffers had gone to Camp David for the weekend strategy session on how to keep the Administration's agenda for the first hundred days in office on track.

"Yes?" Paula said.

"As things start to get tough for us," Del said, "there's some thinking that maybe you should reconsider staying on the bench."

Paula's mood suddenly soured. "That was settled months ago," she said with finality.

"For Jim's sake."

"Jim will be just fine. After all, he's got *you* to watch after him."

Del ignored her comment. "He needs you by his side. In the White House. Day in and day out. I'm sure you'd be missed in the courtroom, but the country's got enough bright federal district court judges. If you stepped down, you'd be giving some other female lawyer a chance at the bench. What the country really lacks is a full-time First Lady now."

"Why is it I think it's *you* who's the only one against

my keeping my job across the river in Alexandria? Everyone has known since the beginning of Jim's campaign that I wasn't giving up my career on the bench. I have no intention of leaving. *Ever.*"

"I'm a pragmatist," Del said cagily. "My political instincts tell me everyone would be better off if you were supporting Jim in the White House."

"I've made this decision," Paula said. "Jim and the children support it. I don't see there's anything more to discuss."

Jim was wrapping up his phone call: "Thank you, Senator. And I look forward to seeing Martha there, too."

"Just think about it," Del said quickly as the President hung up the phone.

Jim at first looked pleased with himself. Then he saw the faces of his wife and political adviser. "What?" he said. "What did I miss?"

"How'd the phone call go?" Del asked.

"I invited Fountain over for lunch in the private dining room off the Oval Office," Jim said. "He and his wife both. I figured maybe having her come along will help soften him up a bit. She's never been to the Oval Office."

"Really? How'd you know that?" Del asked.

The President looked at his wife. "Apparently it's a sore point for her, considering how long her husband's been in the Senate. When we had lunch on Capitol Hill after the Inauguration with the congressional leadership and their spouses, Paula was seated next to Martha Fountain and pumped her for any useful information." He winked at his wife. "Always looking out for my interests."

Paula caught Del's eye and made sure he had understood the implication of what Jim had just said, that she was an asset to his career.

The helicopter was over downtown Washington now, making its final approach to the White House grounds.

"Soon as we land," Jim Candler said, pointing a finger at Del, "clear my calendar for lunch with the Fountains. Make it as soon as possible. It's critical we keep the momentum going to get our domestic plans implemented."

Marine One was slowly descending. The view of Washington from Paula's window was breathtaking. The White House and the surrounding buildings were tinged a deep pink from the setting sun. The helicopter's rotor wash kicked up snow as they landed on the South Lawn.

A Marine guard opened the door as soon as the rotors had stopped. President Candler stood in the doorway surveying the scene for a moment, then walked down the steps and gave the guard a snappy salute.

Paula joined him with the children and Jefferson. Chip and Missy ran ahead through the snow with the dog. Jim and Paula Candler assumed a more dignified walk and waved to the photographers and TV cameramen from the White House press corps. A handful of staffers and Secret Service agents trailed behind.

"I'm going on over to the Oval for a while," Jim said as they walked inside. Del and I have got a couple more hours at least working on that speech. I'm not going to bed until I've nailed it."

Paula read her husband's face: the same determined look as when he had announced to her that he had truly decided to make the run for the White House. The ambition to come to Washington that had been a part of their lives for so long, something they had talked about even before Jim had been elected governor of Virginia, had first dared to whisper as a dream across the pillow twenty years earlier.

"Okay, I'm going to eat with the kids," Paula said.

"I'll stroll with you for a second."

He draped an arm over Paula's shoulders, and they walked slowly down the wide corridor, down the hallway where other men and women of enormous power had walked. The long road to the White House seemed a blur, but here they finally were, and it was even better than Paula had ever imagined it. She and Jim, partners in the long struggle. After all the work, the years of late-night meetings, boosting Jim up the political ladder, the onerous fund-raising, lost weekends spent hustling votes, the time away from each other.

Victorious. Paula was elated, not just at all that she and Jim had accomplished together, but at her family's happiness. All together, healthy, and excited about their future. And her own career had survived—despite the sacrifices she had to make for the campaigns and the family. She saw on a daily basis in her courtroom the heartbreak of families torn apart by desperate situations, and she took nothing for granted. She was thankful for Jim and her life with him, her career, and most of all, her precious children.

Jim stopped Paula and held her gaze for a moment. "We done good, haven't we, babe?" he said with mock folksiness.

"Not bad at all, Mr. President."

He looked hard at her, placing his hands on her shoulders. He had sensed her mood change since the beginning of the flight home. "Something bothering you?"

Paula considered for a moment telling him about her argument with Del about remaining on the bench. "Nothing I can't handle myself."

Chapter 2

Scott Betts squinted through the rain pelting the windshield of his battered Pontiac Firebird as he cruised through an old postwar neighborhood near the southern portion of Washington's Capital Beltway. Ahead of him, the dimly lit front of the two-story building. Eight months' work, thousands of man hours, and almost a million dollars spent.

In the glow of the dashboard he checked his watch: exactly ten minutes after nine.

Scott casually wheeled the car into the driveway and drove to a space in the middle of the potholed parking lot in front of the building. He switched off the headlights, gunned the engine once, cut the ignition, and waited for the ill-tuned car to rumble to a stop.

The sound of the rain beating down onto the roof of the car was deafening. The late March cold snap was over just as quickly as it had arrived, and the snow which had looked so beautiful during the day was turning to slush.

Through the grimy, rain-streaked plate-glass window Scott saw a man leaning over the front counter reading a newspaper. There was a small television on to the side.

The man turned the page of the paper and warily looked up in Scott's direction. Even through the filthy haze of the glass, Scott could make out now that he was smoking the butt end of a fat cigar. An enormous belly rested on the counter. Comically large ears protruded through thin, greasy hair. Scott had never met Salvatore "Dumbo" Cerutti, but he felt he knew him like an old friend.

Scott reminded himself that the clock had started ticking. Unseen, people were already moving into place. All the planning, the round-the-clock listening with headsets, the weeks of rehearsals in the mockup of the building, and it still came down to one scared person's decision. *His* decision. Was this the moment? Was it safe?

Gotta hustle, he told himself.

His eyes darted across the front of the building. The rusting sign bolted to the postwar brick exterior read BT&P INC.—Beltway Tool and Parts, formerly a retail store, which county corporate records indicated was now a wholesale distributor.

A rat scurried along the base of the building through the feeble light. Other than that, there was no sign of life outside.

As Scott had practiced dozens of times before, he punched in the cigarette lighter on the dash. He unfastened the outside pocket button on his jean jacket and got out a hard pack of Camels. He lit the cigarette with the glowing end of the lighter, cracked the window, drew on the cigarette, and blew smoke out the window. The guy inside would see all that. As Scott replaced the pack in his pocket, he lifted the cigarette to his mouth again. That hid the slight movement of his lips as he spoke softly into the microphone hidden in his denim sleeve: "Just the one bad apple in the front room."

He waited for an excruciatingly long minute before he heard a crisp reply through a speaker concealed in the dash: "Roger. Signal check."

Scott felt a buzz in his trouser pocket, like an incoming message on a beeper set to the inaudible vibrating mode. If anything went wrong from here on, that would be his only alarm to get the hell out.

"Roger check," he said.

Another moment of silence, then the order: "Go, WELDER."

He reached down to the floor of the passenger's side, picked up a bundle of greasy rags, and used them to lift a metal auto part out of an oil pan. He felt for something hard buried in the rags, grabbed hold of it.

He shot a glance at his rearview mirror. Nothing.

He inconspicuously swiped his hand over his mouth. Using his code name, he said in a low voice, "WELDER's going in."

No turning back now, he thought.

Clutching the rags and the auto part, Scott pushed open the car door with his foot and stepped into the streaming rain. All during the long, slow walk across the thirty feet of dark, wet parking lot, Scott never took his eyes off the hands of the man inside. Scott was still in the shadows. So far everything was going the way it had been rehearsed.

Scott felt Dumbo's eyes fix on him as he stepped from the dark into the light of the big window. Scott had planned exactly what Dumbo would see at that moment: a trim young man in his late twenties, unshaven for several days, wearing faded blue jeans, worn-out Nikes, a bulky Redskins sweatshirt underneath the jean jacket, and a grubby baseball cap pulled down low over his eyes, hiding most of his face, only the glow of the cigarette visible underneath. He looked like one of the hundreds of other construction workers on the nearby Springfield Interchange project.

As Scott got within ten feet of the front door, Dumbo perked up, fidgeted with something under the counter.

Scott strained to hear any suspicious noise. All he

heard was the rain relentlessly drumming on the tin roof of the building.

Damn it. We didn't rehearse it in the rain! If only it could have been another night . . .

Mistake number one.

He had never heard rain make such a loud noise on a roof before. If someone was coming up behind him, he'd never know it—and he wasn't about to take his eyes off Dumbo's hands.

Scott's raw senses took it all in: the ferocious sheets of rain, the sound of his own heels crunching on the broken pavement, his feet splashing through the puddle, the pounding heart.

Then he got more focused than he had ever been in his life: the feel of cold steel in his right hand under the rags, and Dumbo's widening eyes as he approached.

He stepped under the awning at the entrance, wiped his sweaty palms on the rags before awkwardly grabbing the doorknob. He threw the cigarette into the puddle. A slow volley of thunder rumbled in the distance and shook the plate-glass window.

He pushed through the front door and walked up to the counter, facing Dumbo. The TV was tuned to women's roller derby with the volume turned up loud.

They stared at each other a moment in silence, Scott with his hands in his dirty rags, Dumbo with his hands on something under the counter. Dumbo looked perturbed about the oil dripping off the car part onto the floor.

"Yeah?" Dumbo groused.

He was uglier than the enlarged black-and-white photographs taken by the telescopic camera. Thick tufts of hair grew out of his nostrils. His teeth were stained dark yellow. Scott was so close now he could see the tiny veins running through Dumbo's ears.

"I saw the sign," Scott said in his best Southern twang,

conscious of not overdoing the accent. He pointed with his head to a sputtering neon sign. "I was on my way over to get a beer and thought I'd see if you had an intake manifold for a '75 Firebird."

Dumbo looked Scott up and down, took the cigar out of his mouth, kept one hand under the counter. "Think again, bud. We're wholesale only. We don't take business here off the street anymore."

"It's an auto-parts store, ain't it?"

The rain on the metal roof was even louder inside. The fat man made no attempt to turn down the volume on the blaring TV. Scott pictured the layout of the back room in his mind, just as he had seen it when he had broken in to install the bugs, then measured and photographed the place so the mockup could be built. Did he hear voices back there?

Dumbo was about to say something, then paused as if he too heard a commotion in the back room.

Dumbo half turned away, and Scott's mind was filled with a vision of the moment when he would have Dumbo safely out from behind the counter, spread-eagled against the wall, his twitchy hands exposed, handcuffed, reading him his Miranda rights.

Scott tried to concentrate on his crucial role at this stage of the operation: make sure Dumbo was unable to warn anyone in the building, and neutralize him before the rest of the team took down the players in the back room.

"Aw, come on," Scott said, trying to engage Dumbo in conversation again. "Make an exception, will ya?"

At that instant Scott felt the vibration of the silent alarm go off in his pants pocket. Something had gone wrong with the raid. Then the sound of gunfire.

They weren't supposed to come busting into the back until I have Dumbo subdued, Scott thought.

Mistake number two.

Raised voices filtered through the rainstorm. Dumbo's eyes widened as he too realized there was trouble.

Get out! a voice in Scott's head screamed.

Dumbo made a swift motion with his arm under the counter.

Ohhhhh, shit!

Scott dropped to the floor, scrambled to the side, and withdrew from the bundle of rags the .40-caliber Glock semiautomatic loaded with a clip of hollow-point bullets. The greasy manifold clattered to the floor.

At the same moment a loud explosion tore through the front of the counter just over his head, sending splinters and acrid gun smoke into the room.

Someone just fired a gun at me!

Dumbo had disappeared behind the counter. Scott listened carefully during a lull in the driving wind, thought he heard a shell being loaded into the breech of a shotgun. If Scott popped his head up over the counter to look, he'd lose it. Ditto on around the corner.

Now there was yelling from the back room. Then a bright flash of light flooded the interior of the room, and all the electric lights went off. It was completely dark, inside and out. The TV was silent. Almost immediately a loud clap of thunder shook the building.

Scott pushed himself as close to the base of the counter as he could.

I'm a dead man, I'm a dead man! Think, think!

Scott was absolutely still. The rain on the roof was relentless. More shouting from the back room. A gunshot. Then another. Now automatic weapons chewing up the air, splintering through the door to the rear.

Between the gusts of wind Scott thought he heard Dumbo's labored breathing and the fat man's knees creaking as he lifted himself off the floor.

One chance, and one chance only.

Scott waited until he was certain Dumbo had had enough time to hoist himself completely off the ground.

Now?

Then Scott felt a drop of something fall from above onto his face. A leaking roof?

No—a fat man's sweat—garlic and fear oozing out of his pores.

Scott pointed his Glock straight up into the pitch black, held his breath, and pulled the trigger.

A flash from the end of his gun. A great bulk fell backward against a wall and was silent.

Scott listened, heard nothing but the rain and confused shouting in the back room.

But is he dead?

The lights came back on, startling Scott, the electricity suddenly restored. The TV was blaring again, the sound of the women screaming and shouting at each other as they raced around the roller derby rink incongruous with what was going on.

Scott moved away from the counter a few inches. At first all he could see was a swirl of smoke rising above the counter. He froze, breathed in quietly through his nose.

Mingled with the acrid scent of gunpowder was cigar smoke.

The son of a bitch is still alive!

Before Scott could respond, the door behind the counter separating the reception area from the back room burst open. Scott aimed his gun at the end of the counter.

"Oh, *shee-it!*" swore a familiar voice. "Betts?"

Scott relaxed, pointed his gun off to the side. "Down here."

At that moment something wet splattered onto

Scott's cheek. He wiped it away and saw blood on his fingertips. He looked up and saw the spray of blood and gore on the ceiling.

"What the hell are you watching?" It was the voice of Supervisory Special Agent Craig McNary, the squad leader and his boss while Scott was on loan from St. Louis to the Washington FBI field office. "Get up," he ordered brusquely. "Turn that damned thing off."

Scott slowly stood and stuck the gun into his waistband. Even through the boot black covering McNary's face, Scott could see the veins bulging in his neck.

Scott switched the TV off. He finally looked over the counter in the direction of the smoke.

"Fuckin' mess," McNary said.

Sal "Dumbo" Cerutti was sitting on the floor upright against the wall, legs splayed, one hand on a sawed-off shotgun, his gargantuan ears seeming even larger with the top half of his head blown away, the smoldering cigar still clenched in his teeth.

Sirens screeched into the parking lot outside. Red and blue lights flashed around the interior of the room. Two teams of paramedics rushed in and ran to the back laden with emergency equipment.

Scott looked through the door—a grisly scene of butchers working in an abattoir. One set of paramedics worked quietly with their backs turned to him, blocking his view of their victim, while the others worked desperately on a young woman. Two lifeless figures were slumped against each other near the doorway. A dozen FBI agents stood about quietly, guarding the scene and watching the progress of the paramedics.

"I think we lost Paige," McNary said, shaking his head. "Fuck." He spat. "Fuck, *fuck*."

"God, no. Not Paige."

Scott fought a wave of emotions—rage, sorrow, disbelief. Paige Wentworth was his oldest friend in the Bureau. They had graduated from the FBI Academy together.

"And Alan caught one, too," McNary said. "Son of a bitch!" he said, smashing his fist into the counter.

"What the hell went wrong?" Scott asked.

"Everything," McNary answered vaguely.

"But what?" Scott demanded angrily.

McNary shook his head. "Remalli and those other two had guns drawn when we entered."

"How could that be? After all the careful preparation, none of this should have happened. The whole purpose of training was to give us the advantage of surprise and make the arrests without anyone getting hurt."

McNary put a hand on Scott's shoulder. "Let's just concentrate on wrapping up the arrest, okay, Scott?"

"Then you got Rimshot?"

"Slightly wounded. Those other two goons of his are dead. He saw me dropping down through the roof, but we got him. Rimshot and all the records he was about to shred." McNary paused to listen to the rain coming down hard. "It had to be tonight, Scott. Everyone knew that."

Scott looked over at the paramedics working on Paige. They were still trying to force her back to life, but the looks on their faces said that they were just going through the motions. The team hovering over Alan were still pounding at his chest furiously, ventilating his lungs. There was a lot of blood, but apparently he still had a chance.

"But at this price?" Scott said.

McNary hung his head, then rebounded when he heard a low moan from the back room. He yelled through the door: "Get that motherfucker out of there while they're working on Paige and Alan."

Another FBI agent pushed a heavyset man out through the rubble in the doorway. Brooding eyes, a pockmarked, olive-skinned face, the big hands of the dock worker he once was, Tony "Rimshot" Remalli was the subject of the eight-month-long FBI investigation for racketeering, and more recently the murder of a federal judge. He had what appeared to be a flesh wound to the shoulder that a paramedic was trying to mend as the FBI agent held a gun on him.

Rimshot Remalli glared at all the agents in the room. Then he looked at what was left of his faithful soldier Dumbo. Rimshot bent over and took the cigar from Dumbo's mouth with his good arm and stuck it into his own.

"Would you mind keeping still?" the paramedic said impatiently.

Remalli puffed a couple of times on the cigar until it glowed again. A thick cloud of smoke swirled around his head.

"Handcuff that son of a bitch," McNary said to the agent guarding him.

"But, sir, the paramedics—"

McNary slapped the cigar out of Remalli's mouth, then grabbed him roughly by his wounded shoulder and twisted his arms behind his back. Rimshot winced but maintained a stoic silence. McNary clamped the handcuffs on.

McNary got right up in Remalli's face. "I hope you enjoyed it, Rimshot," he said bitterly, stomping out the cigar. "It's your last taste of the good life."

Rimshot smiled contemptuously.

Paramedics wheeled a woman on a gurney through the room. She wore a bloodied jacket with the bold letters FBI in yellow. Her face was already ashen. The paramedic at her feet caught McNary's eye and shook his head.

Scott couldn't believe it. None of this should have happened.

Then he saw something odd. He stood transfixed for a surreal moment by the white cat hair he saw on his dead friend's collar.

McNary shouted at Scott: "What are you standing there for? Read him his rights and get him out of my sight." McNary then yelled at the other agents, who still had their guns trained on Rimshot: "He's already killed one federal officer, and the other one will be lucky to make it. If he makes the slightest hint of a threatening move, shoot him."

Scott pulled the Miranda card out of his jacket and read Rimshot his rights. "Do you understand?" Scott asked Remalli when he was finished.

The prisoner coughed up an oyster and spat it into Scott's face.

Scott had to use every bit of self-control to restrain his urge to pummel the mobster.

"I'll take that as a yes," he said, his voice shaking with rage.

Chapter 3

In a small examining room in the emergency ward of Fairfax Hospital, Scott Betts unlocked Remalli's handcuffs under the watchful eye of three other armed FBI agents. The paramedic had finished stitching up what turned out to be a minor flesh wound. Remalli's arm was in a sling, and he was flexing his massive hand. Scott twitched his nose at the lingering coppery reek of Dumbo's blood, which covered the front of his jacket.

Craig McNary came in. He had wiped most of the boot black from his face, but the creases in his skin were still filled with the grease.

"I phoned the U.S. marshal and told him we'd like the pleasure of processing him here ourselves." He handed a field fingerprinting kit to Scott.

"You did the work," McNary said. "The honor's all yours."

Scott was still in shock. He'd shot a man—actually taken the top of his head off—in a kill-or-be-killed struggle. Before tonight, it had all been practice shooting at silhouettes on a firing range or on the FBI training course at Quantico. Then he'd arrested the most wanted criminal in America: the Mafia don who had killed a sitting federal judge. Now, under the harsh glow of the fluorescent lights at one in the morning, he was being given the "privilege" of inking Tony "Rimshot" Remalli.

"Hey, what's a guy gotta do to get a cuppa cappa-fuckin'-cino around here?" Remalli said.

Everyone ignored him. Remalli grumbled and made the process as difficult as possible. He made Scott work for every fingerprint, stiffened his hands so Scott had to forcibly roll each finger, then, just as they were about finished, "accidentally" smeared the card.

"Sorry," Remalli sneered. With McNary standing over the don, implying physical violence if he didn't cooperate this time, Scott had to start from the beginning.

McNary assembled the letters and numbers on the board and thrust it into Remalli's good hand. "Smile, asshole," he said as he handed a camera to Scott. Remalli held the board under his chin as if he did it every day.

Scott steadied his hands so McNary wouldn't see them shaking. He was still pumped up with adrenaline.

"Tough guy," Remalli said, before Scott could get off a shot. "Whatsa matter? Little blood make you squeamish?"

Scott snapped the picture. "Turn," he said through clenched teeth. Remalli turned for the profile shot.

Remalli threw the mug shot board back over to McNary. "You guys got nothin' on me. Just like before. You've got shit for evidence and chumps for lawyers. I'll get off like I always do."

McNary could barely restrain himself. Scott knew if he and the others weren't in the room, McNary would probably take a couple of swipes at him for what the mobster had done to Paige and Alan. As hard as McNary appeared on the outside, he was clearly torn up inside about what had happened.

McNary opened his mouth and Scott thought he was going to say something he shouldn't, but Scott caught his eye and McNary settled down. If the arrest and processing weren't handled exactly by the book, Remalli's lawyer would find a way to have the case thrown out of court on a technicality. They had all worked too hard to let that happen.

The FBI agents on guard outside the door let in a huge black woman in an immaculate white nurse's uniform. With a look of boredom on her face, she walked slowly over to Remalli and inspected his wound.

"He gonna live," she pronounced.

"What's this?" Remalli said, feigning incredulity. "It'll get infected. I'll sue the hospital. I'll sue *you*."

"Hmmpf," she grunted. She slyly pulled a syringe out of her pocket and suddenly jabbed it hard into his arm.

"Hey!" Remalli protested, his eyes flaring. He flinched involuntarily, but the nurse held tight with hands as large as his. Scott could tell from the look on Remalli's face that it hurt like hell. But she seemed to command more respect from Remalli than did all the federal agents in the room. Finished, she waddled back out.

McNary banged on the door, and another FBI agent came in. "He's the perfect specimen of health. One minute on the phone, then take him over to the Metro and put him into total sep."

"We're talking violation of my constitutional rights," Remalli growled.

McNary reached into his pocket, flipped a quarter over to Remalli. "You've got plenty of friends in low places. Call someone who cares."

Scott was sure Remalli would get the hint. The task force had already been over the procedure. The U.S. attorney prosecuting the case would be seeking to detain Remalli without bond at the detention hearing the next day before the federal judge. Total sep—solitary confinement—was where defendants who were unlikely to make bail were kept.

As the agent was about to lead Remalli away, the mobster turned to Scott. "You know, you guys oughta be real careful. All sorts a bad people prowlin' round the streets. You never know who you're gonna bump into." Remalli looked Scott up and down, then drilled him with his eyes. "Specially *you*, punk."

McNary jerked Remalli into the hallway, then kicked the steel door closed after them with enough force to crack the reinforced glass observation window.

Don Russ took the call on his cellular phone as he hung upside down, stripped to the waist, his face straining, the veins bulging in his neck. With his legs wrapped around the top bar of his exercise equipment in the small gym off his bedroom, he was just finishing a series of fifty vertical sit-ups.

"Russ," he answered curtly.

"Hey, Donato," the friendly voice on the phone said.

The name slightly irritated Russ, but at the same time he accepted it as a term of endearment. Russ pulled himself up by his stomach muscles one more time to complete the set, then let himself hang downward. He wiped his face with a towel. "Rimshot," he said.

"You doin' okay?"

"Exceptional. You?"

"Not too shabby. 'Cept I need you to fly down to Washington and get me out of this stinkin' jail."

"Washington? A little out of your neighborhood, isn't it?"

"Ah, some bullshit about racketeering. The usual, you know? Guess I'm just unlucky like that."

"I don't believe in luck."

"That's what you always say. But this time the cocksucker's talkin' some real shit about some judge who got herself killed. What they want to try to pin something like that on me for?"

"Careful what you say on the phone," Russ warned. "The *Feds* arrested you?"

"Came shootin' their way into my office. Some people got hurt, but what did they expect when they come sneakin' around a guy's legitimate business in the middle of the fuckin' night? Must be a mistake somewhere."

"You have an initial appearance tomorrow in federal district court there in Washington?"

"They said over in Alexandria. Hey, I'll die if I have to spend more than a night in the joint. And they shot me. I was bleedin' all over the fuckin' place. I'm going to sue the bastards."

"But you're all right now."

"I'll live to see the morning. But ya gotta help me."

"Let's deal with your arrest first." Russ checked his watch. "You'll be seeing a magistrate judge sometime tomorrow. It's too late to get a commercial flight out of here to make it there on time if it's a morning appearance. I'll have to charter an early jet down. You good for it?"

"You're asking me if I'm good for it? Come on, you know how I work. I'll have a couple of hundred thousand delivered to your office before you get here. Money's no problem."

"Never has been. No cash, Tony. Just wire it into the firm's retainer account. Have someone call my office for the bank number tomorrow."

"You're the best, Donato. I'm always tellin' people about my good buddy over in Chicago, Donato Russo. 'If you're ever in a jam, call my lawyer. He'll get you straightened out.' "

"I'll see you first thing in the morning. Get some rest."

Russ turned the phone off. He grabbed onto the side-bars and flipped himself down to the floor.

He stood in front of the floor-length mirrors in the corner and studied his physique, not vainly but critically.

Rimshot, he mused. *What a piece of work.*

The racketeering charges were familiar territory to Russ. He had pulled Remalli's nuts out of the fire on those counts before. But whacking a federal judge? He should find out something at Rimshot's initial court appearance. If the government was going to make a case for denying bond, Russ would push for a quick detention hearing and they'd have to tip their hand enough for the judge and the defense to see what they were up to.

His brain was moving into high gear, sorting through the possibilities. The Feds would be throwing everything they had against Remalli, since they had blown the prosecution before. Twice. It would be a matter of pride for some feisty U.S. attorney. If things started heating up, Russ would need an edge. He had some of the best legal talent working in his firm. Now what he needed was a top investigator on the case. Someone as smart and fearless and devious as himself.

In his mind there was only one choice.

At that moment, Russ caught a glimpse of something in the mirror, thought his external obliques still could use a bit more toning. He ran his hand atop his massive head, over his short haircut, not much longer than that of a Marine at boot camp. He scowled back at the intense face staring at him.

He jumped back up onto the exercise machine, hung upside down, and wrapped his legs around the top bars, ready for another fifty vertical sit-ups.

But first he punched in a number by memory on his cellular phone.

*   *   *

Julia Menendez saw the blinking message light on the answering machine as she entered the kitchenette of her South Miami Beach condo. Next to the phone, the floating hands of the brass Art Deco clock indicated it was 5:15 A.M. She ignored the urgent flashing for the moment and relocked the series of chains and dead bolts on the door.

She pushed the spaghetti straps to her short, tight red dress off her shoulders, kicked off her high-heeled shoes, and pulled the nickel-plated Smith & Wesson Ladysmith .38 Special revolver out of her clutch purse, putting it on the small dining table.

Julia's ears were still echoing with the loud thumping of the drum and bass music at Les Bains. Feeling parched, she got a bottle of water from the refrigerator and stood drinking with her hand on her hip as she regarded her reflection in the stainless steel refrigerator door.

She swept the tangle of dark, curly hair out of her large brown eyes. She was hot and sweating, still pumped from four hours of nonstop dancing. But she looked damned good, she thought, and she could shake it. She was a hot little mink, as the Cuban boys liked to say, with a great ass and long, shapely legs. She bent over slightly, shimmied, and jiggled her breasts in a sexy way, a move she usually reserved for the dance floor. Nice tits, if she did say so herself. She pursed her full red lips and blew herself a kiss good night.

She was desperately in need of sleep. In just a few minutes the rising sun would strike the pastel façade of her 1920s high-rise condo building, and another gorgeous sunrise over the ocean could be viewed out on her balcony. It was a view she didn't care to see this particular morning.

She had started on her way to the bedroom, planning to crash until noon, when she remembered the phone message. She halted in front of the insistent red light. It could be any number of people. She looked at the time stamp: the call had come in at 3:07 A.M. Who would call at that time?

She punched the answering-machine button and slumped into a chair.

"Julia," the voice started flatly, "this is Don Russ in Chicago. . . ."

"No way," Julia said in disbelief. It was a habit of hers—speaking back to disembodied voices on TVs, movie screens, and answering machines.

"I've just been retained on a big case and thought you might be interested. My client can pay a thousand a day plus expenses, first-class all the way. I need you to be in Washington, D.C., later this morning, so you'd better stop the mail, clean out your fridge, and pack for several weeks. Find me inside the Alexandria federal court-house as soon as you arrive."

The tape ended.

"The arrogant son of a bitch!" Julia screeched after the message ended.

She paced the tiny kitchen with as much energy as she had had on the dance floor at Les Bains. *Typical*, she fumed. *He thought I'd have nothing better to do than sit by the phone at night waiting for him to call? After two years?*

He made her blood boil like no one else could. That bit about cleaning out her fridge especially infuriated her. He had developed into such a control freak that he could be classified as a subspecies. Just one of his many endearing qualities. She had forgotten exactly which one had finally caused their irrevocable split.

Julia Menendez didn't like being told what to do.

The tone of his voice told her without doubt that it was going to be all business. Of course, that's how it had all started out last time, too.

Julia let out a stifled scream in frustration, turned on her heel, and stomped back to her office in the spare bedroom.

The walls were covered with street maps of Miami and south Florida. On the desk were expensive computer equipment, telephones, and ultrahigh-speed modems. The specially installed metal shelves were crammed with electronics and audiovisual equipment: cameras, telescopic lenses, camcorders and tape recorders, police scanners, two-way radios, a variety of binoculars and telescopes, night-vision goggles, and a dozen highly illegal eavesdropping devices—the tools of her trade.

She plopped down into the chair in front of the computer, turned it on, and dialed up a number that connected her directly with one of the large credit bureaus she subscribed to—quite illegally—under the name of a fictitious consumer finance company she had incorporated herself. It was one of the most efficient means of digging up dirt on or tracking the whereabouts of virtually anyone who lived in the country.

She typed a name in: RUSS, DON. There were fifty-seven entries. She selected the one with the Chicago address on Astor Street. In a moment, his financial life history scrolled up onto her screen.

How much had changed in his life since they had parted ways? He appeared to still be single. It was a bit surprising, then, to find that he still owned that huge, magnificent Arts and Crafts house—according to tax records on her computer screen, now worth 5.5 million—on the Gold Coast, in the exclusive Chicago neighborhood along the shore of Lake Michigan. Once she had walked through the mansion and counted twenty-seven rooms. *Not too big a place, though, when you consider the size of Don Russ's ego.*

How had his businesses fared? Apparently pretty well. His income from the law firm had increased steadily, to just a hair under $750,000 a year—at least that was what he was reporting to the IRS and his creditors. After almost twenty years of practicing law, Don Russ had finally worked himself into the position where he could be selective, taking on only those who could afford the best, and that almost always meant representing either some high-profile, wealthy defendant, or criminals with access to assets with origins he'd rather not know about.

His personal assets were in good shape, too. He kept a hundred thousand in a money-market fund, which he drew cash from; he owned a string of modest downtown and West Side properties valued collectively at over $12 million; and the market rise and shrewd stock investments had left him sitting on equities worth in excess of $10 million. Not too bad for a poor boy from the South Side.

Julia calculated Russ could easily live off his investments. So why was the guy still schlepping a briefcase to the office every day?

She moved to another screen and examined details of his expenses. She saw a standing order for a bank draft in the amount of $20,000 per month to a Susan Russ in Telluride, New Mexico; he was still making alimony payments. And she deserved every penny of it, as far as Julia was concerned.

Another click of the mouse and she was looking at his Visa and American Express records. She scanned them for any telling information. No florist charges. Plenty of restaurant debits, but it was apparent from the small amounts that he was eating alone. She didn't feel sorry for him one bit.

Julia closed out the credit-bureau window and pulled up one of the pay-per-view Internet research services, which contained a wealth of much more personal information. She found the listing: DON RUSS, age forty-five—she already knew that, although anyone guessing his age would have sworn he was in his late thirties. His mother was a Jewish refugee from postwar Lithuania, his father second-generation Italian. College and law school.

Here was something she hadn't known about before: a recent computer dump of public court documents revealed that after his first year in law school, he had legally changed his name to Don Russ from Donato Russo. Why would he have done that?

Julia printed out all the files she had just read and looked over the pages of raw data.

But that isn't the whole story, is it? she mused. Julia slouched down low and swung her legs over the arm of the chair.

After seven years in the business, she knew that databases didn't give the complete picture on anyone's life. That was where the human element came in, and that was why resourceful private investigators such as herself would always be in demand.

Where, for instance, in the computer records did she find the fact that Don Russ had mesmerizing brown eyes, the body of a Greek god with under ten percent body fat, a cute dimple in his chiseled chin that she embarrassed him about to no end, washboard abs, and a tight ass she had dreamed about almost every night for two years?

And where did all the carefully compiled data reflect how the cold bastard had broken her heart?

She had to remind herself that there was a good reason he was divorced. It was the same reason he was still single. Nobody would have the SOB.

Unless maybe it was someone who understood him. The way she did.

She was getting angry with herself. So what was she supposed to do? Dump all the other cases she had going and hop on the next plane to Washington? Fly *north* in winter? When was she supposed to sleep? More importantly, what would she *wear*?

She spun around in her chair and tapped into the Sabre travel reservations system on the computer. She found an empty window seat in first-class on the 7:00 flight out of Miami, arriving in Washington just after 9:30.

With any luck, she'd be in the Alexandria federal courthouse before the judge had gaveled the morning court into session.

Chapter 4

The car trip from the White House to the federal courthouse in Alexandria took around half an hour under normal rush-hour conditions. For security reasons, the Secret Service drove a slightly different route every day.

Young Special Agent Ted Branson was driving as the veteran Richard Mobley talked into his hand-held two-way radio. The small motorcade—including one Chevy Suburban in front of her car and another behind, each with more Secret Service agents—crossed the Potomac on the Fourteenth Street Bridge and headed south on the George Washington Memorial Highway. Overhead flew a Marine helicopter with additional protection.

The gray four-door they were riding in was the same vehicle she had driven for years while she and Jim had lived in Richmond. Paula—code-named by the Secret Service DRAGONFLY—felt awkward sitting in the backseat of the Ford Crown Victoria, letting someone else drive the old family car. She had used it to do normal things that working mothers do: drop the kids off at school, drive to work, attend a meeting on her way home before popping into a store. It was a roomy and reliable vehicle, perfectly suited for their lifestyle then, and definitely not flashy—a good politician's car. When the subject of transportation arose during the transition meetings after Jim's election, she was adamant that the last thing she wanted to do was to trade her car in for a limousine. It would send the wrong signal politically. During the campaign, the President's wife had been portrayed as someone who had wanted to maintain her common touch and be the first First Lady to hold down a "regular" job. How would it look if she were arriving at work each day in a shiny black limo? The Candlers had also offered to help pay for part of Paula's security to and from work, but the Secret Service insisted that would set a bad precedent.

Helen van Zandt, chief of staff of the First Lady's office, sat in the backseat with Paula. She had also run the First Lady's office when Jim was governor, although then she was a staff of one. Shoulder-length natural blond hair intertwined with a few silver wisps framed a pair of eyes that shone like blue diamonds. She and Paula had birth dates only three days apart. She was a former Richmond debutante, and in her former life as Mrs. Roger van Zandt, her connections, wealth, and dazzling beauty would have put her at the center of any social function. But in her new role in the White House, Helen had adopted a more deferential, businesslike attitude appropriate to working for the President's wife.

Helen showed Paula a file of letters.

"We're still getting thank-you letters from people about the open house you held the day after the Inauguration," Helen said.

Paula scanned a few of the letters. "As much as I dreaded standing in a receiving line again for two hours, I felt more energized than ever. Those people coming through the White House—they're the people who put Jim into office. It's *their* house."

They had decided to use the precious time together in the car in the mornings to review Paula's schedule.

Helen pulled a copy of the week's itinerary from her briefcase and handed it to her.

"I've loaded you up with official White House functions at night and at least once a week during the lunch recess," Helen said.

Paula looked the schedule over, nodded. "That's exactly how I want it. No one should have any doubt that I'm carrying my weight as First Lady."

"Oh, don't worry. No one could possibly think otherwise. I've made sure of that. You're still just about as big a story as Jim is right now."

"I really don't know what all the fuss is about," Paula said. "Plenty of women manage to hold down a full-time job and help take care of the family at the same time. For me to have quit the bench would be demeaning to what millions of women do every day." Paula shook her head, thinking. "The feminists are still criticizing me for not using my maiden name on the bench, though."

"Well, you just can't please everybody, can you?"

"True. I just don't want anyone thinking I'm not doing a proper job of being a mother or a wife. You know that absolutely nothing is more precious to me than my family."

They rode along for a few minutes, Paula making suggestions about the itinerary as Helen took notes.

Paula caught Helen giving her a thoughtful look.

"Penny for your thoughts?" Paula said.

"Oh, I was just remembering the day you were sworn in as a district judge. It was one of the proudest days of my life. After the unanimous vote of approval in the Senate following your confirmation hearings. I'm so glad you decided not to resign. After all those years of legal training and climbing your way up the professional ladder—what a waste that would have been! You were a damned good lawyer and you're an even better judge.

One day you're going to be sitting on the Supreme Court."

Paula smiled faintly.

"This is something you did yourself," Helen continued, "completely apart from Jim's own political career. Your decision to keep working regardless of the outcome of the election helped swing votes in Jim's favor among all those working moms out there."

Paula looked into Helen's bright face. A few wrinkles were starting to show. Between growing up in a dysfunctional old-money Virginia family and surviving a messy front-page divorce five years earlier, Helen had seen a lot of living. Paula relied on her judgment and common sense when she needed an objective opinion.

Paula patted Helen's hand. "I'm glad I've got such a good friend around to help me out."

Having traveled through Alexandria, the First Lady's motorcade turned onto the Capitol Beltway toward Springfield, then took the first exit and headed back into Alexandria.

Sitting up front was Richard Mobley, the senior Secret Service agent in charge of Paula's security detail. A twenty-three-year veteran of the Service, he had been assigned to the Candlers after Jim had won the Florida primary, becoming the party's front runner and meriting Secret Service protection. Paula had never once seen him break a sweat, even on the hottest days of summer campaigning in the Deep South.

Ted Branson, the agent at the wheel, was barely thirty, face close-shaven to an opalescent sheen. Like many of the Secret Service recruits, he was a former Eagle Scout and a devout Mormon. Whereas Mobley was meticulous in his attention to the smallest security detail, Branson was the more physical of the two, seeming to enjoy shouldering his way through a

crowd to make a passage for his assignments, like the
former college football player he was.

"Look at that, will you?" Helen said suddenly.

Cars and vans with the logos of a dozen different
news organizations were lined up in front of the Albert
V. Bryan Federal Courthouse. A large gathering of reporters, cameramen, and other assorted technicians and
onlookers crowded the steps leading into the building.
Alexandria city police cruisers blocked the street, and
officers were diverting traffic.

"What do you think could be going on there?" Paula
asked.

"I heard talk this morning that the FBI made a big arrest last night. The Mafia guy who killed the judge.
They're getting ready to make the camera run in the
front door."

"Drive around to the back side of the building," Mobley said to Branson. "We'll go in through the garage."

They were picking up speed down the street, following the lead Chevy Suburban. Paula watched parents
drop off their children at the day-care center that had
just opened for federal workers.

Suddenly Paula saw a quick motion on the sidewalk. A
small boy pulled loose from his mother's hand and ran
between two parked cars.

She screamed. The mother screamed.

The lead car came to a sudden stop just before the child
ran into the street in front of it. Branson slammed on the
brakes, barely missing the bumper of the Suburban.

The mother dashed out and retrieved the boy. She
took him back to the sidewalk and scolded him. Every
mother's nightmare. The boy was laughing at her, oblivious to how near to death he had come.

Branson's jaw was set, his eyes fixed ahead. It had
been a very close call—both for the child in the street

and for their own car. Mobley took a deep breath and turned in his seat to face Paula. "You all right, ma'am?" he said coolly.

"It's okay, it's okay," she said, burying her head in her hands. "Just drive slowly."

And her day hadn't even begun.

Del Owens looked up from his desk at the half dozen televisions in his corner West Wing office, just down the corridor from the Oval Office. The sound was turned down, but Del recognized the federal courthouse in Alexandria on CNN and Fox News. He adjusted the volume up.

In a few more seconds, the TV camera found the Candlers' familiar gray Crown Vic coming down the street. Paula smiled and waved as she sped by the reporters and gawkers assembled on the sidewalk. The news commentator was saying that the FBI had made an arrest in a major federal murder case, and the media were assembled for the arrival of the defendant. The fact that the President's wife just happened to be arriving for work was incidental to the main story, but the cameraman took advantage of the opportunity to show Paula Candler's face once again on national television. It seemed as if the public couldn't get enough of this First Lady, the anchorman was saying.

Del Owens sneered back at the spectacle on the television screens and turned the sound off.

Of course, she was dead wrong about returning to the bench. Her full-time presence in the White House could be used to enhance Jim Candler's image. Del hated the feeling that he wasn't in control, and he was definitely not in control of the President's wife. She had always been her own woman, making her own decisions.

He returned to the folder of invoices he was hur-

riedly signing with an illegible scrawl. Loose ends from
Richmond, mainly bills to cover the transition from
moving out of the governor's residence. He signed the
top invoice, turned to the next one.

It was a mere piece of paper just like all the others, a
statement from a Ford auto dealership in Richmond.
Nothing more than a lousy $8.50 work order and in-
voice for a new set of wiper blades for the car, all of the
spaces neatly filled in with all the car's details: mileage,
car tag, vehicle identification number. But somehow the
bill hadn't been paid, and this new invoice was stamped
in big, bold red letters SECOND NOTICE.

He shouldn't have to be wasting his time on such
small details, but the President expected someone trust-
worthy to watch after his family's affairs while he con-
centrated on weightier matters of state.

Nothing to linger over, Del told himself. He had always
taken care of the Candlers' needs, always managed to correct the problems that inevitably cropped up, regardless
of how big or small they were. All in a day's work in service to the man he helped put into the Oval Office.

He signed the invoice, the pen slightly slippery in his
hand.

"I'm afraid the Secret Service is not going to like this
one bit, Paula."

The Honorable Paula Candler sat at the long table in
the eighth-floor conference room in Judge Malcolm
Crane's chambers. Chief judge of the four active district
judges in the Alexandria courthouse, Malcolm was her
closest friend in the building. A stocky man with trim
graying hair, he was the first and only black judge ever
to be confirmed to the bench in the district.

Malcolm waved into the room a neat little man with
combed-back white hair and a pixie face. Shelby Trim-

ble was a fixture of the courthouse, knew everyone and everything having to do with the courthouse, having been first selected as clerk of court by a long-dead judge over thirty years earlier. He dressed like an undertaker—a black suit and tie, matching patent-leather shoes with a military shine—and wore chunky black-framed glasses so old that they were becoming fashionable again.

"Shelby, did you bring the new cases?"

"Yes, Judge. Got them right here." Shelby handed Paula and Malcolm photocopies. "This is current as of end of yesterday."

Paula scanned a summary. Each judge typically had around four hundred cases pending at various stages, about three times as many civil as criminal matters. Most of these would never make it to trial, ending as out-of-court settlements or plea bargains. Much of the time in and out of the courtroom was spent dealing with a seemingly unending barrage of motions from the attorneys. Paula and the other judges acquired another two dozen or so new civil actions each month and half as many criminal cases.

"Looks like we've got a full calendar, as usual," Paula said. "And the number of indictments Chapman has been bringing has picked up the closer to election time we get." She was referring to the U.S. attorney, Lloyd Chapman. "Otherwise, where's the problem?"

Malcolm nodded to Shelby. He moved spryly around the table and handed her a copy of a criminal indictment—*United States* v. *Antonio Remalli*. It had been stamped by the clerk's office with her name, randomly drawn among the judges, indicating she would be sitting on the case. Paula looked up from the indictment and saw the look of intense anticipation on Shelby's face.

After reading the first page of the indictment Paula understood. "They've finally nailed someone for Eleanor's murder. Thank God."

Judge Eleanor Goldsworthy, whose judicial seat remained unfilled, had been brutally murdered just before Christmas of the previous year at her home in Middleburg, Virginia.

"Shelby tipped me off," Malcolm said. "I didn't want you to arrive in your office this morning and just find it lying on your desk like any other case. Because it's *not* like any other case. It's a trial of a *reputed* Mafia don who *allegedly* killed a federal judge."

Paula noticed how Shelby had cast his eyes down and lost all of his impish charm at the mention of the late judge's name. Eleanor had been a brilliant jurist but possessed zero people skills, especially when it came to handling courthouse functionaries. She abused everyone, but Shelby was more sensitive than most and had suffered more than others. As much good as Eleanor Goldsworthy had done in championing the cause of women in the state's legal profession, Paula could not excuse the way in which she had tormented sweet Shelby Trimble. Paula had heard rumors that he had taken to muttering profanities under his breath every time he passed her door, and kept a drawer full of pencils to snap instead of her neck after confrontations with the judge.

"I wanted to give you an opportunity to think about your next step before it's too late," Malcolm said.

"Meaning what?"

"Meaning before you're fully committed to sitting this case. You and the Secret Service might have legitimate reservations about security issues, both in and out of court. Our U.S. marshals do a helluva job protecting us and the courthouse, and I know the Secret Service wouldn't allow Remalli or any of his cronies to get away with as much as looking cross at you, but as chief judge I still have to voice my concerns for your safety."

"Now, listen," Paula said sternly, leaning across the table, "both of you. I appreciate your concern. But I will not allow the fact that I am the wife of the President to interfere with my work. I'll never allow the Secret Service to dictate my schedule. I thought I made that clear several months ago."

Malcolm pulled a pipe from his coat pocket, turned it over in his hands like some artifact he had just discovered. Shelby checked the shine on his shoes.

"What goes on in my chamber and my courtroom is my business and my responsibility," Paula said. "Is that clear?"

"Yes, Judge," Shelby said. "You're always right. Unappealable."

"And unimpeachable," Malcolm added somberly.

Chapter 5

Scott was at the wheel of the white unmarked van, driving away from the Criminal Justice Center. The morning sun was still hidden behind the downtown Washington buildings. Scott checked his side-view mirror to make sure he hadn't lost the backup car of FBI agents at the last stoplight.

Craig McNary seemed strangely relaxed, the first time Scott had seen him that way in the eight months they had worked together. "Our part's almost over," McNary said. "We play the tapes, testify in court, then we can all get on with our lives. It's an airtight case, thanks to you. Now that we're about done, I can tell you—when I asked Washington for a top black bag man and they sent me you, I had my doubts."

"Thanks a lot."

"Nothing personal. It's just that you were barely out of your training program. I called them back and told them I needed someone with experience. They told me that's not what I asked for, that I had asked for the best. And that's exactly what I got."

Scott smiled. Coming from a veteran like McNary, it was high praise.

"I knew from the beginning that by themselves, the wiretaps on the phones were never going to give us the evidence we needed to get the murder indictment. The Mafia are too smart these days to discuss anything of consequence on the phone. If you hadn't been able to put the bugs in Remalli's offices, we'd never have made the case." McNary exhaled loudly and slumped in the seat. "Jesus, I'm tired."

It was the first time that Scott had ever heard McNary make an admission that he was anything less than the ex-Marine superhuman everyone thought he was. McNary closed his eyes, appeared to be drifting off to sleep.

"About last night . . ." Scott said. He had been thinking of nothing else, and he asked the question that had been chewing him up inside. "After all the trouble we went through to map the place and build the mockup so we could train. The whole idea was that no one would get hurt. What happened in the back room?"

McNary opened his eyes. "The rain happened."

"I couldn't hear *anything* else but the rain as I walked from the car to the building. Then it was even louder once I got inside under that metal roof."

McNary stared vacantly out the window. "Yeah," he said in a faraway voice. "Couldn't hear a goddammed thing."

"But that still doesn't explain how Remalli and his men seemed to know to expect us."

"There was a leak. That's the only way he could have known."

"But how could that be? The only people who knew about the raid were the Bureau and the U.S. Attorney's Office. No one on the inside could have possibly been responsible for tipping Remalli off."

"As soon as we've got Remalli taken care of, I'm making finding the answer to that question my top priority."

Scott checked his mirrors, looking for any signs of suspicious activity. They were on the lookout in case some of Remalli's buddies still on the loose tried to spring him before he got to court.

"The paramedic told me in the hall that Alan was still alive," Scott said.

"He might as well be dead. A bullet nicked his spinal column. He's also lost his entire lower jaw. I'd walk down the hall and pull the plug myself if it were up to me."

"Chapman's got to be happy, at least," Scott said.

"Yeah. Son of a bitch was pushing hard. He was afraid Remalli was getting spooked by our surveillance. If they had packed it up and fled this jurisdiction, Lloyd Chapman would have kicked our butts from here to the other end of the state."

The FBI had worked closely with U.S. Attorney Lloyd Chapman and his office to coordinate the surveillance and arrest.

McNary checked his watch. "Slow down a bit," he said. "We don't want to be early. Chapman's expecting us at exactly 9:05. No use getting there any earlier."

Scott eased off the gas. "There's going to be an investigation, isn't there?"

"Any time people die in an operation, there's an investigation. Someone's got to answer for dead bodies. Don't worry about it. Routine stuff. Once the report's done, we'll turn everything over to Chapman, and he'll make sure Remalli pays for what happened."

Scott thought McNary's response odd, a little too laid-back, considering the losses in the raid. McNary didn't want to talk about the investigation anymore. "Paige?" Scott asked quietly.

"I called her parents as soon as she was pronounced officially dead at the hospital."

Scott had considered asking McNary to let him make the call himself. He had met Paige's parents at the graduation ceremony at the Academy. They were really decent people. He thought maybe finding out about their daughter's death would be easier hearing it from one of Paige's good friends rather than from someone they didn't know. In the end, though, Scott had decided it was more McNary's place as her superior to make the call. Plus, he didn't think he would be able to get the words out without choking on them.

"You and Paige were pretty close, huh?"

"Yeah. We were thrown together in defensive tactics at Quantico, then stuck together after that. We were in the same study group. She was a really great person. I can't believe she's dead."

"I'm sorry, Scott. She was such a bright young woman. I suppose the only good thing was that she didn't have a family of her own. I was thinking I sure would hate to have been making that call to your wife last night."

"You almost did, you know. I thought I had bought it."

McNary nodded thoughtfully. "So did all of us. So how are those little twins of yours?"

"I don't honestly know. I haven't seen them in two months. You knew Tammy had packed them up and gone to her mother's to stay when it looked like this investigation was dragging out."

"Probably for the best. Not the best situation, being alone with a couple of babies for so long. She going back to work?"

"I hope not. She just about killed herself teaching while she was pregnant."

"Tough job."

"Sometimes I think tougher than mine. I begged her to quit, but we were trying to save up as much money as we could before the twins were born, and she wanted to help as much as she could. At least she understood that taking care of them would be a full-time job, and she wouldn't be returning to the school after they were born. It can get pretty crazy with two infants in the house. They're a handful, even when both parents are at home."

"I can only imagine. It's been a long time since my girls were in diapers. Did you call her today?"

"Naw. She'd just start asking me about when I was coming home. I don't want to get her hopes up until I know something definite."

Scott turned the corner and saw the crowd of reporters and cameramen massed in front of the courthouse building, a ten-story red brick edifice with two lower wings forming a U on the back side. The Tower, as the central part was called, overlooked a wasteland that had once been a railway yard.

"Okay," McNary said. "Here's what's going to happen. Chapman wants us to pull up right in front of the building. There . . . where the Metropolitan Police have the traffic cones." McNary squinted through the window. "Yep, there's Chapman. Right on time. As soon as the rest of the agents are in place, we'll get Remalli out of the back. You take hold of him on one side, I'll grab the other. When the cameras are clicking away, keep your eyes straight ahead and don't show any emotion."

McNary handed Scott a windbreaker with large FBI letters on the front and back. "Here, put this on. The Director wants us to get full credit for bringing this son of a bitch in. No way the cameras can miss these."

The deputy U.S. marshal released Tony Remalli from his handcuffs and locked the door behind him to the interview room, a closet-sized space in the marshal's complex with a counter and two chairs facing each other separated by a steel mesh screen. Remalli rubbed his wrists and sat facing Don Russ.

"Fuckin' zoo out there," Remalli said.

"You knew there'd be a show of making you run the camera gauntlet. You've had enough experience at how these ambitious prosecutors work."

Remalli grumbled, tugged at the front of his uniform. "Prison orange never was my best color. And this sling, what is this? Peachy flesh tone? It clashes."

"We'll get you something more appropriate to wear for your next courtroom appearance."

"Only the best. Think you can have a tailor come by later today?"

"Sorry, it's off-the-rack for now. Unless maybe you can have someone up in New York mail me your best court-appearance suit. You know, the one you wore two years ago for the tax-evasion case?"

"Funny guy. I'll do that. But tie widths have changed since then. Maybe you can pick me up somethin'. I hear there's a Brooks Brothers at that mall near where you're stayin'."

"Sorry, I don't do malls." Russ flipped through the pages of the federal indictment he had just retrieved from the clerk's office. "You been banging someone upside the head again with a pair of drumsticks?" Russ asked as he searched for details.

Remalli grunted and a faint smile crossed his lips. "Everyone needs a hobby." He drummed the counter with his fingers in a fast roll, then hit the screen like a rimshot, just like his nickname.

Russ had heard the story from another of his high-profile clients from New York. When Remalli was only seventeen, he had "made his bones" by beating a nightclub owner to death with a pair of drumsticks. The chump's crime? Failing to cough up the weekly protection money on time.

Russ looked over Remalli's shoulder through the glass panel in the door behind to see if anyone was watching them. "Ah, here it is. This judge you were supposed to have killed. She was shot."

"In actual fact, I never touched the cunt." Remalli shrugged, looked around the bare walls. "My guess is that it was a robbery that got fucked up. I looked at houses there in her neighborhood myself. Nice spreads—big lots, good place to raise kids, 'specially if you're into the horsy set. But ya know what they say: no place is safe these days."

"Washington isn't New York, Tony. A local federal judge gets killed like that, and it stays on the front pages more than a day. What the hell are you doing down here anyway?"

"Setting up a business."

"What kind of business?"

"I bought a franchise."

"What kind of franchise?"

Remalli feigned enthusiasm. "A Snap-on Tools franchise. I'm the new distributor for the area. Good demographics. It's a booming economy here."

"You don't know shit about tools."

Remalli answered cagily: "I brought some fellas down with me who know the trade."

"Yeah, right." Russ flipped through a copy of the indictment. "I didn't see anything in here about dope."

"Or racketeering or tax evasion. They wanted to try a new angle this time. I'm not even sure there *was* a federal murder statute last time. Otherwise they would've tried that one back then, too."

"The feds wouldn't have arrested you if they didn't think they had enough evidence to nail your ass to the wall this round. Not after trying you twice in five years and losing both times."

"Hey, I was found innocent by a jury of my peers."

"You were found not guilty. There's a difference."

"I had a good lawyer."

"You had the best. But there must be a whole lot of people on the government payroll thinking at this very moment that maybe Rimshot Remalli's time has finally run out."

"Well, fuck 'em. They work for me, don't they? I pay taxes just like the next guy."

Russ grunted. "If you can call sending in an estimated payment when you feel like it paying taxes. By the way, did you ever get yourself a real accountant like I told you?"

"I prefer to keep the work inside the family." Remalli grinned.

"Jesus." Russ shook his head, stashed the copy of the indictment into his briefcase. "This isn't an IRS audit, Tony. You're charged with killing a federal judge. It took every resource I could pull together last time to get you off. The feds have almost unlimited resources at their disposal to throw against a defendant in a high-profile case like this. Dozens of lawyers and FBI agents and the FBI's forensic labs. The odds are stacked against you from the beginning."

Remalli leaned in close to the mesh. Russ could smell his last meal on his breath. "You've beat the shit outta federal prosecutors in every major jurisdiction in the country—New York, Los Angeles, Atlanta, Chicago. That's why *we* keep you on retainer. Eh? Come on. This is *Washington*, for chrissake. Buncha sissy lawyers running around lobbyin' for tax breaks. Piece a cake."

"Which makes me wonder. This is hardly your kind of town. What the hell is Tony Remalli—the quintessential New York wop—*really* doing down here?"

Remalli sat back in his chair, folded his arms proudly across his chest. "Okay, okay, you're on to me. I'm an engineering consultant."

"A *what*?"

"I help people out with their construction problems. You got problems with labor or need some cement, some asphalt, you come to me. I'm an ombudsman." He spat when he said the word.

"Where'd you learn a word like that?"

"Sounds better than a 'fixer,' don't it? Hey, people here are looking to get rich. They need help. They're looking for partners. I'm not a greedy guy. All I want is a percentage."

"So what's the lure? Why Washington? Why now?"

"You think I don't read the papers back in Brooklyn? I know what's goin' on down here. Didn't take a fuckin' genius to figure out where all the money is. All ya have to do is get in your car and drive."

Russ's eyes lit up. "I get it now. It's the Springfield Interchange, isn't it? The $350 million state construction project on the Capital Beltway I was reading about on the way down here. You smelled a pile of money and thought you'd muscle in." Russ shook his head in disbelief. "No one ever said you weren't ambitious."

Remalli beamed. "It's the fuckin' land of opportunity, ain't it?"

"And you're the biggest opportunist of them all. The Snap-on franchise?"

"An amusement, a sideline. Somethin' to occupy the time of my fellas. Some of them lack the manners it takes for front-office work. They're better off ridin' the routes. But they're provin' useful to help persuade some of the other people in town how serious I am about our role in the project." Remalli laughed, then did another finger drumroll on the counter and a rimshot on the mesh.

"Oh. I'm beginning to see. The guys on the trucks are the muscle."

Remalli cocked his head as if to say, "There ya go."

"So what's next? I'm ready to get out of here."

"You know the ropes. First stop, initial appearance, then detention hearing. Has someone from pretrial services been around yet to get your personal history?"

"Yeah, I told 'em to go fuck themselves."

"Good. That was probably the best response, considering the predicament you're in. It will give the government some leverage, though, if they want to string out the detention hearing for a while to let you get a taste of life in the local jail. They think that softens some defendants up, makes them more willing to talk."

"They don't know me."

"No, they don't. Don't get your hopes up. The U.S. attorney will say you're being uncooperative. They have up to three days to prepare for the hearing. He's going to do everything in his power not to let you out."

"But you can do it."

"Depends on the evidence they produce at the hearing. And who the magistrate judge is. That could make a big difference."

"Yeah, well, let's choose one who's going to be our friend for life."

"As you recall, it doesn't work that way. The clerk's office randomly assigns a magistrate judge to hear the preliminaries and a district judge to hear the case." Russ checked his watch. It was almost ten o'clock.

"I ain't worried 'bout nothin'."

"I've brought Mike Fein down with me. He should be here soon from the clerk's office with the judicial assignments for your case."

"Mike's a good boy. Did a great job for you on the tax case, didn't he? Maybe he'd like to come work for me. I'm in a growth business, ya know. Lots of opportunities for a go-getter like that. I'm always lookin' for new talent. We could use a smart Jewish kid in my organization. Like you."

Russ shot him a look.

"I don't mean anything by it. But isn't it true that if your mother's a Jew that the kid's considered a Jew? Even if the father's Italian? You're the best of both. Got the brains from your mother and the good name and blood from your father. You're practically one of us. I still think you shoulda left your name Donato. Donato Russo. It had a certain . . . poetry comin' off the lips." As Remalli said it, spittle flew off his moist lips, landing on the screen between them.

"I don't want to hear that kind of talk again," Russ said. "Keep it to yourself."

"Touchy, aren't we? I always meant to ask you: did the fact your grandfather was from Sicily and your father went to jail have anything to do with the fact that you changed your name?"

"*Died* in jail," Russ corrected him. "Died of a heart attack in a stinking county jail after spending nine years behind bars for a crime he didn't commit. Forced to confess to being the driver in a bank robbery that went wrong where a teller was shot. He had an idiot for a lawyer and was being framed for felony murder by a district attorney trying to make a name for himself because he was running for election later that year and needed a few quick convictions to shore up his pitiful resume. For a man who barely graduated from the sixth grade, the alternatives presented him were pretty straightforward: either admit to a crime he didn't commit and get a life sentence, or die in the electric chair. All politicians are bastards. Just make sure when you're talking to me in front of someone else, you get the name right. It's Don Russ."

"Yeah, sure, Donato. Anything you say." Remalli laughed.

A key rattled in the door behind Russ. The marshal let in a tall, dark young man dressed identically to Russ except for his tie.

"Not good," Mike Fein said. He showed Russ a copy of the indictment.

"Welcome to Washington, Mikey," Remalli said through the screen.

"Hello, Mr. Remalli."

Russ examined the indictment. Stamped at the top were the names of the federal magistrate and district judges assigned to the case.

"You'll be appearing before Judge Murchison for your initial appearance and detention hearing," Russ said. "I want to go ahead and have your arraignment at the same time so you'll spend less time in the county jail if we fail to get you out on bond. You'll plead not guilty, of course."

"Nope," Remalli said.

"What do you mean?"

"I'll plead not guilty, but it won't be before that magistrate judge. They're all down in Florida this week for a circle jerk. Some kinda conference. One of the marshals told me."

Russ studied the other judge's name. "That means the district judges are hearing preliminaries, then. We may be in a shitload of trouble."

"Why's that?"

Russ held up the paper, showed Remalli the name of the district judge. "Ring a bell?"

Remalli's face fell. Judge Paula Candler.

"Don't worry. I won't let this be my first loss to the feds. Point of pride." Russ craned his neck to Fein. "Of course, we have to tell him that, don't we? Rule number one of client relations: Never let 'em see you sweat."

Remalli gave them both a shit-eating grin. "Fuck you both. I got a business to run. Now get me the hell outta here."

Chapter 6

Scott hunched over the U.S. attorney's table in the empty courtroom and cursed the uncooperative cassette player. Why was it the equipment never seemed to work properly when it really counted? The government's entire strategy for ensuring Remalli stayed behind bars during the trial hinged on the contents of the recorded conversations from the auto parts shop. No screw-ups allowed, McNary had warned.

Scott turned off the external speakers and put on his headphones—his "golden ears," as the others on the squad called them—and fast-forwarded the tape until he got a signal. He rewound a foot, marked the position with the counter, then hit the Play button.

He heard his own voice on the tape: "Special Agent Scott Betts on December sixteenth, oh-two-forty hours. Venue is Beltway Tool and Parts, Inc., at 138 Farraday Avenue, Annandale, Virginia. Subject is Tony Remalli. Conversation recorded by court order number 99-5667, issued by U.S. District Judge Eleanor Goldsworthy."

Scott felt a tap on his shoulder. He abruptly turned the machine off and spun around to face McNary. Scott removed his headphones.

"The Buddha is smiling on us today," McNary said. He was always using lingo he had picked up in the Marines. "Chapman was saying we'd be really lucking out if we drew Judge Candler."

Just then two men with heavy briefcases simultaneously pushed through the courtroom doors. The taller one, in his late forties, with a squared-off forehead and sleek black hair, was Lloyd Chapman, the U.S. attorney for the Eastern District of Virginia. From what Scott had seen of him in their task force strategy meetings, Chapman was every bit as arrogant as he looked. It seemed as if he were always posing for some imaginary camera nearby. McNary had more than once muttered his suspicions of Chapman's political motives in pushing the FBI investigation so hard. Before Tony Remalli had made the mistake of setting up shop in his district, Lloyd Chapman had lacked a juicy case for public consumption—Saint George without the dragon, as McNary put it. The rumor that he was planning to run for Congress made a lot of sense. McNary's take was that Chapman was going to use the publicity generated from the Remalli case to catapult himself into the minds of the voters. By the time Remalli was sentenced, Chapman would be a household name in the district.

Chapman's assistant, Ted Savage, was a younger clone of his boss. He was politically well connected, the son-in-law of a powerful state representative, and former president of the state's Young Lawyers Bar Association. Like Chapman, he was dressed in a charcoal gray suit with a blue shirt and a nearly solid tie that filmed well on television. He matched Chapman's swagger up to the table step for step.

Chapman bit his upper lip and frowned. "Remalli's arrest," Chapman said to McNary. "What an abortion. What the hell happened?"

"We're not exactly sure yet."

"I'm sorry about that girl working for you."

"Paige."

"Yeah, Paige. We'll be presenting evidence to the new grand jury for indictments to cover her murder. And also for your other agent, if he doesn't make it. There's nothing I'd like better than winning another conviction against Remalli. As soon as I see the final report on what happened, of course. You'll be getting that in ASAP, won't you, McNary?"

"Uh, yeah, sure. Soon as I can." McNary's voice had gone up an octave.

"You're not anticipating any delays, any problems, are you?"

"No, Lloyd."

Scott sensed that the U.S. attorney had also picked up on the slight doubt in McNary's voice. Scott thought the uncertainty was curious. McNary had always been so direct and confident in every aspect of his professional dealings. Was McNary holding something back? Even after Scott had pumped him for details on what had gone on in the back room during the raid?

"Whatever," Chapman said. "Just as soon as you can." Chapman looked at his watch. "Judge will be here in ten minutes. We were just a little concerned because we got word Candler would be handling the preliminaries rather than the magistrate judge. I was afraid it wouldn't give you enough time to set up in here."

Magistrate courtrooms were smaller and not so exquisitely furnished. The courtroom of a federal district judge was much grander, especially some of the older rooms like the one they were in. The audio equipment hookups were a bit more complicated.

"Would you like to hear how it sounds on the speakers?" Scott asked. "I was just about to do a sound check."

"No, no," Chapman replied. "You boys are the black bag pros. The game plan's still to waive our three days to prepare for the detention hearing. There's no reason the judge can't get a taste of what's on these tapes today. You make sure the equipment's working. I'll make sure this creep isn't released back into the community on bond." Chapman did pick up a copy of the transcript, however, and scanned it quickly. "This is exactly what we talked about yesterday upstairs?"

"Word for word," Scott answered.

Chapman smacked the rolled-up transcript on the table. "Remalli's going to fry this time."

"The press is already three deep out in the hall waiting to get inside," McNary said. "Between a President's wife being the sitting judge and the publicity your office has been cranking out . . ."

"Just enough to reassure the law-abiding citizens of the district that their government representatives are doing their utmost to protect them." Chapman was sensitive about being too transparent in blowing his own horn over a trial that was being staged to further his political ambitions.

"Yeah, well, good news about the draw," McNary said.

The two attorneys nodded. *"Great* news," Chapman said. "And just as lucky we didn't get Judge Crane."

"We don't need a left-leaning jurist on this case," McNary agreed knowingly. "Not after all we went through to get these tapes." He pointed to Scott. "Not after all *this* guy went through."

"You're going to be our star witness on the stand," Chapman said to Scott.

"Not to mention losing a fine, young agent."

They paused at the mention of Paige's death again.

Chapman continued. "We would have done okay with Judge Crane, but Candler is a straight up-and-down law-and-order judge. No surprises. She's not going

She was relieved that the proceedings appeared to have just got under way. The judge, a woman in her mid-forties wearing half-moon glasses who looked very familiar to Julia, was shuffling papers. She had impeccably groomed shoulder-length brunet hair and the classic facial beauty of a former Miss America. She glanced over her glasses at the people sitting at the two tables in front of her, then looked out over the observers beyond the bar. The moment she removed her glasses, Julia recognized her: Paula Candler, the new President's wife, the First Lady who had decided to keep her job as a federal judge. Julia hadn't realized until now that this was where the judge presided.

Judge Candler spoke: "Our first item this afternoon is the initial appearance in the matter of *The United States* versus *Antonio Remalli*. Mr. Remalli, I see you are represented by counsel this morning?"

Don Russ rose, smoothing his silver tie with his left hand as he buttoned his black Armani suitcoat with his right. "Don Russ, Your Honor." He nodded to the young attorney seated next to him. "And this is Mr. Fein. I am representing Mr. Remalli and requesting bond today so that I may work with my client to properly develop an adequate defense—if that turns out to be necessary. We would also like to enter a plea."

"All right, Mr. Russ. And the plea is?"

"Emphatically not guilty."

"Fine, thank you. I've made a note of that. Mr. Chapman, I see, representing the Government. Do you have any information you'd like to bring before the court concerning the request for bond, or will you want a delay?"

Chapman rose. "Thank you, yes, Your Honor. The Government will waive its three days for the detention hearing."

"Fine. May I see a copy of the pretrial services report?"

"The defendant refused to cooperate, Your Honor," Chapman said. "He wouldn't answer any of the questions."

"I see. Mr. Russ, that does not bode well for your client relative to your application for bond."

"I understand."

"And is there some reason you'd like to offer the court for Mr. Remalli's refusal to cooperate?"

"It's very likely the Government would misconstrue any information Mr. Remalli might offer about his personal history to shore up what we will show to be a flawed case. Your Honor, I'm sure you know my client has always been happy to appear in court."

The judge looked doubtful.

"If I may . . ." Chapman held out a paper for the court security officer to hand up to the judge, and another copy for Russ. "Bank records we have obtained through court orders clearly demonstrate that Mr. Remalli has access to substantial resources, which would make him a serious flight risk. We have relevant excerpts from copies of taped conversations of Mr. Remalli that underscore this, while also indicating he would be a continued danger to the community."

"Very well. Proceed."

The U.S. attorney produced a stack of papers for the judge and the attorneys at the defense table. "Special Agent Scott Betts will play portions of taped conversations that were made pursuant to a Title III court order acquired by the FBI permitting them to install hidden listening devices at Antonio Remalli's place of business. The defendant is speaking with an associate, Salvatore Cerutti, also known as Dumbo. You'll find copies of the court orders attached to the transcripts. The government contends that Mr. Remalli and his associate were speaking of the murder of Judge Eleanor Goldsworthy. I might want to warn Your Honor and any observers in court that some of the language is rather offensive." Chapman turned to the courtroom spectators and made a face indicating his disgust.

Judge Candler nodded. She put her glasses back on and opened the transcript.

"All right, let's hear it," she said.

The prosecutor nodded toward Scott, waiting beside a cassette player. He turned the machine on, and there was a hiss over the speakers set up on the wall behind the bench. The courtroom went dead silent.

Then Julia heard the voice of a man whom she knew from the last time she had worked with Don Russ. She craned her neck to get a better look at Tony Remalli, sitting next to the attorney. He was unshaven, his arm in a sling. On the phone message, Russ had given her no clue about his client or the case. So what kind of trouble had the famous Mafia don got himself into this time?

REMALLI: Fuck's that?

CERUTTI: I picked up some papers on the way over. Thought you might want to see. [*Sound of paper rustling.*]

REMALLI: Yeah. Where's my name? Did you see my name anywhere?

CERUTTI: I haven't read it yet. I just saw the pictures in the machine at the gas station.

REMALLI: Will ya look at that? Hey! Look at this!

CERUTTI: How do they get away with printing pictures like that?

REMALLI: They'll print *anything* these days. The photographer musta snuck in the same way I did, round back of the stable. Musta had a cop on the take, though.

See? Somebody let him in. The police tape there? Right *there* . . .

CERUTTI [*laughs*]: She ain't got no more brains to think with. Look, Tony . . . it's dark, but can you see little bits of her brain all over the wall?

REMALLI: Geez, I see it. I see it. Man . . .

CERUTTI: You popped her good.

REMALLI: I whacked her good. . . .

Julia thought: the President's wife, a Mafia don, a dead federal judge . . . As seriously as she had earlier considered backing out of working with Don Russ again, there was no way she was going to miss out on being a part of this.

REMALLI: She got it where she deserved it—inna fuckin' mouth! Sometimes I get carried away like that when it's personal. I don't understand why a judge like that wouldn't have some guards around, or dogs or somethin'.

CERUTTI: 'Specially when she knows she's pissed someone off as bad as you.

REMALLI: Shit. I'da done it for the exercise. That's one bitch who won't be signin' any more court orders for the feds to tap my phones.

CERUTTI: We got wised up on that just in time. How'd ya know she was doin' that? Aren't those court orders supposed to be secret?

REMALLI: Hmmm . . . yeah . . . I got my sources. Anyways . . . you'd think someone as important as a federal judge would pay someone to shovel the shit out of her barn. Look . . . there . . . that's shit she's lying in. See that pitchfork? The bitch tried to kill me with that thing! Plus she's married to some rich Jew. She coulda had someone do that and she wouldn't be lyin' facedown in a pile a shit. I'll tell you one thing, I wouldn't do it. I don't care how fuckin' much I paid for the horse. . . .

Julia saw the back of Don Russ's head finally move. He looked over at his client, and she was able to get a good look at his profile for the first time in two years. His hair was cropped closer and his tan had deepened, but it was the same hardened face of the man she left standing in the lobby of a New York hotel.

Julia glanced at the man drawing the picture of the courtroom. He had a laminated tag clipped to his jacket front that said PRESS—obviously a sketch artist for one of the news organizations. She pointed to the figure of Russ he was just filling in with a colored pencil.

"You don't have his nose quite right," Julia whispered to him. "Make it look like it got smashed once." She pounded her fist into her other hand. "By me."

The artist cut his eyes at Julia, ignored her advice, shifted in his seat so she couldn't see his drawing pad anymore.

CERUTTI: Yeah, that's why you've got dumb fucks like me workin' for you. [*They laugh.*]

REMALLI: Yeah, you're dumb, all right. That's why you're called Dumbo. [*More laughing; sound of papers folding.*] These federal judges think they're so goddammed smart. If the bitch was so smart, she'd still be alive.

CERUTTI: She was dumb. I know plenty of dumb lawyers.

REMALLI: I do, too. Lawyers is all dumb fucks really. She was one of them. The bitch did have a real nice mouth, though. But that crazy horse started actin' up and I had to shoot it and she got really worked up and started fuckin' pokin' me with that goddammed pitchfork. I ain't never had someone come at me with a fuckin' pitchfork! Ya should'a seen me. Buddy, I was *mad*. Plus, I wasn't lettin' no *girlie* judge send me up—

The FBI agent switched the tape machine off with a loud click.

All eyes were on Judge Paula Candler. Even from the back of the room, Julia could see how she was struggling to control her anger.

Judge Candler carefully closed her transcript and put it aside. "Bond is denied," she said succinctly.

Russ shot to his feet. "I have another motion, Your Honor."

"Yes?"

"I move that the venue for these proceedings be changed. It's inconceivable my client can get a fair jury trial here in the state. The victim was far too well known in the community, and there has already been an extraordinary amount of media coverage, which will be prejudicial to my client." Russ glanced over at the reporters in the gallery.

"I'll be happy to review any such motion, but in written form. For now, however, your motion is denied."

"If Your Honor will permit, I have one final motion."

"Go ahead."

"I respectfully ask that Your Honor recuse herself from this case."

Judge Candler was visibly perturbed. She drew a deep breath. "On what basis, Mr. Russ?"

"On the basis that Your Honor is married to the chief law enforcement official of the United States government, whose prosecutors and investigative authorities are sitting at that table." Russ pointed at Chapman.

There were audible gasps from the journalists. Judge Candler turned crimson. She took her glasses off and glared at Russ.

"You'll have to do better than that, Mr. Russ. The law is clear on that point, and I will tell you frankly that some of the best legal minds the President could assemble have already reviewed the situation you allude to and concluded that your reasoning is flawed. But let's get it into the record if that's where this is going. Put it in writing, and we'll handle it in the normal manner. I'd ask you to withdraw that motion for the time being. As a favor to me."

She looked expectantly at Russ. It was the kind of favor no defense attorney could refuse a judge. She could make his life difficult if they ended up in an extended trial together.

"Certainly, Your Honor."

"Thank you, Mr. Russ. Is there any other business on this case before the court at this time? Susan?"

Judge Candler was handed a piece of paper by her case manager, who then let the court security officer give copies to Chapman and Russ.

"All right. Susan tells me the docket is very full over the next three months. Status conference is on Friday in the third week of April. Is that too tight for you, Mr. Russ? Motions still have to be to me thirty days before that, so it doesn't give you much time."

"No problem, Your Honor."

"All right. Trial date is set for two weeks later. Is everyone satisfied with that?"

"Yes, Your Honor," Chapman said.

Russ nodded. "Fine."

Paula Candler shot a wary eye at Russ, then looked at her case manager. "Next case?"

"The defendant's counsel called me to say he was running late."

The judge rolled her eyes. "Then we'll take a short recess until counsel sees fit to grace us with his presence."

Judge Candler stood up.

"All rise," Susan called out.

As soon as the judge had left the room, the sketch artist stepped over Julia and followed the gang of reporters walking as quickly to the rear door as courtroom etiquette allowed. Julia jumped up from her seat and headed toward the front, squeezing through the crowd clogging the central aisle on their way out.

Russ was talking to Remalli with a federal marshal standing nearby waiting to take him back to his cell. Julia made it to the row of seats behind the defense table just in time to hear the U.S. attorney remark on his way out: "You're going to lose this one, Russ." Remalli barely concealed an obscene gesture at Chapman, which prompted the marshal to insist that his handcuffs be put back on immediately.

The FBI agents filed out behind Chapman. As they passed by, Remalli spoke softly to the one who had been working the tape player. "Think you're so clever, don't you? Invadin' my privacy." His voice rose as they walked out. "Hey, hotshit. Better keep your eyes open a friend of mine doesn't pay you a visit sometime."

Russ gave Remalli a sharp jab in his meaty ribs. "What the hell do you think you're doing?" he said. "You want to end up charged with intimidation of a witness, too?"

Remalli rolled his eyes.

"Don," Julia said, lightly touching Russ's shoulder.

Russ turned and saw her. He took a deep breath. "Give us two minutes, please," he said to the marshal.

"Tony, you remember Julia Menendez," Russ said.

"Certainly," Remalli said. "So why you bringin' this bimbo in? I thought you two had some personal problems in workin' together. Do I really need this spic from Miami?"

Julia's eyes were narrowed to a slit. "It's 'Cuban-American.'"

Russ got up close to Remalli, out of earshot of the ̇aiting marshal, and said in a quiet but harsh voice, "Ms.

Menendez is a lot more expensive than a whore and infinitely better at what she does. After hearing those tapes, her talents may be your only hope of avoiding death row. Especially in light of your frank opinion of the legal profession. By the way, which dumb lawyer were you referring to?" He held up a copy of the transcript with the remark "Lawyers is all dumb fucks" circled.

Remalli looked sheepish, waved it off. "It was all talk."

"And that's what got you into trouble in the first place," Russ said. "I'll come by to see you about this later this afternoon."

Russ nodded to the marshal, who led Remalli away.

"I'm Mike Fein," Russ's associate said to Julia. He shook her hand, holding on to it a little longer than necessary.

"I remember, Mike," Julia said. "New York, two years ago. You had just got out of law school. You're all grown up now."

The young attorney blushed.

Russ stared at Julia. She searched his face for a clue as to what he was thinking.

"You're late," he finally said, filling his briefcase.

Julia let him have it: "Not '*Thanks* for coming on such short notice,' or '*Good* to see you again,' or 'How ya doin', Julia, it's been a *long* time'?"

They were jostled by the defense attorney trying to set up at the table for the next case.

Russ said to Fein, "Why don't you go on over to the Georgetown Law School library and get started on the recusal issue? Talk to some people in the legal community. See what you can find out about her legal background."

Fein took a long, lingering look at Julia before he left the courtroom. "Good to see you again," he said.

"You, too."

"Nice-looking kid," Julia said after Fein had left. "Kinda reminds me of you."

Russ shook his head. He grabbed Julia's arm and led her toward the back of the courtroom. "Come on," he said. "Let's go somewhere we can talk in private."

"Honest to God, Don, I thought she was going to throw her gavel at you," Julia Menendez said.

She was exploring the interior of Don Russ's spacious suite on the executive floor of the Ritz-Carlton Pentagon, a posh hotel close to the Alexandria courthouse. Through the windows were sweeping views of the National Mall.

Don Russ was seated stiffly in a Chippendale-style chair at a table, watching her poke her head into one of the two bedrooms off the sitting room, offended by her assumption of familiarity with his living space. She disappeared again, her voice coming from the interior of the other room: "I can understand your tooling up on that U.S. attorney, but a judge you never met before in your life?"

Russ drummed his fingers on his briefcase, considering his courtroom performance dispassionately. "I knew *exactly* what I was doing," he said. "After hearing those tapes, I doubt we're going to win this case on its merits. My first priority is to get us a new judge who'll be more sympathetic to a defendant. I'm also laying the groundwork for a possible appeal if that becomes necessary. Paula Candler was against us before we ever walked into her courtroom. As soon as I found out she'd be sitting on the case, I had Mike Fein run a Westlaw report so I wouldn't be walking into her court blind. She wrote more than two dozen law review articles from the time she was in school through her days as an associate law professor while she was partner in Bennington-King, the Richmond firm she joined just before her husband was elected governor. Zero tolerance. Three strikes, you're out. All the old arguments for the death penalty. She's a shameless apologist for law and order."

Julia emerged from the first bedroom holding a heavy terry-cloth robe to her face. "Nice bathrobes," she said.

"Have you heard anything I've said?" Russ replied.

"I'm listening, I'm listening," she said, and ducked into the second bedroom. "What about her Senate confirmation hearings?" she called out.

"Totally uncontroversial. Flawless testimony before a respectful subcommittee. No one voted against her when the vote came to the floor—just a handful of abstentions from liberal holdouts wanting to make a statement. I made a couple of phone calls on the flight down. Not surprisingly, she was a big rainmaker for Bennington-King. You'd expect a governor's wife to be able to pull a slew of juicy new clients into the firm, and apparently she did. She cut way back on the litigation, but kept her teaching job at the University of Richmond Law School even after they moved into the governor's mansion. My guess is she was trawling for potential associates for the firm, and bright, energetic workers for the presidential campaign that she must have known was coming." Drawers opened and shut. "*Julia . . .*" he said, with some annoyance.

Julia reappeared at the bedroom doorway. "If it's okay with you, I'll take the room on the right," she said.

"No, it's not okay. How about sitting down so we can talk? I've got a pissed-off client sitting in a stinking jail and a private jet idling on the runway to take me back to Chicago, where there's an entire firm awaiting my return."

Julia circled the couch, then settled gracefully, crossing her legs in an obvious show. Russ couldn't help noticing.

He had been so intent on the issues of the case that he hadn't really *seen* her except as an appendage to his legal strategies. Now he was seeing her as a woman again. The thought of her lying naked in a tangle of bedsheets made the back of his knees sweat. She still had her dancer's legs. She shook her hair, tucked her chin, and looked at him seductively through her bangs.

"Furthermore," Russ added, ignoring her flirtations, "her record on the bench indicates she's no friend of defense attorneys. She consistently refuses to allow motions on procedural issues which might benefit their clients. Fein tells me, though, she's never been overturned on appeal."

Julia took out a pen and a legal pad from her leather portfolio and struck a serious pose. She was all business now. "Okay," she said, "what's the next step?"

"I'm flying back to Chicago this afternoon to get my associates cranking on the legal research. We don't have much time to pull together a brilliant brief to convince Judge Candler that she should remove herself from the case. Although the procedural rules say technically we've got some latitude about when and how often we can file, realistically we've got one shot at this. We need to do it before the trial. And it's *got* to work."

Russ was pleased to see that Julia had been taking notes as he had talked. He read her neat script upside down: little bulleted points outlining everything he had said, even while she was wandering through the other rooms. She *had* been paying attention.

"So," she asked, "what's my assignment?"

"We're dealing with a highly unusual situation, what with the judge being the President's wife. I'll cover the legal issues with the guys at the firm. Who knows? We may be breaking new legal ground here. I'm counting on *you* to dig up the facts we can use to demonstrate

Paula Candler's bias—not so much a prejudice against Tony Remalli as a defendant as her prejudice in favor of the prosecution as the President's wife. I need substance for our brief. Specifics, details, hard evidence."

Julia didn't look up from her furious scribblings. "Do you have any idea where to start?"

Russ thought for a moment. "We need some lateral thinking, especially because of our severe time constraints. I'm trying to imagine myself in the place of a judge who knows that she's going to be petitioned to step down from a case. 'How does defense counsel demonstrate bias? Exploit my legal, my professional career? My *personal* life?' " Russ sat up and leaned over Julia's notepad as she wrote. "Now, there's an interesting tangent to explore." It was almost as if he were dictating to her now. " 'What would I fear most? What incident from my past, or association with other people, or personal indiscretion would I least want surfacing in a document submitted in open court? Where are my weaknesses? Who are my enemies? What deep, dark secrets are lurking in the closet? More to the point, *what do I most dread my family and the public finding out?*' "

Julia took a moment to catch up writing with all he had said. "Geez, Don," she said, "you're talking about a federal judge—who happens to be married to the President of the United States. This ain't just some *shmuck* who's been cheating on his wife I'm investigating."

"And that's exactly why I brought you in on the case." Russ could see Julia was thinking through the implications. "What makes Paula Candler so different from anyone else?" he continued. "Everyone's got a past that can—given the right spin—be exploited. Everyone has something in their background they're not proud of."

"Yeah, Don," she said, "what about us? We've got a

past, all right." She smiled wickedly at him. "But have we got a future?"

"That's not what I meant."

"You're changing the subject."

"I need to know everything there is to know about Judge Paula Candler. I'll supply the brilliant legal reasoning, you supply the dirt. I don't know how you're going to do it, but it's got to be done. Quickly."

Russ dug into his suitcoat pocket and produced a key. He held it up for Julia to take. She broke out into a big smile and flicked her eyes toward the bedroom.

"My room key," she cooed.

"That's right. Suite number 217 at the Patriot's Inn, a little farther west of here."

She was disappointed, but had never really expected they would be sharing a hotel suite together. "Sounds quaint."

Russ smiled knowingly. "I assume the feds will be snooping around, keeping an eye on me, now that they know who's representing Tony. They've got too much at stake to take any chances on blowing this case. I don't want to raise their guard by tipping them off that I've got a high-powered private investigator already working with me. I've decided it's better if we're not seen together. I don't want you attending court sessions, either. It agitates Tony unnecessarily."

"Are you sure it's not *you* who's being agitated?"

"I'm going to ignore that."

Julia frowned at the key. "It's okay, really. You just don't trust yourself around me," she teased. "I'm a woman; I understand those things. We wouldn't want a replay of two years ago, would we?" She capped her pen and stood. "At least promise me this: I get you the evidence you need to have this judge thrown off the case, and you'll let me buy you a drink. I noticed there's a very nice lobby bar downstairs. Couple of martinis . . . a little piano music . . . who knows? This is beginning to look a lot like the way things got rolling in New York, isn't it?"

Russ dialed the phone to summon a taxi to take Julia to her hotel. He turned away from her to hide his bewilderment. *She never gives up.*

"Later," he called over his shoulder. "Much later. The only commitment I'm going to make at this point is to my client."

Julia smiled. "But I sense you've left yourself an opening, Counselor."

Chapter 7

A little after nine o'clock at night in the downtown Washington FBI field office on Fourth Street, Scott finished checking over the handwritten draft of his incident report on the Remalli raid. He tore a dozen pages from his legal pad and paper-clipped them together. Out in the hallway, he could see the lights from several offices still on, other agents like himself who were completing a mountain of paperwork after a long day working cases in the field.

Scott put his report into his secretary's in-box for typing the next morning. The word from the FBI headquarters in the J. Edgar Hoover Building several blocks away was that the Director wanted to see the write-ups of every agent involved in the Remalli raid on his desk by noon.

Just about to return to his office before setting out for home, Scott noticed a file folder on top of the stack of folders on the corner of the secretary's desk. It was labeled with McNary's name. Scott hesitated for a moment, looked to see that no one was watching, then picked up the file and opened it. Paige's death had been weighing heavily on Scott. He had to know everything that had happened in there.

Along with various typed memos to McNary's superiors was his own version of the Remalli incident report. It was marked CONFIDENTIAL.

All he needed was a fast peek. If the memo had been

about anything other than why Paige had been killed, the thought of reading his boss's confidential memo would have never crossed his mind. . . .

He quickly scanned the seven-page report. Then he read the section at the end headed ACCOUNTABILITY.

Jesus Christ, he thought. *What is this?*

"Scott," came a voice from down the hall. Scott nearly jumped out of his skin.

It was McNary, briefcase in hand. Scott quickly closed the folder and threw it back onto the desk.

"Time for you to go home, sport," McNary said.

"I'm right behind you."

"All right, see you tomorrow," McNary said.

"Night."

As soon as McNary was out the door, Scott grabbed the folder and reread McNary's narrative of the Remalli raid. *Paige died because of me?* Scott asked himself. *Because of what I did last night?*

Why hadn't McNary mentioned that before? How could he just pass him in the hallway without saying anything about it?

What the hell is going on?

Paula, Missy, and Chip Candler sat in the family's private White House dining room. Jim Candler's place was set at the table, but empty. Word had come that DAGGER—as he had been code-named by the Secret Service, possibly an allusion to his skills as a college fencing champion—was on his way, but they should start without him.

Paula was still turning over the day's events in her mind as the first course was served by Navy stewards. The word "recusal" still rung in her ears. Having had the entire afternoon to think about it, she had only gotten madder about the defense attorney's arrogant behavior.

That son of a bitch, she thought. *Damned cocky*

lawyer comes into my courtroom and asks me to remove myself just because I'm the President's wife!

Missy was frowning at her. "About the spring formal, Mom . . ." she was saying.

Her voice broke Paula's trance. "I'm sorry, sweetheart. What were you saying?"

"You don't think Dad will have any problem with me going, do you? I mean, I am in ninth grade, after all."

"I think you'd better ask him yourself."

"Well . . . I was kind of hoping you could talk to him first. Soften him up a bit."

Chip broke in. "If she needs a lawyer to represent her, she must be desperate."

Missy shot him an angry look. "Am not!"

"Changing the subject," Paula said, passing the potatoes around. "How was school today?" After much agonizing over the public versus private options, she and Jim had decided to send the children to the Quaker school used by several of the previous Presidents' families, mainly for security reasons. Providing protection for Chip (code named DRUMBEAT) and Missy (known as DIVA) would be much simplified.

"We start indoor training for cross-country next week," Chip said.

"That's good. You still like your teachers?"

Both the children nodded, although Chip somewhat less enthusiastically.

"*Tons* of homework," Missy said between bites. "But the classes are great."

Just then the door opened and Jim Candler came in. He looked preoccupied, then grinned upon seeing his family gathered around the dinner table. "Hello, everyone," he said hoarsely.

"Your voice is terrible!" Paula said with alarm. "I haven't heard it that bad since the campaign."

"Yeah," he croaked, taking a seat at the table. "We've been working on that speech for tomorrow night all day. I was given orders to return to the residence forthwith to rest."

"We're glad to have you," Paula said. "Regardless of your condition."

Chip and Missy talked more about school as they finished dinner. Jim was prepared to wave off dessert as the Navy steward returned, but was instead presented with a message.

"What is it?" Paula asked.

"I have an urgent request to go to the Situation Room."

"Okay," Paula said to the children, hustling them out of the room. "You two go on and get started on your homework."

After Chip and Missy were gone, Jim said, "This could mean another late night in the West Wing. Since we may not get to talk later, I wanted to ask you about that mob case you drew. Del told me you've been asked to recuse yourself?"

"As far as I'm concerned, it's a matter before the court, just like any other. There's case and statutory law covering the recusal issue. Our legal advisers covered all that during the White House transition. I'm not going to be bullied by some slick defense attorney into removing myself from a case just because I'm your wife, if that's what you're asking. That runs against everything I stand for."

"I'm glad to hear that," Jim said. "I want you to know I understand the pressures you're under because you've taken on the responsibilities as the First Lady."

She smiled at his concern. He was, as usual, irresistible, even if he could barely talk.

A knock on the door, then a Secret Service agent

stuck his head in. "Sorry to interrupt, Mr. President. They're asking for you back in the Situation Room."

"Tell them I'll be right there."

Julia Menendez picked at the chipped oak veneer on the edge of the dining room table and squinted at the dim image cast on the wall by her portable microfilm projector, the only source of light in the room. At 2:43 A.M., she was numb from information overload. She hadn't discovered anything consequential in the public—and not-so-public—records that defined the life of Judge Paula Candler, the totality of which had been reduced to the photocopied, disk-copied, and microfilmed contents of an empty cardboard Jack Daniel's liquor case.

Julia's bloodshot eyes searched the gloom of the living room. Dun walls, beige carpeting, brown curtains—such were the inspiring distractions of the homey Patriot's Inn, a small budget extended-stay hotel within walking distance of the King Street Metro station. Quaint, it definitely was not. Don Russ had obviously selected it because it was one of the last places in Alexandria that anyone would ever suspect the five-hundred-dollar-an-hour lawyer would be putting up one of his staff.

Earl, the live-in manager who read used paperback murder mysteries with lurid covers behind the front desk, had carried her suitcase up the stairs to her room overlooking the liquor store across the street. No room service, but there was an all-night convenience store around the block. Laundry in the basement, no unescorted guests past the reception, and don't ask any questions about the other residents.

Julia focused again on the projection, a microfilm roll of back issues of the glossy *Richmond Magazine* she had "borrowed" from the public library for the evening. She was halfway through scanning a feature article entitled "Paula Candler: Woman of the Twenty-first Century." An accompanying photo layout depicted her excelling in the many aspects of her busy life: adjusting the bow tie of her husband—the then governor—while attending the Daughters of the American Revolution's annual ball; dropping the kids off at school just like a regular mom; glaring over half-moon glasses at an unfortunate defendant in her courtroom.

Over the past dozen hours, Julia had amassed an impressive pile of data on the judge's life. She had photocopied articles from the library and financial information from all the major credit bureaus. From several on-line subscription databases she had downloaded onto her laptop computer additional information on the judge's assets—home and car purchases—and a list of the trivial civil and criminal matters she had been involved in: a lawsuit against a building contractor settled out of court, a ticket for rolling through an intersection at a stop sign while she was in college—nothing worth immediately pursuing. The complete records of Paula Candler's phone calls over the past four years—private calls made in the governor's mansion and the judge's chambers—were procured for a substantial fee through an embittered telephone company employee in Jacksonville, Florida, whom Julia and several other Florida private investigators regularly used.

From what she had seen in the documents so far, Paula Candler's life seemed *too* perfect, like the way the judge wore her hair: too trim, tidy, set in place. People like that made Julia highly suspicious.

She was confident that somewhere in that mass of data something would eventually pop. Something she could hand over to Don Russ for his recusal motion to get Paula Candler off the Remalli case. She just had to keep digging.

The only thing Julia lacked at the moment was copies of the canceled checks from the judge's personal bank account. She knew whom she had to call, and she absolutely dreaded it.

She dialed a number in Miami.

"Raul," she said sweetly. "One more favor, *por favor*? Pretty please?"

She listened to him talk and cringed.

"Yes," she answered, "I know my IOUs are piling up on your desk. It's just that I'm in a real fix and I need something . . . tomorrow."

She winced as he ranted in rapid Spanish.

"Okay, okay," she relented. "It's a deal. Just as soon as I get back into town. Anywhere you choose."

Raul mellowed, spoke to her with a new intimacy. She bit her lip and lied: "I wouldn't have it any other way. I've got just the thing in mind. The black microskirt— you know, the one I had my picture taken in on the hood of my Vette for the newspaper after the Herrero trial in September? We'll go dancing anywhere you want to go, all night long, you and me, babe. Just let me explain what I need. . . ."

Raul was a source in the banking industry—a Cuban-American like her, living in Miami, who made five times his salary as a skip tracer in a bank by accepting outside "consulting" jobs for Julia, his only private-investigator customer, and several less reputable South Americans, presumably with ties to money laundering and drug running.

Raul seemed to understand what she was looking for. "Yes," Julia said, "of course we have an arrangement. I'll even spring for drinks."

Raul seemed pleased. Maybe he'd actually do what he promised he would by the next day.

"What other thing?" Julia said. ". . . Oh, come on. I told you I'd go dancing with you. Can't we just leave it at that?"

Raul was trying to change the terms of the bargain.

"For God's sake, Raul! All right, all right!" She took a deep breath. "Lap dance. But no touching. And this is for you only; I don't want this turning into a stag party. You'd damned well better have me those checks by tomorrow."

Raul said something smutty to her.

"You know something?" she replied. "You really are despicable. But I'm going to keep my word . . . as long as you keep yours." She slammed the phone down. "You greasy piece of shit."

She hated herself when she got off the phone. She hated Don Russ worse.

Chapter 8

Julia Menendez signed the courier's log for the parcel from Miami at 9:07. Earl stood behind the front desk twitching, ready to pistol-whip the delivery man if he didn't leave quickly.

"Thanks, Earl," she said politely, but without too much familiarity. She felt his eyes watching her legs as she climbed the stairs back up to her suite.

From the air bill slip she could tell the package had been put on the early flight out of Miami. It was much heavier and larger than she had expected. She tore through the large envelope.

"Ha!" she laughed.

One small box containing the roll of microfilm. A second, larger box of fabulously illicit Cuban cigars, Cohiba Lanceros. A handwritten message on a Post-it note: *With compliments, Raul.*

Now she owed him big-time. She wouldn't be able to refuse his next request to take her dancing in South Beach. Maybe if they went someplace really dark, no one would notice his harelip and Sansabelt trousers. *That was cruel*, she chastised herself. She'd never even met the guy in person. He just sounded like such a creep on the phone.

Two and a half hours later, and her third cigar smoked, she was still at it. Frame after frame of canceled checks from Paula Candler's personal bank account. Groceries. Dental bills. Magazine subscriptions. One boring transaction after another—all of which helped build a picture of the judge's life, although nothing startling had emerged so far. Don Russ would not be very pleased. And she sure as hell wasn't doing this for Tony Remalli.

Julia had started with the most recent checks and worked her way backward. Paula Candler was methodical, noting in a clear hand without exception the purpose for each debit in the lower-left-hand corner of the check, probably for tax purposes. Not everyone was as meticulous a record keeper as she was, but Julia supposed it came from her training as a lawyer and judge to make note of the smallest of details.

Julia rolled to the next frame and stared at the check made out to Dobson Ford in the amount of $282.97 in September two years previous. The notation indicated it was for a 24,000-mile maintenance checkup on her Crown Victoria. An ordinary transaction, just like the hundreds of others she had looked at. So what was it that bugged her about this particular check?

She wound the roll to a period six months *later,* among the checks she had already examined. She found one she recalled seeing before—made out to a different car dealership, Riverside Ford, also for a car checkup, but this time the mileage was only 12,000 miles on the Crown Victoria. Julia ran the microfilm forward in time once again, and found a second 24,000-mile maintenance check at the same dealership. *Two 24,000-mile services on the same car, but at different places?* Julia was certain she'd only seen on-line database records for a single car owned by the family, and she knew the governor almost always had been driven by a state trooper or borrowed a vehicle from the state motor pool. To be certain, she rewound the film back to the time before

Judge Candler had taken the car to Dobson Ford. Just as curious, there was also a *second* 12,000-mile checkup.

What was going on?

If she had found anything meaningful to pursue, she would have let this oddity drop until later. But at the moment—until something leaped out of the data—she had nothing else to work on.

Julia reexamined the database reports and found the VIN—the vehicle identification number—for the car. It was listed as a gray Ford Crown Victoria, registered to the Virginia executive residence address in Richmond.

So had Paula Candler bought a second car? *Another* Crown Victoria? Julia rechecked the records and found only the one vehicle.

She exchanged the microfilm roll for the one with the feature article on the judge in *Richmond Magazine*. The accompanying photo clearly showed her driving a Crown Victoria in one shot, and this was during the period when she would have presumably been driving the first car, the "high mileage" Ford. Julia rummaged through her box of photocopies and came up with a newspaper article from the period of the second car, the "low-mileage" Crown Victoria, showing the judge and governor arriving at a party, driving an identical car.

There was a three-month gap between the dates the car had been taken in for checkups at the two Ford dealerships. Which also raised the question, why change garages for the auto checkups? Either someone, sometime during that period, had mysteriously rolled the odometer back, or there were in reality two different cars.

Julia pulled all her other records out and focused on those few months. It was just a hunch, but it was all she had to go on.

There was nothing remarkable in the credit card

records. The phone records were all over the place, and without more time it would be next to impossible to evaluate them for any peculiarities. She'd go digging there later if something emerged elsewhere.

She copied down the Ford's VIN, placed it in her purse, then decided she needed a shower to clear her head before she left the hotel.

She turned the hot water on in the shower. She stripped naked and breathed in the steam, cleansing her lungs of the heavy cigar smoke. She adjusted the shower temperature and got in.

Damn it all, she fumed as she lathered her hair. She was beginning to wish she hadn't taken the job. Digging up dirt on federal judges who just happened to be married to the President wasn't her usual gig. She was still mad about having to provide "favors" for Raul so she could meet the demands of her client. Being seen with a total geek in the South Beach clubs would do absolutely nothing to bolster her carefully cultivated image as one of Miami's hippest chicks.

Her client, she mused. Always keeping the client happy. Just how far would she stoop for a second chance at romance with Don Russ?

Paula had been in chambers since seven in the morning, reading motions for the cases pending in her court, then going over the speech she was giving at the League of Women Voters lunch. Marla buzzed her at eleven-thirty to say Helen van Zandt was downstairs in the car.

There were always crowds wanting to get a glimpse of the First Lady, but Paula was still amazed when she saw the mass of people outside the Sheraton National Hotel in Arlington, the site of the League's function.

"You're the hottest ticket in town," Helen said. She held up the morning newspaper and showed her an article. "Every table was sold out weeks ago. You've become a real hero to working mothers. They want to get a look at the woman who's got it all."

Agent Branson steered the car through the police cordon. The crowd was mostly women, pressing forward to try to see Paula in the backseat. The car stopped at the front entrance and the Secret Service agents in the Chevy Suburbans hurried into position, joining the police and advance agents already in place. As Branson opened the car door for her, the women began clapping. Paula stood tall and they began to cheer and call her name. "Judge Candler! Judge Candler!"

She was immediately enveloped by a protective ring of Secret Service agents, their eyes scanning the crowd from behind dark glasses. Helen trailed behind. The women surged forward, holding out their hands for her to shake. She reached out and touched several of them. Their faces were full of wonderment and joy.

If it weren't for the thorough preparation of the Secret Service, it could have quickly turned into a mob scene. Agent Mobley radioed that DRAGONFLY was coming in, then politely urged her onward through the front entrance.

Inside, it was no different. Women everywhere, clapping and insistently calling her name. The hotel staff all stopped what they were doing as she passed down the corridor toward the meeting rooms. Television camera lights swung in her direction, and a group of reporters rushed forward as she entered the cavernous Commonwealth Ballroom. No one was seated, everyone looking expectantly at the door. The place was filled to overflowing, standing room only around the perimeter packed five deep. As soon as she entered the clapping began again—loud, enthusiastic clapping as she hadn't heard since election night. It was exhilarating.

The usually staid League of Women Voters lunch had taken on the excitement of one of the campaign rallies. Paula saw the chairman on the dais looking thrilled.

"Judge Candler!" cried one particularly insistent voice. "Judge Candler!"

Paula turned to look. A woman with a microcassette recorder caught her eye—another reporter. She looked vaguely familiar. "Judge Candler," she said breathlessly, "is it true that the reason you're continuing to work and not serving full-time as the First Lady in the White House is that you and the President are having marital problems?"

"What?" she said incredulously.

Now she remembered. The reporter with a tabloid, one of the papers that had unsuccessfully tried to dig up dirt on her and Jim during the campaign.

Flustered, she had opened her mouth to respond when Agent Mobley swept the reporters and their gear out of the way and gently pushed her back with his hand.

"Ignore it," he said. "Just keep moving."

On the street outside, Julia Menendez stood expectantly among the other women hoping to catch a glimpse of the nation's First Lady as she left. Julia was dressed as inconspicuously as possible—blue jeans tucked into short boots, a hand-decorated sweatshirt of the kind usually bought at country craft fairs, and an oversize leather bomber jacket. It seemed all the professional women were inside attending the lunch, while the soccer moms and tourists were jostling outside.

Many of the women had cameras, so Julia wasn't the only person carrying a 35mm camera with a telephoto lens. She was certain, however, that no one else was using a Nikon F5 with a bulk back holding a hundred feet of film and a motor drive capable of blowing through over eight and a half frames per second—one of the several pieces of equipment she had brought from Miami.

A car sped out of the driveway and a buzz of excitement swept through the crowd. People began pushing each other for a better position to get a picture of the judge. Julia had claimed a spot on what would be the driver's side of the car as it approached.

"It's not her," someone said as the car approached, and everyone groaned.

Julia kept her eye on the camera's viewfinder, adjusted the focus on the car's dashboard through her lens. She checked to make sure the polarizing filter was in place to reduce the glare from the windshield.

Three more cars came speeding down the driveway.

"It's them!" a woman shouted.

The first car was one of the Chevy Suburbans that accompanied the judge's car wherever she went. Julia trained the lens of her camera on the driver's-side dashboard of the second car, unmistakably Paula Candler's gray Crown Victoria. She held her finger down and heard the whir of the camera over the voices excitedly calling out all around her: "Judge Candler!" "Over here!" "Wave!" "There she goes!" Then, finally, "Awwww, shoot, honey! I didn't even see her face!"

Julia had missed Judge Candler's face, too, but that was never the point.

Julia was fast-walking to her rental car before the taillights of the judge's Crown Vic had disappeared down the street.

Destination: a small neighborhood photography shop she had found near her hotel.

Chapter 9

Gathered in the sitting area of the Oval Office was a small group of the President's closest military and intelligence advisers talking in hushed voices. The seat at the head of the group was still empty.

An aide entered the Oval Office and increased the level of the lighting in the room, signaling the arrival of the President. The group of advisers stood as Jim Candler came in with Del Owens by his side. The room was immediately energized by the presence of the chief executive.

The President motioned them all to sit. He dropped onto the coffee table a well-thumbed background paper prepared for POTUS—President of the United States—as Jim Candler was known in internal White House documents.

Del sat on the President's right. Without wasting any time, the director of the National Security Agency, an intense academic with horn-rimmed glasses, launched into his presentation. He drew an arc with a pointer across the face of a map of the Middle East.

"Our analysts have concluded from satellite reconnaissance that he's moved over twenty rocket launchers out of hidden underground tunnels in the past two days. We've also detected unusual movement along transportation routes from a pharmaceutical plant outside the capital city, which they adamantly insist is only being used to produce desperately needed medicine."

"Mr. President," Del said, "that's bullshit. They've tried hiding behind that humanitarian crap before. I've reviewed the intelligence. It's a biological weapons laboratory."

The Vice President, a stout, graying man from Utah, sat on the other side of Jim Candler. Chosen to balance the ticket, he owed his position partially to Del, who had urged Jim to select him as his running mate.

The CIA director, a hawkish former hotshot undersecretary for defense in an earlier administration, leaned forward. "Mr. Owens is correct, sir. We've picked up rumblings through our agents on the ground that he has been able to revive his biological weapons program."

"Are the rockets armed at the moment?" the President asked, looking at the CIA director.

"As far as we can tell, no. But it's just a matter of time. He can't be more than a couple of weeks away from having everything in place to install the warheads."

Jim Candler nodded thoughtfully. "The likely target?"

"Nominally Israel."

"He wants to see what the new American president is made of," Del chimed in. "He's testing you. Obviously he believed all that nonsense your opponent was spewing last year about your lack of foreign policy experience."

The other advisers looked at Del with awe and disbelief at his candor. The President took the assessment without the slightest indication that Del's objectivity had ruffled him in any way.

"You're right," Jim said. "We're not going to let him get away with threatening our allies in the region, but we're also not going to give him the pleasure of the knee-jerk response he seems to be after. If this escalates to the point where we'll have to respond with military action, fine. I'll not hesitate to respond appropriately." He pointed a finger at the defense secretary. "Draw up contingency plans for an armed response. I'll call the Israeli prime minister and inform him what's going on. Then we start letting our other allies know. We want to start building international support in case we do need to take military action. And we'll need to start working the phones with the congressional leadership. It wouldn't hurt to go ahead and get them in here for an intelligence briefing—I don't want them left out of the loop until the last moment. Agreed?"

Enthusiastic nodding all around.

"Del will coordinate all government departments and agencies. You have a question, you call him. I want to make sure this young administration doesn't stumble in the face of its first crisis."

"Thank you, Mr. President," the advisers said in chorus; then they left. The Vice President hovered for a moment until he realized he was no longer needed. Del and the President were left alone.

Jim Candler eased into the chair behind his desk.

"Jim, you realize what a godsend this is?" Del said, sitting down. "You've just been presented a golden opportunity to shore up your credentials as a strong and decisive leader. Move decisively, forcefully, and foreign governments will be reassured of America's leadership position on international relations. Better yet, swift, firm action sets a precedent for the rest of the term with Congress. Makes the job of moving our domestic program through Congress all the easier."

"I hate like hell that it takes a foreign threat like this to give us some leverage with Congress over our budget priorities. But those are the cards we've been dealt."

Jim Candler rose from his chair and looked out onto

the Rose Garden. Del stood beside him, and the President put his arm around Del's shoulders.

"I sure am glad you agreed to come to Washington with me," Jim said. "Can you imagine where we'd both be if you had decided to become a Baptist minister like your daddy wanted you to be?"

Only several blocks away, near the Patriot Inn, Julia hunched over a workbench with a magnifying glass in the darkroom of the Kim Foto Lab. "Mr. Kim," she said, blinking back tears from the fumes of photographic development chemicals, "can you make out these last two numbers?"

Mr. Kim unhurriedly pulled another sheet of photographic paper out of the tray of fixing solution and clipped it to an overhead wire to dry. He looked over her shoulder. "Maybe nineteen? Seventy-four? Good thing you take lots of pictures. Here, take a look at these."

He unclipped another half dozen prints from the other end of the wire and spread them out for her side by side on the counter.

Of the 143 frames she had taken of the judge's speeding car outside the hotel, over half were totally unusable, either out of focus because of the target's movement or distorted by the camera-flash glare off the windshield. But by piecing together portions of the remaining photos she had almost completed the task of assembling the different segments of the car's vehicle identification number from the stamped metal plate riveted to the top of the dashboard.

Julia examined all the enlarged photos that Kim had laid before her. "Seventy-four," Julia pronounced. "That's it. I've got the entire number now."

She checked it against what she had copied down from the on-line database. It was as she had suspected:

a different car from the Crown Victoria registered to Paula Candler. There were two cars, to the casual observer identical to each other.

It was eight o'clock before Julia got back to her hotel. There were five messages on her answering machine, all from Don Russ, his voice growing increasingly agitated with each unanswered message. Don would just have to wait a few minutes.

Julia accessed one of the on-line databases on her laptop computer. She punched in the VIN she had constructed from the photographs of Judge Candler's car. She tapped the desk impatiently with her long red fingernails as she waited for the host computer to find the record.

Several things really bugged her about the car business. Why would the judge buy an identical car—a *used* car—when the one she already owned had such low mileage? If the original car had been sold, or even wrecked and unloaded as scrap, a record of the transaction would exist. The car was still around somewhere. What did it all mean?

In less than half a minute she had her answer. Paula Candler's car had been purchased used in November two years earlier from Slocum Automotives in Bledsoe, Virginia, odometer affidavit sworn as 10,166 miles, titled in the name of Delbert P. Owens.

Julia checked her notes: the purchase date fell neatly between the time that the personal checks were written for the two maintenance visits.

But Delbert P. Owens? What was the President's wife doing tooling around in the car of some redneck named *Delbert*?

Then the name began to sound familiar. *Delbert . . . Delbert*, she repeated to herself. *Del*. It was *Del*.

She remembered in a flash: Del Owens, the President's campaign manager and now chief of staff.

The phone was ringing, the Caller ID panel indicating it was Don Russ again. She let the answering machine take the call. Don cursed to himself, but declined to leave another message this time.

She rang the reception downstairs. She had a hunch to play. She asked Earl what time the main library in Alexandria closed. He said if she hustled, she had a few minutes before they closed for the night.

Hustle was something she knew about.

She flew down the stairs past the reception and out the door, leaving Earl to ponder what the mysterious, exotic woman in Room 217 was doing running out into a winter night. He nodded knowingly to himself and turned another brittle yellow page of his pulp fiction murder novel.

Chapter 10

Scott scanned the small parking lot below his office window. It was six-thirty and the lot was virtually empty, the bulk of the federal workers already headed for home.

Scott was still upset from reading McNary's memo the previous night. The thought that he himself had been responsible for Paige's death really shook him up. McNary claimed that it had been Scott's responsibility to call off the raid after he got inside the auto parts place and realized that Dumbo might be able to give some secret signal to the back room to warn of a possible raid. That much was true. The plan had been that if Scott found anything the slightest bit suspicious, he'd terminate the operation.

McNary's memo cited a buzzer hidden under the front counter found by the FBI the day after the raid, which was how the mobster apparently tipped Remalli off that something was going down out front. That was news to Scott. McNary claimed in his report that with the rain pounding so hard on the metal roof, Scott was unable to hear the buzzer, and he should have known to withdraw.

It was a convoluted crock of shit.

If McNary thought Scott had been responsible, why hadn't he said anything to him directly?

It was clear McNary had been avoiding him. He'd had

his door closed the whole day. He had his phone calls forwarded to his secretary, who told Scott he wasn't taking any meetings. He had his lunch sent in. *He probably pissed into the trash can*, Scott thought, *to keep from running into me on the way to the rest room.*

Scott needed answers. McNary was playing fast and loose with Scott's career, trying to pin the blame on him. What really torqued him, though, was Paige's death. Scott hated that he didn't know for certain himself if he was to blame or not.

Scott confirmed that light was still coming from under McNary's door before he went down the stairs and out of the building. He headed for McNary's car, a seven-year-old Honda Accord he had been driving since his divorce settlement five years earlier. Scott made sure no one was looking, then pulled a Swiss Army knife from his pocket and selected a stubby blade. He moved to the front of the car, dropped quickly to the ground, and reached up underneath. With a well-positioned thrust of his arm, he punctured the radiator.

"Aw, shit," McNary said, seeing the large puddle of fluid spilling in front of his car. "What the hell is that?"

Scott had hung out in his office until McNary had at last emerged. Scott caught up with him at the elevator just before the doors closed in his face. It was a quiet ride down.

McNary had muttered something about the weather as they walked together to the parking lot. Then he saw the problem with his car and realized he wasn't going anywhere fast.

"Looks like a radiator leak," Scott said. "Come on. Give you a lift home."

"You don't live anywhere near me."

"Doesn't matter. I'm in the mood to drive."

McNary stared at his useless car for a moment, then relented. He threw his briefcase into the backseat of Scott's car.

Scott pulled out onto the main road. "You eaten yet?" he asked.

"Naw."

"Me either. Want to grab a bite somewhere?"

McNary was obviously torn between his desire for food and his extreme discomfort with being in Scott's company. "I'd better go on back home."

"There's some stuff behind you."

"Really?" He perked up. "What've you got?" McNary said, reaching into the backseat.

Scott had made a quick run at lunch to stock up on some of the junk food McNary used to eat on stakeout.

McNary unwrapped a sleeve of miniature powdered doughnuts and offered one to Scott.

"Pass, thanks."

Scott glanced at McNary's gut straining against the seatbelt. He must have put on fifteen pounds since the beginning of the Remalli operation. Some people stopped eating when they got stressed out. McNary kept feeding his face.

"So, you get your incident report all finished?" Scott asked.

McNary popped another doughnut into his mouth. He took his time finishing it.

"Yeah. All done yesterday. You?"

"Same here."

"That's good. Headquarters appreciates getting them sent in promptly. Sure you don't want one of these doughnuts?"

"No, really. Thanks." *Shit*, Scott thought. *This is going nowhere.*

McNary brushed a lapful of powdered sugar from his

trousers. He was trying to skirt the subject of the incident report.

"What's the latest on Alan?" Scott asked. "Is he going to be in any position to help the investigation?"

McNary was clearly uncomfortable with the question. "Unfortunately, I don't think Alan's ever going to be in a position to help shed any light on what happened. When I talked to the hospital this afternoon, there hadn't been any change in his condition. They're not giving him much chance of pulling through."

On the other side of the White House, Scott headed west on Pennsylvania Avenue, passed the turnoff to his furnished rental apartment in Foggy Bottom, and headed north, in the opposite direction from McNary's house in Prince William County.

"Think you should have hung a left back there, sport."

"It's okay. I'll make the next one." Scott was driving and in control. He had McNary trapped in his car.

Soon Scott swung onto a road lined with two-story brick apartments. "Paige lived somewhere around here," he said.

Lots of Georgetown University off-campus parking stickers on the car bumpers. Paige was younger and single and liked living among the college kids.

"She was dating a graduate student, wasn't she?" McNary said.

"Yeah. They'd been talking about getting married when he got out of school." Scott slowed the car. "Up there," he pointed.

They looked at the front window of her place, an inside light still on. A cat was standing between the window and the curtains, looking down on the parking lot.

Now Scott remembered: the cat hair he had seen on Paige's collar as the paramedics had wheeled her through Remalli's front office. She was always going on about her calico tom. And McNary was always on her case about all the cat hair she came into the office wearing on her clothes.

"I'll call the apartment manager in the morning to do something about the cat," McNary said.

Scott stopped the car. "Craig, that's nice of you, but something's been bothering me."

"Oh?"

"I've been torn up inside about Paige's death. We were as close as two friends could be."

Scott turned off the engine and cut the lights. He wiped the condensation off the windshield and rolled down his window.

"And?" McNary said.

"What *really* happened in the back room at Remalli's place? I've got the feeling you're holding out on me. If there's something I need to know, I'd really appreciate it if you'd just tell me. Now's as good a time as any."

McNary was watching the cat's tail swishing back and forth. "This afternoon I got the third degree from Chapman about how Remalli could have known to expect the raid. He's convinced there's a leak. And he's adamant that it's no one in his office. Which implies it's one of us. We both know that's bullshit. Of course, the bigger question is—"

"Craig—"

"—how the hell did Remalli know that Eleanor Goldsworthy was the judge who signed the paperwork authorizing us to tap his phones and install the bugs back when all we were doing was trying to nab him on racketeering charges?" McNary refused to be drawn into the subject. "It's ironic. She signed the papers that allowed us to bug his joint and tape her own killer's confession. You should have heard Chapman—"

"Wait!" Scott shouted. "Wait a minute. I was asking you about what happened in the raid!"

"Scott," McNary said calmly, "did you fill out your incident report recounting what happened to the best of your memory?"

"Yes, of course."

"Well, so did I. We send in our reports to headquarters and let them sort it out. It's just that simple."

"Just that simple," Scott repeated. "That's it. You're not going to tell me anything else?"

"Afraid not, sport. It's out of my hands. If you want to get worked up about something, why don't you start by finding out who tipped off Remalli? That'd tell you who's ultimately responsible for your girlfriend's death, wouldn't it?"

Scott glared at him.

"Back off that other stuff," McNary said sternly. "And start the car. I want to go home."

Returning from her East Wing office, Paula heard her husband's raised voice through the door of the President's Study next to their bedroom.

She knocked, then entered to find Jim Candler red-faced, pacing in front of the window. Del Owens sat on the couch, clenching his teeth.

"What's going on?" Paula asked.

They both stared at her.

"Seems that someone in my administration has a serious conflict of interest," Jim said angrily. "Wouldn't you say that accepting large gifts from a defense contractor poses a bit of an ethics problem?"

Paula looked at Del for answers.

Del said, "Peter Lambuth at the *Post* pulled Kevin Hadley aside"—referring to the President's press secretary—"and asked if there was any truth to the rumors that our new CIA director had been on the take while he was undersecretary of defense."

Paula sat in the armchair next to the couch. "And was he?" she asked.

"Apparently our man became overly friendly with a couple of defense contractors while in government the last time. The allegations include free trips for himself and his family. He also allegedly was a paid consultant to the same companies directly after he was out of office, in violation of federal revolving-door ethics statutes. I've heard rumblings about secret bank accounts in Europe. This is serious stuff."

The President was still incensed. "Mister Squeaky Clean! This was the man who sat in our meeting this morning pushing like hell to get us into a major military conflict! What's he getting? A percentage on every bomb we'd be dropping?"

"I think he's right on the merits of his arguments, but obviously he's lost the moral authority to be so hawkish. He's got to go, Jim."

"You're damned right he's got to go! This type of moral lapse is totally unconscionable . . . unacceptable," the President said. "I don't want this administration to wallow in mire when we should be sprinting. On top of our problems with a certain fossilized Appropriations Committee chairman, we don't need a potentially crippling distraction like this, especially when there's a major armed conflict looming. I was elected to help raise the ethical standards of politicians in this town. What's Congress going to think when they find out my CIA director is a paid mouthpiece for the defense industry? It gets directly at the question of good judgment. Let's not underestimate the seriousness of this problem. Something like this could undermine my presidency. It reflects directly on me. It calls into question our credibility, and our ability to govern the country. And if Peter Lambuth at the *Post* knows, the whole world's going to know."

"I'll take care of Lambuth," Del promised. "The director's history, but I'll make sure it gets the proper spin. Don't worry, I'll fix everything."

"And another thing," the President said sternly, pointing his finger directly at Del. "No more surprises like this that are going to damage my presidency. We've all worked too damned hard to get here to have it blow up in our face. Got it?"

Del didn't dare look away from Jim Candler, but he saw Paula nodding out of the corner of his eye.

"Got it," Del answered. "No more surprises."

The only other people still in the public library at eight-fifty were two winos seeking warmth in out of the cold, pretending to read week-old issues of the *Wall Street Journal*.

Julia was at a computer terminal, racing to log on to the word-search program for the *Richmond Times-Dispatch*. She selected the three months spanning the time between when Paula Candler's two conflicting car maintenance checks were written, then added a couple months in each direction just to be sure. She entered the words "Crown Victoria."

As she waited for the computer to display the results, she reminded herself it was still only a hunch. She had nothing else to go on, but it couldn't hurt. She didn't even know what she was looking for.

In a few seconds, the screen was filled with every reference to a Crown Victoria that had appeared in the newspaper over the seven-month period she had specified. She paged down, scanning the story headings, looking for any clues. Most of the references were among long columns of stolen cars or cars being sold at auction by the police department. Several mentions were made of the car in descriptions of accidents. A few articles appeared evaluating the new year's car models.

She was just about to start checking the vehicle identification numbers of the stolen cars listed against the ones Paula Candler owned when she found what appeared to be a series of related news articles from around the time when the purchase of the Crown Vic by Del Owens had been recorded.

"Closing time in ten minutes," a woman's shrill voice called out from behind the library's circulation desk, startling the two drunks.

Julia stayed focused on her task. There were three articles referenced in the local news section of the paper, plus an obituary. Words from the article headlines flashed in front of her eyes: "tragedy"—"death"—"bereaved family"—"unresolved crime."

Her heart was still pounding with excitement. She scribbled the dates down on the back of her hand with a pen.

Julia bounded from the terminal to the file drawers where the microfilm was stored and pulled the boxes corresponding to the dates she had copied down. She turned on a microfilm reader and threaded the film through the sprockets. Out of the corner of her eye she could see the winos stirring, folding their papers, heading toward the exit. Julia ignored the woman coming in her direction, the ribs of her corduroy trousers rasping as her fat thighs rubbed together.

"I'm sorry, miss, we're closing. You'll have to come back tomorrow."

Julia didn't look up, but fast-forwarded the film, stopped it to check the date, fast-forwarded it again.

"*Miss . . .*"

"Thank you. I heard it the first time," Julia replied calmly, still intent on finding the first article.

"We close at nine o'clock," the woman insisted curtly.

Julia turned slowly in her chair toward the librarian. She spoke evenly, in a hushed tone appropriate to the setting: "By the clock on the wall, it's eight fifty-two. That's time enough for you to march your happy ass right back to your designated work station so I can make a copy of these three articles before closing time. You bother me again before the big hand's on the twelve, and I'm gonna follow you outside on the way to your car and slap the shit out of you. *Comprende?*"

The librarian reeled backward, then stormed back to the desk. She picked up the phone and dialed—the cops, Julia figured.

Julia didn't have time to read what she found. She scrounged for dimes in the bottom of her purse and dropped one into the machine. She pressed a button and suffered through an agonizingly long wait for the photocopy as the librarian glared at her. She found the second article, made another copy, and did the same for the obituary.

Two uniformed policemen came through the front door as she was waiting for the copier to spit out the last sheet of paper. The cops were met halfway across the room by the librarian. They nodded and looked in Julia's direction.

Julia stashed the photocopies into her briefcase. She walked smartly past the policemen, who were fixated on her chest.

"Evening, Officers," she said with a lascivious smile and a wink. She heard them laughing as she hit the street. She glanced back through the window and saw the librarian standing alone, fuming, wondering what the hell had just happened.

* * *

Back in her hotel room, Julia sat on the floor and skimmed the newspaper articles in chronological sequence. The first was barely two column inches buried on page 7 of the local news section: the suspected hit-and-run of a fourteen-year-old boy. The second was an obituary, an announcement of a simple graveside service and interment of the child at Hollywood Cemetery. The third was a feature interview with the boy's mother. Last was a follow-up piece several weeks later.

Julia reread the end of the interview piece:

Cathy Tisdale, the boy's mother, said that there had been no responses to the family's offer of $100,000 for any information leading to the conviction of the person responsible for her son's death. But she has not given up hope.

"Someone out there knows something," she said. "I pray to God that whoever it is steps forward. It would mean everything to our family. It would give us peace of mind to bring this awful tragedy to conclusion. We want to know what happened to our boy."

Richmond Police Department spokesperson Madeline Kramer confirmed that the investigation into the death was ongoing, but admitted the detectives had few solid clues to pursue. After consultations with the chief of police's office and the deceased's parents, she did agree to a partial release of the results of the preliminary examination by the forensic pathologist, in the hope that a member of the public may be persuaded to come forward with additional evidence.

Specifically, Kramer said that detectives were following up on the results of a forensic report analyzing paint chips found on the clothes and personal effects of the boy, which indicated the car that likely struck the boy was a gray Ford, either a Taurus SHO or Crown Victoria, manufactured within the past six years. Anyone with relevant information is asked to contact Detective Paul Gacey of the Richmond Police Department directly.

Julia could barely absorb all that she was reading.

The phone rang, and she jumped. She took a calming breath, picked it up, knowing who it would be.

"Why didn't you return my phone calls?" Don Russ demanded angrily.

"Gimme a break, why doncha?" she shot back. "I just walked in the door."

"What the hell's going on down there?"

"I need another day or two to check things out," she answered nonchalantly.

"We don't have it," he snapped. "Tell me what you've got—*now.*" He sounded almost desperate.

"I take it your crack legal research team in Chicago ain't doing so hot. Looks like I'm going to be pulling your nuts out of the fire this time, too."

"Julia, damn it! You've found something, haven't you? Don't even think about doing this to me again. I've got a client facing the death penalty, and we're trying to pull together a motion to remove a federal judge from a murder case. This isn't Dade County divorce court."

Julia took a moment to think. Would she let him have what she knew tonight, or take the time she needed to confirm what she appeared to have stumbled onto?

"Don . . ." she purred. "Baby . . . You're not going to have to worry about bumping Judge Paula Candler from the case. You may not even have to worry about how to keep that son of a bitch Tony Remalli off death row by the time I'm through."

"But—"

"Better get your buns back to Washington. I'll call you at the Ritz-Carlton end of the day tomorrow and let you know how things are shaping up."

"Julia! Don't hang up!!"

She hung up. And took the phone off the hook.

She had him exactly where she wanted him. Again.

Chapter 11

At nine-fifteen the next morning, Tony Remalli sat down hard in the chair behind the screen in the interview room of the U.S. marshal's lockup in the Alexandria courthouse building. Usually a defendant awaiting trial in the federal system would have been sent to one of the jails in the surrounding counties. Only special security risks like Remalli merited round-the-clock observation as a guest of the U.S. marshals.

Don Russ thought the prison orange jump suit was comically small for him, which only made him meaner.

"This is gettin' old real fast," Remalli grumbled.

"I've got a new set of clothes for you for your next court appearance," Russ said.

"My people send down somethin' from home?" Remalli asked hopefully.

"Yeah."

The scowl from Remalli's face softened for an instant.

"But I'm not about to let you wear one of those pimp suits you parade around in in New York. You're going to look exactly like one of the conservative local attorneys. I got you a dark gray suit and rep tie from Brooks Brothers. And a blue shirt. It's supposed to make you more likable."

"What are you doin' back down here so quick? I thought you said you hadda go back up to Chicago?"

"I've got meetings." Russ wasn't about to let on that Julia Menendez had summoned him back. "I thought I'd take this opportunity to go over a few things, even though you're not due back in court for a few weeks. Are you paying attention?"

"You see me looking at you?"

"Here are the rules, just like the last time we went to trial. No wisecracking, no smirking when you're in court. Thank the marshals politely after they've led you inside. Smile to the spectators before you take your seat, but don't ham it up. The media will want to portray you as a slimeball; we need to show them your human side."

Remalli flashed a cheesy smile.

"Try for something a little more sincere. Keep both elbows on the table so you don't slouch."

Remalli held up his arm in the sling.

"Just do your best," Russ said.

"Yeah, yeah, yeah."

"I'll arrange for a barber to come in the day before your court appearance to give you a nice haircut, wash that grease out of your hair—"

"Hey—"

"—and trim your nose and ear hair. Your eyebrows look a little sinister. They'll need shaping, too."

Remalli leaned in closer to the screen, lowered his voice. "You know, Donato, I seen that government attorney on TV last night. He's tryin' to become some famous fuck, havin' me arrested. I'll bet he wants to run for governor or somethin'."

"Congress, actually."

"See? I was right."

"He's just like all the other crummy politicians out there. Unfortunately, you happen to have walked into his sights before an election."

"Shit, why don't I just make a contribution to his campaign? Maybe he finds a way to drop the charges."

Russ was shaking his head. "This isn't a traffic ticket you can get fixed at city hall. You've been charged with murdering a federal judge. And while we're on the point, knock off those idiotic threats to the feds. What are you thinking? Chapman would love nothing better than to add a witness-intimidation charge against you."

"My people'd do anything I asked them to do to help me out."

Russ flushed with anger. "I sincerely hope you're not thinking about doing something stupid. Where are all your people anyway? The ones you said you brought down for your so-called tool distributor business."

Remalli shrugged, then took an interest in the file folder Russ had on the work space in front of the partition. "Whatcha got there?"

"It's your file—why?"

"What's in it?"

"Why do you want to know?" Russ asked suspiciously.

"It's *my* case file, ain't it?" Remalli tried a less emotional tack. "The government give you their list of expert witnesses yet?"

Russ shook his head in disbelief. "Oh—no. I'm not letting you get your mitts on that! Not after the last time. Forget it. I know what happens to government witnesses when Tony Remalli gets hold of their names."

"What?" Remalli feigned innocence. "I'm just trying to take an interest in my own case!"

"Dammit, Tony, don't make this any more difficult for me than it is. Forget it."

Remalli quickly changed the subject. "You still gettin' me a new judge for the case like you said? I don't think I really want the President's wife or any other girlie.

They probably wouldn't take it too good that someone whacked another chick judge."

"I'd advise you to keep that kind of sexist talk to yourself. We're still working on the recusal issue. It's not looking very good now, though."

"Okay, then, so what's Julia Menendez doin' to earn her fee?"

Russ was wondering the same thing. He had checked in with his office a half dozen times since leaving Chicago earlier that morning and still hadn't had any messages from her.

"You let me worry about Julia," Russ said.

He stood up to leave, stepped to the door, and knocked to have the marshal let him out.

"Keep your chin up, Tony. I'll take care of you. Hey, and don't bend over if you drop your soap in the shower."

By nine-thirty Julia Menendez was already halfway across the state of Virginia. The Appalachian Mountains rose in the distance before her. As she was driving she reread the photocopy of one of the newspaper articles about the boy who was the hit-and-run victim, then she punched a number into her mobile phone.

A man who sounded as if he were chomping on a cigar answered. "Gacey."

"Detective Paul Gacey?"

"Who is this?"

Julia turned on her most businesslike voice. "Detective Gacey, my name's Vivienne West. I'm a producer with LayLow Productions, perhaps you've heard of us?"

"Um, I'm not really sure. Maybe so. What can I do for you?"

"As you probably know, we have a history of producing successful true-crime shows for television. We have a large booth at most of the national law enforcement conventions. You've been by, haven't you?"

"Uh, yeah, probably."

"I thought so. I was sure your name was familiar to me. Anyway, for our upcoming season, we've decided to create a new show focusing on unsolved crimes. One of our regional freelance researchers sent us a file of clippings of possible ideas, including one from Richmond. I don't need to tell you the unsolved crime TV shows have been instrumental in finding dozens of criminals all over the country. The reason I'm calling you today is that we'd like to help you out."

"That's mighty generous of you."

"Not at all. That's our business."

"What did you say your name was?"

"Vivienne. Vivienne West."

"Right, okay, Miss West. You said there was a particular crime you were interested in?"

Julia flipped the stapled pages until she came to one with names highlighted.

"Yes. Do you remember the William Tisdale case a couple of years.ago?"

"The hit-and-run? Sure. I was lead detective on that. It got a lot of play in the media because it was such a tragic case. I can tell you, I was given a pretty hard time about it. The politicians and my then-boss wanted suspects to be questioned, but there just weren't any. We worked every possible angle, and we still came up empty-handed."

"And no new leads since then? Still unsolved?"

"Technically it's still an active case, but we've got nothing, I'm sorry to say. I see a lot of heartbreak in my line of work, but this was one of the saddest cases I've ever come across. Such a bright young boy. Really nice family. They'll never be the same. And the perpetrator is still driving around out there someplace."

"I'm looking here at an article," Julia said. "It says here that you followed up on every single possible car in the area that might have been involved. You had the suspect's car narrowed down to a Taurus SHO or a Crown Vic?"

"That's right. We found paint chips from the car on the buckle of the boy's book bag and on his clothes. That was the main evidence we had to go on. We ran a computer match against all possible cars registered in about a fifty-mile radius. It was a huge operation, but as I said, there was a lot of pressure to find the killer. We visited hundreds of homes and businesses to see for ourselves if the cars showed any signs of having been in the accident."

"How long after the accident did it take to complete all the car checks?"

"Several weeks."

"You don't think a few slipped through?"

"No way. Everybody on our list got checked out."

"Regardless of who it was?"

"What do you mean?"

"Well," Julia said cagily, "I was just wondering. I know this is a bit off the wall, but it's no secret the then-governor's wife drove a gray Crown Vic."

The cigar chomping halted.

"Just stop right there," he said. "If this is the direction this conversation's going, we're finished. As department policy, we don't discuss suspects with the media, but I'm gonna tell you this right now, lady. As far as the governor's wife is concerned, I personally checked out that car and there was not a thing wrong with it."

Of course there was nothing wrong with it, Julia thought. *By the time the police got around to looking at the car, it had been switched!*

"Let me tell you something. You're wasting your time. The press were all over this state looking for dirt on Jim and Paula Candler and didn't find shit. And never will, 'cause there ain't none. Thank you for the offer to help us with the Tisdale case, but I'm afraid we're going to have to decline. Good-bye, Miss West."

The detective hung up on Julia before she could say anything else.

She stepped on the gas. She knew she was definitely onto something.

The brakes of the tractor-trailer rig that had been riding Julia Menendez's tail ever since leaving the interstate ten miles back squealed as the truck skidded to a stop behind her at the town's only stoplight. She looked in her rearview mirror, frowned at the rebel flag painted over the truck's grille, and checked her inclination to flip the redneck a bird. The trucker was signaling right, so Julia turned left as soon as the light changed, throwing up gravel.

Julia drove until she had left behind the single diner, a brick-fronted bank, and the shabbily merchandised windows of the stores in the town center. She had a rural route box number, but no other way of locating the address listed for the Crown Victoria registered to Delbert P. Owens of Bledsoe, Virginia.

In less than a minute, she was heading back out into the countryside, definitely feeling out of her element. Rural Virginia was a world away from the streets of Miami.

She passed a succession of aluminum buildings bolted down to concrete slabs outside the sign for Bledsoe city limits. A beautician. Taxidermy. Small-engine repair. A bait and tackle shop. Another sign indicated a boat launching ramp on the Shenandoah River just three miles ahead. She had decided to turn around and make her inquiries back in town when she rounded the next bend in the road and saw a gravel parking lot, surprisingly packed even in the morning with pickup trucks. She slowed and turned in, parking next to a pickup with jacked-up monster tires and a roll bar with fog lights on top. The shot-peppered sign swinging from a rusted pole by the road read CLUB 606. Neon signs for Budweiser and Miller High Life flickered in front of a blacked-out window.

What the hell, she thought. Looked like a good congregation of locals. And she could use a beer—even if it was only ten in the morning.

All eyes were on her as she pushed through the front door. It was dark inside, the air thick with cigarette smoke, the only light coming from the television screen suspended by chains from the ceiling in one corner. A half dozen men in hunting gear and manual work clothes sitting on bar stools turned back around and watched Julia's reflection in a wide mirror as she crossed the floor. The tough woman of indeterminate age working behind the bar looked like their collective mama.

"What're you havin'?" Mama asked humorlessly, revealing a set of rotted teeth.

"A beer." Julia looked down the length of the bar to see what the others were drinking. "Budweiser."

Mama got a can of beer from the ice chest and popped the top. Julia sat on a stool with the stuffing coming out of the vinyl seat. On the wall next to her was a calendar published by a tool company showing a busty woman in frayed blue jean shorts straddling a gargantuan wrench. Julia took a long drink and watched stock cars racing around a dirt track on the TV screen.

Mama busied herself attaching small bags of pork

rinds to a clip strip on the wall by the cash register, right next to a gallon jar of pickled eggs. She let the ash fall to the floor from the cigarette between her lips. She finished and leaned across the bar to Julia. "Just passing through?" she asked.

"Looking up an old friend," Julia answered. A few heads tilted in her direction. She had never been shy about going into a club or bar by herself, but had never in her life been more self-conscious about her Latino accent. "Maybe you could help me."

"Depends. Who you lookin' for?"

"Del Owens."

Heads at the bar inclined in her direction. Julia glanced quickly at the mirror behind Mama and saw the whites of one pair of eyes studying her particularly hard.

"Might know who that is," Mama said vaguely. "He doesn't come round here much anymore. We used to see him a weekend every couple of months till he moved to Washington. Course, you probably know all about that, being an old friend."

"Oh, yes."

"We got lots of famous people from Washington coming out here, 'specially on the weekends and in the summer. They all got houses down yonder on the river. Half these dumb rednecks you see sittin' at the bar here are millionaires. Done sold their useless land along the Shenandoah River to the developers, and now they got nothing to do but sit in here and drink all day."

"Beats sittin' at home with my ugly ol' lady," one of the men spat out. The rest of the patrons nodded and laughed.

Mama moved the grease around the counter with a filthy rag. "We also get lots of politicians." She leaned in conspiratorially and winked. "See, it's out here they bring their honeys."

One of the men chuckled coarsely as another made a crude gesture with his fingers. They sniggered like teenagers.

"Nothing personal, but we got to be real careful what we say to strangers," Mama continued quietly. She turned the volume up on the TV with the remote so no one could hear them talk. "The people who bought the river houses come here and spend money. *Cash* money. That means a lot to people like me and some of the people in town, barely scraping by to make a living. And it also means no credit card receipts or canceled checks for the little woman at home to find, see? We'd be just another wide spot on the road to nowhere if it weren't for the river houses and the big city folk. They aren't our kind of people, but we feel right protective of them just the same, for obvious reasons. Wouldn't do anyone any good if we were to tell every woman who comes up here where to find a man's hideaway, would it? Might be a wife, or worse—another girlfriend. You understand what I mean."

Julia discreetly pulled a twenty-dollar bill out of her purse, making sure Mama saw it. Mama snorted. Julia kept pulling twenties out until she had two hundred dollars folded over.

"I understand the part about the cash," Julia said. "And I know it would mean a lot to Del. I know he'd be sorry to miss me."

Mama looked Julia over carefully. "I have no doubt he would, honey." She took the money and slipped it into her pocket. "It's none of my business, but I didn't think he had time for a wife or girlfriend. They says he's married to his work." Mama gave Julia another suspicious look. "Like I said, he ain't there. I'll tell you how to get to his place, but all you'll find is a house with windows boarded up for the winter. He inherited that and the broken-down boathouse on Indian Cove when his daddy died about five years ago. Just let the kudzu take over the whole damn place. Real eyesore."

Julia noticed the calendar on the wall next to her was still on the previous month. She tore the page off and flipped Miss February facedown. "Draw me a map," Julia told her.

"Hey, you motherfucker," the man said sinisterly over the phone.

"Who the hell is this?" Del Owens said.

"It's *me*, goddammit! You're out of the state less than a month and you forget your best friend?"

Del relaxed into the high-backed chair in his West Wing office. Henry, one of the boys from back home in Virginia, shot the shit about the old days when they had gone squirrel hunting together in the Appalachians.

"All right, Henry, why the hell are you calling me out of the blue like this?"

"Woman problems," he said.

"What's new? Who you knocked up now?"

"Not me, goddammit. *You.*"

"What are you talking about?"

"Well, you sure as hell got some woman on your tail. She's been around here asking all about you. Where you lived, when you were last here. 'Course, Mama was blabbering like an idiot as soon as a roll of twenties was waved under her nose. No telling what she told the woman."

Del froze. "When did this happen?"

"She done left Club 606 not more than an hour ago. Seemed pretty keen to get out to the river. Your daddy's place was where she was headed, I reckon."

"Holy shit," Del swore. "Okay, Henry. This is what I want you to do. Meet me at the intersection of the interstate and the highway that leads to my daddy's place at six o'clock, got it?"

"Anything for my ol' buddy. What's up?"

"I need you to help me out with something. Just be there, okay?"

Del slammed the phone down hard.

"What the hell is *this*?" he wondered out loud. "I don't need this shit." He glanced at his planner. Full of meetings for the next six hours. "Especially not now."

He drew a big X over his schedule and all but ran out of the office, promising his secretary he'd be back on time for the evening strategy session in the Oval Office.

Del cursed and stammered and beat the dashboard of Henry's pickup truck for the entire half hour they had been driving. Then he slouched down into his seat, stared out into the black countryside. He looked over at the speedometer and punched Henry lightly in the arm. "Keep it right on fifty-five. Last thing I need is to be caught breaking the law in Buttfuck, Virginia, while I'm supposed to be tending to important business on behalf of the nation back in the capital."

"Del, you're talking about the place where you grew up. And where I still live."

"Yeah, right. Sorry."

Del stewed, trying to figure out what could be going on. Who was this woman who was asking Mama all these questions?

"I'm going to snatch that bitch bald," Del said.

Henry kept silent, watching his speed.

Earlier in the day Del had been working the phones in his office in the White House. Now he was back where he started almost thirty years ago. Back to the part of the country where people bought their groceries at service convenience stores and where liquor by the drink had failed on the last county referendum. Hadn't he spent a lifetime trying to get away from this place? It wasn't that he didn't value his Southern roots. In his travels he had discovered there were rednecks in every culture. Even if he couldn't lose his Appalachian twang—for which the Sunday morning news commentary shows scrambled to book him—he didn't have to wear a Rebel Yell whiskey baseball cap. Not like his daddy, Lee Owens, God rest his soul.

"Slow down, Henry, you'll miss it," Del said.

Just before coming into Bledsoe, Henry downshifted at an intersection with a gravel road, unremarkable except for the dozen or so wooden signs—most in the shape of fish—with fanciful hand-lettered names for hideaways along the nearby river. Del made a mental note to pull down the sign with the wood-burnt name SHANGRI-LEE on his way out.

"You still own that property with the barn across the state line?"

"Sure. Why?"

"We may need to take a little road trip there tonight."

"Tonight? We'd have to bulldoze our way in through the brush. It's been years since I've set foot on the place. Hell, it was before you moved to Richmond with the governor."

"Oh, we'll get in there. If I have to chop a path myself, we'll do it."

"What you got at your daddy's place that's so important?"

"Never mind. Drive, Henry. Stop talking and drive."

They wound through the pitch dark down the road until emerging on a wide, level piece of ground. Fog completely obscured the river, which Del knew lay only a few yards down a bank on his left, and made driving along the narrow road following river's edge dangerous.

The road cut back suddenly away from the river. There was no sign marking the entrance to Indian Cove, just a different feel of the road under the tires as gravel gave way to heavily rutted dirt. The truck bounced along roughly until they saw the peak of the small A-frame house in the headlights.

"Wait here," Del said.

He got out of the car with a flashlight. Everything looked normal from the front. Same old pile of scrap lumber banged together in the name of leisurely retirement and the pursuit of catfish and crappie. He checked around back and found all the windows still boarded up, the door secure.

He walked in the direction of the sound of water lapping at the bank. Out well beyond the entrance to the cove he could just barely make out a light moving eerily above where the surface of the river would be. The water sloshed harder. A large boat was quietly motoring westward.

At the water's edge, his daddy had built a boathouse, an amateur but effective engineering job which—attached to poles sunk deep into the muck—rose and fell along with the water level. Between Shangri-Lee and the boathouse was a thick tangle of kudzu vines, which had claimed most of the quarter acre of riverfront property during the past three summers since Del had decided to let it consume the structure, hoping that it would make it less noticeable. There was no way to get from the cabin to the boathouse other than tramping clumsily through the vines.

Del kicked his way through the overgrown vegetation and shone his light on the front of the structure. His first indication that something was wrong was the crushed kudzu and fresh tire tracks leading off from the boathouse toward the access road. Upon closer inspection of the double wooden doors, he found a broken padlock on the ramp connecting the boathouse with the bank. It looked as if it had been snipped with a pair of bolt cutters.

Henry had obviously been right. The woman—the one described as good-looking with a funny accent—had been intent on snooping around the place.

"Goddammit," he swore. Mama at Club 606 always did talk too much, loved to name-drop, and couldn't resist a fistful of cash under the table. He couldn't even trust his own people. Del supposed the problem was that they were his daddy's people, though, not his anymore. He had turned his back on that lot the first chance he got.

Del pulled open the doors. His flashlight illumined an algae-covered pontoon boat bobbing at the end of a large wooden deck, whose walls were lined with mildewed fishing gear.

The deck was just big enough to store a car—even one as big as a Crown Victoria.

All that was left now, though, was an oily spot on the floor.

"Sheee-it!" Del cursed.

Chapter 12

"This is *absolutely* the last time we're working together," Don Russ was saying as if it were a blood oath.

Julia Menendez was at the wheel of the car, maneuvering slowly through the rain-slicked streets of the University of Richmond campus. She checked the clock on the dash, ignoring Russ.

"Your conduct has been utterly unprofessional," Russ said. "No communication with your client for two days. On a case as important as this? If your behavior at home's anything like what it's been with me, I don't know how the hell you can support yourself down in Miami."

Julia patted his knee. "Save it for your junior law associates, sweetheart. While you've been sipping Diet Cokes around your big polished conference table up in Chicago, I've been out in the real world collecting solid evidence you can use in the courtroom. Take a look at that file on the dash."

Julia turned on the interior light. She wound around campus as Russ read the packet of typed notes and photocopies. He didn't look up until she had stopped in front of a large university building.

Russ read aloud from a neatly arranged timeline in the file: " 'October twenty-seventh, five P.M.: After adjourning court in Alexandria early for the day, Judge

Paula Candler drives back to Richmond and arrives at the University of Richmond law school to give a talk to students and faculty. The campus newspaper records that she was accompanied by Del Owens, the governor's chief of staff.' "

Russ looked at Julia with a growing appreciation of what she might have been up to since they had last met.

"Keep reading," she said.

" 'There was a brief reception afterward. Paula Candler and Del Owens mingled. Like most of the other people attending the function, they were delayed in departing due to heavy thunderstorms. She and Del Owens finally leave at six twenty-five to drive back to the Executive Mansion. Paula Candler is planning to eat dinner with her husband and children as usual.' "

"Check out the time," Julia said.

Russ looked at the clock on the dash. "Six twenty-five," he said. "Same as when Paula Candler and Del Owens left the law school."

"On a night not too unlike tonight. Cold, dark, wet, just after a heavy storm. Follow along with my notes."

Julia put the car in gear and drove among the academic buildings and dormitories until she was off campus. Don Russ continued flipping back and forth through the file contents.

They stopped at the intersection of Highway 147 at the edge of campus, waiting for an entrance into the oncoming postwork traffic from downtown.

" 'Six thirty-five P.M.,' " he continued: " 'Their car turns right rather than left toward the city to avoid the traffic, then heads south across the James River. They make several turns, skirting an upscale neighborhood. The homes are bigger, spread out on huge lots, fewer street lights, narrower roads.' "

Julia watched her speed, pacing herself against landmarks and the clock. They rode in silence as Russ waited for five more minutes to pass.

" 'Six-forty: They pass Glenview United Methodist Church on her right.' "

Russ paused to verify they were indeed passing the church, then resumed reading: " 'Meteorological reports for that evening indicate that the severe thunderstorms have passed by that time, but unseasonable cold and high humidity resulted in fog patches in low-lying areas—such as around the river running nearby—and visibility would have been considerably reduced.

" 'They approach a sharp curve in the road—' "

At that moment Julia swerved the car close to the edge of the road, throwing the papers loose from his hands.

"Hey!" Russ said. "What was that?"

Julia slowed the car and pulled as close to the side of the road as she could without allowing the wheels of the car to slip off into the small drainage ditch. She turned the emergency flashers on and set the parking brake.

She collected the notes from the floor and handed them back to Russ.

Russ smoothed out the wrinkled papers and finished reading. " 'Before they realize what is happening, they have momentarily let the car come too close to the edge of the road. The local medical examiner estimates time of death for William Tisdale, age fourteen, to be between six and seven P.M. on that same night. Further credence is given to this report due to the smashed wrist watch on the boy's arm, which stopped at precisely six forty-two. The boy had two broken legs and minor internal hemorrhaging, but the ultimate cause of death was asphyxiation—he died unconscious, lying facedown in a shallow pool of water. Forensic samples obtained from the boy's clothes indicated the vehicle that struck the boy was a gray Ford, either a Taurus SHO or Crown Victoria."

Julia pulled from the back of the file Russ was holding a copy of the *Richmond Magazine* photo showing Paula Candler in her gray Crown Victoria from the days when her husband was still governor. Russ looked at the picture hard for several moments without saying anything.

Julia retrieved a flashlight from the glove compartment and got out of the car. Russ followed, clutching the file tightly. At the bend in the road, hidden in a thicket of tall dead grass near the curb, Julia pointed out a small marble memorial with the name William Tisdale, a cross, and the date he died. Don Russ stared at the polished black slab, sullied from the spray of mud from passing cars.

"The scene of the crime," Julia said. "But just the *first* crime—as I now know that there was a cover-up—a conspiracy."

Don Russ maintained his silence for another moment, then uttered quietly, "Damn. Paula Candler has been covering up for Del Owens all this time. She *knew* he killed a kid that night. She was hiding it so she wouldn't be involved in a scandal which might affect her husband's chances in the presidential race. Is that it?"

Julia turned and motioned for Russ to follow. "Back in the car," she said.

They drove parallel to the river for another fifteen minutes, made a few more turns, then crossed back over the James River and entered the congestion of the downtown traffic. Julia stopped the car and left the engine idling across the street from the gated entrance to an elegant building next to the state capitol. The sign read EXECUTIVE MANSION.

Julia took the file from Russ's hands and read out

loud: " 'The Virginia state trooper manning the security hut recorded the car's return at precisely six fifty-five.' "

Don interrupted her. "That means they didn't stay at the scene of the accident, right? They wouldn't have had time. He hit the kid and drove on."

Julia put the folder down. "No, Don. That's not what it means. That's what I thought at first, too. Take a look at this." She handed him a photocopy of a credit card receipt.

"Paula Candler's signature."

"That's right. I found that not an hour before meeting you tonight. I neglected to include one crucial fact in that narrative you were reading. They made a quick stop for gas back on Highway 147 just after crossing over the river when they left the campus. I talked to the station owner on the way over here. He remembers when they drove in that night, because he recognized her name, then asked her if she was the governor's wife. Don—Del Owens wasn't at the wheel of the car when they pulled out of that gas station. It was Paula Candler."

Russ gazed out the window to the lights blazing inside of the Executive Mansion. Julia picked up the story again in summary fashion: "Del Owens very cleverly procures another car—a car of the same make and model as the one which the judge was driving when she hit the boy. He makes the switch, and no one has any reason to suspect that anything unusual has happened. Life goes on as normal for Del Owens and the governor and Judge Candler. . . . Unlike for the family of William Tisdale."

Julia handed him back the file folder.

"Yes," she said, "I believe Paula Candler not only covered up killing the kid with Del Owens, she was the one who was responsible for his death. At first, when I found out about the car switch, I was sure the judge was responsible, then covered it up with Del Owens's help. Then when I found out they had both attended the law school function, I just assumed like you did that Del was the one who drove. Now I'm certain she was the driver. *And* the killer."

"Is this factual or conjectural?"

"I've done my homework thoroughly. It wasn't difficult finding out what Paula Candler was doing on that night. All I had to do was run a computer word search for her on the local newspaper's database and I found a brief mention of her speaking at the law school. What you've just read is eighty percent factual, twenty percent beyond a reasonable doubt conjectural. The records are all there in the file—plausible timetables, cash withdrawals, registrations on the two cars. People have fried in Old Sparky on less evidence than you're holding in your hands."

"This is good," he said, his voice trailing off in further contemplation of all she had provided him. "*Real* good." Then he snapped out of it, and resumed with the full vigor of a forceful trial lawyer: "Even so, having a stack of photocopied newspaper articles and illegally obtained bank records hardly makes for admissible evidence in a court of law. It's a tidy paper trail, and certainly compelling reading, but as a criminal attorney I can tell you the weakest point in your argument is how you go about demonstrating that it was the judge's car, and not some other of the thousands that might match the paint chip, that was involved in the kid's death. You have no case without physical evidence."

Julia put the car into gear.

"Where are we going?" Russ asked.

"Just sit tight."

As she steered them onto the interstate around the city, she recounted everything to Russ, how she had slogged through the stacks of records on Paula Candler's personal life and discovered the one serious mistake in her past, which she had up to then managed to keep hidden.

She headed east along I-64 until almost at the airport, then exited in an area of light industry. She turned into a driveway of a business announced by the sign AIRPORT SELF-STORAGE. She gained entry to a security gate by punching in a code, then proceeded through a narrow corridor of storage units.

Julia whipped into the space in front of Unit 43. They got out of the car, and Russ waited as she opened the padlock.

"Give a girl a hand?" Julia asked.

Russ shoved the metal door open with one powerful upward jerk of his arm. It banged loudly against the ceiling.

The bright mercury vapor security lamps around the perimeter of the storage facility flooded the interior of Unit 43. Dust settled onto the gray Crown Victoria which was backed into the space.

Julia said, "Do you know what it took to find and convince a flatbed wrecker to drive all the way over from Charlottesville to pick up this car?"

Julia shone her flashlight onto the right-front corner of the car. "Here," she said.

There was a gash, and a rusting streak along the front passenger side door where it looked as if metal had bit into the paint. "The lab found paint in the clasp of the kid's backpack."

Russ walked around the car, inspecting it closely.

"Del Owens had it stashed at his old man's fishing hut out in the middle of nowhere," Julia said. "The car he used for the switch he got through an old high school buddy's used car business in the nearby town. I checked at the library: Crown Victoria was a top-selling model that year. That silver-gray was one of the most popular colors. It wouldn't have been hard to find an almost identical car to substitute."

Russ circled the car once more. "Damn fine work," he said. "I'd say you earned your fees. So far."

"This ought to be enough to get the judge thrown off the case, don't you think? How you want me to handle it? Call the Richmond police detectives or the local D.A.?"

Don propped his foot up on the front bumper, wiped the dust from his shoe. "No. First I want you to find a better-quality lock for this door, one that can't be snipped so easily with a bolt cutter. And take some pictures of the car. Lots of pictures."

"Already done it from every possible angle."

Russ nodded thoughtfully, looked hard at Julia. She felt he was sizing her up.

"You want to help me win this case?" he asked her.

"Of course," she answered without hesitation.

He moved away from the car until he was right in front of her. His head was backlit by the harsh parking lot lights. She couldn't see his face to get a read on what he was thinking.

"I mean," he said, "do you *really* want to help me win this case?"

"Is there something I'm missing here?"

He moved his hand as if to brush her face and she closed her eyes. She felt nothing. She opened her eyes again and he had pulled back.

"I've thought a lot about you since New York," he said.

"Oh, yeah? I wouldn't have known, would I? Not a single freakin' phone call."

Russ gently took hold of her shoulders, squeezed them lightly. "I know now that was a mistake. I think we make a great team. It's just that I'm not sure . . ."

"What?"

"I'm not sure what your level of commitment to me would be. I mean my professional life. You know how important my work is. You know, my last wife didn't really understand me. . . ."

"What do you want me to do?"

"Show me that you care enough not to let this case go down the toilet."

"Anything."

"Anything?"

"What do I have to do? Kill someone?" Julia joked.

Russ wasn't laughing. "If I asked you to cross the line, would you do it?"

Julia rolled her eyes. "What do you think I do every day of my working life?"

"This is different. I don't mean just cracking someone's computer files or breaking into some philanderer's love nest. The stakes are higher. What I'm looking for is a full partner."

"Just give me the chance," Julia said eagerly. She intertwined her fingers with his. Her hand seemed so small.

"All right." He broke away from her again, all business. "Let's get to work. I'll stay on top of the legal maneuvering. You I want back in D.C." Russ looked at the scrape on the side of the Crown Victoria. "I've been thinking. Here's what you'll need to do. . . ."

Del Owens spun the dial on the wall safe in his office and heard the last tumbler fall into place. He turned the handle and yanked open the heavy door, reached into the back of the safe, and felt around until he found the small clasped envelope.

Next he checked that his office door was locked and forwarded all his phone calls to his secretary. Then he turned on the shredder beside his desk.

He had to get rid of the evidence. Anything linking him with that goddamned car.

He had all but forgotten about it. At one point—before Jim Candler's move from state governor to the President had been assured—Del had considered the contents of the envelope his "insurance policy."

He took one last look. He spread the contents of the envelope on his desk. Some folded-over newspaper clippings, a receipt for eighty-eight hundred dollars, and an official-looking document. It was a car title for a four-year-old Ford Crown Victoria.

He flipped it over. The back showed the transfer signatures from the auto dealership in Bledsoe, Virginia, to Delbert P. Owens. Somewhere among the personal possessions of the Candlers in a bank vault he would never be able to get to was an identical document showing that Paula Candler owned an identical car.

That goddamned car. No one other than himself had any idea about its existence or what it represented. Del had made the switch when he volunteered to take Paula's slightly damaged car into the shop for the repairs after the "accident" that night. Of course, he never took it to the shop to be fixed, but simply substituted one car for the other. The old family car was actually a bit worse for wear than the one he had acquired from a used car dealer. What few minor differences there were between them Del had been able to explain away as the result of having the car thoroughly cleaned inside and out after the dent was fixed.

He fed the car title through the shredder, then the cash receipt. Now there was only one car title, although there were still two cars.

Then, without even reading them, the newspaper clippings detailing the sufferings the Tisdale family of Richmond had to endure after the hit-and-run death of their young son, William. Now their tragic story was nothing but so much pulp. His detailed knowledge would be enough if the shit ever hit the fan and the Candlers forgot who had brought them all the way to the White House.

But all that was irrelevant now. The only thing that mattered was that the only physical evidence linking Paula with the accident that night in Richmond was missing.

"Goddammit!" he swore to the four walls.

Scott sat at his desk surrounded by stacks of audio cassette tapes. The last time he had locked himself in his office with hundreds of hours of Remalli's taped conversations, he had been listening for evidence of racketeering—and had found evidence of Judge Goldsworthy's murder. Now he was listening to the same tapes with a new mission, searching for some clue that Remalli might have inadvertently dropped that would lead Scott to the person who had leaked information about the FBI's imminent raid.

Scott rewound the last tape and put in a new one.

During the thousands of hours spent listening in on the mobster's conversations, he had come to know Rimshot pretty well: his personal likes and dislikes, his preferences in food, women, cars, murder weapons, his particularly foul-mouthed turn of phrase. He and the other FBI agents on the case were so familiar with the Mafia don that they could all do a mean imitation of him. Many times in the control room hidden in the back of an antiques store five blocks away from the auto parts shop, Scott and his fellow agents would shout out the dialogue before Remalli could get the lines out himself. But it was altogether different seeing Tony Remalli in person. Even after all those months of listening to his swearing and bloodcurdling oaths on the phone taps and bugs, he wasn't prepared for that face-to-face meeting with the killer.

And what was it Remalli had said to him at the court hearing? Something about "his *friend*" paying Scott a visit? Remalli must have figured out that Scott was the one who had bugged his place. McNary had told him the threat was nothing but talk. He wasn't going to mess with a federal agent.

Right.

Scott had already decided to take extra precautions. He'd be even more vigilant to and from work. And his semiautomatic handgun would never leave his side, even in the apartment.

Hour after hour he listened to Remalli's voice. Finally, well after everyone else had left the office, he found a telephone conversation that he had previously dismissed as being merely a call from one of Remalli's nameless flunkies phoning the mobster about one of the many criminal enterprises Remalli controlled.

REMALLI: Yeah?

UNIDENTIFIED MALE: It's me.

The voice was weak, thin, and, Scott thought, probably disguised.

REMALLI: I know lotsa mes.

UNIDENTIFIED MALE: We met a while back about a certain mutual acquaintance. You were very interested in the papers I brought you. You told me how grateful you were, and—

REMALLI [*suddenly agitated*]: Hey, hey! Dumb fuck! Didn't I tell you never to call me?

UNIDENTIFIED MALE: Yes, but I thought you should know—

REMALLI: You goddamned idiot! You fuckin' *know* the phones—

UNIDENTIFIED MALE: And that's why I'm calling you from a phone booth—

REMALLI: Not *your* phone, you prick! You wanna talk to me, you set up a meeting like last time!

UNIDENTIFIED MALE: I'm getting scared. And I had to get in touch with you fast because—

REMALLI: Scrawny piece a shit!

Remalli hung the phone up hard.

Scott wondered: Could the papers the man referred to have something to do with Eleanor Goldsworthy? He checked the date of the recording: two weeks before the judge's murder. Could this be the person who had originally tipped Remalli off to the phone taps?

Scott had a precise date and time of the phone conversation. The wiretape logs ought to indicate the origin of the incoming call.

Scrawny piece a shit?

Wasn't much of a clue to work on. Maybe the phone trace would give him more, even if the call was from a phone booth.

"It's dawn in the Middle East," the Vice President said.

Del stole a look at his watch: 7:35 P.M. Through the Oval Office window he could see the Washington Monument lit up, American flags snapping smartly in a stiff wind. Del's mind was not on the hastily called meeting on the growing military threat in the Mideast but on his lightning-fast trip to western Virginia.

After a Navy steward finished pouring coffee for everyone, the national security adviser presented the President with a red file folder labeled EYES ONLY POTUS, then handed similar folders to Del Owens and the rest of the group. Inside were black-and-white satellite photographs of a desert location indicating the position of rocket launchers.

"Just got these in. They're definitely poised at Israel. Another dozen moved out of the hidden bunkers overnight. This is as serious as it gets, Mr. President."

An aide slipped quietly into the room and handed Del a note. As gatekeeper, Del decided who could and could not interrupt the President's critical meetings. Del shook his head. The aide bent over and whispered into his ear. With great irritation Del told him to wait.

He scooted to the edge of his chair, about to stand up. "You've still had no reply from that scumbag through any of the regular diplomatic channels?" he asked.

The secretary of state shook her head. "Nothing so far. I summoned their ambassador this morning and asked him point-blank what they were up to with the rockets. He said he didn't know, but he'd get back to me. That was over ten hours ago and I've still heard nothing. Several other governments have been making similar inquiries on our behalf, but so far there has been neither an official nor unofficial response."

"Better tell the Israeli prime minister to start passing out the gas masks," Del said.

"Right," the President said. "Here's what I suggest we do. It's time we go public with what we know. It can't be much longer until word of what's going on leaks, anyway." He addressed the secretary of state: "Draft a statement we can issue at tomorrow's regular White House press briefing. Keep it low-key. We don't want to encourage him, but now's the time to start building public support for any military action."

Everyone nodded in agreement.

Del finally looked at the note. Paula was waiting outside. The President was supposed to be at a small ceremony in five minutes where Paula would present citations to a group of volunteers who operated a shelter for runaway kids.

Del caught Jim Candler's eye and motioned to his watch, mouthing his wife's name.

The President stood immediately, then Del and everyone else. "I think we're done for tonight," he said. "Anyone hear anything before tomorrow morning, beep Del immediately. Right now, though, it's business as usual. I'm meeting my wife for a presentation in the East Room. And I'm certainly not going to be late for that."

Laughter all around as the group started to leave.

As Paula came into the room, Del's mind was a thousand miles away. The faint ticking that had been in his head for the last couple of years had grown almost deafening in the past few hours. He knew what that sound was. It was the sound of a bomb about to explode.

That goddamned car.

When would the bomb go off? A phone call from a journalist? During the President's press conference on the Middle East situation? At Paula Candler's presentation in less than five minutes?

The bomb ticked even louder, seeming to fill the room.

He shook it off. No, he told himself. There was a country to run. A war to avert. After all, it was probably just some redneck who'd broken in and stolen the car. With any luck, they'd get liquored up on Wild Turkey, run head-on into a semi tractor-trailer rig, and the whole car would burst into flames.

Chapter 13

Tunnicliff's Bar and Restaurant on Capitol Hill was owned by a real-live Cajun from Louisiana who said he had opened the joint because Washington didn't have enough places to party and New Orleans had too many.

Julia Menendez sat on a stool at a bar festooned with purple and gold banners and swung her foot to the Dixieland jazz blaring from the speakers. All around her, Brooks Brothers and Talbots mannequins sloshed drinks and leaned in close to each other to be heard over the loud music. It was the first time she had been to the nation's capital, and she wasn't sure she liked it.

Tunnicliff's was supposed to be one of the hip places where the nation's power brokers raised hell hidden away from the tourists, but this crowd was far too uptight for her Miami temperament. The conversation was either politics, the Washington Redskins, or sex. It was hard for her to imagine any of these people actually falling into bed and rubbing bellies with each other after a few drinks. She felt like kicking off her shoes, climbing on top of the bar, and giving the assembled nerds a lesson in what real partying was all about. That would liven the place up a bit.

But she kept her seat, demurely sipping vintage champagne, a perk of working on a case with as yet no discernible upper limit to the expense budget. Don Russ had given her specific instructions about where to stay, what to wear, and how to spend her money once she got back to town. Her spacious room at the venerable Renaissance Mayflower—rented just for the day, however—cost almost four hundred bucks a night. Three chic new outfits with plunging necklines and barely legal skirt lengths from the boutique near her hotel totaled almost two thousand dollars. She should be seen consuming only the best the city had to offer in the way of food and wine. Russ had told her to pretend she was a classy chick on the make in D.C.; Julia replied she wouldn't have to pretend.

It was nearing ten-thirty when she noticed a buzz around the front door. Backslapping, handshaking, high-fiving. It was either a sports hero or a demigod from the Hill. Julia held her position at the bar and waited to be engulfed by the swarm coming her way.

He was offered a seat at the end of the bar. He was surrounded equally by men and women, the sycophantic types in suits. They laughed at his animated stories, listened carefully and nodded as he imparted wisdom. He turned to accept a drink on the house, and she immediately recognized his profile. Her man had finally arrived.

Julia ordered another drink. She sipped slowly and waited. She kept busy fending off men who only an hour earlier had lacked the courage of their drink to approach her.

The celebrity eventually wearied of holding court and turned on his seat to talk with the bartender. The adoring crowd had dispersed, paired up for the rest of the evening, staggering out the door.

There were four empty stools between her and the man at the end of the bar. Julia made a show of crossing her legs and started swinging her foot again in time with a slow, trembling clarinet solo. It took less than a minute before she caught him admiring the curve of her inner thigh.

He was far too cool to give her anything more than a quick grin. She could tell he wanted to take another long look at her legs as he struggled to keep his eyes on the bottom of his brandy snifter. He was concentrating so hard on swirling the cognac around in the glass that he failed to notice when she slipped up behind him.

She put down her bottle of vintage Krug between them, and he finally looked up.

"Hi," she said.

"Hi," he answered noncommittally.

She offered him her hand. "I'm Roberta Fuentes."

He took her hand, held it a little longer than most ordinary men dared. "Del Owens. Nice to meet you, Roberta."

Julia motioned for glasses. "I just ordered a nice bottle of champagne, and I hate drinking alone."

"Drink with me, then," he said, and scooted the stool out for her to sit on. "I don't think I've seen you before. You live in the area?"

"Just in town for a couple of days on business."

The bartender set down another champagne flute next to Julia's glass. Julia poured for them both. They raised glasses and clinked. *"Salud,"* she said, and they drank.

"I take it you're Latino," he said.

"You take it right. I take it you're not the typical uptight Anglo."

"Hmm," he mused. "Do you know who I am?"

"Yes."

"Is that why you came over here?"

God, he was as conceited as he was ugly. But she supposed he had to be careful. Julia shrugged. "You're not married and you're not gay as far as I can tell. You've got a steady day job. So what's the big deal?"

Del grinned at that one. "You smell good," he said.

"You're a man who appreciates the finer things."

Del Owens narrowed his eyes and took a deep breath. He checked his watch. "It's getting late. School night." He drained his glass quickly and made motions as if he was about to go.

"I thought we might go somewhere quiet and talk," Julia said. She dangled a key in front of his face. Del Owens didn't flinch.

"Where you staying?" he said.

"The Mayflower."

"Good address." She could tell he was thinking hard about it, weighing the pros and cons, the risks and returns. He looked around to make sure no one was listening. "I could meet you there in half an hour. Probably a good idea if we're not seen leaving together."

Julia gave him her sexiest look. "Probably so." She pulled a couple of hundred-dollar bills out of her purse and put them onto the bar. "Keep the change," she told the bartender. She slid off the stool and smoothed her skirt.

"Room 532," she said. "I'll bring the champagne." She pressed the key into his palm and closed it with her hand. She grabbed the bottle and started walking toward the door, making sure that all her parts were in gear.

Del shook his head as he watched her hips swaying, then took his first good look at the key.

"Hey!" he called after her just before she got to the door. She turned and came back close enough so he wouldn't have to shout. The poor dear looked so terribly confused. "This isn't a hotel key," he said.

"No, it's not. It's a copy of the ignition key to a four-year-old gray Crown Victoria. Thirty minutes. Don't keep me waiting."

Then she vanished.

"Here are the terms," Julia Menendez said. "Very simply, Tony Remalli walks, or we turn over everything we've got on the dead kid to the local commonwealth attorney in Richmond and to the press. This is not open for negotiation. Don't cooperate, Judge Candler is yanked off the case, and we're still better off with a more sympathetic judge. We're prepared to take our chances with whoever we draw as her replacement."

Del Owens slouched on the sofa in the woman's hotel room in the Mayflower. Julia stood in front of him with her arms crossed. He looked up from the file folder on the coffee table. He couldn't believe what he was hearing. Not only did this woman seem to know almost everything that had happened on the night of Paula Candler's accident, she had all the documentation to prove it. *And* she had the car.

A Polaroid of the Crown Victoria's damaged right-front panel lay on the coffee table. *The goddamned car!* He thought he had taken the more prudent path by locking it up in the sticks and not risking the police finding it if he had dumped it in the river, as he had originally planned. In hindsight, he should have done whatever was necessary to destroy it, even if it meant tearing it apart himself with a pair of pliers and blow-torch. This was much worse than he had ever imagined after discovering the car was missing from the boat-house.

"I don't understand," she continued, "what there is to think about. Either you work with us or you don't."

"I'm not saying one way or the other," Del said. "I'm just trying to figure how it might play out." The truth was, he was so dazed by the revelations that he could not properly focus his thoughts.

The woman was relentless: "Plus, *you're* deeply involved in this yourself. You hid the old car, obtained a replacement, and were instrumental in the cover-up. It's in your own self-interest to make sure the judge gets on board."

Del's mind was racing. He was grasping at anything: "You'd be ruining the career of the President, a man who's spent his entire political career fighting sleaze and corruption," he told her forcefully. "This has nothing to do with him."

"Seems to me the President could have done better in picking his close friends and advisers. I'd even question his choice of a wife at this point."

"That kind of attitude really chaps my ass."

Julia shrugged. "My concern is with my client's welfare."

"And you'll do whatever's necessary to free a murderer?"

Julia scoffed. "You're telling me you wouldn't do the same in our situation? You covered up killing a kid, for chrissake! You'd do whatever is necessary to protect the President."

The patriotic appeal was going nowhere. "Okay, okay." He waved her off. "Specifically, what do you want her to do?"

Julia sat down across from him. Even her all-business demeanor couldn't completely negate her powerfully alluring physical presence.

"First," she said, "Remalli needs to be freed in a court of law on the basis of the facts, so that he can't be tried again on the same charges. Second, whatever happens inside the courtroom needs to be as credible as possible. We'll go through the motions so no one's the wiser."

"How are you going to do that?"

"Don Russ will take care of everything; he's working on it right now. All the judge has to do is play along. The proceedings need to have the legitimate stamp of authority so none of this comes back to haunt us ever again."

"And supposing we do go along with you—what's to stop you from trying this again? Isn't that always the dilemma of someone being blackmailed? Because that's exactly what this is." Del was coming out of the fog; now he was starting to get mad. "What guarantees do I have that you won't try to leverage this same knowledge against me, the judge, or the President again and again?"

"I can't give you any. But what choice do you have?"

Del shook his head. He couldn't see how to weasel out of this one.

"Paula Candler is her own woman," he said. "You know as well as I do how strong-willed she is. I'm not in a position to make any commitments on her behalf."

"But you'll certainly take our proposal to her."

Del nodded.

"And put our case forcefully to her."

"Yes. Of course. This may take a few days."

"We don't have it. Russ is thinking sooner than later. I need an answer tomorrow."

Del's back was up against the wall. He had settled down enough to see what was at jeopardy: his own hide and that of the President. Paula Candler's considerations had become secondary.

"We leave the President out of this," Del said. "I can handle everything myself."

"That's entirely up to you. And while we're on that subject, we need to insulate the principals. Don Russ's contact with Paula Candler will be strictly limited to the courtroom. I'll represent him, and you'll represent the judge. I think you'll agree with me on that."

"Of course." Del ran a hand with irritation over his bald head. "Anything else?"

"This room's already been paid for in cash under a false name and I won't be here two minutes after you leave the hotel, so forget about having me traced or followed. And it should go without saying, but I'll say it anyway: first hint you've called in anyone else—and don't underestimate our resources to ensure you're playing fairly—we start leaking bits of this to the press."

"Don't lecture me. I have no intention of getting anyone else involved."

Just then Del's beeper went off. The message indicated that the White House was trying to get in touch. More developments in the Middle East.

Del wrote something on the file folder cover, stood to leave, and handed it to her. "This is my beeper number. As much as you'd like it to, this is not going to happen overnight. I'll need a few days."

"They're in court tomorrow."

"No, they're not," Del said. "They're not due back in court for weeks. I heard it on the news."

Julia looked smug. "Don't believe everything you hear."

Del rose to leave, even more confused.

"Not staying for that champagne?" Julia asked.

Del turned, gave her the warmest, most sincere smile he could manage. In his deepest Southern drawl he told her, "Go to hell, lady."

Chapter 14

"You don't have to prove anything to anyone," Malcolm Crane said quietly, although his baritone voice resonated throughout the room.

His substantial presence filled a corner of the great oxblood leather couch in his chambers office. The red morning sun lit up his dark skin like rich mahogany. He was lighting a pipe. He was already in his robe.

Paula Candler sat in the armchair facing him across a coffee table covered with pipe smokers' artifacts: a crumpled pouch of sweet-smelling tobacco, a heavy ashtray, a decorative stand with an odd assortment of expensive hand-carved Meerschaums and drugstore-bought Dr. Graybos, a packet of pipe cleaners, and a multipurpose tool for tamping tobacco and fiddling with the pipes. Strictly speaking, smoking was prohibited in all federal buildings, but since Malcolm was the chief judge he had wide latitude to set his own rules. Paula detested being around cigarette smoke, but the pungent aroma of Malcolm's pipe brought back pleasant memories of her days in graduate school at the University of Richmond. For a fleeting moment, she felt as if she were no longer a federal district judge and the First Lady, but a law student again, sitting at the feet of the great constitutional law professor in his cluttered office.

"I'm just trying to do a job, Malcolm," she answered. "The same as you and the rest of the judges."

Malcolm nodded thoughtfully, blew a cloud of smoke toward the ceiling. "Uh-huh," he uttered noncommittally.

"If this is about the Remalli case—"

Malcolm cut her off. "I was just speaking in generalities. But if you want to discuss the Remalli case—"

"Malcolm, I have no intention of passing it on to another judge. In fact"—Paula waved a note—"I had a message waiting on my desk from the defense attorney in the case, and I've already agreed to his request for an early status conference in court today. I'm afraid it's a moot point. I'm due there in twenty minutes."

Having followed Malcolm to the bench three years after he was confirmed, Paula owed much of her courtroom demeanor to studying his style. Like Paula, he had taught at the University of Richmond before being nominated for the bench. But whereas Paula had been a partner in a city law firm and had only been an adjunct professor teaching upper-level criminal law classes, Malcolm had been a full professor of constitutional law for over a decade. Malcolm had served ably for four years as chief judge and was seen by court observers as a likely candidate for elevation to the U.S. Court of Appeals.

Malcolm spoke unemotionally. "I understand you are likely to be formally petitioned by the defense to recuse yourself."

"You read the piece in the *Post* this morning? It's sure to be picked up by the wires, so then it will be national news, but it's really no big deal. I'm a very high-profile federal district judge sitting on a very high-profile murder case. I accept that. The media scrutiny won't go away just because I beg off from this one. If it's not this case, it's going to be some other. I can't walk away from the tough ones."

· Malcolm gestured at her with his pipe. "I knew you'd feel that way. Paula, I don't mean to interfere. Just because I'm chief judge doesn't mean I have any right to meddle in your affairs on the bench. The responsibilities that go with the title are mainly administrative, as you know. All I'm saying is that it's not too late for me to reassign the case."

"I *knew* that was why you wanted to see me. Malcolm, I wouldn't have returned to the bench if I hadn't expected to have to make a few tough decisions because of Jim's election. One side or the other is going to be unhappy with my decisions—that's always the way it is."

"I'm just letting you know you have options," Malcolm said. "Before it's too late," he added with some emphasis.

Paula stood to leave. "Thank you anyway, Malcolm."

Malcolm took a final puff from his pipe and escorted her to the door leading to his outer office, where the secretaries were seated. As he opened the door, the two Secret Service agents outside rose.

Shelby Trimble, the clerk of court, entered the office humming an old Broadway show tune. Paula couldn't help smiling. The man really loved his work.

"Hello, Judge," he said enthusiastically.

"Hello, Shelby." Her day already seemed a bit brighter for having run into him.

"I passed your secretary in the hall on the way here," Shelby said, "and she asked if I wouldn't mind delivering this note since I was coming down here anyway." He handed her a plain envelope.

"She said it was urgent, but she knew you were in with the chief judge."

Paula opened the envelope and read the note on unsigned White House stationery: *Under no circumstances start your afternoon court session without talking to me first.* She instantly recognized the handwriting.

Shelby gave her an impish wink and held the door open for her. "I believe he's waiting for you in your office."

"What in God's name are you talking about?" Paula said.

In her private chambers, she gripped the edge of her desk as if for dear life. Del sat ramrod straight across from her, both feet on the floor, briefcase on his lap. At any other time, the politico would have had one leg slung casually over the arm of the chair.

Paula was using every bit of self-control to contain the flood of emotions washing over her. "I am not believing what you just told me. This—is—*not*—real! I haven't killed any child!"

"I'm sorry, Paula. I honestly thought that I could take care of everything so that it would never come back to haunt you."

Paula stared out the window as Del talked.

"I went back to the scene after you returned to the executive residence," he said. "The boy was already dead. There was nothing anyone could have done at that point."

Paula raged at him. "How do you know? How do you really know that?"

Del was as calm as Paula was emotional. "I know. It was an accident, Paula. Let it go at that. It happened."

"So you decided—without even telling me—to cover the whole thing up? Couldn't you have at least told *me*?"

"Why? So you could tell Jim, who'd then have to tell the police? No, Paula. It was an *accident*. It wasn't your fault. I had to make a decision. There was no sense in ruining even more lives. Do you think Jim would be sitting in the Oval Office right now if it had come out that his wife was a child killer, even if only by accident?"

"This is not right," Paula muttered, shaking her head. "Not right. Something's wrong here. Wait—" She sprang up, pacing the room. "I remember now. This is the child who was in the news? The one whose parents offered the big reward? But it's insane. It can't be! You got out and checked after we thought I might have hit something that night. *There was nothing there, Del.* You told me so. I trusted you. I completely put it out of my mind until right now. It never in a million years would have occurred to me—"

"What do *you* remember about that night?"

Suddenly, Paula was in the driver's seat of the old Crown Victoria on a rainy night in October over two years ago.

"The dark, the rain. The sound of the wipers. The last thing that vividly sticks out in my mind about the drive is passing the Methodist church on Glenview. There was a bright light over the parking lot which I used as a landmark at night to remind myself that the sharp curve was just ahead. We were laughing about what was on the church sign. Then it happened just as I rounded the curve. Something ran out from the side of the road. I screamed. I swerved and felt the tires on the roadside gravel. I stopped the car and you said you'd get out to see what it was. You came back and told me there was nothing there. That it must have been a stray dog or some small animal that had bolted from the brush. It probably wasn't even hurt, you said. It had run off into the woods."

"I lied," Del said.

"You mean you saw the boy when you got out of the car?"

"No, I couldn't find anything along the roadside. But I was pretty sure it wasn't just some animal. I didn't know for sure it was the kid until I went back later."

Paula still could not believe what Del was telling her.

"I never gave it a second thought after you got out of the car and told me it was nothing. I forgot all about it—until today. Now you're telling me that it was a child? I killed a child? I don't believe it!"

"Believe it, Paula."

Paula dug into her pocketbook. She found her keys and threw them onto the desk. "I know one thing. I'm not driving that car anymore. Not if what you're saying is true."

Del drew a deep breath. "It is true, Paula. But, in fact, that's not the car that hit the kid."

Paula looked confused. "But you just said I hit the child with my car."

"And so you did. . . ." Del explained how he had replaced Paula's car with another one. He watched her carefully. Did she realize what he was holding back from her about that night? *It certainly doesn't hurt matters if Paula believes she's responsible for killing that boy,* Del thought. *Especially since the blackmailers think the information they have fingers her as the killer. Better her than me.*

"This is all just too absurd to believe," Paula said. "Why are you telling me this now? After all this time?"

From his briefcase he pulled out all of the evidence that the woman at the Mayflower Hotel had given him: photocopies of her old bank statements, credit card receipts, newspaper articles, VIN records confirming that her present car wasn't her own.

"What's all this?" she asked.

"You're being blackmailed."

"What do you mean?"

Del passed Paula the Polaroids of the old Crown Victoria's registration plate and damage to the right front panel. "They now have the car. I had it someplace safe, but they located it and now it's in their possession."

"Who are 'they'?" Paula shouted.

"Everything I've shown you here was assembled by someone who approached me late last night."

Del then explained what had happened, demonstrated how someone really clever who was digging could pull together the seemingly unrelated scraps of information to devise a damning scenario. He related the terms that had been presented to him by the Latino girl.

"Didn't I tell you not to go back to work?" Del said. "Didn't I tell you to dump that car in favor of a limo?"

Paula was at first devastated, then defiant.

"No," she said quietly with great resolve. She placed the Polaroids facedown. "This is not happening . . . I shouldn't even be discussing this with you," she said indignantly, her voice rising. "It's a violation of judicial ethics. I will *not* have my judicial integrity compromised by this sort of . . . unlawful intimidation."

"Paula . . ." Del maintained his characteristic condescending smirk in the face of opposition. "You don't have any choice but to talk about it. It's not going away by itself. You're in serious trouble. But I'm here to help you."

Paula stared at the photocopies of her credit card receipts and checks.

"My God!" she said indignantly. "How does someone get hold of my personal records like this?"

"When the stakes are high, people get mighty motivated. She's obviously very good at what she does."

Paula flipped the pictures back over again and glared at them. "Who *is* this woman?" she snapped.

"As I said, she seems to be working for that mobster, but she refused to say who exactly is pulling her strings."

"So who do you think she's working for?" Paula spat impatiently. "The mob? Remalli himself? The defense attorney? Maybe she's in this for herself. What's her real agenda, Del? It makes a huge difference, doesn't it? Have you even thought this might just be some political payback by someone you trampled on the road to the White House?"

"Believe me, I've thought about it. If any of our political opponents had this kind of stuff before now, they would have used it before the election."

"So I'm supposed to just roll over for some bimbo you meet in a Capitol Hill bar who approaches you with some feeble blackmail attempt?" Paula tossed the photocopies back across the desk. "It's all conjecture. As a lawyer and a judge, I'll tell you that there's not enough there to establish probable cause for a crime, much less constitute enough weight for any reasonable prosecutor to go ahead."

"With what? Indictment? Prosecution? Because if we—you and I—don't address this situation now and make it go away very quickly, that's what's on the table."

Paula grew quiet.

"Listen to me," Del said. "You're in denial. I was, too, only twelve hours ago. I can't believe this is happening, either. These people are in a position to cause great difficulties for all of us. My advice is to play along with them for the moment until we can figure out who's really behind this. Let's find out what they're really after. It can't be as simple as getting that mafioso off the hook."

"I cannot in any way go along with this. First of all, I still don't believe you—"

"Read my lips," Del cut in. *"You—don't—have—any—choice.* What's the alternative? Risking the originals of all these documents being turned over to the media or some zealous prosecutor? Can you imagine what Lloyd Chapman would do with something like this?"

Paula was out of rebuttals for the moment. "Unless we do what?"

"She said something about Remalli's lawyer—"

"Don Russ."

"Yeah, Don Russ—going to make a few motions today in court."

"I just granted his request for an early status conference this afternoon. Five minutes from now, to be precise. I'm expecting him to submit a formal petition for me to recuse myself."

"Well, she didn't say anything specifically about that, but she did say that you needed to go along with whatever it was he was requesting."

"I will not!"

"Paula . . . stop. Think for a moment."

She was already out of her seat, coming around to Del's side. "All right," she said. "Now you listen to me. I am a United States federal district judge. I do not—repeat, do *not*—administer justice in my courtroom on the basis of coercion from the defendant."

Del sighed, reached into his briefcase, and pulled out another photocopy.

"What's that?" Paula asked.

Del handed the paper to her. Her shoulders slumped and her hands started to shake as she looked at it.

"This is him?" Paula said quietly. "The boy?"

"Yes."

It was the picture printed in the Richmond newspaper. William Tisdale in his Little League baseball uniform, a bat slung over his shoulder, sun-bleached hair, a toothy grin on his face.

"Why are you showing this to me?"

"To make it more personal. Less of an abstraction. I don't think it's registered yet how serious the situation is. You're responsible for that boy's death."

Paula looked at the picture another moment. "I can't be. Not . . . him."

"His mother called him Billy."

Paula shot back, "You didn't have to tell me that."

"We need to find a way to work with these people, Paula, whoever they are."

"No one," she said through gritted teeth, "is above the law. No one."

Del looked at her, started to say something, then changed his mind.

"What?" she demanded.

"Does that apply even to yourself?" he asked.

Paula felt herself burning crimson.

"Look, Paula . . . we go back a long way together, you and Jim and I. You're thinking about this thing all wrong. You're all worried about maintaining the integrity of the judicial process, and I'm here to tell you . . . Let me put it this way: I didn't leave Jim's side to come over here to have a chat about some little matter in district court—"

"Don't trivialize it," Paula said icily.

"Okay, okay. I'm sorry. Yes, everything you said about justice and the law are all true. You're a very powerful woman in your own right. And you have a very important job to do. But, lady, right now you're just another woman in trouble. From my perspective, if you don't find some way to accommodate these blackmailers, not only is this the end of your career, but it will be the end of Jim's presidency. It could be the shortest term in office of any president since William Henry Harrison caught pneumonia giving his inauguration speech and died a month later."

"I've got to tell Jim," she said.

"No," Del said forcefully. "Jim is the last person you need to tell. He has a country to run. He's trying to get his domestic agenda through Congress. There are crises looming. And you and I both know what Jim would want to do. He'd want you to come clean, tell all, get it out into the open."

"And that's exactly what I want to do, also."

"The problem with Jim is that he believes that by doing the right thing, everything else will work out. But it won't. Not this time. His presidency would be at grave risk if this ever became public. At least give me a little time to work on this, Paula. Don't tell Jim. Not yet."

Paula bit her lower lip, watched the second hand sweeping around the face of the clock on the wall. She was trying to think through the next steps logically, but found herself slipping back into waves of disbelief, then rage, then sorrow. For once in her life she was at a complete loss for words.

Del was watching her intently. "So, Judge, what are you going to do?"

Chapter 15

"The cuffs are a bit long, doncha think?"

At the defense table in Judge Candler's courtroom, Tony Remalli shot the cuff of his new suit for Russ and Fein to see. His filthy hospital sling had been replaced with a dark paisley silk cloth. He had been barbered and groomed so that he resembled a sleek greyhound.

Fein was deeply involved in going over his notes. Russ kept his eyes fixed on the courtroom door from which the judge would emerge, ignoring anything Remalli had to say. Russ flicked his eyes once over to the government's table to check out the competition. Lloyd Chapman had his head together with his assistants, whispering intensely.

Russ leaned over to Remalli, Fein listening. "You're going to have to sign some papers today. And the judge is going to ask you some questions."

"What kinda questions?"

"It doesn't matter. Just pay attention to what I'm saying and follow my lead. If you're unsure, look to me."

Fein furrowed his brow. "I still don't know why you got this early court appearance," he said to Russ.

"I don't have time to explain now." Russ turned back to his notes.

"Oh, by the way," Remalli said eagerly, "did ya get 'em?" Neither of his attorneys responded. "Did ya get 'em? Guys?"

Fein looked at Russ, who nodded. Under the suspicious eyes of the marshal sitting behind them, Fein opened his briefcase, took out a small metal box not much larger than a pack of cigarettes, and slid it across the table.

Remalli's eyes lit up. "Of all the things I've missed while being shut up in that stinkin' jail . . ."

The cover of the box was decorated like an old-fashioned patent-medicine box, the words reading AL-TOIDS—CURIOUSLY STRONG MINTS. He opened the lid and popped one of the large white flat mints into his mouth.

"I just love these things," Remalli said, rolling it around his mouth.

The judge's door opened, and the clerk came out. "Good," Russ said. "Now shut up and stand up straight."

"All rise," the clerk called out. "The United States District Court of the Eastern District of Virginia is now in session, the Honorable Paula Candler presiding."

Paula Candler left the small conference room attached to her chambers office and entered a packed courtroom. She settled into her chair and put on her glasses.

She glanced at the agenda on the bench that had been prepared by her clerk Susan, who was taking her seat below her on the left. Paula's court reporter sat poised on the edge of his chair, ready to begin typing.

The words on paper confirmed that she had still not awakened from the nightmare that had become reality only minutes earlier. Without looking up she announced, "The first matter before the court is *The United States* versus *Antonio Remalli*." In her peripheral vision she saw Don Russ shooting to his feet; Paula ignored him, and he sat back down. "Before we get started this afternoon . . ."

She paused to look up and carefully survey the room. U.S. Attorney Lloyd Chapman had apparently found it necessary to make an appearance himself at what should normally have been a matter handled by a junior member of his staff, a half dozen of whom were backing him up with thick, black, meticulously tabbed three-ring binders filled with every possible legal obstacle that their boss might ever require. Chapman craned his neck, adjusted his tie, and somehow managed to look both tense and supremely bored.

At the defendant's table, Don Russ sat motionless, strangely relaxed, eyes fixed on her. The defendant was dressed in a conservative suit, his arm in a sling. His good hand was at his mouth, cleaning his fingernails.

The gallery was crammed with a mixture of slovenly dressed crime and political reporters from the local market, plus a dozen faces she recognized from the national news organizations. There was a buzz of excitement, as if a celebrity were in their midst. Under normal circumstances, she might have enjoyed the extra attention. But one look at Del Owens, seated in the back row next to the door, staring without expression at her, reminded her these were anything but normal circumstances.

"I realize the public's interest in this case and acknowledge the need for these proceedings—preliminary as they may be—to be available to all interested parties. That being the case, we will dispense with the usual method of handling matters like this with counsel at the bench and will conduct the business in open court. Therefore, I would ask counsel to address the court from your tables or the lectern, and speak clearly so that you can be heard over the speakers."

Paula took a calming breath before addressing the defense table. She could barely bring herself to look at Remalli's attorney. "Mr. Russ, you asked for this meeting today, well ahead of the scheduled report date. Would you care to enlighten us as to your purpose?"

Russ stood. "Thank you, Your Honor, we do have a couple of matters to address with the court."

"You may submit them. Ken . . ." Paula nodded toward the court security officer, a retired police officer on the payroll of the U.S. Marshal's Office, to get the papers from the defense table to distribute to herself and the prosecution.

Don Russ appeared confused. "I'm sorry?" He had nothing for the officer.

"This court was expecting your formal petition for recusal. You brought it up at the time of Mr. Remalli's arraignment."

"I understand now. No, we will not be making any such motion."

"Not even later?"

"No, Your Honor."

There was a slight murmur from the gallery. Paula shot them a warning look and the noise immediately subsided.

She felt an unsettling mixture of relief and anxiety. Had the threat as outlined by Del passed so quickly?

Russ continued. "What I was going to say was that I'm afraid the trial date given earlier this week is not going to work out for us, Your Honor."

"And why not? Have you not already been given access to tapes and transcripts from the government?"

"Yes, the FBI promptly delivered copies of the tapes and transcripts to me already. It's not that. We're not looking to push the date out. I'm requesting that the trial date be moved *up*. We're ready to go."

Out of the corner of her eye Paula saw confusion at the Government's table.

"And you believe that your client's interests are best served by reducing so drastically the amount of time you have to prepare for trial?"

Paula saw Russ's legal assistant looking at his boss as if this was the first he had heard of this unorthodox maneuver.

"With all due respect, my client's interests are best served by freeing an innocent man as quickly as possible."

"And what did you have in mind?"

"If it pleases the court, we were hoping to begin next week."

Chapman was already on his feet. "Your Honor, really. This is farcical. The Speedy Trial Act guarantees trial within seventy days from the date the defendant makes an appearance with an attorney, not two weeks. We want to move this along, too, but what the defense is requesting is totally unreasonable. The Government strenuously objects."

The other lawyer with Russ was trying frantically to tell him something, but whatever it was, Russ wasn't paying any attention.

Russ countered: "The law was meant to put an outside limit on the time a defendant is brought to trial. It does not address the issue of how quickly a trial may begin if the court is able to accommodate the defendant."

Remalli's lawyer was correct on that point of law. But Paula was highly suspicious of his real motives, especially after having just learned of the blackmail attempt against herself.

Chapman was up again. "Your Honor . . . the date originally set seems perfectly adequate and reasonable for all parties. I'm not sure I understand why the Gov-

ernment's case should have to suffer just to accommodate some hidden personal agenda that Mr. Russ seems
to have."

"My concern, if I may," Russ interjected, "is with my
client. He is, as he sits here, an innocent man, proven
guilty of nothing; yet he is forced to remain in solitary
confinement in what is—with all due respect to the
many fine federal employees working in this building—
a squalid jail cell that is hardly fit for human habita-
tion—"

Chapman interrupted and said wearily, "Your Honor
has seen the U.S. marshal's facilities and knows that
they are state-of-the-art and maintained at an extremely high standard."

"Well, then," Russ said, "perhaps the Government's
attorney wouldn't mind spending a night there himself?"

Chapman sat down shaking his head.

"All I ask is for the opportunity to have the charges
against Mr. Remalli addressed at trial at the earliest possible date so that he may be freed. I do not believe I am
asking anything unreasonable of the court."

"Mr. Chapman," Paula said, "as you recall, it was you
yourself who urgently insisted to this court that the defendant be held without bond."

"Yes, but also, Your Honor—"

Russ chortled. "Frankly, it sounds as if Mr. Chapman
does not have a compelling case with sufficient proof to
bring forward against my client. It makes me wonder
why he sought this indictment in the first place if he
wasn't already prepared to go to trial."

"Indeed," agreed Paula. "Mr. Remalli, do you understand what your attorney is requesting of the court?"

Russ prodded Remalli, who stood. "Uh, yes, Your
Honor."

"And you realize that you are entitled to at least thirty days to prepare for your defense, and that by waiving that right, you would not subsequently be able to cite that as a reason for prejudice against you?"

The defendant looked at Russ, who nodded. "Yes, Your Honor."

Paula looked across the space from her bench to the defense table and tried reading the look on Remalli's face. He was at least attempting to be well behaved in court, and there was nothing to suggest that he had any knowledge of the blackmail attempt.

"Fine, Mr. Remalli, you may be seated."

Paula was trying to focus on the law, not allowing the supposed coercion from the defense team cloud her judgment. "The government should already be in a position to present its evidence. Susan, hand me the calendar, please."

There was much concern among the U.S. attorneys as Paula studied the dates for the next several weeks.

"The calendar is very, very tight, Mr. Russ."

"Yes, Your Honor. I'm sure my client will not take it personally if you are unable to find any time."

Paula was busy looking at the dates and wasn't sure she heard him right. *What was that? A threat?*

She used the laptop computer on her desk to discreetly scroll back in the court reporter's notes to confirm that she had really heard him say what he did. It looked even more menacing in black-and-white.

Is this what I'm in for?

Paula flicked her eyes over the heads of the lawyers toward the back of the room. She saw Del slowly nodding his head. She tried to convince herself that she was making decisions solely on the basis of good jurisprudence.

"Mr. Russ, what you're asking is highly unusual, in

light of the fact that I have seen none of the motions that one would expect a defense attorney to file in a case like this. I couldn't possibly agree to so quick a trial date if, for example, you were planning to file a suppression motion. There's absolutely no way I can refer it to a magistrate judge for a hearing or review it myself."

"We won't be filing any such motions, Your Honor."

Paula was becoming more and more confused, just as it appeared the Government's lawyers were and, indeed, even the other defense lawyer.

"All right, then, Mr. Russ, perhaps I should formally ask the Government if they are planning to enter the tapes from the hidden listening devices and wiretaps. By statute, the defendant's attorney must be given at least ten days to review the tapes and transcripts before trial."

"Not necessary, Your Honor," Russ responded. "Thank you, though, for pointing that out to me."

"Yes . . ." Paula was thinking Russ was every bit the smartass he was reputed to be. "So how long does the Government expect to take in presenting its proof?"

Chapman stood, extremely agitated, but holding his tongue. "It's a fairly straightforward case. Roughly a week."

"Does that include cross-examination?"

"In a normal case it would, Your Honor. Obviously, I have no way of knowing how long Mr. Russ will take with each of our witnesses."

"Mr. Russ?"

"Our proof could possibly take about the same amount of time."

Paula examined her calendar closely for another moment. "It seems to me," she finally pronounced, "that the defendant's rights as well as the public interests are best served if we do, indeed, keep this matter on what has admittedly become the fast track. I am setting a new trial date for next Wednesday. Mr. Russ, I assume both you and your client are willing to sign a waiver of the thirty days you're normally allowed to prepare for trial?"

"Yes, ma'am."

Paula nodded to her case manager, who produced the appropriate form and gave it to the court security officer to hand to Russ.

"Fine, we will begin jury selection on that date. Is there anything else?"

Russ spoke up. "Actually, yes. The court could go ahead and schedule the start of the actual trial on that date rather than jury selection."

"And why is that?" *Now what's he up to?*

"Because my client wishes to exercise his right to request a nonjury trial. We ask that Your Honor be the finder of fact in this matter."

Paula noticed the look of dismay on the face of Russ's legal assistant. Chapman was huddled with his assistants. They appeared in further disarray.

"Mr. Chapman?" Paula said.

Chapman rose. "Your Honor, we'd like time to confer about this."

Russ shot up. "Judge, this appears to be just another instance of the Government's reticence to give my client an opportunity to prove his innocence quickly. My purpose in making this request is merely to speed up and simplify the entire process. I am surprised by Mr. Chapman's wanting a delay. I have yet to hear of a U.S. attorney who would turn down the chance of prosecuting a case with the judge as the finder of fact. Prosecutors usually love nonjury trials. Surely the Government's case is not so shaky that it would not allow Your Honor to hear the case?"

"Mr. Chapman," Paula said, "Mr. Russ has a point. I

see no reason to further delay these proceedings. But technically, according to the statutes, a nonjury trial must be with the Government's consent as well as with the approval of the court. You must make up your mind now."

Another few moments of confusion at the Government's table. Apparently there was no consensus emerging among the lawyers.

"Mr. Chapman?"

"Sorry, Your Honor. I wish the Government had more time to consider the request, but if we have to decide now, we would not want to antagonize the court by opposing a nonjury trial, if that is, indeed, what Your Honor wishes."

Paula fought hard to choose the right words. She had just realized what Don Russ was up to with pushing for a nonjury trial. That confirmed he was behind the blackmail. *This is real*, she told herself. *It's happening.*

Paula looked down at the afternoon's agenda. There were a half dozen more report dates scheduled. It was looking blurry. She began to feel warm and light-headed. Her hands were cold, yet damp. She poured a glass of water and took a sip to quell the queasy sensation rising up her throat.

"Mr. Remalli, I must ask you again for the record if you really want to waive your right to a trial by jury."

Remalli stood. "Yes, Your Honor. Whatever my lawyer says."

"But I'm asking *you,* Mr. Remalli. Are you yourself absolutely certain that you want to have me listen to the evidence in this case and make the decision as to whether you are guilty or not guilty?"

Remalli looked at Russ. Russ nodded, then looked directly at Paula. Remalli cracked a thin smile. "Yes, Your Honor. I'm sure."

"And you understand that if you waive the jury, that I will also decide the sentence in the case, which could include the imposition of the death penalty?"

Remalli answered with somewhat less conviction. "Yes."

Paula took a deep breath. "Fine. You still have in front of you the form which you signed to waive your thirty days to prepare for trial. At the bottom you will also find another section concerning your waiver of trial by jury. Read it—then you and Mr. Russ need to sign it."

Remalli signed the form and slid it over to Russ, who did the same with a great flourish. The court security officer retrieved the paper and handed it to Paula.

"If that's all, this court will be in recess for an hour," Paula managed to say before bolting from the bench.

"All rise," Susan called out, weaker than usual, obviously caught off guard.

The two Secret Service escorts barely had time to catch up with Paula as she walked swiftly through the door of her chambers. She waved them back as soon as she was inside, passed Helen, who was supposed to meet her for a late lunch, then made it around the corner and into her private rest room just in time before she threw up.

Chapter 16

"Genius," Paula uttered softly. "Pure, evil genius." She had finally recovered from being sick after presiding over the court session. Paula and Del sat facing each other on opposite ends of the couch in her office. She had told Helen their working lunch was off—an urgent matter of the court. Helen had looked dubious as Del was ushered into Paula's office and the door firmly closed in her face.

Paula traced a raindrop streaking down the window as a storm over the courthouse lashed at the window behind them. The horror had finally begun to sink in.

"Your run-of-the-mill mobster is not above attempting jury tampering," she said, "usually without the knowledge of his attorney, although that's not always the case. All he has to do is secretly get to one of the twelve jurors and that's enough to result in a hung jury—no unanimous verdict, no conviction. There's a mistrial; it buys the mobster some time. He gets a new trial, or possibly the prosecution even decides it's not worth retrying the case. The brilliance in Remalli's approach is that without a jury seated as the finder of fact, all he has to do is somehow compromise a single individual—the judge—and he definitely walks."

Paula looked at her judicial robe hanging on the back of the door. She thought back to the first day she had worn it, remembered how proud she was when taking the oath of the office to uphold the laws of the United States. After she had supported Jim in his quest for higher political office, that had been *her* moment, what she herself had accomplished. Even after three years on the bench, she still was in awe of the responsibilities she held.

"It doesn't matter how overwhelming the evidence is against him," she continued. "If the judge finds him not guilty, there's no way to overturn that decision or retry him on the same charges. He's a free man."

Del added, "And there's virtually nothing that can be done to a sitting federal judge, except impeachment by Congress, and that's not even a remote possibility unless the bribe—or blackmail—is discovered. By then it's too late to do anything about the defendant's original charge."

Paula nodded. "*If* their assumption is that we're going to cave in to their demands," she explained, "then this is a brilliant strategy. I have no doubt now that this was done with Don Russ's input, if not at his instigation. It required very deft legal maneuvering."

"Their vision is that you'll preside over the prosecution's case, Russ will take a few shots at the evidence and witnesses to make the defense's efforts seem plausible, but they know you'll ultimately find Remalli not guilty. The outcome will shock the U.S. attorney and the public will be dismayed, but none of that will matter. They will have won and a murderer will be set free."

"But that's not going to happen."

Del looked doubtful.

Paula stood up and started pacing. "You know," she said, "up until about an hour ago, I'd always felt so in control of my life. It seemed like everything had gone according to some master plan. Law school, marrying Jim, the kids, the career—I felt like I could shape my own destiny. That's especially true when you're a judge. Lawyers, court officers, defendants, all have to do what you tell them to do, whether they like it or not. I make decisions every day that affect people and their families for the rest of their lives. The judgment is solely mine. I have real, life-altering power. Now I realize how unimportant all that is. I can see how going through something traumatic could give someone on the bench a new perspective. It would make a judge more thoughtful, more sympathetic to the defendant."

Del nodded impatiently. "Those are nice sentiments, Paula, but I'm afraid now's not the time to agonize over your judicial philosophy."

Paula shuddered, rubbed her shoulders. "Since you told me about the blackmail attempt, I've mentally run through dozens of different scenarios of how this thing will play out. And none of them includes my letting Remalli free if indeed the evidence shows beyond a reasonable doubt that he's guilty of killing Judge Goldsworthy. I will *not* be compromised."

"Then you may find yourself answering some very tough questions from the Richmond Police Department about the death of Billy Tisdale. Because there is no doubt in my mind that these blackmailers are serious."

"Del, I've got to do what my conscience tells me to do. I must take responsibility for what I've done. And the sooner the better."

Del was agitated. "Paula, this is not really about you. Let me put it to you another way—help you get focused—and I want you to think very, very hard about this question: is your going public with this to assuage your guilt worth bringing down Jim's presidency? Putting the country through the agony that you know will result if this gets public? Is that what you want for Jim? After everything you two have done to get to the

White House? To do the things for this country that millions of voters put you there to do?"

Paula had an important decision to make. Similar to judgments she had to render in court, she was being asked to balance the public and private good. Deliver a considered opinion that could affect not just herself and her family, but all those people who had shared their hopes and aspirations for a Jim Candler presidency.

The answer was obvious. There were even larger considerations, wider constituencies involved than just the Candlers.

"We need to fight," Del said confidently. "Fight to save yourself but, more important, fight to save Jim."

As much as Paula hated to admit it, she needed Del's help. She could see no way to avoid the terrible consequences of her actions, one way or the other.

"Then help me, Del," Paula pleaded. "Find a way to fix this, just as you've always done in the past. If you need to, sacrifice me, but keep Jim and the kids out of it. There's got to be a way out."

Del nodded. "I've been thinking about that. I heard what Russ said to you today in court about his client taking it personally if you couldn't move the trial date up. I caught the menace in his voice, and I sensed you flinched. Russ is clearly as much a part of this blackmail attempt as his client. That being the case, it might behoove me to make a few discreet inquiries into his background, and of that woman of his. All of us have our Achilles' heel, don't we? I just need to find theirs." Del tapped his watch. "I need to get back to the White House."

Paula walked Del to the door.

"Nothing needs to be said to anyone, Jim and Helen included," Del said.

"Unfortunately, I agree. For now, at least. I hate this. I want this behind us as soon as possible."

"Me, too."

"Thank you." She managed a weak smile.

"Thank me later. A big Paul Bunyan breakfast at the Music City Roadhouse would do for a start. I've been missing a decent plate of country ham with red-eye gravy."

Paula watched the only person who could save her walk out the door.

Now she felt truly alone.

The slam of the door was still reverberating around the room as Lloyd Chapman launched into one of his legendary tirades. "What the hell was that all about?" he demanded.

The question was directed at everyone who had assembled in the large conference room back in the U.S. Attorney's Office suite. Scott tried to remain inconspicuous, sitting with several other of the supporting staff of FBI agents and assistant U.S. attorneys in the chairs lining the wall. Craig McNary occupied a seat at the large boardroom-style conference table directly across from Chapman, along with the other major players, including Chapman's right-hand man, Ted Savage, who was furiously making notes on a legal pad.

"I'd like to know what the hell Russ thinks he's doing in pulling the trial date up to next week, then requesting a nonjury trial in front of the most consistently law-and-order–friendly federal district judge in the circuit. Anybody?"

Neither Scott nor any of the other subordinates dared meet Chapman's eyes as he scanned the room for answers.

"Nobody in this roomful of legal geniuses got any ideas? Russ was awfully cocky in court, especially considering he's now had a chance to review the tapes and transcripts of his client we turned over. Obviously he thinks he knows something we don't. What could that be?"

"Something his client told him?" offered Savage.

"Maybe," Chapman said. "But what could Remalli possibly tell him that would make Russ opt for a legal strategy that at least appears to jeopardize his client's best interests?"

One of the assistant attorneys near Scott finally spoke up: "Perhaps he's considered the weight of evidence against Remalli and convinced him that the only way of even having a chance to escape a certain death sentence is to cooperate with us to help develop an even bigger case. You know, something that cuts across several big organized-crime outfits."

Chapman nodded, impressed. "That's novel thinking. So all this dazzling legal footwork today was just a smoke screen. What he really wants is a deal. But right now he's raising the stakes, making us think the case is still ours to lose, although he's really just laying the groundwork for future negotiations. And, of course, he knows he'll have more leverage if I approach him, rather than the other way around, so he's remaining aloof." Chapman nodded thoughtfully. "A bit convoluted," he continued, "but very impressive reasoning. And not implausible, knowing Russ's background. Except for one thing."

"What's that?" the assistant said.

Chapman shot back with an intensity unusual even for him: "There's no way in hell I'm going to work a deal with that son of a bitch to let his client off from killing a federal judge!"

The young government attorney withered as Chapman became increasingly wound up. "Think of the kind of awful precedent that would set. Kill a federal official, but hey, that's okay. My hotshot attorney can get me off this one. All I have to do is go through the motions of a stiff defense, then work a deal with the Government, turn over a few names of assholes in rival crime families I didn't get around to whacking myself, then I can walk in a few years on good behavior." Chapman was pounding the table. "No way. This case needs to do just the opposite. We're sending a message to every creep out there who makes the mistake of thinking he can violate the laws of the land, then twist them to his own advantage in a legal system that's too easy to manipulate. This is where we take a firm stand, my friends."

Scott saw McNary's eyes starting to glaze over. Chapman was on his soapbox again, rehearsing some press interview or Rotary speech he would be giving in his congressional race.

"Frankly," Chapman said, "my biggest fear in this case has always been the unknown. As you all remember, we went to extraordinary lengths to ensure there would be no wriggle room for Remalli by the time we made the arrest. No legal loopholes he could jump through later with the help of a crafty defense attorney like Don Russ. I'm convinced that by my office working together so closely with the Bureau we did everything humanly possible to develop a watertight case. But after almost twenty years of prosecuting, my gut tells me we've got a problem.

"I keep thinking about the tapes. That's our main evidence. We've developed our case around Remalli's almost-admission that he killed Judge Goldsworthy. If they've found some way to discredit the tapes, we're not left with a hell of a lot. But you'd think they would have done that in a suppression hearing, which they're not. McNary, you get any insight you'd like to share?"

"I think you pretty much said it all, Lloyd. We're on solid ground with the tapes. If there's something we've missed, I don't know what it is. We're happy to help in any way we can, Lloyd, but you know at this point, we've handed over everything we've got and it's pretty much in your hands now."

Chapman gave McNary a look bordering on disdain. "All right," he said, finalizing the meeting with a clap. "Anyone think of something new, e-mail it to Ted Savage, and we'll have a look-see. The U.S. Attorney's Office doesn't have a monopoly on bright ideas, so send 'em in, folks."

The meeting started to break up. McNary motioned to Scott to join him by Chapman's side.

"What's up?" the U.S. attorney said.

"Tell him what you told me before we walked in here," McNary said to Scott.

"I went back through most of the tapes we had on Remalli. He got a call that—in light of all that happened with the raid—looks like he was being tipped off. I had the phone company run a trace on the incoming call."

"And?"

"It's from a gas station around the corner from here. Our guess is that someone from inside the courthouse called Remalli."

"You got a copy of that tape we could all listen to? Maybe we could identify the caller."

"I'm pretty sure it was a male voice, but it was disguised. I've already sent the tape over to the lab to have the voice reconstructed. Should be a few days. They promised they'd make it a priority."

"Damn right it's a priority," Chapman said. "What else?"

"I've had a quiet word with the U.S. marshals who are watching over Remalli. They're supposed to get in touch with me the moment he makes any phone calls or receives any visitors."

"Good work. You've been a tremendous asset to the team."

"Thank you."

Chapman clasped McNary on the shoulder. "Can I talk to you alone for minute?"

The two men huddled in the corner as the rest of the group filed out of the room. Scott hung back, pretended disinterest by busying himself with his notes, just within earshot of their conversation.

"What's up?" McNary said.

"I've got a funny feeling about what went down in court. Did you catch what Russ said when the judge asked him how long he'd need to present his proof? He said it *could* take a week. Not it *would* take a week, but it *could* take a week. Is he playing word games? Without reciprocal discovery, we have no idea what his strategy's going to be. It's worrisome, that's all I'm saying. And frankly, we really did need more time to think over the issue of letting Remalli have a nonjury trial."

"Having second thoughts?"

Chapman shrugged. "I didn't want to show any doubts in here in front of the bigger group. But I've been wondering: maybe we should get us some insurance."

"Don't follow you, Lloyd."

Scott strained to hear Chapman's words as he lowered his voice. "Despite what I just told the big group in here, I don't think your work's quite over yet."

Try as he did, Scott was unable to hear the rest of what Chapman was telling McNary. The U.S. attorney was sticking his finger into McNary's chest as he spoke. As they finished talking, Chapman looked meaningfully at Scott and gave him the thumbs-up. "Keep up the good work," he said. Then he winked at McNary.

"One of the world's great assholes," McNary muttered as soon as the attorney was gone. He asked Scott, "You coming in to the office tomorrow? I know you've worked just about every Saturday for the last few months on this case."

"Sure. If you need me to."

"We need to have a little chat."

Scott couldn't get rid of the image of McNary and Chapman standing behind him, daggers drawn.

I'm about to be seriously abused.

"You're the boss," Scott said, forcing a smile.

Mike Fein sat behind the wheel of his car, waiting for Don Russ next to the arrivals curb at Chicago's O'Hare airport. Russ read the dismay on his junior associate's face even through the dazzling glare of a shuttle bus's taillights on the front windshield.

Russ jumped into the passenger side. Fein gave him a quick look. Russ stared straight ahead. "If I told you, I'd have to kill you," Russ said. "You've got twenty minutes to get me back to the office. Drive."

The car squealed off without another word said.

Russ glanced over at his associate as he merged into the interstate traffic off the ramp. The young man was angry. That was good—it meant he gave a damn about his work.

They headed toward the city at night in silence. Fein handled the car like a pro, weaving in and out of traffic. The kid was so much like him it was scary. Russ could tell he was about to bust a gut, wanting to ask why the hell Russ had done the things he had done in court today down in Washington.

The Chicago skyline loomed large. "One day, when you're running your own show, you'll find yourself in situations where it's best not to explain," Russ finally said. "For your client's sake, and for the sake of the people working for you. And most of all, for yourself. Just keep plugging away on the forensic issues. And make sure I've got plenty of ammunition to fight back with when they start playing those tapes."

"It's okay," Fein said somewhat sulkily. "By the way, your secretary told me to let you know that someone named 'Boobjob' sent you an e-mail message to the firm marked Urgent to your attention."

"Boobjob?"

"Yeah, that was my reaction, too."

Russ dialed his Internet service provider on his cellular phone, then flipped open the back to reveal the small computer screen. He got into his e-mail reader. The firm regularly used PGP, an easily available form of encryption that was supposedly indecipherable even to the code breakers at the National Security Agency. Russ entered his key password and decoded a message from Julia Menendez:

> *Potentially big problem ... Rumors circulating here in Washington that a medical examiner was beat up really bad this afternoon when he got home from work. He's in the hospital on life support. . . . Heard he was on the Government's expert witness list for Tony's trial. Also overheard one of the U.S. attorneys on the case talking about how his car was broken into at lunch—they're thinking someone got a look at the witness list he left in his briefcase. Except this list wasn't the one he turned over to you—this one had everyone's home and work addresses. There's no way Tony had a copy of the list, RIGHT?*

Russ hit the dashboard. "Damn that Tony. I'm going to kill him myself."

He finished reading Julia's message.

By the way, saw you on CNN emerging from the courthouse scowling—you need to try smiling, baby! But also heard you did brilliantly before the judge. Great being your partner—in more ways than one! Still furiously digging away—time to REALLY squeeze the lemon! I'll get reaction and confirmation of the deal. Enjoy the pic.

XXX Julia

Russ saw there was a file attached to her message. He double-clicked and the image started developing from the top of the screen.

Fein flicked his eyes over to the screen.

"Eyes on the road," Russ warned.

The picture was a nude woman with breasts of bizarre proportions. Julia's face had been seamlessly electronically pasted on top of the body. Russ suppressed a chuckle.

"You get real lucky, and something like this can be yours one day, kiddo," Russ said.

Fein looked again at the computer monitor. "Actually, I'm more of a leg man myself."

"So am I," Russ replied, then zapped Julia's message and the picture. "So am I."

Chapter 17

With a start, Paula sat bolt upright in bed. Her heart was pounding. It was totally dark. Her hair was damp with sweat. And for a moment she was disoriented by the surroundings of her White House residence bedroom. She checked the alarm clock: 3:13. Jim was sleeping soundly.

It had been a nightmare that had awakened her, but she couldn't remember the specifics. All she knew was that something was terribly wrong. Someone was hurt. Crying out for help. Paula was unable to help. And she was the cause of all the pain.

Then she remembered: *This is not just a bad dream. It's my life.*

She had been shaken from sleep by the vision of Billy Tisdale's smiling face, the picture Del had shown her from the newspaper.

Paula shuddered. There was no way she would be going back to sleep.

She felt claustrophobic. She needed air. Needed to get out of that room for a few minutes to rid herself of the nightmarish thoughts that had been haunting her.

Paula rose from the canopied four-poster as quietly as she could and put on her robe. She walked barefoot across the carpet to the door, opened it.

Paula walked down the wide corridor, one foot in front of the other, in a daze. She didn't really know where she was going or what she was going to do. All she knew was that she couldn't lie awake in her bed for the next three hours, thinking about what Del had told her about that poor child.

She padded down the hall, past the President's Study and the children's bedrooms, past the Monroe Room. The revelation earlier in the day had by now completely overwhelmed her. She had been grieving for Billy Tisdale as if he were her own child. Yet she had not been able to share her grief with anyone—she had followed Del's advice and said nothing about it to Jim or Helen.

Paula entered the portion of the second floor reserved for special guests, where a distinguished visitor might be allowed to spend the night in the White House, or where the very fortunate were occasionally invited for an intimate reception. On her left, the Rose Guest Room, where foreign dignitaries were usually put up. On her right, the historic Lincoln Room.

Paula turned the knob to the Lincoln Room, pushed open the door. It was completely dark inside. Standing in the doorway, she caught sight of something that made her gasp, setting her heart galloping again.

She flipped on the chandelier lights and saw what had startled her: her own reflection in a full-length mirror on the opposite side of the room.

Paula entered the room and shut the door behind her. She switched on the small table lamp beside the massive bed and turned off the harsh overhead lights.

Although now a bedroom, it was originally used by Abraham Lincoln as his personal office and cabinet room. During the Civil War, the walls were covered with military campaign maps. It was here he signed the Emancipation Proclamation, freeing the slaves. The room was filled with historical furniture, including some of the original chairs from his administration and a few pieces Mary Todd Lincoln had brought in to refurbish the residence. All of this was looked over by the brooding portrait of Lincoln himself on the wall.

Paula sat in the rocking chair near the window. Although the White House heating system was pumping out warm air, she was chilled. She wrapped her arms around herself and rocked.

Paula closed her eyes. After what she had learned of her past, it seemed a blasphemy for her to be in this room, which had witnessed such profound decisions being made.

Yesterday I was a good mother, a supportive wife, a respected federal judge, and First Lady—and now? Now? I'm a child killer? What's happening to me?

She needed to get a grip. Paula opened her eyes, sat up straight. She had a duty to her family, her job, her husband—and, yes, to the country.

There was another portrait in the room, one of Mary Todd Lincoln. She had weathered so many storms in her life with her husband. Years of disappointment as Abraham Lincoln fought one losing political campaign after another, until his move to Washington as a congressman, then his successful and fateful rise to the presidency. The debilitating war. And the assassination.

But before her husband's death, she'd lost a son. He had died in the White House at the age of eleven from typhoid fever. Little Willie Lincoln died in that very same massive carved rosewood bed now in the room.

Mrs. Lincoln was never the same after the boy's death. Years later, Lincoln's ghost was seen by several First Ladies and Presidents. But before that, Mary Todd Lincoln claimed to see the ghost of her son every night at the foot of her bed.

In the end, the President's wife could no longer cope.

She brought spiritualists, mediums for consultations into the White House. There were séances. Mary Todd Lincoln turned her back on reality and sank further into a world of fantasy and denial.

That's not going to happen to me, Paula swore. *Never!*

Paula shut her eyes tight, willing herself the strength to confront the blackmailers and to do what was right. Regardless of the consequences.

But when she opened her eyes, she had attracted a ghost of her own.

The vision of Billy Tisdale rose before her—a pitiful child in a lonely wood, battered, bloodied, drowned, a life cruelly snuffed in its prime.

She rose to leave.

She realized it had been a mistake to come to this room. Too many ghosts. Too many painful associations. It was the worst place she could have gone to seek solace.

Then—with one hand on the doorknob—she realized she wasn't trapped in this room or any other place. There was no place she could go to hide from her past.

She would forever be a prisoner of her own deeds.

There would be no escape.

Chapter 18

Early Saturday morning, Del checked the in-box in his office, then sprinted up the stairs two at a time to the second floor of the West Wing to pay a visit to Marianne Applebaum, who he knew would be cranking hard, even on the weekend. She was on the phone with her back turned as Del stepped inside her office and quietly closed the door.

Marianne was a large, unattractive woman whose best feature was her gleaming gums. She kept a jumbo dispenser of waxed dental floss on her desk and was often seen emerging from the ladies' rest room with toothbrush in hand. She dressed in well-tailored black suits every day—which showed off the dandruff on her shoulders beautifully—and wore no makeup or nail polish or jewelry. The only splash of color was the red AIDS ribbon on her jacket. She was best kept inside, away from public scrutiny, but her performance for the campaign had merited her a tiny office upstairs.

Marianne swiveled in her chair and motioned him to sit.

Her official title was Special Assistant to the President for Administrative Affairs. Her real function was much as it had been during the campaign: to handle all the dirty little jobs that needed to be delegated to someone who knew how to discreetly make her way through or around the system. She had been in charge of opposition research, a fancy title meaning digging up dirt on Jim Candler's opponents—just in case they needed to use it, which in the end they hadn't.

"I'll call you back," she said in a husky voice into the phone, then hung up.

"A favor," Del said, sliding down into the chair in front of her desk.

"Wait, tell me this first. You in for sponsoring a table at the Gay Pride dinner?"

"Talk to our special-issues people about that. You can go in my place."

"Acres of stud muffins there," she teased.

"Pass."

Marianne got a notepad out, ready to write. "Okay, so what can I do you for?"

"A criminal defense lawyer named Don Russ out of Chicago. You know, the one who's representing the mobster who's up on a murder charge before Paula Candler. I want to know everything there is to know about him, especially his vulnerabilities. Personal, legal, financial, whatever. What's going to make him not just flinch but double over with pain and pass out."

"What else?"

Del pulled a sealed envelope from his corduroy coat pocket and handed it over to her. She felt the heft and held it up to the light.

"A key," she said. She started to open the envelope.

"Don't touch it," Del warned. "Have the prints checked out on that. You'll find mine and those of a woman, early twenties, Latino, smart, very pretty. She gave me the name of Roberta Fuentes, but I have a hunch it's not real. I need to know her name, what she does, who she works for, every boyfriend she's ever slept with, her complete medical history, police record, and anything else you can think of. What's her relationship to Russ. I want

your expert assessment of her pressure points. Her worst
nightmare. What keeps this girl lying awake at night."

"Resources?"

"Hire an outside firm to do the leg work. Go through
a third party to make sure no one's able to trace any of
this back to you or me or the White House. Be creative.
Charge it against the campaign fund. I've already called
the finance director to let him know you'll be sending
him bills. Big bills. Marianne, I need thick files *fast*."

"How soon's that?"

Just then Del's beeper went off. He checked the read-
out and scrolled through the message: *"Be at the McPherson Square Metro station on the westbound platform at 8
P.M. Tuesday. We need your definite answer by then."*

It was the Latino girl from the Capitol Hill bar.

"Try day after tomorrow," Del answered. "On the girl.
I'll give you an extra day on the lawyer."

"Gee, thanks a lot."

"Come on, Marianne. You've done it before. You're
not going to let this be the first time you've disappointed me, are you?"

"Keep this up, buddy, and you'll find your name and
private phone number in the bathroom stalls of every
gay bar in town."

"You wouldn't do that," Del joked.

Marianne fished in her desk drawer and pulled out a
black marker.

"Wanna bet?"

Scott made the call from a phone booth a block away
from the FBI field office. Technically speaking, he was
going over his boss's head, and if he had phoned from
the office there would have been a record of his call.

"Firearms Identification," the man's voice on the
other end answered.

"It's me. Glad I could catch you working on a Saturday," Scott said.

"Hey, buddy, I *live* here."

Lee Barrington was an old friend who worked in the FBI's forensics lab. They used to play a rough game of basketball together at lunch in the gym when Scott was doing his rotation at headquarters before his first field assignment.

"Did you get it?" Scott asked.

Silence on the other end of the line.

"Well?"

"I'm really sorry about Paige," Lee said. "And that other guy. I didn't know him at all. It's just that I've had second thoughts. I know I said yesterday I'd do you a favor and check—"

"Just tell me, Lee. I have to know."

"Scott, you've got to realize . . . the Director has asked to see the report as soon as it's complete. If it ever got out that it was leaked—"

"Hey, it's *me*. Your buddy. Remember, the guy who runs circles around you on the court?"

"That'll be the day. Next time you're over here I'll whip your ass."

"Lee, I gotta know for sure. Just tell me that it was Remalli who killed Paige."

Another moment of silence.

"Can you call back in half an hour?" he said.

"*No*. I have to know right now."

"Hang on."

Scott shuffled his feet in the phone booth and watched nervously for anyone who might see him as he waited the two minutes for Lee to return to the phone.

Lee lowered his voice almost to the point where Scott couldn't hear him. "The evidence sent over from the raid on Tony Remalli's place—"

"That'd be the bullets and the handguns."

"Like I told you yesterday. The case has been assigned to someone else. Just so that you know: I can't just waltz into the other lab and ask for a copy of the report—"

"You're stalling."

"Okay, okay. There was just the one bullet from the hospital, the one that got Paige. The two bullets that hit Alan passed through. The holdup's been that all the bullets were damaged so badly. Hollow points, you know. They've made a preliminary determination, but they're still waiting for confirming results. It's not the kind of thing you want to be wrong about."

"Dammit! Just tell me, Lee."

Lee's voice was a harsh whisper. "The bullet that killed Paige came from McNary's Glock semiautomatic. Ditto for the bullet that got Alan. Satisfied?"

Scott felt a warp of pain in his chest. The news that McNary was responsible for pulling the trigger on Paige and Alan left him reeling. Even though McNary had acted funny about the whole friendly fire issue, Scott had always thought his boss was just being overly defensive about anyone trying to sully the Bureau's reputation.

"Not satisfied," Scott finally said. "Sickened. Thanks, buddy. Don't worry. It's between you and me."

"I've been quietly checking out people close to Eleanor Goldsworthy," Scott said. "I hit a wall investigating the people who used to work directly for the judge. Just a couple of women—her secretary and administrative assistant—and a law clerk from Louisiana who was chubbed out from eating shrimp poor-boys."

It was a rare sit-down lunch in a real restaurant for Scott and McNary, even when working on a Saturday.

Any other day and they'd be eating sack lunches at their desks, trying to catch up on the mountains of work. They had a booth in the back near the kitchen at Las Palmas, a bustling Mexican restaurant. And McNary was paying, which made Scott even more suspicious of his motives for asking him out to eat. This was evidently the "little chat" McNary had told him they needed to have today.

McNary nodded, his mouth still half full. "Damn, this is good." He wiped the guacamole from his chin and took another big bite of his overstuffed taco. He held a finger up for Scott to wait while he chewed another few moments. He swallowed. "So you've turned up no *'scrawny* piece a shit' like Remalli called the guy on the phone?"

"I'm certain no one working in the judge's office made that phone call to Remalli trying to tip him off to the raid. The leak's somewhere else."

"I'm afraid that part of our investigation is going to drag on a long time. Goldsworthy pissed a lot of people off in the courthouse building. Which brings me to why I wanted to talk. I want you to back off looking for the leak—for now."

After listening to what Lee Barrington in forensics had to tell him before lunch, Scott could barely stand to sit at the same table as his boss. But he wanted to keep McNary talking.

"The John Gotti case, back in the early nineties," McNary said. "Gotti's regular defense lawyers were disqualified from the trial because they were ruled to be too involved with the evidence—if not the actual crime—to properly defend their client."

"Lloyd Chapman's going to try to get Remalli's attorney thrown off the case?"

McNary pointed to Gary's plate of burritos, which he had barely touched. "You're not eating."

The truth was, Scott had lost his appetite. The firearms identification report made it hard to even look at food. "Is that what your powwow with Chapman was about yesterday?"

McNary nodded. "Even before that Virginia medical examiner who's on the Government's witness list got beat up, Chapman was thinking there's something screwy going on here, and he's made up his mind that Don Russ is at the center of it. Yeah, maybe someone totally unrelated to the case broke into that assistant U.S. attorney's car, but odds are, it was someone looking specifically for names and addresses of people who were going to be called to testify against Remalli.

"Chapman hypothesized that Russ has gotten too close to his client's business over the years. He's a mob lawyer, so you'd kind of expect that might happen. I told Chapman I was certain we hadn't come across anything in our investigation, but that I'd check again."

"I think I would've remembered something like that. I can run a word search on the transcripts when we get back to the office if you'd like."

"Can't hurt."

"Was that it?"

McNary was being cagey. "Maybe some background would help. You need to understand, Chapman's got to make sure he's a winner on this one."

"How so?"

"There's still the matter of what went wrong with Remalli's arrest. I'll catch some hell on that, but your name figures pretty prominently in the investigation, too."

What a contemptible jerk, Scott thought. *Still hiding the fact he sent in the memo directly blaming me for the raid disaster. Does he have any idea it was his sidearm that felled Paige and Alan?*

McNary used his fork to mash his refried beans together with his rice. "Paige's death is going to have to be answered for," he continued. "The bureaucracy in Washington demands an answer when an agent gets killed. It tears me up having to tell you this, and if you ever say we had this conversation, I'll deny it. I'd hate for your career to be over before it's had a chance to get off the ground. But, frankly, once your name gets associated with an operation gone bad—Waco, Ruby Ridge—certain career paths get cut off. Unofficially, of course, and there may never be a single negative citation written into your personnel record, but you've got to be aware of what's called institutional memory—nobody ever forgets who was on duty when the bad press started and the Bureau ended up with a black eye again. Even if it was Remalli who actually pulled the trigger that killed Paige. It's unfortunate, but that's the way it operates."

Scott had already made up his mind to play along with McNary. Let him think he was scared shitless over what might happen.

"When I first came to your unit," Scott said, "you and I talked about how this was going to be my first big career break with the Bureau. Looks like now it's a career-ending move."

The SOB isn't denying it.

"So how does all of this relate to Chapman and his hypothesis about Don Russ somehow being involved?" Scott said. "And me?"

"Chapman and I talked. We don't have to just sit back and wait for things to happen to us. We can still be proactive, take control of the situation. It's not too late for us to come out of this as real heroes. But it's not me I'm really talking about here, it's you. I'm much too visible to be able to do the kind of field work that needs to be done." McNary leaned across the table. "Scott, listen closely. I'm giving you an opportunity to salvage what up until last week had been the makings of a stellar career in the FBI. You following me?"

"Just tell me what I need to do."

"You remember your courses in legal ethics from law school, and you remember the lectures on proper procedure from the FBI Academy. Now, I want you to keep all of that firmly in mind after we've had this discussion, because I don't want it ever said that I encouraged you to do something that was illegal. Do you understand that?"

"You want me to do what, exactly?"

"If, in the course of our follow-through on the Remalli case, you happened to come across evidence of his lawyer's involvement in criminal activity, it would be proper to share that information with your superiors, who would then pass along this information to an extremely grateful U.S. Attorney's Office. Likewise, if you happened to be out on your own in the evening, and you just happened to come across Don Russ around town, you might want to prick your ears up. Or lift a pair of binoculars to your eyes. Or take whatever steps that you might reasonably believe to be required given the circumstances."

"Oh," Scott said. "I get it now."

"You may have only one shot at getting your career back on line," he said. "I suggest you don't blow it."

If Scott could have belted McNary and got away with it, he would have. He decided to channel his emotions into something more productive. Like making sure Paige didn't die in vain. Like putting Remalli away for a long, long time. And keeping Lloyd Chapman and Craig McNary from saddling him with the blame for the botched raid.

Jefferson, the Candler family's well-fed yellow Labrador, stretched lazily in the early afternoon sun and moved beside Paula's couch in the solarium on the third floor of the White House. The old dog was partial to her because she spoiled him with table scraps and rawhide treats. She reached over and stroked the old dog's belly, but he moved away, apparently disturbed by her trembling hand.

The rage Paula was feeling from the blackmail attempt still left her shaken. She was having a difficult time containing all of the conflicting emotions. Her concentration was totally gone, and the stacks of court documents on the coffee table remained unread.

It had taken until dinnertime yesterday for the realization to set in of what was really happening. Not just the possible consequences of the blackmail, but the knowledge that she had . . . She could barely bring herself to think the words: she had *killed* a child.

"Hey," a voice said softly, making her jump. She had been so deep in her own thoughts that she hadn't noticed Jim sticking his head in the door. He stepped into the room, holding a briefing book. He looked tense. "They told me I'd find you up here."

She made room for him on the couch.

"Sorry, we're moving over to the Situation Room," he said. "Where'd the kids go?"

"They're at a school basketball game."

Paula could barely look Jim in the eye. She pulled up the collar of her turtleneck sweater to hide the deep red splotches on her neck, another physical manifestation of her inner turmoil.

"What's going on?" he said. He knew something was bothering her, just from her tone of voice. Paula motioned to the paperwork. "Same old stuff." She managed a weak smile.

He nodded slowly, waiting for more.

She couldn't remember a time when she had outright lied to her husband.

"Sure?" he said.

For an instant she felt that she should tell Jim everything—be out with it now rather than later, let him know the full extent of her culpability so that he could both help her and assess what impact her actions would have on his own position.

"I'm busy," he said, "but I'll make some time for you if you need it."

Paula felt an almost rapturous relief, a great burden lifted. Jim was the only person she completely trusted. He would help her. She felt ready to tell all. Despite her promise to Del, why shouldn't she confide in her own husband?

The best way was to start at the beginning, explain what happened that night, how Del had told her it was just some animal she had hit, how it wasn't her fault. She caught herself, a bit ashamed, because now she was beginning to think like Del.

If ever there was a moment to come clean, it was now, before she got sucked into something that was even more out of her control.

She opened her mouth to begin. The look on Jim's face told her he was expecting something important.

"You can tell me," he said with infinite patience. "Whatever it is."

She nodded. It was definitely time. "Sometimes, you know, it's difficult—"

A commotion at the door interrupted her. Someone in the hallway giving the President a message.

"All right," Jim said. "I'll be right down." He turned back to Paula. "I'm really sorry. You were saying?"

In those few seconds of disruption, she had experienced an awful flashback to the recurring nightmare scenario she had been playing over and over in her mind. It was the vision of her being arraigned in a courtroom. She was led before the judge handcuffed just like any other criminal who appeared before her. Her children sat in the gallery and cried, then ran out of the courtroom as she was found guilty of killing the Tisdale boy. Her husband turned his back as she was being led away.

It would hurt him so much. She would do anything to prevent that.

She shook her head. "Nothing, Jim. Go on. We'll talk later."

Jim wasn't buying it. But he knew enough not to push. "When you're ready," he said.

Chapter 19

Three nights later at 8:15, a cold wind swept through the underground tunnel at the McPherson Square Metro station. The platform lights flashed, signaling the arrival of another train. Del, sitting on a bench with his head buried in the *Washington Post,* looked up. A dozen or so weary men and women headed for the platform edge as the train stopped. The train doors opened, and the government workers rushed in out of habit, even though the train was only half full. The train departed, and Del was alone again on the platform.

For the past half hour he had been waiting for the Latino woman. Over the next few minutes more people entered the station. Del recognized no one, and he took care to keep his face well hidden behind his newspaper so no one would recognize him. He would give it another fifteen minutes, then give up.

He looked toward a small commotion at the other end of the platform. A very short, unshaven man in an oversized suit with no tie was pestering people for money, slowly making his way toward Del. He was unsteady on his feet, tripping over his baggy trousers, swaying dangerously close to the edge of the platform. Del stuck his face into the newspaper and hoped the bum would ignore him.

Suddenly Del was aware of the presence of stale alcohol breath and unwashed flesh.

"Got a dollar?" he heard in heavily slurred speech. Del looked over the top of his paper. It was the drunk, squinting hard at him.

"Sorry," Del answered tersely. He shifted in his seat and craned his neck to see if a train might be coming from the other direction.

"Got a minute?" the man tried again.

"Pardon?"

"You *are* Del Owens, aren't you?"

Del was jolted. The grizzled man held a picture of Del that had been clipped from the previous week's copy of *Time* magazine. The drunk looked back and forth between the picture and Del.

"Why do you want to know?"

"Sorry I'm late. Had to make a stop on the way." He patted his coat pocket, where a pint liquor bottle was visible in outline. "A lady promised me twenty bucks if I found you and gave you this."

"What did this woman look like?" Del asked as he accepted a grubby page of newsprint folded over.

"Cute, young. Hispanic. Pretty mouth. Great legs. Nice piece of ass."

Del opened the paper and saw that it was torn from the *Washington Blade,* the gay weekly newspaper. Circled was an ad for Remington's on Pennsylvania Avenue. Del read out loud:

" 'The finest queer country-western club on the East Coast.' Great. Just how I wanted to spend my Tuesday night. Thanks." Del pocketed the ad and walked briskly toward the exit.

"Hey, mister!" the drunk yelled out after him. Heads turned.

Del was afraid someone was going to recognize him. He went back to the man. "What is it?" he asked irritably.

"She told me *you'd* be paying me the twenty bucks."

"Aw, shit . . ." Del dug a twenty out of his wallet and handed it over.

"Thanks, man," the bum said.

"I don't think I've seen *you* in here before," a delighted cowboy told Del.

Standing just inside the door at Remington's, the cowboy looked like the Marlboro Man—lean, hard body; hat, blue jeans, boots, leather vest and chaps—except that his hair and mustache were trimmed a little too neatly.

"And you won't again, with any luck," Del answered as he pushed his way through the crowd to the dance floor.

The woman he had last seen at the Mayflower Hotel was nowhere in sight. He checked out the bar but saw only more men.

Then he thought he saw a flash of skin through the crowd of denim. He looked again and saw her seated on an overstuffed sofa in the lounge, bouncing her crossed leg up and down in time with the music. She was wearing a black miniskirt and a skintight black Spandex midriff-baring top. The boots she was wearing were more appropriate for a heavy metal concert than a rodeo. She was drinking a Corona and seemed to be enjoying herself watching all the cute guys having fun.

"Thanks a hell of a lot," Del said, plopping down beside her. "Why did we have to meet in *this* place?"

"It's one of the few nightclubs I've found where the men wouldn't hit on me. And I assumed you wouldn't know anyone here."

Del scrutinized the faces at the bar. Pairs of men in western garb sipped light beers and fruity mixed drinks. On the dance floor, a couple of dozen others were performing a line dance to a Garth Brooks song. "You're right about that," he said.

"Glad you could make it. Brilliant performance in court last week. Very cooperative of Paula Candler to press the U.S. attorney to go along with Russ's request for a nonjury trial."

"I didn't have anything to do with it. I have very little influence. I'm just the messenger."

"I seriously doubt that's true."

"I'm sure Judge Candler did what she thought was right under the circumstances. I don't have a lot of time. What is it you want?"

Her mood quickly darkened. "It should be obvious what the judge needs to do. She's off to a great start. Tell her she can give the defense attorney as hard a time as she likes during the trial. In fact, it shouldn't look too easy. As long as in the end she returns a not guilty verdict for Tony Remalli."

Del smiled condescendingly at her. "You're awfully sure of yourself, aren't you?"

"I have a gray Crown Victoria in storage that tells me I have good reason to be. You know, a judge should drive more carefully, especially at night in bad weather—you never know who she might hit."

"All right. I'm listening."

"I'm not going to play games. My purpose in meeting you is to get your unconditional guarantee that Paula Candler will cooperate fully."

Del spoke with the practiced, unhurried response of a political pro. "I'll do whatever is necessary to prevent this from becoming a public issue."

"Cut the crap; you're not on TV. You didn't answer my question. All I want is a straight yes or no answer. And we don't really care about what *you* will do anyway. It's what the judge will do that counts."

"You know, that's very interesting. That's the first time you've used the word 'we.' Who are you working for? Don Russ? Tony Remalli? Yourself?"

"It doesn't matter. I'm just like you, I'm the bona fide representative. And I've got the car and the information linking Paula Candler to the hit-and-run. I'm the person you have to deal with."

"I don't respond real well to pressure."

"Hey, I wasn't the one who helped cover up the judge killing a kid. You're in deep shit yourself."

She definitely had a point, but Del wasn't going to let her see him sweat.

"Look, you're probably a very nice girl, and I'm sure you're a lot of fun, but you're in *way* over your head. Why don't you do yourself a favor, just pack it up and head back to Miami. Okay . . . *Julia*?"

She almost dropped her drink. "Miami? And where do you get off with this 'Julia' business? The name's Roberta. Roberta Fuentes."

"Julia Menendez, twenty-four-year-old daughter of Felipe and Carla Menendez. The same Felipe Menendez who abandoned his wife and two-month-old baby daughter and hasn't been heard from since. The same Carla Menendez who lives in public housing, redeems U.S. government food stamps at twenty-five cents on the dollar in cash at a bodega in Little Havana to help support a drug habit, and draws $537.66 a month unemployment, even though she takes in almost that same amount in cash under the table at the Sea-Do Hotel on Collins Avenue in Miami working as a maid."

"Leave my mother out of this," Julia snapped.

Del knew that Marianne Applebaum's sleuthing was dead on target.

"You're a private investigator licensed by the state of Florida. Eighty percent of your work is divorce cases, spying on suspected cheating husbands and wives. You were suspended once after pleading guilty to invasion of privacy and criminal trespass when you were caught installing a hidden video camera in your own client's bedroom after you started dating her husband and wanted to find out if he was cheating on *you* with his own wife."

"We've since broken up."

"Up to your eyeballs in debt," Del rattled off. "The clients who do pay you are usually late. You spent thirty percent more last year than you declared on your federal tax return. You buy expensive clothes at specialty boutiques, make outrageous car payments, and you're two months behind on your apartment rent. Your phone service has been disconnected twice in the past three years for nonpayment."

Julia was now speechless.

"Two years ago you had an abortion." Del slowed down his pace. "This followed a monthlong stay you had in New York. Also working on another Mafia case; Antonio Remalli was the client then, too. Also on assignment for Don Russ. You had adjoining rooms at the Helmsley Plaza. Did Russ know about the baby?"

Julia still couldn't speak.

"I'm thinking he did. You've been on some kind of special retainer with his law firm, receiving a thousand a month for no discernible work. You know, the IRS frowns on claiming payoffs to old lovers as a business expense. People go to jail for things like that."

A cowboy who had been pacing in the area took advantage of the lull in their conversation to interrupt. "Care to dance?" he asked.

"You talking to *me*?" Del said.

The cowboy nodded enthusiastically.

"Get bent."

The cowboy hurried away.

"I suppose that's what allows you to barely hang on to that posh South Beach condo," Del continued. "Nice place. I'm not too wild about how you've decorated it, though. I've never been much for that fifties retro look. I might have furnished it with elegant upholstered furniture and art deco accessories, in keeping with the style of the building. The bird's-eye maple frame in your bedroom with the picture of your parents on their wedding day is a bit sentimental, don't you think? And by the way, when you get back to Miami, you need to have someone take a look at that leaky sink faucet in the back bathroom—you know, where you've got your G-strings hanging up to dry over the tub? Nasty stains—on the porcelain, that is. Something about the minerals in the water down there."

Del reached into his pocket and pulled out a G-string, spread it like a spider's web over the outstretched fingers of his hands.

Julia's eyes grew large with the recognition of the panties taken from her own apartment.

"Coochie-coochie," Del said humorlessly, jiggling the G-string.

Julia grabbed the underwear away.

"So, how does it feel to have the tables turned?" Del asked.

"I have nothing to hide," Julia shot back.

"Then you wouldn't mind my turning your mother's name over to the Florida state welfare fraud investigators. Or my making an anonymous tip to the IRS about Russ's fraudulent tax returns claiming monthly payments to you as a business expense."

Silence.

"What is it that motivates you?" Del asked. "The risks are too high for the money you're getting. Have you let yourself be drawn into this because of some relationship you still have with Russ?"

More silence. Del shook his head in disbelief.

"You seem to have forgotten who you're dealing with here," he said. "It's one small criminal law firm in Chicago and a Latino PI from South Miami Beach against me, my access to almost unlimited financial resources, and the entire force of the United States government, if it comes to that. Don't ever threaten me again, lady. Same for Don Russ, or Tony Remalli, or whoever it is you work for. And leave Paula Candler the hell alone."

As the dance floor filled with cowboys coupling as the Texas two-step began, Del left Julia Menendez sitting on the sofa.

They both knew she was so wrapped up in her feelings for Russ that she'd do anything for him. Despite his warning, Del was certain he hadn't seen the last of Julia Menendez.

Chapter 20

Don Russ entered the U.S. marshal's lockup facility Wednesday morning with a grim face. He would make his opening statement in an hour and a half.

"I'd like to see the log of telephone calls my client has made out of here," he told the deputy marshal.

The marshal was over a half foot shorter than Russ, wearing blue jeans and a cheap poly-cotton button-down shirt. He stroked his thin mustache and regarded Russ's impeccable appearance with disdain. "Sorry, we're only allowed to show the U.S. Attorney's Office. Unless, of course, you've got a court order."

Russ bit his tongue and turned away from the marshal. He saw Remalli already waiting on the opposite side of the mesh screen in the interview room.

"Jesus Christ," Russ said, spinning back around. "You don't really want me to have to tell the judge that some chickenshit deputy marshal is denying me proper access to my client's records, do you?"

The marshal left Russ standing alone in the hallway. He returned in a minute with a sheet of paper still warm from the photocopy machine.

Russ looked at the records of Remalli's outgoing phone calls with the number and name of each recipient neatly recorded. First, the cliché call to his attorney after his arrest, followed by a call to his home back in New York. There was also a Jewish deli, several calls to

Russ's Chicago office, and a final call to a number traced to a cellular phone registered to PDB Enterprises, Inc., the company that Russ knew fronted for a variety of Antonio Remalli's various business interests, including his client's new Snap-on Tools franchise.

Russ folded the paper and stuck it into his coat pocket.

"We refused delivery of the 'hoagie' he ordered from the deli," the marshal said in a distinct Virginia accent. "Whatever *that* is. I ain't lettin' nuthin' through the door I never heard of."

Russ smiled condescendingly as the marshal locked him into the interview room facing Remalli. His client was outfitted and groomed according to his earlier instructions. Russ kept the smile on his face until the marshal was out of sight.

"You stupid dago son of a bitch!" Russ whispered harshly.

"Wha? Wha?"

"I just looked at the log of your phone calls. Which one of your goons did you call to beat up that medical examiner?"

"Whaddaya talkin' about?"

"Don't play innocent with me. I know exactly what happened. You had one of your boys break into that assistant U.S. attorney's car and get a copy of the witness list. Dammit, Tony—we don't need to do it that way."

Remalli dropped the pretense. "Fuck you," he spat. "You're not the one facing the death penalty here. You lose the case, you still get your dough and you get to walk."

Russ vigorously shook his head. "No, no, no! Promise me no more of this or I'm off the case."

"Hey, hey . . . whaddaya wanna talk like that for? We're just about to go to trial."

"Then start taking my advice and let me handle things, Tony."

"It's just that—"

"What?"

"Seems like you're keepin' me in the dark about lots of stuff. You didn't used to do that. We used to talk strategy. I don't understand what you're doin' in there. I feel helpless. I'd hate to lose this case knowin' there was somethin' I coulda done."

"Now you think you're a legal mastermind? Drop it, Tony. Your way's not going to work this time. It's too big. This isn't tax court, where we can negotiate a percentage settlement. You whacked a federal judge."

"Okay, okay," Remalli said contritely. "Just, I couldn't help thinkin' . . ."

"What?" Russ said impatiently.

"Ya know. No witness, no evidence, no case."

"Oh, Christ . . ." Russ stood up abruptly, banged on the door for the marshal.

"Where ya going, Donato?" Remalli pleaded, up on his feet. "You can't walk out on me now."

Russ slammed the door behind him. Remalli slumped back into his chair.

Assistant U.S. Attorney Ted Savage turned quickly on his heels and pointed a finger at the defendant. "Your Honor, Antonio 'Rimshot' Remalli, the man who murdered Judge Ellen Goldsworthy."

Paula Candler had listened for over an hour as Savage presented the government's opening statements. The courtroom was packed. The summary of the case had been a clean, unemotional outline of the evidence the prosecution would present to convict Remalli. One of the medical examiners who performed the autopsy would show that Judge Goldsworthy was murdered with a gun. An FBI forensic scientist would then explain how evidence gathered at the scene corroborated the medical examiner's testimony. The key to the case would be the tapes of Tony Remalli made by the FBI, which showed Remalli's motivation for killing the judge and which also contained what would be unambiguously interpreted as his admission of the murder.

Lloyd Chapman cracked a tight-lipped smile and nodded in approval. "Opening, Mr. Russ?"

Don Russ rose and addressed the court from the defense table. "Your Honor, it's unseasonably cold outside," he stated matter-of-factly. His legal assistant smirked as if he knew what was coming. "In fact, it's so cold that as I was running early this morning, I noticed ice forming along the banks of the Potomac. Now *that's* cold. On my way into court, I literally had to step over hungry and homeless men huddled together for warmth, seeking shelter on the steps of the Albert V. Bryan Federal Courthouse. It made me wonder: why is it that the United States Government—your government and my government—has wasted millions of taxpayers' dollars to frame an innocent man when there are so many other ways in which that money could have been put to use? Ironic, isn't it?"

Paula glanced at the Government table, saw the collective rolling of eyes.

"I thought about that, and then I open today's *Washington Post* and find my answer."

Russ pulled a newspaper from his briefcase, made a show of finding the page, and read dramatically: " 'Lloyd Chapman, touted as a likely candidate in next year's congressional race, sees his political fortunes rise or fall today with the start of the Remalli trial.' "

Don Russ shook his head in disgust.

"What we have here is a modern-day witch hunt by a

smug, ambitious, career-minded prosecutor who would put his own political interests ahead of the law. So we're going to allow *this* man"—Russ turned and pointed an accusatory finger at Chapman—"this man, to run roughshod over the constitutional rights of my client just so he can set up office on Capitol Hill? I don't think so, Your Honor. Not in *this* court."

Lloyd Chapman stiffened.

"Now, about the so-called damning evidence that Mr. Savage alluded to in his opening remarks. Your Honor, during the course of the next few days, you are going to hear a lot about some tape-recorded conversations of my client. The Government will attempt to present a highly conjectural misinterpretation of these tapes as proof of Mr. Remalli's involvement in the heinous crime which was committed against Judge Goldsworthy. But I am *confident* that after the court hears the tapes for herself, Your Honor will realize that these tapes are nothing more than the intrusion upon the privacy of a legitimate businessman participating in harmless conversations with his work associates."

Russ put a hand on Remalli's shoulder.

"I have the privilege and honor of being asked to defend Mr. Remalli. Family man, entrepreneur, philanthropist. These are the qualities of the man I and many others who have known him for years well recognize. Yet the Government has used every available resource in an attempt to portray my client as some monster." Russ looked at his notes. "It's instructive to look to the public words of the U.S. attorney. Last week Mr. Chapman said on local television stations that he would vigorously prosecute any Mafia from outside the area attempting to set up shop in his jurisdiction. What exactly does that mean?

"I think we have to break it down. First, we know

that 'Mafia' is often a code word for 'Italian' or 'Sicilian.' So Mr. Chapman has made a presumption that people of Italian ancestry belong to a class of individuals deserving special scrutiny by his office. That seems to me to be prejudicial to my client and others with Italian names. What about others he might target in the community?" Russ picked up a local telephone book from the defense table, flipped pages as he read names circled boldly in red ink: "Battaglia, Coosinata, Denelli, Gambino—*Ippolito* . . ." Russ looked up to gauge Paula's reaction.

The last name jarred Paula.

Ippolito was Paula's grandmother's maiden name. Russ obviously had done some digging into her background to find that piece of trivia from her past. *How much farther have these people dug into my personal life?*

"Perhaps even Your Honor has some Italian blood in her own distant background?"

Russ paused just long enough for the implications of his hypothetical question to sink in. He left Remalli's side and walked to the lectern so that he was only ten feet away from Paula.

" 'Outsiders,' " he said with disdain. "Now what do you suppose that could mean?" Russ looked at Chapman and shook his head once more. "Yet another code word. Try inserting the word 'Yankee.' I remember overhearing a joke the other night. What's the difference between a Yankee, a damned Yankee, and—if you'll allow me—a God-damned Yankee?"

Paula knew the answer, as did most everyone in the court. Russ was playing to the media at this point.

"A Yankee, of course, is someone from the North. A *damned* Yankee is one visiting the South. And a *God-damned* Yankee is one who comes and stays."

There was some laughter from the gallery; apparently a few people hadn't heard the joke after all. Fein nodded with a broad smile. Remalli grinned.

"Well, Your Honor," Russ said, raising his voice for the first time and thumping the table for emphasis, "I'm here today to tell you that this is *one God-damned Yankee who ain't goin' away*. I will not leave until I see Mr. Remalli cleared of these charges so he can walk as a free man out those doors."

There was dead silence in the courtroom. Russ had locked onto Paula with his eyes and wasn't turning loose. No one at the Government's table nor any of the spectators could see the menacing look on Russ's face.

Russ broke the stare and paced in front of the bench. "I have no doubt that the Government will attempt to portray Mr. Remalli as a career gangster." He shook his head again. Remalli was looking appropriately indignant.

"Well, Your Honor, part of my job is to show the other side of my client. The human dimension. We all have some thorn in the flesh, some frailty, some secret knowledge or burden to bear that the public may not be aware of." Russ stopped in front of Paula and said with the most sincere face possible: "My client's son happens to suffer from a learning disability—dyslexia."

Paula sat up straighter. Russ wouldn't let her look away. He had touched a nerve and he knew it. *Is this merely a coincidence? Is it possible he knows of my son's struggle with dyslexia?*

"For years Mr. Remalli has worked with his young son in his home, helped him to learn how to live with this affliction. They spend hours together, poring over his homework, just like any normal father and son. And once a week after school—taking time out of his extremely busy schedule—Mr. Remalli drives his son to a special tutor."

Paula couldn't believe it. That was what she used to do with Chip when they all lived in Richmond.

Russ turned back to the defense table and picked up a piece of paper. "The pretrial services office has been kind enough to provide me with a copy of my client's arrest and conviction record. Not very exciting reading, I can tell you." Russ paused to look over the page. "In fact, the only charges for which Mr. Remalli has ever been found guilty were eight years ago for speeding in upstate New York while taking his family on a vacation to the Poconos, and last year when he was pulled over for failing to maintain a safe vehicle when his rear turn signal wasn't working properly. Hardly the record of a hardened criminal. In fact, I'd put his record up against that of anyone else in the room—Mr. Chapman . . . *and* Your Honor included."

It was a daring thing for a defense attorney to say in open court. Russ was obviously feeling in control.

"Perhaps," Russ continued, "in his haste to get to the office one morning, Mr. Chapman has once innocently overlooked the speed limit while rushing along the interstate? Or—if I may be so bold—Your Honor may have quite innocently rolled through an intersection, failing to come to a complete stop where a police car unfortunately happened to be waiting? Of course, these are only hypotheticals, and I wouldn't want to infer that either the U.S. Attorney or Your Honor is a regular scofflaw."

Paula's heart was in her throat. Russ had somehow managed to get his hands on *her* police record as well. The one violation she had ever been charged with was the one he had just mentioned, a stupid mistake she had made in her college days.

Paula noticed Lloyd Chapman squirming in his chair. Russ had probably also nailed the U.S. attorney for the speeding violation just mentioned.

Russ strode back to the defense table. Tony Remalli wore a smug smile, pleased with his attorney's performance. Russ held up the paper with Remalli's arrest record. "An innocent mistake," Russ said. "Could happen to anyone in this courtroom. We're all human here. No one's perfect. I just wanted to remind the court that none of us is infallible. Charging my client with the murder of a federal judge is a mistake. Contrary to what the Government will tell you, Mr. Remalli is just as much a caring, law-abiding citizen as you are, not some monster who goes around killing people."

Paula was stunned by the direct comparison of the killing of the Tisdale boy and the murder of Judge Goldsworthy. No one else in the courtroom could have understood the impact it made on her. She was being likened to a cold-blooded mob killer.

Paula foresaw everything now. How the intimidation would be unrelenting and in her face, day after day of the trial. The blackmail attempt had seemed abstract, something that Del was taking care of. Now, for the first time, she felt personally threatened by the famous criminal defense attorney and his client.

"That's all, Your Honor," Russ said. "For *now*."

Scott had Don Russ in his sights from the moment the attorney crossed the lobby of the Ritz-Carlton Pentagon City and climbed into a waiting taxi at nine fifty-five on the evening of the trial's first day.

Scott used all the counterespionage skills learned in Quantico to follow the crazed taxi driver through congested traffic over the Potomac and into Georgetown. As soon as the taxi stopped at the busy intersection of Wisconsin Avenue and M Street, Scott made himself a parking space in a no parking zone and prayed his car would be there when he returned.

Hands thrust into pockets, Russ headed along the sidewalk of M Street, Scott cautiously following a half block behind. Even on a frigid January night in the middle of the week the sidewalk was crowded, providing plenty of cover for tailing the lawyer. Russ had changed out of his business suit and was wearing blue jeans and a black leather jacket, fitting right in with the crowd of college students and out-of-towners. Scott felt more conspicuous in his suit and tie, although he could have easily been one of the businessmen trolling the area for music and drink.

At his fast pace, Russ passed a blur of boutiques, bars, discos, cafés, and restaurants. After keeping a close eye on Russ's comings and goings for four days without seeing the lawyer so much as commit a jaywalking violation, Scott had a hunch that this brisk evening walk was more than a stroll to stretch the legs.

Scott shadowed Russ as far as a Vietnamese restaurant near Thirtieth Street, when he crossed to the opposite side of the street, then quickly doubled back, looking to see if he was being followed. Scott dropped and tied his shoe, hidden from Russ's sight by the mass of revelers on the sidewalk.

He popped up to follow Russ another hundred yards, past Garrett's Tavern, past the Old Stone House, crossed a side street; then, suddenly, Russ disappeared.

Scott half-ran to the spot he had last seen Russ. Above the sidewalk where he stood sputtered an old neon sign. SCHWANGO'S, it read. POOL—DRINK—MUSIC. A couple came out the door, followed by the sound of a lively rockabilly band.

There was no other place Russ could have gone. The move had been too quick and deliberate. The door opened again, and Scott saw the band was set up on a small stage directly in front of the blacked-out window, with everyone inside turned to face the direction of the front door.

Scott paced back and forth on the sidewalk, wondering how he could get inside without being recognized from court. Just as he was about to head off to see if there was a back service entrance, a group of a half dozen boisterous college boys who had just emerged from a bar across the street made a beeline for Schwango's. Scott pulled his tie off and fell unobtrusively into the back of the group as they pushed rowdily into the bar.

Inside it was very dark, except for the colored spotlights trained on the band. The lights temporarily blinded anyone coming in the front door, and Scott could barely see where he was going. He groped his way to the back of the long, narrow room with the rest of the college boys, unbuttoned his shirt collar, and climbed onto a stool at the end of the bar.

His eyes began to adjust to his dim surroundings. In between drumbeats Scott heard the clacking of balls on a pool table in the next room. The only drinks on the bar were long-neck beer bottles. The band on the minuscule stage was young and enthusiastic—one guy on drums, a lead singer who belted out tunes as he worked magic on the guitar, and a third slapping at his tall bass.

Apart from the long bar, people were seated at small tables or in chairs lining the room. There were some tourists and businessmen, but it was mostly college kids.

Scott found Russ easily: he was sitting sullenly alone at a table for two, halfway toward the front, the only person in sight not grooving to the music. Even in his jeans and leather jacket, he looked way too clean-cut and uptight to be in a joint like Schwango's.

Scott ordered a beer and kept an eye on Russ in the big mirror behind the bar. Russ fidgeted, checked his watch, tried finding something to do with his hands, somewhere to look. He obviously hadn't come for the music.

After a fifteen-minute break, the band started up again at eleven and more people came into the bar from the sidewalk. The place was packed to capacity, standing room only. Scott noticed something interesting. Every time Russ was asked if the chair was taken, he said yes.

Even more people joined the party from outside. By eleven-thirty the place was really jamming. So much so that Scott was having a hard time keeping a clear line of sight to Russ in the mirror.

The front door popped open and Scott couldn't help noticing a very pretty tanned girl who came in unaccompanied, wearing a long coat. Definitely not a college girl, unless she was hooking to make tuition. The colored stage lights lit up her lustrous black hair. She headed straight for the bar and squeezed in between two men only a few seats away from where Scott sat. She was uncommonly attractive, exotic even, and attracted a lot of attention from both the men and the women in the bar. Once she was seated, there was a low whistle from one of the tables of fraternity boys. She bought two beers and was quickly lost in the crowd. Scott was sorry to lose sight of her.

Then he realized she was hovering over Russ's table.

Scott swiveled on his stool as if to get a better look at the riff the guitarist was playing. Now he had an unobstructed view of where Russ sat. The attorney not only relinquished the chair opposite him, but stood up and pulled it out for the woman.

She took off her coat, revealing a dress with an extremely low-scooped neckline, cut high on the thigh. Scott was thinking she must be awfully cold on a night like this dressed that way. When she crossed her legs, he thought he'd have to look away out of modesty, even though all the other men in the place couldn't take their eyes off her.

The great Don Russ rendezvousing with a call girl?

He'd give anything to hear what they were saying, but couldn't risk moving any closer.

"I am really, really sorry," Julia Menendez said, having to almost shout to be heard over the band. "If you hadn't put me up in that hole of a hotel, it might have been easier to get a taxi. I'll bet they're lined up in front of your hotel."

"Just stop. You know we can't stay at my hotel because the feds are probably watching the place. By the way, what the hell are you wearing?"

Julia was offended. "What, you don't think it looks nice?"

"For a South Beach rooftop party maybe."

"A girl likes to be noticed. What's it to you, anyway?"

Russ kept looking between Julia's cleavage and the perky lead singer of the band. Their music really grated on his nerves. "Why did we have to meet here?" he said.

"Do you think anyone from court would come into a place like this?"

Russ took a look at the kind of people surrounding them. Not the usual sort he socialized with. And not an attorney or fed among them, at least as far as he could tell. Russ knew she was right. She was right much more often than she was wrong.

"Did you get a commitment from Del Owens on the judge?" Russ asked impatiently.

"Not exactly."

"What does *that* mean?"

"He's . . . not cooperating. I thought at first he was going to go along, but when I met him he basically told me to go to hell."

Russ was disbelieving. "How can he do that? With all the evidence we've got?"

Julia looked everywhere in the bar but into Russ's eyes.

"What?"

"Look, Don. They've been snooping around. Doing background checks on me. You're probably next. Del Owens knows things he shouldn't be able to know. Highly embarrassing things."

"Like what?"

"Like it's too personal to tell you." She lowered her eyes, tugged at her dress in a self-conscious effort to better cover herself.

"Out with it."

Julia drew a deep breath. "For one thing, he knows about my mother. She's a welfare and tax cheat."

"Screw 'im. I don't give a rat's ass about your mother, and neither do you."

"They talked to my friends, guys I dated. They got hold of my tax and financial and medical records. Someone broke into my apartment. They've been in my bathroom, my bedroom. That's getting too close, Don. I'm not liking this."

"What did he say about me?"

"Not much. It was more what was implied. . . ." Julia got quiet again.

"What?" Russ said.

"They know about *us,* Don. The monthly payments you've been sending me."

"That's business. You're on retainer with my firm."

"No, it's not, and you know it. He said something about how the IRS might be interested in our arrangement. I got the impression he knows a lot more, too."

"Christ!" Russ exploded.

"It's obvious to me," Julia said, "they've got their own

investigators working. They've got more resources than we do. More than you could ever pull together, even with all of Tony Remalli's money. Think about it, Don. Owens can probably raise more cash to fund an operation in one afternoon of working the phones than you and I will see in a lifetime. Or at least what *I'll* see in a lifetime. He's the President's closest aide in the White House. All he has to do is pick up the phone and he's got every government agency in the country at his disposal."

"Yeah, but don't ever forget, the final move's ours, no matter what else happens. We hold the trump card. We've got the car, and we've got all the evidence linking Paula Candler to the kid's death. Sooner or later, they've got to give in. They're not sliding out of this that easily."

"You can say that now, but you're not the one they've been digging dirt up on. Not yet, at least."

"They're bluffing. Del Owens is smart. He's buying time, improving his playing position. It's a negotiating ploy. If I were in his position, I'd do the same thing."

Julia took a long drink of her beer. "Tony still doesn't know anything about this?"

"Nothing. He's better off knowing as little as possible. Tony's got a big mouth. That's what got him into trouble in the first place. He's still scratching his head over what happened in court, but he's got confidence in me. I just shove him a mint and tell him to shut up and sit up straight when we're in court."

"I'm beginning to get a little worried, Don. About my role in all of this. I think you're going to have to get personally involved with Del Owens."

"No way. That's what I'm paying you to do. If the principals get too close, this whole deal could blow up. I'm not talking directly to Owens, just like Paula Candler isn't going to talk to me. That's far too dangerous."

"Just listen to me for a moment," Julia pleaded. "I've been thinking about something Owens said. He told me I was in way over my head. At first I was angry about what he said; then I started thinking about it. He's right. I'm a private investigator. Hey, I can do a lot of stuff, but there are some commitments I can't make on my own. I don't have your credibility. At some point, you're going to have to meet him face-to-face."

"That will *never* happen. I'll keep the pressure up on Paula Candler in court. She's going to have to deal with me day after day. I could tell from the look on her face this morning I was beginning to get to her. She's picking up on my not-so-subtle hints. Eventually, I'll just wear her down. I'll bet it won't be more than a couple of days before she gives word to Owens that we've got a deal. And I'm having a ball driving that son of a bitch U.S. attorney crazy. They don't know where the hell I'm coming from."

"Don . . ."

Russ could tell she had been badly shaken by what Owens had told her.

"Right now," she said, "Del Owens thinks he's got the upper hand."

Russ shrugged. "He's overconfident, is what he is. That, or he's in the bluff of his life. Judge Candler will cave, and after she's done that, so will he. Just wait until you see what happens in court tomorrow."

"So what do you want me to do in the meantime?"

"Stay available, but at a discreet distance. Whatever you do, don't show up in court, and don't contact me directly. I've really stirred up the hornet's nest, and I wouldn't put it beyond Lloyd Chapman to orchestrate something against me outside of court. I'm just waiting."

Russ scanned the faces of the people around the bar. "Don't worry about Del Owens. I'm not. After tomorrow, I guarantee you, he'll be begging to talk to us. Here,

take this." Russ took an envelope from his jacket and
put it on the table between them. "I need you to mail
this tonight. Put it into a box inside the main Alexandria
post office so it'll be delivered with tomorrow's mail."

The envelope was already stamped and addressed to
Judge Paula Candler, marked boldly PERSONAL & CON-
FIDENTIAL in the corner. "What is it?" Julia asked.

"I selected a few key bits from the other information
you found during your research of Judge Candler. More
incentive for her to come to her senses and make a deal
with us quickly."

Julia drained her beer. "Anything else?"

Russ handed her a folded piece of paper. "I need you
to dig up a couple more items."

Julia looked at the paper, stashed it into her purse.
"No problem."

"I assume I can get in touch with you at the Patriot's
Inn," Russ said.

"Sitting by the phone, waiting for you to call."

"As it should be." Russ zipped his jacket. "We'd better leave separately. Just to be safe. I'll go first."

"Good luck tomorrow," Julia said. She gave Russ's
hand a squeeze. He felt a pang in his gut and quickly
withdrew it.

Scott saw Russ slide the envelope across the table to
the girl. He half stood up on his stool so he could get a
better look at what was going on over the shoulders of
the bar patrons who clogged the floor.

What was in the envelope? A prepayment on a night
of bouncing the bed springs? It could have been anything. Drugs, pictures, documents.

The girl didn't bother opening the envelope, but
stuffed it into the pocket of her overcoat slung over the
back of her chair. Russ got up from the table and

promptly left the bar, so quickly and unexpectedly that Scott hardly had a chance to think what to do next.

Scott had expected them to leave together, but Russ was already gone. Scott had a quick decision to make. Follow Russ or the girl?

Follow the envelope, he decided.

An envelope that size could contain a hell of a lot of cash, more than even a beautiful girl like her would command for an evening's entertainment. What if Russ had asked her to make a purchase before coming up to his room? With that kind of money, it was either a couple of cases of vintage champagne—or drugs.

Scott's pulse pounded with the exciting prospect of making an anonymous call tipping off the Arlington County narcotics squad and having them raid Russ's room at the Ritz-Carlton. That would be front-page news. It would be difficult representing a murder suspect in court from a jail cell.

Five minutes later, the girl buttoned her coat and left the bar. Scott counted to fifteen, then followed her outside.

She zigzagged her way back and forth along M Street, doubling back, stopping to look into the reflections of windows to see if there was anyone behind her. She was being extra cautious, acting as if she were trying to shake anyone tailing her, which made Scott's task all that much harder.

She was walking fast. She turned down Thomas Jefferson Street, past the Chesapeake & Ohio Canal Visitor Center, then quickly ducked into the entrance to the Foundry Mall Cinemas.

Scott darted across the street to get a more direct view. He saw her disappear through a door marked LADIES.

"Damn," he spat. Now what?

Scott carefully made his way back to the side of the street where the movie theaters were. He found a dark doorway and tried to make himself inconspicuous without looking too much like an out-of-town businessman looking to score some drugs.

She emerged from the rest room and ordered a cup of coffee from the concessions bar. She sat on a bench against the wall and sipped, looking out through the front windows into the night.

Every half minute he peeked around the corner, checking to see if the girl was still there. Ten minutes went by. Then twenty. After a half hour she was still sitting inside, staring out into the street.

It was already past midnight. But he'd wait until the sun came up if he had to.

Scott checked again—and saw she had disappeared.

He walked slowly, very cautiously, past the front of the cinema complex. They were closing up after the last show. She was definitely gone.

He had lost her.

"Shoot!" he swore under his breath. How could that happen?

He walked to the next street corner to get his bearings.

He turned and saw the girl heading in his direction.

There was no place to hide, and she had already seen him, so he decided to walk toward her. He would let her pass, give himself a few moments, then turn and resume following her again. It was obvious she had no idea who he was. Otherwise she wouldn't be approaching him so brazenly.

He kept his head down so their eyes wouldn't meet. He heard her footfalls getting closer on the pavement. Still about twenty feet away now, he figured.

"Hey, you!" she said suddenly.

Scott stopped and looked up.

She was holding something in her hand. Even at that distance in the semidark, Scott could tell it was too small to be a gun. It looked more like a can of pepper spray. He told himself she was too far away for it to be effective. She pointed it directly at his face.

Suddenly he was dazzled, blinded by an intense red light. He shut his eyes, but it was too late. He could see nothing.

"Creep," her voice seethed over him. "That'll teach you to follow women around at night."

Scott heard the echoes of her running away. She must have known all along she was being followed.

Blinded, he stumbled forward a few feet, then tripped over a crack in the sidewalk and fell. His eyes were open, but still he could not see.

He was completely helpless.

Chapter 21

Late the next morning, in his cross-examination of the medical examiner, Don Russ dropped the first hint in open court as to the direction of the defense's legal strategy: "Is it not true, Dr. Reynolds, that the injuries sustained by Judge Goldsworthy are also entirely consistent with suicide?"

Dr. Reynolds considered Russ's question. "That's highly unlikely."

"But possible."

"I suppose."

"Yes. *Very* possible. Is it not true that most women who commit suicide use a gun?"

"By a slight statistical margin over poisoning, pills."

Dr. Reynolds was not originally on the Government's list of expert witnesses. Although it had not been formally brought up in court, Paula knew from the media that the lead medical examiner on the Eleanor Goldsworthy case had himself fallen victim to tragedy. The unfortunate Dr. Balthazar had apparently surprised a burglar upon his return home from work and had been severely beaten. At least that was the official story. Paula had heard through the grapevine that the witness was probably pummeled by one of Remalli's associates, but since nothing could be proved, the Government had chosen not to make it an issue. Perhaps Balthazar would have fared better under Don Russ's cross-examination than the present witness, another one of the medical examiners in the same office who had assisted in the forensic evaluation of Eleanor Goldsworthy's corpse.

Paula followed Russ's line of questioning closely. Yet at the same time it was not uncommon for a judge with too little time in the day to do everything that had to be done to bring a stack of mail into court and go through it while listening to the proceedings. No one could see what she was working on behind the front of the desk. Her quickly jotted instructions on yellow Post-it notes to Susan atop the already opened correspondence looked as if she were taking notes on the trial.

Russ continued with his questioning. "Are not most suicide gunshots to the region of the head?"

"Yes."

"Often through the mouth?"

"Yes."

"Judge Goldsworthy was killed with a single shot, was she not?"

"Yes."

"A close-contact wound in the back of her mouth?"

"Yes."

"Both characteristic of suicide by a handgun?"

"Yes."

Russ picked up a photocopied document off his table. "Your Honor, may I approach the witness?"

Paula nodded.

Russ flipped through several pages and pointed at a paragraph. He showed Dr. Reynolds. "In your autopsy report, you indicated that there was gunpowder residue on the judge's left hand?"

"Yes."

"And you had information from her family that confirmed she was left-handed?"

"Yes."

"Did you find any evidence in the autopsy that suggested specifically that Judge Goldsworthy struggled with an assailant?"

"There were minor abrasions and bruises on both hands, which might have been the result of her efforts to fend off an assailant's attack."

"Listen to the question, Dr. Reynolds. Did you find any evidence that suggested *specifically* that Judge Goldsworthy struggled with an assailant?"

The blood drained from the medical examiner's face. He looked at the Government's table for support, but saw only Lloyd Chapman and his assistants looking down at their legal pads, making notes. He would have to withstand this attack on his own.

"I'm sorry?" Dr. Reynolds said.

"Is it not entirely possible that the minor abrasions and bruises on Judge Goldsworthy's hands could have resulted from something else? Her working around the horses?"

"Yes, I suppose that's possible."

"Thank you. Now, then, Dr. Reynolds. As part of your work as a county medical examiner, do you sometimes perform a postmortem psychological evaluation?"

Dr. Reynolds was momentarily thrown by the question. "Occasionally."

"And what is the purpose of these evaluations?"

"Usually to determine the state of mind of the deceased at the time of death."

"Would these evaluations normally determine such things as whether the deceased had a history of personal problems which might tend to suggest suicide?"

"Mmmm . . . yes."

"And would these evaluations also address the issue

of the extent to which the deceased was under any special emotional pressure at the time of death?"

"Yes."

"You do not carry these evaluations out yourself?"

"No. They are performed by an outside consultant."

"But as a medical examiner, it would be your responsibility to request that such an evaluation be made?"

"Yes."

"And you did not make such a request in the case of Judge Goldsworthy?"

"No."

"And no one else in your office did?"

"No."

"Why not?"

"We were working under the assumption that this was a murder."

"I see. You *assumed* that the judge was murdered. How did you form this assumption?"

"Because in my professional opinion, based on my training and experience, Judge Goldsworthy was murdered."

"Dr. Reynolds, how did you come to learn that the FBI had claimed jurisdiction in the investigation of Eleanor Goldsworthy's death?"

"I believe we were still performing the autopsy with Dr. Balthazar when I received a message."

"Isn't it true that you were told by the Washington FBI field office that the death of Ellen Goldsworthy, a sitting U.S. federal district court judge, was a murder investigation?"

The witness did not immediately respond. "I can't recall exactly."

"Did you ever suggest that the FBI perform a postmortem psychological evaluation of the judge?"

"At that point—as soon as the physical autopsy was

complete—my office was done. It really wasn't my place to suggest anything to the FBI because it became their investigation."

"Do you have any knowledge of the FBI performing any type of analysis which might have included suicide as a cause of death?"

"That's something you'd have to ask them."

"And I certainly will." Russ flicked his eyes over to the Government's table. "Let's get back to your role in the autopsy. I just want to confirm for the record: you neglected to perform a postmortem psychological evaluation of Judge Goldsworthy."

"I wouldn't use the word 'neglected.'"

"But you yourself have no way of determining whether she was under considerable stress at the time of her death."

"That's right."

"Or whether she had a history of personal problems?"

"Correct."

"Come now, Dr. Reynolds, weren't you the one who certified the cause of death on the death certificate as a homicide?"

"Yes, that's right."

"And in the copy of the death certificate already entered into evidence by the Government, did you not indicate that the judge died from being shot by another person?"

"Yes."

Russ addressed the bench. "Approach the witness, Your Honor?"

Paula nodded assent. As Russ strode to the witness stand, Paula came to a manila envelope in the stack of mail. Unlike the others, it was unopened, and was marked in large letters with the words PERSONAL &

CONFIDENTIAL. The postmark indicated that it had been processed on the same day in Alexandria. Paula tried to open the envelope as quietly as she could as she kept an eye on the defense lawyer.

Russ flipped through pages of a document. "I see here that your toxicology report revealed blood-alcohol levels consistent with consumption of approximately two ounces of alcohol?"

"Yes."

Paula got the large envelope open, finding inside two other letter-sized envelopes, marked simply #1 and #2. She opened the first one.

"And in your professional opinion, how many drinks would that be?"

"Two drinks," Dr. Reynolds answered.

Paula studied the contents of the envelope. There were three photocopies. At first she didn't recognize them for what they were; then suddenly it hit her. First, a copy of an old American Express card statement with a charge to a business named VTS highlighted with a yellow marker. Out to the side were the words "Virginia Tutoring Services," which she recognized as the company name for the woman who helped her son Chip learn to cope with his dyslexia.

The next item, a copy of her grandmother's birth certificate, indicating her maiden name as Ippolito.

And finally, a copy of the computer-generated arrest record for Paula Candler, showing the date of the charge and guilty plea for running a stop sign—a violation over twenty years earlier.

All pieces of her past that Don Russ had alluded to in his last courtroom appearance.

She realized that Russ was waiting for her attention before asking the next question.

"And also in your professional opinion," Russ said,

"are two drinks enough for a female of Judge Goldsworthy's weight to result in impaired judgment?"

"Any amount of alcohol consumed will result in some degree of impaired judgment."

Russ turned away from the witness. In one quick instant he looked up into Paula's face until he was sure she was returning his gaze.

Then—unbelievably—he winked at her.

Paula almost gasped. *How can he do that?* she asked herself. He must have known she had opened the envelope. He was brashly signaling that he was the person responsible for sending it to her.

Paula was both incensed and mortified. *How can I let him get away with continuing that kind of behavior in my court? And sending me things in the mail?*

Russ frowned. "Thank you. So in summary, Dr. Reynolds, you really cannot conclusively determine that Judge Goldsworthy did not kill herself."

Dr. Reynolds waited a long time to answer.

"Dr. Reynolds?" Russ said.

"No."

"Thank you, Doctor."

Russ returned to his seat. Remalli was smirking, but Russ maintained a steely composure.

The U.S. attorney was already on his feet. "Redirect, Your Honor?" Chapman said with no small amount of irritation in his voice.

Paula nodded. She was so angry she was unsure what would come out if she opened her mouth to speak.

"Dr. Reynolds, in your fifteen years as a forensic pathologist, have you ever come across a situation in which a victim was murdered, yet had gunpowder residue on his hands?"

"Yes."

Paula's hands were shaking so hard she could barely

hold on to the second envelope. The thought of Russ prying into her private life and using it to intimidate her so blatantly enraged her beyond anything she had experienced. Still she wondered: *What could he possibly be sending me in addition to the photocopied proof of how he has delved into my past?*

Chapman asked the witness, "Could you explain to the court how this could be possible?"

"If a victim is attempting to thwart an attacker and grabs part of a gun as it is fired, it's certainly possible that powder residue will be present on the victim's hands."

Paula tore open the second envelope, laid the contents out before her on her desk.

Chapman continued. "So gunpowder residue on the hands of the deceased is not something you would see exclusively with suicides."

"Certainly not."

"Thank you. No other questions."

Paula didn't hear what had just been said. She stared down at three items: a small section of paper cut from a map and two Polaroid photographs. The map fragment she instantly figured out was the south side of Richmond. A circle was drawn around the area where the accident had been. The photograph was a recent picture of the bend in the road just past the Methodist church where Billy Tisdale had been killed by a car. The second photograph was of a small marble marker by the roadside: the name William Tisdale was clearly visible.

"Your Honor?" Chapman said.

Paula saw then that everyone was waiting for her to say something. Don Russ looked at her with a chilling, knowing smirk.

She consulted the clock on the wall. "It's almost

noon," she said between clenched teeth. "We'll recess for lunch until one-thirty."

Hands trembling, she still was able to manage to slam the gavel down hard on the bench.

"Ohhh, *yeahhhhh,*" the woman cried out, almost in pain. "That's it," she panted. "Almost got it . . . AH!" she gasped. "You're in me now . . . Oh, *God,* yes. . . ."

Although Scott Betts still could not see very well, there was absolutely nothing wrong with his hearing. In fact, he had in the past twelve hours become a firm believer in the old adage about a blind person compensating for a loss of sight by developing a more acute sense of hearing. And Scott had heard an earful in the last thirty minutes, including the disembodied voice of some woman named Angel giving phone sex to a man driving the southern portion of the Capital Beltway.

Scott sat behind the wheel of his car, parked in an urban wasteland near the courthouse, a former rail yard, exposed to the open air on a painfully sunny day, listening on a radio frequency scanner to the chatter of self-important businessmen and housewives. Technically what he was doing—intercepting private cellular phone conversations—was illegal without a court order, which he happened not to have.

Scott lifted the extra-dark sunglasses he usually wore on stakeouts and wiped his eyes, still weeping from being dilated during an excruciatingly thorough ophthalmological examination earlier in the morning. He had spent an hour in the office of an eye specialist. The retina had not been permanently damaged and the prognosis was good, although he was told that it might be several more days until his vision was entirely back to normal.

The doctor had wanted to put a patch over his eye to

give the retina a chance to heal, but Scott insisted that he not. A man with a patch over his eye was not an inconspicuous FBI agent on surveillance.

Scott had already figured out what had caused the half hour of complete blindness the previous night, even before the doctor offered the likely source: a miniature laser used as a pointer by lecturers, but being bought at an alarming rate by a variety of criminals. The intense red light was the tip-off. The doctor told him he was lucky: he estimated that Scott had been zapped by a 10-milliwatt beam, not by one of the more powerful pointers, which produced a 50-milliwatt beam, strong enough to instantly cause permanent damage.

Scott had left a message on McNary's office voice mail well before daybreak explaining that he had injured his eye, but would be able to make it to court that afternoon. He was one of a half dozen FBI special agents on standby to give testimony on the Remalli case.

Scott had *not* gone into detail about how he came to be lying helpless on a downtown sidewalk at one in the morning. Nor how he had fortuitously been picked up by a sympathetic cop whom he was able to convince he had just been out for a late-night drink in one of the nearby bars, but had become disoriented and a victim of an apparent mugging attempt. Scott had also not volunteered to the patrolman that he was an FBI agent, which might have led to further embarrassing inquires being made.

Scott was unsure how much of his story he would eventually share with McNary, although his boss would be anxious for any scrap of news about his surveillance of Don Russ. So far Scott was empty-handed, although the meeting with the woman was at least intriguing and might lead elsewhere.

Scott had seen Russ using a cellular phone as soon as the attorney had emerged from the courthouse the previous day following the opening statements. It was highly unlikely that Scott would actually catch Russ in the commission of some illegal act. Scott needed to jump-start his investigation. Perhaps by listening in on Russ's telephone conversations Scott could pick up a clue that would point him in the right direction.

Scott checked his watch. Court would be reconvened in less than a half hour, and he still hadn't intercepted any calls to or from Russ. Scott knew exactly where Russ was at the moment, and he had seen him retrieve his cellular phone from the security lockup at the courthouse entrance. Scott had thought Russ would certainly be using his phone during the lunch recess, but so far he was wrong.

"... Do me now.... Come on, babe ... you can do it again.... Do it *hard*."

Scott thought about how glad he'd be when he could finish up his work in Washington. Eight months all alone in an empty apartment. He really needed to get back home soon to Tammy.

"... That's it ... that's how I like it...."

Scott hit a button to permanently block Angel's channel.

With growing impatience, Scott watched the scanner display cycle through the frequencies. Then the digits on the display froze. The sound of a ringing phone. He prayed this time he'd hear the familiar caustic, streetwise voice from Chicago.

Don Russ sat alone at a table in the Trucking Association's cafeteria. An odd place for a five-hundred-dollar-an-hour lawyer to be eating lunch, but he had chosen it hoping to find a quiet place nearby, away from the prying eyes of the courthouse crowd. It seemed an unlikely place for any of the government attorneys or FBI agents to be patronizing.

Russ picked at his tuna salad as he read through his notes in preparation for the afternoon's cross-examination of the FBI's forensic scientist. From the list of expert witnesses the U.S. Attorney's Office had given him, Russ knew that the Government had also failed to have anyone at the FBI perform a postmortem psychological evaluation of Judge Goldsworthy. The witness would get the same grilling on the issue as the local medical examiner had.

He answered the warble of his cellular phone.

"Russ."

"It's Mike."

His assistant had flown to Chicago for the day to make a previously scheduled court appearance on behalf of another client.

"What's up?"

"I thought you'd want to know. The FBI just came into the office two minutes ago with a search warrant."

"What the hell for?"

"They're looking for all records pertaining to the filing of Medicare claims for the Boyne Medical Group, Inc."

"*What?*"

"I got a call from your accountant just as they were coming in here. They're executing an identical warrant simultaneously at his place, too. Just a sec. . . . My secretary handed me a note saying you just got an urgent call from some guy named Sandy Ellman saying he's got the feds busting into his office as well."

Russ put his fork down hard and shoved his salad away. "Sandy freakin' Ellman," he said. "President of Boyne. Before you joined the firm years ago, I success-

fully defended him against federal charges of filing
fraudulent claims for nonexistent patients and bogus
procedures at his company's chain of psychiatric hospi-
tals in the Midwest. It was a close case—the government
produced a mountain of evidence, but the prosecutor
was green and screwed up in court. All that was supposed to be cleared up, though. What time period is covered by the search warrant?"

"Last eighteen months."

"Which happens to coincide neatly with when I made
a sizable investment in the company myself."

"What kind of probable cause could they possibly get
to have a judge sign off on the warrant?"

"Who signed it?"

"Kowalski."

"Figures. He'd sign a Polish sausage if it was put under
his nose. Either Sandy's been engaging in some creative
accounting the federal bureaucrats can't decipher again,
or this is an outright setup. Either way, I find the timing of
this search warrant peculiar. It's not like the Chicago FBI
office isn't aware of what's going on down here. We're
only on the national news every night. This is intimidation,
pure and simple."

"What do you want me to do?" Fein asked.

"Help them carry the boxes out," Russ said. "Offer
them coffee. Anything, just don't antagonize them.
Have my secretary make sure they don't *accidentally*
pull the wrong files. She'll know the ones I'm talking
about. You hold the door open for them on their way
out and wish them a nice day. I'll take care of this myself in court."

Clerk of Court Shelby Trimble stood over Paula's
conference table and smoothed a crease in an archi-

tect's plan of the sixth floor. Paula nodded with satisfaction.

"Thank you so much, Shelby," Paula said. "I'm sorry we hadn't anticipated earlier how much more room the Secret Service would need here in the building."

Shelby squinted at the plan, fingering a huge ring of keys dangling from his belt. He had a key for virtually every lock in the courtroom complex. He was the only person Malcolm Crane trusted absolutely.

"If there's any way at all you can get them out of that broom closet down the hall, I know they'd be extremely grateful," Paula said. "As would I."

"Consider it done, Judge. I'll have some new furniture delivered and make sure they've got enough telephone lines. Monday soon enough?"

"That would be perfect."

"Let me know if there's anything I can do for you."

Trying to make routine administrative decisions at a time when she was struggling to hold her life together was the last thing she wanted to be bothered with. She was still reeling from the morning court session, her shaking hand unable to hold a pen steady enough even to sign her signature to the letters Marla had typed.

Shelby had jumped on her casual request in the hall only that morning for bigger Secret Service facilities nearby. He had been waiting outside her office for her with a roll of floor plans to review tucked under his arm when she had returned from the morning court session. It was as difficult as always to say no to the ever eager-to-please Shelby.

As he rolled up the floor plan, Marla stuck her head inside the door. "He's on line one, Judge."

Shelby hurried to finish clearing the table and left, closing the door quietly behind him.

Paula picked up the phone. "Where have you been?" she snapped.

For a moment there was silence on the other end of the line. Then a familiar, though unexpected, voice: "*Paula?*"

It was her husband, not Del, whom she had been trying to reach ever since leaving court.

"Jim . . . I'm sorry, I was expecting someone else."

"I feel sorry for whoever it is," he joked.

"Jim—"

"Look, no need to explain. Can you talk? Are you alone?"

Paula's heart leapt. *Has Jim found out about the blackmail?*

"Yes," she said. "What is it?"

"We didn't get a chance to talk before I left this morning. I'm taking a break from meetings on the Middle East situation. I know something's been eating at you, and it's hard for me to stay silent when I know you're suffering."

Paula shuddered with relief. *He still doesn't know.*

"You're a strong woman, Paula. But you're only human."

Paula was torn between telling him and protecting him. She *had* to rely on Del's judgment. Del had always put her husband's career first and would never do anything to jeopardize it.

Paula closed her eyes. She wanted to scream.

She drew another breath and opened her eyes. The light on her phone was flashing, Marla's signal that she needed to talk to Paula.

"Jim . . . You don't know how much it means to me that you'd take time out of your busy schedule to call me. Just knowing that you're thinking of me is a tremendous help. Please, don't worry about me."

The telephone light was flashing incessantly. Paula was worried she might miss the call that was waiting, but she needed to talk to her husband—needed to draw strength from his voice for what she was facing.

"Don't ever forget that I love you," Jim said.

"I never will. I love you, Jim."

She hung up, worried that she had rushed her husband. She punched the flashing button.

"I am furious at you," Paula said. There was no mistaking who was on the other end now. "I have to talk to you. This cannot go on."

"Settle down, Paula," Del said coolly. "I've been with Jim in the Oval Office all morning."

While she talked she pulled out an envelope from her desk drawer and fed the map fragment and photographs of the accident location through a document shredder.

"I know you're busy with Jim, but we've got to take action. Now! I just spent the morning from hell in court. I've never had an attorney behave so . . . *insolently* in my court before. He's mocking me. To my face! But nobody else in the room has a clue what he's doing. He's highly insidious in the way he does it. He brings up words and phrases associated with—"

Del cut her off. "Don't forget someone may be listening."

"—*that* incident." Paula was at her wit's end. "He says things that he knows are going to elicit a reaction from me, but he knows I can't respond because I'm on the bench. Del, I cannot carry on like this."

"Calm down . . . just calm down. I'm working on it. This is a complex situation. It takes a little time. Patience, Paula."

"What are you doing? Whatever it is is having no impact on that man."

"It's not something we can talk about over the phone.

Things are happening . . . *today*. Even as we speak. I can't get into it, but you'll probably hear about it soon enough."

Paula felt like exploding. She struggled to channel her emotions into rational words. "I thought I could just carry on sitting this case as if nothing else were going on. But he's starting to get to me."

"Paula, listen to me. I guarantee you that the steps I've already taken will soften the blackmailers up."

"Del, I'm really struggling with this. You can't imagine how much I dread going back into that courtroom in just a few minutes." She checked her watch. "Actually, I'm already late. Del, I don't think I can go through another week of this."

There was a moment of embarrassing silence.

"Hell," Del finally said, slipping into that folksy manner she heard him use when he was trying to disarm an unwary opponent. "I'm sure you're doing fine. Nothing bad's happened yet. Just do what you normally do. You know, harangue the attorneys, cite someone for contempt—throw the book at 'em, babe. Hey, *you're* in charge."

"No," she answered emphatically. He had really pissed her off now. "This is not business as usual. And don't you ever talk to me like that again. Need I remind you that you're involved in this as much as I am? Call that woman, whoever she is, and tell her in no uncertain terms that I will not cooperate, and have her tell Don Russ to back off."

"I've told her already."

"Then get your hillbilly ass in gear and let's find a way to stop this insanity once and for all."

She slammed down the phone before he could answer.

Her knees were weak and she sat down slowly. Her

hands were shaking so uncontrollably that she couldn't properly punch in the extension to buzz Marla in the outer office to let her know she would be another five minutes.

What she really needed was more like another half hour. The thought of going back out into her own courtroom to face the media, the U.S. attorneys, and . . . *that man* made her physically ill.

She buried her head in her hands and repeated the mantra: This is not real. This is not happening.

Then her clerk knocked gently on her chamber door to remind her it was time.

Julia Menendez pulled the collar of her heavy winter coat up around her neck and shivered. She stood at the base of the George Washington Masonic National Memorial, at 333 feet tall easily the most prominent landmark in Alexandria. The only thought in her mind was getting back into her car and turning the heat up full blast. She thought the people rushing around at lunch in the frigid air were fools, and reminded herself why she never wanted to live outside of south Florida.

She walked up the long flight of steps leading to the entrance and found Don Russ leaning against a stone column, reading *USA Today*.

"Why did we have to meet outside?" Julia said. "It's freezing."

From their position away from the parking lot it would be difficult for anyone to see them.

"I have to get back to court," Russ said. "You sure you weren't followed?"

"As sure as I can be. What's going on?"

Russ folded the paper.

"The FBI raided my office. Pure harassment. Got to be a reaction to the pressure I've been putting on Judge

Candler during court. You should have seen her face yesterday when I started dropping hints that we knew a lot more about her personal life, then today when she opened up that envelope full of documents showing her how deep we can dig into her personal history. If looks could kill . . . You've really come up with some great stuff."

"I don't understand why they haven't rolled over already."

Russ looked out over the city in the direction of the courthouse and narrowed his eyes. "Frankly, that's beginning to concern me, too. I'm not worried, but obviously this isn't going to be as quick and easy as I had thought. I have no doubt whatsoever that Del Owens is behind the FBI crashing my office. They don't know me very well if they think they can intimidate me like that, though. All we're going to do is turn up the heat even more on them. Did you get what I asked you for?"

Julia handed Russ a file folder. "Best look at those somewhere else," she said. "Especially since you've just eaten lunch."

Russ grinned sinisterly. He peeked inside the file folder anyway, saw only the rubber-stamp mark on the back of a photograph: "Copyrighted, exclusive property of Richmond Times-Dispatch."

"Think you're right," he said. "I'll wait."

"That cost you twenty-five hundred bucks," Julia said. Now that her hands were free, she rubbed her arms to keep warm.

"And worth every penny. You do good work."

Julia smiled. "Thanks, Don."

"I've got to get back to court," he said. "Time to tool up on some pathetic FBI forensic scientist this afternoon."

*   *   *

Scott was finally headed home. McNary had been meeting with Chapman all afternoon, and they'd said they were not to be disturbed unless it was an emergency. Scott knew he needed to tell McNary about the FBI's raid on Russ's Chicago office, so no one on the Government's side would be blindsided in court the next morning. So he wrote a note for McNary to call him before court tomorrow and slipped it underneath the conference room door.

He pulled into the dark carport in front of his Foggy Bottom apartment. The photosensitive light which had attracted a legion of moths every night had finally burnt out. He had popped into a video store and rented a tape, ordered food at a Wendy's drive-through. He grabbed his dinner and movie and headed toward the door in the dark.

A cat bolted between his legs at the same time a garbage can spilled over. Instinctively, Scott dropped what he was holding, reached beneath his sweatshirt, withdrew his semiautomatic from a jogger's pouch, and assumed the Weaver stance.

"Who's there?!"

Scott held his breath and listened. All he heard was the cat's meowing in the neighbor's carport. He sniffed the cool nighttime air and smelled the reek of a week's spilt garbage.

He exhaled and relaxed. He stood upright and replaced the gun.

Jumpy tonight, aren't we? he thought.

He bent over to pick up the take-out bag and videotape. As he stood he was grabbed from behind by some unseen bear of a man who pinned his arms behind his back.

Out of the darkest shadows to the side of the carport

emerged another figure, who quickly retrieved Scott's handgun from his waist harness.

A strange thought ran through Scott's head: *These guys eat at the same place as Dumbo Cerutti did.* Their clothes stank of a recent heavy meal in a closed room. The smell brought back all the sensations he had experienced the night of the raid on Remalli's place.

Then another crazy thought flashed through his mind. *I'm about to die,* he thought. *This time I'm really going to die.*

Scott finally got something of a look at the man in front of him as he stepped into the weak, irregular light of the cars passing on a nearby side street. He wore a dark, shapeless suit. A pair of sad eyes protruded through a heavy face that looked more like a caricature of an aging Mafia soldier than what Scott would have expected from a professional hit man.

"You the guy who made the tapes?" the man asked. He spoke with the same Brooklyn accent as Remalli and the rest of his crew.

Scott didn't want to give the mobster the satisfaction of seeing anything resembling fear. *The best thing to do is not panic. Be calm. Talk to them.*

Before he could gather his thoughts, a twisting of his arms at an unnatural angle provided the proper inducement to answer. Scott couldn't help wincing.

"FBI Special Agent Scott Betts," he said.

The man looked Scott over humorlessly, talked with a surprising casualness. "Yeah, well, nice to meet ya, Scott. Someone I know suggested I might wanna meet ya, stop by to say hello, give my regards. We've found Washington to be a very friendly city. And I just wanted you to know you've got a couple of more friends watchin' after ya."

Scott summoned up everything he had learned about hostage situations. If he cooperated, there might be a chance he'd live to see the sun rise.

"Looky here, Scott. The way I see it, you should make yourself unavailable for a few days. I hear fishin's good down on the Chesapeake Bay. Or, you could testify, play your tapes, then you'd spend the rest of your life with a permanent crick in your neck from looking over your shoulder. 'Cause playing those tapes is definitely not a friendly thing to do, and if you and I was no longer big buds, I'd track your sorry ass down, cut your balls off, and shove 'em down your throat so you choked to death on 'em. See?"

Scott nodded.

"Our mutual friend said we'd probably get along. I tried tellin' him that we can't just go around intimidating feds, but he persuaded me that was bullshit. And he was right. He ain't often wrong."

The man looked at the title of the videotape: *"Sleepless in Seattle?"* he sneered. "You pussy. Did you bother reading the box at the store? This is a goddamned chick flick."

The one holding Scott chuckled at his ear.

Scott involuntarily flinched and the hold on him from behind tightened. Something terrible was about to happen.

The man shoved the Wendy's bag and videotape into Scott's stomach, pulled out and pocketed the semiautomatic's bullet clip, and threw the gun over the fence.

"Look at me, Scott." Scott was forced closer from behind. "Look at this sorry excuse for a face. Memorize it. Dream about it. Don't ever forget it. You don't want to see me again, I swear to God you don't. I'm an honorable man, Scott. I keep my word. You testify in court and I'll track your motherfuckin' ass down and stomp the brains outta your head after you're dead with your dick hangin' out your pussy mouth."

He gave a signal with his head, and Scott was suddenly flying toward his front door with a powerful shove. By the time Scott climbed to his feet, the two men were gone.

Chapter 22

"What note?" McNary said.

"The one I put under Chapman's conference room door," Scott said incredulously.

On Friday, the next morning, Scott had just sat down next to his boss in the small, drab witness waiting room. The chairs were an eclectic mix of styles from over the last twenty years, secondhands and rejects from the old courthouse building. New facilities, same old dumpy furniture.

"We weren't meeting in the conference room. We'd gone off-site to prep for my testimony. After seeing how Russ ripped into that medical examiner, I wanted to make sure I knew what the hell I was supposed to be saying in my testimony this morning. Why? What's the problem?"

Quite a few problems, actually, Scott was thinking. He had already decided he wouldn't say anything about being laser-zapped by the woman who had been meeting with Don Russ in the Georgetown honky-tonk. McNary wouldn't want to know.

"Well, besides the fact that a couple of Remalli's thugs roughed me up last night, I was wondering if you had heard anything about the Bureau's Chicago office raiding Russ's office up there?" Scott asked.

"What?" McNary shouted. "We can't let Remalli get away with that! And of course I don't know anything about the Chicago Bureau."

Scott flicked his eyes as a warning toward the doorway where people were going by. McNary lowered his voice. "You know I would have told you about something like that if I knew anything. Jesus H. Christ."

Scott studied McNary's face. It was the face of a good liar. Anything McNary said was highly suspect.

"I'm not worried about myself. But do you think Chapman knows about the raid?" Scott said.

"If I didn't hear about it, I'll bet neither has he. I'd better let him know before he gets going in there."

"There's still a chance," Scott said, checking his watch. "They were running late when I looked in the front doors before coming in here."

McNary pulled a business card out of his wallet and started writing on the back. "Witnesses like us aren't supposed to be sitting inside the courtroom when someone else is testifying," he said. "Maybe I can have one of the marshals slip Chapman a note."

Scott stepped into the hallway and squinted through the fisheye security lens on the outside of the side courtroom door. Lloyd Chapman was already addressing the court. Scott returned to the waiting room.

"Too late," Scott said.

"Damn. I can't hand him this going in in full view of the court." He tore up the note. "This case just gets more and more screwy."

They heard the side door to the courtroom open. Ted Savage stuck his head around the corner and pointed at McNary. "You're on," he said, and ducked quickly back into the courtroom before McNary could tell him anything.

"Can you tell the court, please, Mr. McNary," said Lloyd Chapman, "how Tony Remalli came to be regarded as a suspect by the FBI in the death of Judge Goldsworthy?"

Paula sat on the bench, perfectly composed. She had assumed an almost trancelike state. Blocked from her mind for the moment were the events of the previous day. Unlike yesterday, she was concentrating hard on the words of the lawyers and witnesses to keep her thoughts from straying.

Agent McNary cleared his throat. "We, the FBI team, overheard Mr. Remalli talking about his role in the murder as we recorded his conversations using a hidden mike that was installed subsequent to an amended T-3 application."

Chapman nodded. "I think all of us here understand what a T-3 is, but could you explain for the record?"

"The so-called T-3 is an application under Title III of the 1968 Crime Control Act to allow a law enforcement agency to intercept telephone communications. It was subsequently amended by an act of Congress to also allow the installation of hidden listening devices."

"Thank you." Chapman addressed the bench. "Your Honor, just in case you were wondering, I wanted to inform the court that the Government will not be introducing the taped evidence through this witness, but that we will be doing that at a later time through another FBI agent. The Government believes it's important to clearly establish the context of the murder within the overall scope of the FBI's investigation of Mr. Remalli on other charges. And since Agent McNary is special resident agent in charge of the investigation, he would be in the best position to do that."

"That's fine," Paula said.

Chapman lifted a document from his table. "Agent McNary, which judge was it who signed the T-3 allowing the FBI to surreptitiously record certain of Mr. Remalli's phone conversations?"

"Judge Goldsworthy."

"I'd like to show you a T-3 application. Permission to approach the witness, Your Honor?"

Paula nodded.

McNary confirmed his signatures on the applications to record telephone conversations and install the listening device at Remalli's office.

"Your Honor, at this time I would move these documents into evidence as the Government's next two exhibits."

Chapman continued with his examination. "By way of background, Agent McNary, could you explain why the FBI was so interested in securing surreptitious recordings at Mr. Remalli's place of business?"

McNary spoke to Paula. "The FBI had had Mr. Remalli under investigation for some time for possible violations of the RICO statutes—"

Chapman interrupted. "I'm sorry, but for the benefit of the record . . ."

Paula knew that while the record would not really benefit from the agent's explanation of the statute, Chapman probably believed the media in the courtroom would.

McNary replied, "The Racketeer-Influenced and Corrupt Organizations Act. Basically, it makes it illegal for someone to acquire or operate a business with funds derived from a pattern of racketeering, or conduct the affairs of a business through a pattern of racketeering."

"Fine, thank you. You were saying about the FBI's investigation of Mr. Remalli . . ."

"Mr. Remalli had been under investigation for some time in New York by various law enforcement agencies, including the FBI, before he moved to the Washington area."

"And why did you believe Mr. Remalli moved to Washington?"

"At first we had no idea. Then we learned through an informant that certain members of the Cosa Nostra hierarchy had decided to expand their influence in major construction projects throughout the country. Organized crime unfortunately has some very bright people on the payroll these days. According to reliable sources, the Springfield Interchange project was identified as a target. There's a lot of money to be made over the eight-year project, and the Mafia wanted a piece of the action."

"And how was Mr. Remalli going about gaining influence in the local construction business?"

"Bribery, intimidation, extortion. Protection rackets. They demand a percentage of all contracts, and threaten to hold up work through their influence on the labor unions. The usual Mafia tactics used to muscle in on a business, except on a larger scale."

"Getting back to the recordings, Agent McNary, could you explain, please, about the quality of information you were able to gather from the telephone taps?"

"In the beginning," McNary said, "the quality of information from the phone tap was very good, excellent. It yielded the evidence we needed to go back to Judge Goldsworthy for the second T-3. But then something happened, and Mr. Remalli ceased using the phones in his office to discuss extortion and racketeering business. The nature of his telephone conversations changed suddenly and dramatically. He wouldn't even use the code words he used regularly to refer to his various illegal enterprises."

"Fine," Chapman continued. "Now, the recording in

which Mr. Remalli was discussing the victim whose picture was in the newspaper was from the hidden microphone, not the telephone."

"Correct."

"But at the time of that conversation, you believe he already had knowledge of the telephone wiretap?"

"At the time the recording in question was made, we had concluded that he apparently knew about the telephone taps but not the listening device we had installed during the prior week."

"And you believe that between the time he learned of the existence of the wiretap and the time of his arrest that he also acquired knowledge of the listening devices placed inside his business in the D.C. area."

"That's correct."

"Why do you say that?"

"Mr. Remalli and the man with him on the night of the arrest, Mr. Cerutti, were much more heavily armed than usual, and were—we believe—expecting company."

"Agent McNary, did Mr. Remalli have knowledge of the fact that Judge Goldsworthy was the person who signed the Title III applications authorizing the electronic surveillance of him?"

Russ half rose. "Objection, Your Honor. Calls for the witness to make a conclusion as to the defendant's state of mind."

"Mr. Chapman, please rephrase the question," Paula said.

"All right. Agent McNary, did Mr. Remalli ever say anything in his taped conversations that led you to believe that he had knowledge of Judge Goldsworthy's involvement in signing the T-3s?"

"Yes. He made direct reference to Eleanor Goldsworthy as a judge who was signing papers against him."

"So Mr. Remalli's motive in the murder of Judge Goldsworthy would have been what?"

"An act of revenge, or perhaps intimidation. He might have believed that by killing Judge Goldsworthy, he was sending a message to other judges that he would kill anyone who cooperated with the FBI by signing T-3s."

"Thank you, Agent McNary. Judge, I don't have any further questions for this witness."

Paula noticed what a long time Chapman took in returning to his seat, allowing her and everyone else in the courtroom plenty of time to think about the point he had just made. Somehow Remalli had known Judge Goldsworthy was signing the Title III applications, even though these were under seal and supposed to be confidential.

"Cross-examine," she said.

Russ gazed across the wide space to the witness and smiled faintly.

"Agent McNary, based on your experience, would you please explain to the court who normally has knowledge of the contents of the T-3 applications?"

"That would be myself, the FBI special agents reporting to me, the U.S. attorney, some of his people."

"And is the application made in open court?"

"No, in the judge's chambers."

"And is the application a public document?"

"No. It's under seal."

"So unless you, someone on your staff, the U.S. attorney or someone on his staff, or the judge herself revealed the contents of the T-3 applications, should it not have been impossible for Mr. Remalli to have learned of the existence of a telephone tap?"

"Theoretically."

"Was the telephone tap at Mr. Remalli's business of a nature that he could have detected it?"

"Ordinarily not. The tap is actually performed at the telephone company. There were no wires or anything like that at the premises which Mr. Remalli would have seen."

"And the listening device that was planted . . . where was that?"

"In the ceiling. It was an old building with lots of wires running everywhere. It would have been next to impossible to detect with the naked eye. He wouldn't have been able to find the device unless he was using specialized equipment for that purpose, and to our knowledge, he did not."

"Agent McNary, do you know with certainty how Mr. Remalli learned of the existence of the phone wiretap?"

"No, but—"

"Do you know with certainty how he learned about the listening device?"

"No."

"Fine. So how can you say he had a motive to kill Judge Goldsworthy when he didn't even know of the existence of any of the devices?"

McNary ran a finger around his collar. "That's the Bureau's theory."

Russ added quickly, "But it's only a theory."

"Yes."

"Is it true that the FBI in the New York office attempted to get a federal district judge to sign a T-3 application against Mr. Remalli, but they were turned down for lack of probable cause?"

"I believe that to be the case."

"To your knowledge, how many times was an application refused?"

"A couple. Two or three."

"Yet nearly identical applications citing nearly identical evidence were submitted to Judge Goldsworthy, who then signed off on the application."

"I'm not sure that would be a fair statement. The facts of the case we were investigating were different. Our investigation dealt primarily with Mr. Remalli's activities since moving to this area."

"But wasn't the Bureau investigating Mr. Remalli for possible violation of the RICO statutes, and weren't you attempting to demonstrate a broad pattern of racketeering, including activities in both New York and the Washington area?"

"That was part of what we were doing, yes."

"Okay, then. So, you'd have to say that the contents of the applications were at least of a very similar nature."

"Sure."

"And even though a federal district court judge in New York had refused to grant the FBI an application, your office made a decision to pursue another one once Mr. Remalli entered your district?"

"That's correct."

"Agent McNary, did the U.S. attorney in this district, Lloyd Chapman, ask or suggest in any way that you might want to use some of the FBI's local resources to investigate Mr. Remalli?"

"Mr. Remalli remained a well-known suspect on federal racketeering charges. That didn't change just because he left New York and moved here." McNary shot a glance at the U.S. attorney's table. "There was a interdepartmental task force which coordinated the Remalli investigation in the Washington area. Obviously, that included the U.S. Attorney's Office."

"And whose idea was it to set up this interdepartmental task force?"

"It may have been Mr. Chapman's."

"It *was* Mr. Chapman's, wasn't it?"

"Yes, probably it was."

"Agent McNary, I believe the FBI accounts for its

manpower and other resources spent in each of its field offices, with monthly reports issued of costs listed by major investigations. Am I not correct?"

"You are."

"And how much has the FBI spent to date to investigate my client?"

"I don't have an exact figure."

"Give us a guess."

"Oh, maybe three-quarters . . . of a million. Perhaps a bit more. It depends how you look at the figures."

"I'm sure it does. Upwards of a million dollars of taxpayer money. This was just your office? How much extra had already been spent by the New York office?"

"Again, I don't have an exact number."

"And again, give us an estimate."

"Another half million. Or so."

"So the FBI has conceivably spent over one and a half million dollars investigating Mr. Remalli—"

"Your Honor," Chapman cut in with great irritation, "I'm not sure where this line of questioning is leading. The FBI's budget and the administration of the Remalli investigation hardly seem relevant to this case."

"They're highly relevant, Your Honor," Russ countered. "The purpose of this line of questioning is to demonstrate the lengths to which the U.S. attorney would go to get a high-profile case cooking in his district. It points directly to prosecutorial misconduct. The FBI in New York were unable to make a case against Mr. Remalli, but the U.S. attorney didn't mind wasting another million dollars or so to support his own political agenda."

"Your Honor—" Chapman pleaded.

But Russ was relentless. "Mr. Chapman has pushed this investigation of an innocent man purely for political purposes. He's wasted valuable time and money, and now he's even got blood on his hands. A young female FBI agent was killed in the reckless pursuit of my client, as was a business associate of Mr. Remalli's."

Paula could not let him continue. "Mr. Russ—"

"And furthermore, Your Honor, I received word that even as I was busy preparing to defend my client in this case, the FBI was raiding my office in Chicago."

Paula looked sharply at Lloyd Chapman, whose face showed his complete ignorance about the raid. *So this is the pressure that Del has been working on in Washington?* she wondered.

Rising slowly to his feet, Chapman said, "Your Honor, this is totally ludicrous. Permission to approach the bench."

"I think that may be a good idea," Paula said.

The courtroom was buzzing. A couple of the media people scooted out the back of the courtroom, undoubtedly to get a head start to the phones to report the news of the latest twist in the case.

Both attorneys came to the front of Paula's desk. She flipped a switch to turn off the speakers in the courtroom. Replacing it was a hissing white noise so their comments couldn't be heard.

"What do you know about this?" Paula asked Chapman sternly.

"Nothing!"

"I think the U.S. attorney certainly should know, Your Honor," Russ said. "Perhaps he thinks both of us naive?"

"I can't prove a negative, Russ," Chapman shot back.

"That's enough," Paula said. "For now we'll continue this case as if this incident in Chicago didn't happen. Agreed?"

"Not really, Judge," Russ said. "Mr. Chapman is trying to intimidate me by wreaking havoc in my personal and professional life when I'm trying to defend my client on capital murder charges."

Chapman's face reddened. He bit his lip to keep from saying whatever was on his mind.

"So we can't come to an agreement to continue with this case?" Paula asked.

Russ shook his head.

"If you have some kind of motion to make, you'll need to do it in open court, Mr. Russ. But I don't want to hear any more lectures. Understood?"

"I understand."

The two attorneys returned to their tables, and Paula turned the courtroom speakers back on. She gaveled for order and the courtroom got quiet again. She was about to call on Russ when she noticed that one of the two lawyers had left a file folder at her desk during the bench conference.

"One of you left this folder up here," she said.

Neither of the lawyers made a move to respond.

Paula held the folder up. "Mr. Chapman?"

"It's not mine, Your Honor."

"It must be yours, Mr. Russ."

"No, I'm sorry, Your Honor, it's not."

Paula looked back and forth between them, but neither acknowledged ownership of the folder.

She shrugged and put the folder aside. "Mr. Russ," she said, "you have something for the court to consider?"

Russ rose and walked directly in front of the bench. It was as if the bench conference had never taken place. "Yes, I most certainly do, Your Honor. I do not understand how this court could allow Mr. Chapman to orchestrate this campaign of intimidation against the counsel for a defendant before you."

Paula was going to give Russ exactly ten seconds to

continue with his completely over-the-top speech; then she'd cut him off.

"He has attempted to corrupt justice by coercing me into cowing before him. This man, and his willing accomplices in the FBI—"

Paula nonchalantly lifted the edge of the mysterious file folder and peeked inside. Perhaps it was hers after all? Something Carol had left for her to review?

Then the horrific images grabbed her, and she felt her heart lurch.

A half dozen eight-by-ten glossies, stamped on the reverse with the name of the photographer from the *Richmond Times-Dispatch*. She turned them over one by one. Graphic color shots. First from a distance of twenty feet, encompassing the trunk of the massive hickory tree and a crumpled body in a blue pullover sweater underneath. Then a series of shots zooming in closer and closer, until the camera was directly over the boy.

His leg at a sickening angle to his body. The backpack with its contents strewn nearby. A head barely discernible as human on its side in the root water, hair matted.

Russ had deliberately left the folder, probably even bringing the proceedings to such a fevered pitch that he knew a bench conference would be called so that he could leave the file on her desk.

"Your Honor," Russ finally concluded, "I would respectfully move that Mr. Chapman be removed from this case."

Paula looked at the final picture: the boy turned over so that he was staring up at the camera, eyes open and filmy, the face bloated, wrinkled from being in the water, the features of the boy beginning to swell from the bacteria that had already consumed his body and begun the decomposition of the youthful flesh. The close-up shot revealed the dark spots and lines on his face to be flies and slugs.

Paula swallowed hard, closed the file folder, and shut her eyes tight. She felt a wave of nausea pass over her body and thought she was going to faint. Somehow she managed to gavel for order, but the noise continued unabated.

Finally she was able to utter between breaths: "Both of you . . . in my chambers . . . *now*."

Lloyd Chapman was still visibly shaken, the color completely drained from his face.

"First, *you*," Paula said, glaring at Don Russ across her desk. "You are out of line, Counselor," she said sharply. "You have an issue like that to raise, you do it in chambers. Understood?"

Paula was as close as she had ever been to telling the two attorneys that she was removing herself from the case. She couldn't shake the images of the dead boy from her mind, and she had serious concerns about how she could continue, subjecting herself day after day to Russ's mind games.

Russ was slouched slightly in his chair, his fingers templed, scrutinizing her intently. Paula was struck by how disturbing she found Russ's physical presence. It was an attitude that was too casual, just this side of disrespectful, she thought. His posture was not normal for a defense attorney summoned into a judge's chambers. It was as if he considered himself to be her equal.

Russ nodded.

"I take that to be a yes?"

"Yes, Your Honor," he said begrudgingly.

The smug son of a bitch, she thought.

Her other concern at the moment was to make sure that Chapman didn't think something was going on behind the scenes. Not until Del could sort things out.

"Now *you*," she said, turning on Chapman. "Is this true?" she demanded. "Did the FBI raid Mr. Russ's office?"

"I honestly don't know, Your Honor. No one's discussed it with me."

Paula believed him. She was at the same time incensed and relieved about the raid: incensed that the FBI—who should know better—had taken steps that would complicate an already complex trial. Relieved because it meant that Del was starting to take action. And Russ had taken notice.

The look on Russ's face told Paula that he, too, believed Chapman when he said he knew nothing beforehand about the search. Russ could have guessed that Del was behind the FBI's busting into his office. The only one in the room confused about why the FBI had chosen this particular moment to storm into Russ's law offices was Lloyd Chapman, the one person who should have had all the details.

Paula pounced on Chapman. "Well, I strongly suggest that you get the facts. On the surface, at least, this doesn't look very good for you. A good case might be made that the Government was indeed interfering with his client's right to counsel. If I find out that you or someone in your office was responsible for initiating this action against Mr. Remalli's attorney during the middle of a trial, there will be hell to pay."

Chapman was still bewildered. "Yes, Your Honor."

Now Russ looked confused. Although he had raised a legitimate issue of prosecutorial misconduct, Paula assumed that Russ knew Del was behind the Chicago raid, and that Paula would be inclined to give the Government a pass. He must have been wondering why she was now coming down so hard on the U.S. attorney, especially when he clearly didn't know anything about the situation.

Paula knew that every step she took as judge on this case was being meticulously scrutinized by the media. Her actions were also being closely observed by her brethren on the bench. She was determined to maintain her credibility as a jurist.

More important, by coming down so hard on Chapman, she might be able to put enough doubt in Russ's mind that he would question how closely she and Del were working together.

Although only that same morning she had begun to have doubts about her ability to try the case fairly, Paula felt emboldened by what Del had been able to achieve. He was by her side, after all. They were going to beat back this blackmail attempt. She just had to force the images of the boy from her mind. *It was an accident,* she kept telling herself. *An accident. It could have happened to anyone.*

"And furthermore—and I'm talking to both of you—if I find out anyone on either the Government or the defense has been interfering with the business of this court in any way, I will not hesitate to administer the appropriate sanctions to ensure that you will not have the opportunity to make that mistake again. Am I making myself clear?"

A dark expression came over Russ's face. Although directing her words to both of the attorneys, she knew Russ would understand that she was really addressing the intimidation issue to him.

She gave Russ a warning look for good measure. She felt empowered again.

Chapman starting coughing. He motioned to the credenza on the other side of the room. "Mind if I get a drink?" he said between spasms.

Paula nodded.

Chapman crossed to the credenza and poured water from a pitcher.

Paula looked across the desk at Russ. It was the first time they had been in any sense alone.

Russ stared back at her. He held her with his eyes and would not let go. Paula was determined not to let him stare her down.

Chapman resumed a hacking cough. He poured a second glass of water. As he did, Russ narrowed his eyes, leaned in a few inches closer, and said just under his breath, "You and your husband are finished unless you cooperate."

Chapman returned to his seat. He looked back and forth between Paula and Russ, trying to figure out if he had missed something.

"Sorry, Judge," Chapman said meekly. "Tickle in the throat."

Russ pulled a box of Altoids out of his pocket and offered one to Chapman. "Mint?"

Chapman must have recognized them as what Russ had given to Remalli in court to shut his client up. He wasn't accepting any favors from the defense attorney. "No, thanks."

Paula was nearly catatonic. *Did he really say what I thought he said?* The idea of an attorney personally threatening her—and in her own chambers—was inconceivable.

But it had just happened.

Any new confidence she had regained because of Del's successes had been wiped away. In the space of a couple of minutes in the sanctity of her own chambers, Don Russ had gained the psychological upper hand again.

"Get out," Paula said in a monotone. She was still half-dazed.

"Judge," Chapman tried, "what time do you think—"

"Get out!" Paula snapped.

Chapman backed off and hurried out of the room.

Russ took his time walking to the door. He left without giving Paula a second look.

Chapter 23

Back at his office during the noon recess, Scott learned that Alan Griffith had awakened after almost two weeks in a coma. He made an excuse to avoid lunch with McNary and drove to Fairfax Hospital.

Two U.S. marshals were posted outside the intensive-care room. After the medical examiner's beating, Lloyd Chapman had insisted on the protection, as Alan was not only a victim but a witness to what had happened in the raid. Chapman was thinking ahead to the indictment he expected to get for Paige's murder. Scott wondered how long it would be until Chapman learned through official channels that the bullet that killed her was actually fired by McNary.

In the room, two nurses were finishing giving Alan a sponge bath and changing his bed linens. He was hooked up to a half dozen monitors, with wires and tubes flowing in and out of his body. The lower portion of his face was covered in bandages. Scott was sure he noticed a spark of recognition in his colleague's eyes when he moved to his side.

Before leaving them alone, the nurses explained that the doctors had ordered them to begin withdrawing Alan from the cocktail of painkillers so that they could assess his mental state before the surgeons began the long process of reconstructing the lower half of his face, which had been blown away.

Scott pulled a chair next to the bed and sat so he was at the same level as Alan. The wounded man could communicate by tapping out words on a small laptop computer on a tray swung over his lap.

"I'm so sorry for what happened," Scott said. "Everyone at the office is pulling for you."

thanks, Alan typed. His eyes roamed around the room, taking in the sight of dozens of flower arrangements.

"Is there anything you need?"

Alan had never learned to type properly, and his pecking at the keyboard with two fingers was slow going. *luv a cheeseburger.*

Scott laughed, but not too hard. "I'll be the first to take you out to Wendy's as soon as they get you fixed up with a new set of chompers."

"Your wife and kids okay?"

sheila's been here every day . . . she finally took a break to look after the kids at home when they told her she wasn't going to be collecting insurance on me yet.

"Not for a long time, I'm sure."

Scott noticed that the hair falling down into one of Alan's eyes was bothering him. He smoothed it back.

thanks, Alan typed. *ur a pal.*

Scott was as relieved as anybody that Alan seemed to have pulled through the worst. He had argued with himself all the way over from the office about what he would say to him. Did Alan know that the botched raid was partly Scott's fault?

As if Alan had read his mind, he began typing again. *mcnary never should have let us go in.*

"What do you mean?"

after remalli knew something was going on in the front where u were . . . after the warning.

"McNary heard the warning buzzer?"

yes.

"Even from outside with the trapdoor on the roof closed?"

unmistakable . . . it was loud.

"But McNary told me he couldn't hear any buzzer over the sound of the rain on the metal roof."

??????!!!!

Alan furrowed his brow. What McNary had told Scott didn't make any sense.

"You know that Paige is dead?"

i figured . . . bullets everywhere . . . remalli already had his gun pulled and fired as soon as she broke in . . . mcnary and I tried to provide cover from the trapdoor in the roof . . . i saw her hit as she stepped thru the door.

"You two were on the roof together. Why didn't McNary call the raid off according to our operational plan if he knew Remalli suspected problems and was loaded for bear?"

? asked him that myself . . . the last thing he said to me was that we were going to take remalli that night or never.

Scott couldn't believe what Alan was telling him. All this time McNary had been trying to pin the blame on Scott for not warning the team that Dumbo had hit some warning buzzer. If McNary had thought Alan would never recover from his wounds, there would have been no one to contradict his version of what had happened.

mcnary tell u otherwise? Alan asked.

Scott nodded reluctantly.

that son of a bitch . . . i never liked him.

"Have you told anyone else this yet?"

ur the first to come by.

Scott was thinking about what a waste of life. Paige had died unnecessarily.

whatever anyone says, it's not ur fault, Alan typed. *i'll testify to that.*

He winced as if in pain. The anesthetics were wearing off.

Scott squeezed Alan's hand. "Thanks. You have no idea how much that means to me."

Scott couldn't have been any angrier, but fought hard to conceal the fact from everyone back at the office. He needed to keep a cool head. Make sure he didn't tip anyone off that he knew he had been royally screwed by his own boss. The FBI was an organization for team players, not mavericks. Scott still had a career to think of. He needed to make sure he ended up a winner when the smoke cleared.

When Scott returned from the hospital, his secretary told him McNary had spent the entire lunch break in his office with his door closed again with orders not to be disturbed.

McNary emerged twenty minutes before they had to be back at the U.S. Attorney's Office for a debrief with Chapman's people. Scott had never seen him so nervous before.

"Chapman's freakin' out," McNary said with a nearly panicked voice as they walked to the parking lot. "He got beat up pretty badly in chambers by Judge Candler on the intimidation issue. He just spent fifteen minutes reaming me out on the phone for not warning him about the Chicago FBI busting into Russ's law offices. I still haven't been able to convince him it was news to me, too. Of course I didn't tell him I had just heard about it from you. Headquarters knows we've got this high-profile case going. At the very least they should have given us a heads-up. I don't understand the lack of coordination. The only answer I could get out of headquarters was that the order to move on Russ's offices came from high up. On top of all that, Chapman's watching the testimony of his witnesses crumble before his eyes under cross-examination."

McNary tossed the keys to his car to Scott to drive. He was obviously still too shaken by the defense attorney's courtroom attack to operate heavy machinery. His vacant stare and white-knuckle grip on the armrest said it all. But with Scott's newfound knowledge of what had really happened during the raid on Remalli's place, he was totally unsympathetic to any discomfort McNary might be experiencing.

McNary turned in his seat as they drove. "Listen, Scott. The real reason I wanted you to drive me over to the courthouse was that we needed to talk out of the office."

"Oh?"

"It's Chapman. He's really spooked by what's going on with the trial. He's leaning on me hard to come up with something on Russ. The knockout punch. He was wondering if you've made any progress. Sure would be a feather in your cap if you could get a clue as to whether Russ is actually involved in this thing to a degree that we could help Chapman get him thrown off the case. A little payback would be nice, too."

The last comment really incensed Scott. There was plenty he could have told McNary, but as everyone was looking out for number one, he held his tongue.

"Sorry, Craig. I've been watching, but so far Russ has been sticking to the straight and narrow."

The sun broke through the cloud cover as they cruised through Old Town Alexandria. The glare was murder on Scott's injured eyes.

McNary shook his head slowly. "Chapman had told me to expect a straightforward cross-examination about how we set up the surveillance on Remalli's place. That attorney made a goddamned fool out of me, Scott. He chewed my butt good on the stand. And there wasn't a damn thing I could do about it. He almost makes me want to question our own case. All that preparation yesterday for my testimony. What a waste. Russ came at me from a totally different angle than we'd expected. I have never been so humiliated in my entire life. Criminal defense attorneys are the biggest slimeballs on earth. Worse than some of the clients they're defending."

Scott was thinking, *Not as big a slimeball as someone who tries to shift the blame for a colleague's death to somebody else.*

"I don't want to jinx you, but you'd better be prepared for some major abuse when you climb up into the witness box next week. I'd make sure you knew your stuff backwards and forwards. Because sure as hell, Russ is going to make you wonder if you even know your own name."

Scott turned into the parking lot behind the courthouse. He parked and cut the engine.

"Great," Scott said. "That's exactly why I joined the Bureau—to be made a fool of by some mob lawyer."

McNary started getting out of the car.

"By the way," Scott said, "I guess you heard that Alan's come out of it. Looks like he's going to be all right."

McNary sat back down. "No," he said cautiously, "I hadn't heard."

"Yeah," Scott said nonchalantly, "I paid him a visit at lunch."

"Really?" McNary fidgeted with the lock on his briefcase,

"Yep. He's sitting up already. He's alert, but still in a great deal of discomfort. They say he'll be out in a few weeks, although he'll obviously never be the same again, even after reconstructive surgery. I thought you'd want to know."

"You're right. I'm glad you told me. I'll have to go by to see him myself after work."

McNary started to get out of the car again, then stopped as Scott spoke again. "They've got him this nifty laptop computer so he can type out a conversation."

"Oh?"

"He and I had a nice long discussion about what really happened the night of the raid."

McNary slowly lifted his eyes. Scott sensed real fear.

"He told me you didn't call off the operation, Craig, even though you knew Remalli had been warned something was going down. You led Paige and Alan into a death trap."

McNary's face betrayed his fear. Then he waved it off. "Alan's confused. It's probably just the painkillers talking."

"Unh-uh. And by the way, have you heard anything from firearms identification yet?"

"Scott, listen to me. You're in no position to be making judgments. You don't have all the facts in front of you—"

"Bullshit!" Scott exploded. "I have enough to know that you're trying to cover up the fact that not only did you lead us unnecessarily into that bloodbath, but I highly suspect that *you* killed Paige!"

"Dammit, Scott! You're out of line! *Way* out of line! I think I see exactly what's going on here. You're letting your relationship with Paige cloud your judgment. I strongly suggest that you keep your mind on the business at hand."

Scott was indignant. "Oh, don't worry. I'll be ready for my testimony. And I'm going to stay on top of Don Russ, just like we talked about. But I'm also going to stay on top of you. And Lloyd Chapman. To do everything in my power to make certain you two don't let your own personal agendas get in the way of making sure that Remalli is locked away, so Paige didn't die in vain. And to make sure that the blame for the screwed-up raid gets put where it belongs."

Scott yanked the keys out of the ignition and tossed them to McNary.

"Drive your own damn self next time."

Scott got out of the car and slammed the door so hard a hubcap fell off one of the front tires.

Paula and Del walked side by side along the jogging path on the South Lawn of the White House grounds. Secret Service agents followed behind at a distance.

The crisp air was filled with the sounds of young voices just outside the fence. Yellow school buses idled on the street nearby. The children had come to the White House on a class field trip to see where the President of the United States and the First Lady lived. To surreptitiously touch the walls, scuff their shoes on the floor, take home a leaf fallen from a White House tree.

Paula caught a glimpse of one of the children pressing his face against the fence. It was a young boy in a school uniform, similar to what the boy she had killed had been wearing. She felt her chest seize up.

Killed. The word had assumed a horrible vibrancy. The flashback to that night stopped her dead in her tracks.

Del touched her arm. "It's okay," she said.

They strolled past trees that had been planted by former presidents. Andrew Jackson's magnolias. Franklin Roosevelt's lindens. Dwight Eisenhower's pin oaks.

Paula checked over her shoulder at the Secret Service agents to make sure they were still out of earshot.

"I hate this," she said. "Everything about it. Mostly I

hate deceiving Jim, and putting him at risk. We're the two people he trusts the most. That's why we must make sure he is never touched by this."

"Now maybe you're beginning to understand what I've done for him all these years. I take the heat. I make problems go away so he doesn't have to know about them."

Paula stopped walking. "I can't believe you think I'm that naive. I know what you've done for him over the years. It's just been that I also didn't want to know about all the problems you've taken care of." She started again, slowly, along the path. "Your intervention in having the FBI raid Russ's Chicago law offices threw everyone for a loop—including me," she said.

"Just made a few well-placed, discreet phone calls, that's all. My investigators do good work. Everything else took care of itself."

"I thought at first it might cause Russ to withdraw, but after his behavior in my office today, I know now that he's not going to be scared off like that. He knows he's holding the trump card, and whatever you or I do to try to thwart him ultimately doesn't matter. He's been extraordinarily careful to cover his tracks. As long as there's no way to directly link him with the blackmail attempt, there's nothing we can do."

The shouts of children climbing back onto the school buses made Paula shudder.

"These mobsters . . . Del, if anything should ever happen to the children . . ."

"Just get that kind of thinking out of your mind. No one's going to touch the kids. Certainly not Remalli's people."

"I just can't help thinking. If you had called for help when you saw the Tisdale boy, he might have lived."

"Don't even start, Paula. He was dead."

Paula couldn't think of anything to say.

Del got them talking about the trial again. "Russ has been pretty aggressive in court," he said. "He's doing a lot better than most people thought, considering the FBI's case was supposedly so solid."

"The tapes haven't been played yet."

"Look, Paula. I heard about what Russ said in court in his opening remarks about the tapes. They're ambiguous. They're subject to interpretation. *You're* the one who has to decide that. I don't suppose it would be viewed as extraordinary if in the end you might have some doubt as to whether Remalli really did kill Judge Goldsworthy. Hey, remember the O.J. trial? What's the standard that the U.S. attorney is up against? Beyond a reasonable doubt? I understand that Russ can be terribly persuasive in court. Would it really be so terrible if you kept an open mind about Remalli's innocence or guilt?"

Paula was offended. "I'm the finder of fact on the case. My mind *is* open."

Del stopped walking.

"Well, don't you think you could keep it . . . a little more open?"

"You're asking me to make up my mind now on the case."

"I have a message I haven't returned yet from Julia Menendez. I was thinking if I could tell her that you're leaning toward a not guilty verdict, it would take a lot of pressure off everyone. Wouldn't it be nice to get back to having a sane trial without all these histrionics every time you step onto the bench? If you made a decision now, you'd have all that worry behind you. And I could return to helping Jim full-time."

"I can't believe you're proposing to cooperate with those blackmailers."

"Can you honestly tell me that at least some doubt hasn't been placed in your mind already by Russ's cross-examination of the medical examiner and that FBI supervisor?"

Paula wasn't going to admit that to Del, but it was true. Even factoring out all of Russ's deviousness in attempting to intimidate her, he *had* been powerfully effective in starting to tear apart the FBI's credibility.

"I haven't heard all the evidence," she said.

"Paula, I honestly don't know how much longer we can keep this up. Day after day of unrelenting pressure on both of us? At some point we're going to crack. If you could hear yourself on the messages you left on my voice mail . . . Come on—who needs this grief? Not guilty doesn't mean innocent. In the end, I'll bet that reaching a not guilty verdict isn't going to be much of a stretch."

"I did not call you to meet with me to finalize a deal with these criminals."

"Well, what in God's name did you have in mind?"

The Secret Service agents had perked up to the sound of the raised voices and had closed the gap. Paula led Del beneath a stand of maple trees planted by Grover Cleveland. She turned her back to the agents for added privacy.

"I have been over this in my mind a thousand times. I have decided unequivocally that I am not giving in."

"Paula—"

"Listen," she snapped. "I take full responsibility for Billy Tisdale's death, if that's where the blame lies, but I'm not going to end up a blackmail victim for the rest of my life."

Del drew his mouth into a pucker and found a distant spot on the horizon to stare at.

If she only knew what really happened, he was thinking. *But she doesn't need to know. She's much more easily manipulated thinking she's the killer.*

Del drew a breath. "Okay," he said. "Talk."

"Don Russ has been successful in remaining above this because he's got the help of this Menendez woman. Yes, he's been sneering at me and trying to frighten me with allusions to the accident, but basically he's letting the girl do all his dirty work for him. He's smart. He's kept himself well insulated from the action. I mean, what do we really have to prove that he's involved in the blackmail? Nothing. We need to lure him out, show him to be an active participant in the crime."

"So what are you proposing?"

Paula pulled out of her purse what looked like a folded-over magazine. She handed it to Del.

He opened it. It was a thick catalog for spy gadgets and accessories.

"Where'd you get this?" he asked.

"There's a shop in town. Helen picked it up for me at lunch. I told her I was looking for a gag birthday gift for Jim."

Del leafed through the pages.

"They're open late," Paula said. "We could be in business tomorrow."

"What exactly did you have in mind?" Del asked dubiously.

"We're going to turn the tables on the blackmailers. Catch them in the act. We need evidence—artifacts, tapes—proof of *their* crime. Something to hold over *their* heads. They need to be sweating this out, just like us. We need our own leverage. But just trapping Julia Menendez is not going to cut it. We need Russ's head. He's the key."

Del shook his head dismissively. "Julia's already told me that Russ would never meet with me. For all the reasons you just cited. Nice try, Paula, but it won't work."

"You miss the point."

"Okay . . ."

"I'm going to lure Don Russ out from behind that woman's skirts with a face-to-face meeting. Just the two of us." Paula thumped the catalog. "Along with a few goodies."

"And by the way, you can call off that creep you've had following me," Julia said into the phone. At eight-thirty that night, Del Owens had finally returned her phone call. "That kind of intimidation on me works just about as well as your Chicago FBI ploy did on Don Russ."

"Sorry?"

"The guy who was shadowing me the other night. He got a little close and I had to teach him a lesson."

"I haven't had anyone tailing you here in Washington."

"Yeah, right. Just like you didn't break into my apartment. When are you guys gonna learn we're not backing off?"

"That's why I called," Del said. "To arrange a meeting."

"We've done meetings. We've got nothing to talk about. If Judge Candler doesn't come up with a not guilty verdict, the news on the kid's death is in the hands of the Richmond Commonwealth Attorney and the press within fifteen minutes of her decision. I've got photocopies ready to distribute."

Julia lied, because she knew it would never come to that. There was no way the judge wasn't going to cooperate.

"Not you and I," Del said. "Don Russ. And the judge."

"Don would never agree," Julia said emphatically. "And I'd advise him not to go. It's too risky."

"It's that or nothing," Del said. "Paula Candler wants a one-on-one meeting with him to sort things out."

"He's not going to change his mind."

"That's not why she wants to meet. She wants to cut a deal directly with Russ. Only the principals involved; no intermediaries. No meeting, no deal."

"There's no reason why you and I can't work this out ourselves," Julia said.

"I'm just the errand boy. Same as you. It's time for us to get out of the way and let them thrash this out themselves."

"Don's not going for it."

"No feds. Just the two of them. I promise."

"All I can do is pass this along and get back to you. When and where?"

"It's got to be somewhere that they can talk without her Secret Service escort interfering. Or the media."

"I don't know where you think you'll be able to find a place where either of those don't follow her."

"I've already thought about that. You got something to write with?"

"Yeah," she said reluctantly. "Go ahead."

Julia listened, wrote down what Del told her.

"You're a very clever guy, you know?" she said when he was finished.

Chapter 24

The four members of the Candler family were in Paula's White House bedroom in various states of undress. Clothes cleaned and pressed by the White House staff had been carefully laid out by the valet. Jim Candler, exquisitely attired in white tie and tails, was the only one ready to go downstairs to the diplomatic reception. He was helping Chip knot his first real bow tie. Paula was still in her slip. Jefferson the Labrador crawled under the bed as Missy began wailing melodramatically.

"Mom, I can't get my hair to work!"

She handed Paula a brush, removed the clip, and shook her hair loose.

"Come here, sweetheart," Paula told her. "Let me fix it."

Missy was trying so hard to be the sophisticate, but at fourteen she was in many ways still just a little girl.

"I think the kids had fun at the Smithsonian today," Jim said.

"Yeah, the Air and Space Museum was great!"

"I would have preferred high tea at the Hay-Adams," Missy sniffed.

Paula and Jim exchanged looks. "Maybe next time," Paula said.

"Well, when's *that* going to be?"

Paula was stung not just by her adolescent tone of

voice, but by the realization that she couldn't give her daughter an answer. It was taking every ounce of strength she had to make this public appearance, in the face of all the pressure she was under. She could barely think beyond the next day now. She was having to deal with the blackmail one day at a time.

"Don't be smart," Jim warned gently. He got down on one knee to make an adjustment to Chip's tie. He grimaced, having difficulty getting the ends even. "You're sure you don't want to try one of those clip-ons? Nobody will notice."

"No way. They're just for little kids. Everybody will know."

"Come on, Chip," Missy said. "Wear the clip-on. We're going to be late!"

"Nobody's going to be late," Paula said.

"Finally," Jim said, standing back to admire his work. "These things are almost impossible to tie yourself anyway. Try doing it backwards!"

Paula finished putting up Missy's hair. They both admired it in the mirror. Finally Missy smiled.

"Okay?" Paula asked.

"Thanks, Mom." Missy gave her a hug.

"All right," Paula said, "you two go amuse yourselves so I can finish getting dressed."

"They both think they're about four years older than their actual age," Paula said after the children were gone.

Jim carefully maneuvered his coattails and sat on a vanity stool. He watched Paula sort her clothes out.

"What are you looking at?" she said. She didn't mean it as sharp as it came out. It was just that she wanted some privacy to finish getting ready.

Jim didn't let on that her tone of voice bothered him. "The most beautiful woman in the world."

"Always the charmer."

He didn't deny it.

Paula took her dress off the hanger and stepped into it.

"The kids were really excited you spent the whole day with them," Jim said. "They really do know how busy you are. And they told me you said you'd drop them off at school Monday. I know what you have to do to rearrange your morning schedule at the courthouse to work it out. It means a lot to them."

Paula didn't answer. She was having a tough time zipping the dress. "I don't know why I let Helen talk me into wearing this."

"It's gorgeous."

"Not if I can't get this zipper to work."

Jim got up and walked over to her. "Here, let me help."

Paula was one huge bundle of nerves. Maybe that was why there was something so erotic about having him help her with the dress. The way his hands steadied her bare shoulders. His warm breath on her neck. The way he smelled, a clean, masculine smell.

"In case the British ambassador corners you, I've already made apologies on your behalf about the prime minister's wife," he said, while still working on the stubborn zipper.

Paula instantly let slide any amorous thoughts she might have been having. "And what for, might I ask?"

"She's visiting next week and was wanting to have coffee and a chat here at the White House. I think she was hoping you'd be here to give her the tour."

"Doesn't she read the papers? Doesn't she know I have a full-time job as a judge? I can't be hanging around here giving politicians' wives tours, for God's sake!" Paula saw Jim looking at her questioningly in the mirror. "Well, it's not like my not being here is going to cause some diplomatic row, is it?" she said.

"No," Jim answered quietly. All the brilliance had left his voice. "As I said, I just thought I'd mention it in case the ambassador brings it up so you won't be blindsided."

Paula sighed. She knew there was no good reason she should be behaving this way toward her husband. "If it comes up," she said, "I'll just tell him Helen will straighten it out. We'll find time, even if it's at night or on a weekend. Even if I have to come back over here during lunch recess."

Paula felt a tug at her back.

"Oh, damn," Jim said.

"What?"

"It broke."

"It broke? How could it break?"

"It just broke."

"You were forcing it."

"I wasn't. It just broke."

Paula pulled away from him, turned in the mirror to examine the damage.

"Damn," she uttered. "What else can go wrong?"

Jim placed his hands on her shoulders from behind, and she instinctively flinched. He dropped his hands to his sides and walked around in front of her.

"Don't you think you're overreacting just a bit?"

"No, I do not."

Paula sat down hard on the edge of the bed. Jim alighted more gracefully.

"I've had this feeling for a while," he said, "that there's something you're not telling me. You keep telling me no, but I don't believe you."

Paula was shattered. She buried her face in her hands. Her whole life had become a sham. Ever since finding out she had hit that little boy. Faking it as a dispenser of justice from the bench. Posing as the President's wife. If people only knew the truth about her.

She fought hard to remain rational. She had to give her husband some kind of credible explanation for her erratic behavior.

"Did it ever occur to you that I might miss spending time with you? The kids? Everything's changed."

"Well, sure. No, wait. I'm confused. You've been working ever since we've been married, and moving at lightning speed. We're all busy, but that doesn't mean we can't talk anymore about what's going on in our lives."

Paula was an emotional wreck. The blackmail was swirling around her, affecting every part of her life. Tell him and she would feel instantly relieved of the weight of the guilt she had been carrying by herself. If she didn't have confidence in her plan to turn the tables on Don Russ, she would have told him at that moment.

"I love you," he said. "When you want to talk, we'll talk. You have to do what you think's right. I'll back you up, no matter what."

Paula half smiled. He had no idea what she was having to deal with.

"No matter what?" she said.

"Absolutely. Promise me one thing, though."

"What?"

"We've always been honest with each other. Let's not stop now. There's a problem we need to talk about, let's not hold back. Okay?"

Paula nodded. "I promise," she lied.

Jim kissed her cheek. "That's my girl. Now about that dress . . ."

"I'll call Helen. You go on down to greet our guests. It may be a while."

"No way. I'm not going down without you. I'll be waiting in the study."

* * *

"Hold still," Helen said. "If you move again I'll draw blood."

With the help of one of the White House valets, Helen was sewing the back of the dress together where the zipper had torn. She finished and stood back to assess her work.

"An expert job if I do say so myself."

"Thanks," Paula said listlessly. The valet left.

"You'd better perk up before you go downstairs. Jim may be the President, but you're the hostess."

Paula straightened up. Helen was right. She had to carry off being the charming First Lady tonight.

"You're right. You're absolutely right."

Helen stayed in the dressing room as Paula finished getting ready.

They started out the door.

"You're being awfully secretive these days," Helen said.

"Is that supposed to be a joke?"

"I just noticed you're spending a lot of time off-itinerary with Del."

"That's really my business, isn't it?"

Paula could feel the chilliness set in. Helen had got the hint. God, she hated to do that, but she had to prevent the topic of her closeness to Del from coming up again.

They walked down the corridor toward the President's Study. Paula took her friend's hand. "I'm sorry, Helen."

"No, I shouldn't have said anything."

Paula gave Helen's hand a little squeeze. Maybe when this horrid mess was over, there would be some way Paula could explain her atrocious behavior.

"By the way, thank you for weaseling me an invitation to Tanya Pickering's dinner party tomorrow night," Paula said.

"She freaked because of the last-minute acceptance, but of course she's over the moon that you're coming."

Paula got Jim, and they went to the Green Room on the State Floor to form the receiving line. Both of them were assigned protocol officers who whispered into their ears the name of over a hundred ambassadors and chiefs of mission and their spouses who had come to meet the new President and his wife. Jim worked the line as if he were still running for office, giving his guests the impression that they had each just made a new best friend.

Fake it, Paula kept telling herself. *Smile. This will all soon be over.* With her mind on anything but small talk with the dignitaries and their spouses, she smiled and kept an eye out for the one person she really needed to see.

A half hour later, Del appeared in the room and stood in her line of sight so she would be able to see him. Making eye contact with him and with a slight nod of her head as she greeted the French ambassador's wife, Paula gave the signal that the plan had been put into motion. Del nodded back and slipped out to begin his part.

Now there would be no turning back.

Chapter 25

At one-thirty on Monday afternoon, Paula took a phone call in her office. Helen van Zandt's voice sounded strange over the phone. "Paula, are you having special difficulties of some kind we need to talk about?"

Paula had a white-knuckled grip on the telephone at her desk. "What do you mean?"

"I had a very strange message left on my voice mail when I got back from lunch," she said cautiously.

"And?"

"It was a conversation you were having with Chip and Missy. It sounded like when you were dropping them off for school this morning. I'll be honest with you—it really gives me the creeps. I kept asking myself, why would you tape yourself like that? And, then, why would you phone in a copy? It was you, wasn't it?"

Paula frantically tried to recall the details from that morning when she had accompanied the children to school. They drove in the Crown Vic, got out in front of the school, and walked in together. She could remember nothing that would have tipped her off that she was being spied on. Paula was scared. Now someone was following her children?

"I didn't do that," Paula said vehemently. "I would never do something like that."

"I didn't think so. Which makes me think maybe you've got even bigger problems."

There was an embarrassing silence between them.

Oh, God, Paula thought. *If she only knew.* Paula was almost afraid to ask: "Was there anything else on the message?"

"Nothing."

"What am I saying on the message?"

"Mainly you were talking to the kids about how nice the school looked. You asked them if they were embarrassed pulling up with their mom in the motorcade like that."

Paula's words came back to her. Someone was obviously using special equipment to pick up their conversations, because Helen had ensured there would be no media people with microphones jammed into her face as she escorted her children into the school.

"Paula, that message scares the bejesus out of me. At first I thought maybe it was some kind of cry for help, like you had cracked. But if you didn't make a tape, that means someone else did. Someone's following you. Or the kids. We need to have the Secret Service look into this right away."

"No," Paula said definitely. "Don't do that. I'll handle it. It's probably just some media scum snooping again. Like we talked about, remember?"

"Yeah. You're probably right. But what about the children, Paula? Do you think they're in some kind of danger?"

Paula was thinking: Surely Don Russ wouldn't stoop so low as to involve her children.

"Don't you think it's worth having it looked into for their sakes?" Helen asked.

It was for the children as well as her husband that Paula was going to such extraordinary lengths to stop Russ. All she needed was another day. *Just one more day.*

"Let's not do that," Paula said calmly. "Not yet. I don't want to cry wolf over something as important as a threat to the children. It's the tabloids, you know it is. It's a slow news day. Let's not mention it to anyone yet, okay?"

"You're probably right. You'd think people would know better than to try something like that against the President's family. Just thought you'd want to know."

"You did the right thing. Thanks."

Paula hung up the phone. And said a little prayer that she had made the right decision. She would know in another few hours.

"I'm stuffed," Paula said, loosening her seat belt. "Too much dessert."

Secret Service Agent Branson turned around from the front seat of the Crown Victoria and smiled at her.

When Paula had originally declined Tanya Pickering's dinner invitation, she had been able to do so legitimately because of the conflict with her workload. But, she'd known, too, there was no way she could possibly fake civility as the Remalli crisis engulfed her.

And yet fake it tonight she had. As the new President's wife, Paula had been the top celebrity at the dinner for eight at the Georgetown town house. She made a special effort to be the sparkling dinner guest. She was witty and erudite, holding forth on matters of art and science. She stayed clear of politics and the law. Most of the people at the dinner party had attended at least one of the inaugural parties in Washington, but she was still able to dazzle them with inside tales of the White House, even though she had had next to no time to explore it herself.

The car was cruising east along M Street in Georgetown in the direction of the White House. The Washington Memorial loomed over the skyline.

"Too much dessert," Paula said again, "and I'm afraid

too much coffee on top of all that water. Ted, would you mind if we made a pit stop before we got back to the House? Maybe right up there?" She pointed at a row of stores.

"Here?" Agent Mobley asked.

"Sorry," she said sheepishly. "Emergency."

The car slowed, and Mobley radioed the agents in the Chevy Suburbans what was going on.

"I think the bookstore's still open," Paula said, squinting through the window. "Yes, I see a few people inside. There's a rest room at the back of the store. This will be fine."

The car swung into the parking lot, along with the other two vehicles. The Secret Service agents escorted Paula inside.

It was nearly eleven o'clock, almost closing time. There were more employees than customers at this hour in the independent bookshop. No one seemed particularly to notice their coming in. With Mobley and Branson on her heels, Paula made a beeline for the rest room, trying not to catch anyone's eye.

Mobley nodded. "We'll just wait here."

"Hold on, ma'am," Branson said.

Paula stopped and turned.

"Better check," Branson said.

The look on Paula's face must have told him how anxious she was to make it inside.

"Won't take but a second," he said. "Just to be safe."

Branson banged on the rest room door. "Anyone in there?" he said loudly. He cocked his head to listen for a response, but there was no sound. He took a quick look inside. Empty.

"Okay," he told Paula. He let her pass by. He joined his partner to take up a position guarding the entrance to the ladies' room.

*   *   *

Del Owens wore a faded Redskins baseball cap pulled down low over his eyes. From his position, seated on a footstool in the art section of the bookstore, he peered over the edge of an oversize volume on Georgia O'Keeffe paintings. He could just barely make out the shifting feet of the two Secret Service agents positioned by the rest rooms.

Del was worried because Paula was running so late. Just a few more minutes and she would have found herself locked outside the bookstore. If that had happened, Del knew he would never be able to arrange a second meeting with Don Russ.

Worse, there had been no sign of the attorney. Del feared he was a no-show.

Del could see only a few heads sticking above the bookshelves throughout the rest of the store, mostly employees straightening up before closing. In the middle of the store rose a wide, gleaming wooden staircase leading to the children's and reference sections and a coffee shop on the second floor. A balcony ran around the upper level, overlooking the floor below.

Del had carefully cased the place before taking his position in the art section. There were only two customers left upstairs: one pathetic-looking guy with his nose stuck in a self-help book who looked like he'd be sleeping in a cardboard box later in the night, and a man finishing his decaf cappuccino over a book of poetry at a table. No one upstairs or down- looked like a member of the Mafia. And there had been no sign of Julia Menendez.

Del checked his watch. Paula had been in the rest room for less than a minute.

Paula stood in front of the mirror, fiddled with her hair, adjusted her skirt. She smoothed her suit jacket, checked her lipstick and makeup. She glanced in the reflection at the scene behind her: everything looked normal.

Russ will never make it now, though, she thought. Not past the two Secret Service agents. He was late. They'd immediately recognize him if he tried to get through. But he wouldn't do that. He'd see them standing there and turn back.

Del had told her he had secured a firm commitment from Julia Menendez that the lawyer would be there. The farewells at Tanya's dinner party had run long. Then they had been stuck in the usual awful Georgetown traffic.

And now it was too late.

Paula really did need to use the toilet, but thought she could hold out until she reached the White House. She would wait another few moments to give the appearance of having been busy, then leave.

A voice suddenly boomed around the tiled room. "Your Honor."

Paula started and spun about. A man was emerging from one of the stalls. She gasped.

In his blue jeans and leather jacket, she didn't recognize him at first. She was so accustomed to seeing Don Russ in a business suit.

He had none of the swagger of his earlier courtroom appearances. His face was a blank, unfathomable.

She instinctively backed up a step as he approached her. She bumped against the sink counter and was trapped. He reached toward her, and she involuntarily put a hand out to repel him. "No . . ." she uttered. She thought he was going to grab her.

He gave her that familiar condescending grin. He reached past her and turned on both water taps full blast.

"What are you doing?" she asked.

"Covers our conversation better in case someone's listening outside the door."

Paula regained her confidence. She crossed her arms. "An old trick you learned from one of your clients, no doubt," she said.

"No doubt."

They stared at each other in silence, the water splashing in the bottom of the sink.

"Well?" Russ eventually said. "*You* called *me*."

Paula had rehearsed the lines over and over again. With time so precious and the situation so hostile, it was important to know exactly what to say to elicit the words she needed for him to speak.

"I just can't believe what Del Owens has told me about you," she said. "I find it difficult to understand why you're doing what you're doing. I had to hear it for myself."

Russ played it cool. "There's nothing I can add to what's already been said."

Paula's mind raced. Russ was being a good lawyer for himself. He wasn't going to say any more than he absolutely had to. But she was prepared for this. She'd figured she would have to pull it out of him.

"You may have a certain reputation in the legal community for your work on behalf of criminal defendants, but that means nothing to me as a judge," she said. "All I want is to sit on this case as I would any other and apply the law to your client as fairly as possible. But this . . . this is all so incredible."

"But it's become very straightforward. A simple quid pro quo. We each have something the other wants. I'm willing to trade. Problem is, I'm not getting any cooperation. Is it you or Owens who's the deal killer?"

"There *is* no deal," she said.

Paula screwed her face up in anger. She paced in the small area in front of the sinks.

"I received the WestLaw prize my first year in law school for contract law," Paula said. "If I remember correctly, one of the basic elements for an agreement is that there be a meeting of the minds. I'm afraid we're not anywhere close to that. If you don't tell me specifically what it is you want from me, and what you're willing to give me as consideration, then we don't have a contract. Spell it out, Mr. Russ. I want to know what your terms are."

Russ's eyes clouded for an instant. A storm brewing within. He was conflicted, but trying terribly hard not to show it.

"Okay," he said. "Here's the deal . . ."

Del heard a commotion at the front door. The manager was locking up, not letting any new customers in. But someone outside was knocking loudly. The manager was trying to turn the person away, but whoever it was was insistent.

Then Del recognized the pleading voice. Julia Menendez.

At that moment the manager relented, and Julia rushed inside.

She walked quickly straight toward the back of the store. Then she ran. She saw the two men blocking her way, but didn't slow down.

"Excuse me, miss," Branson said, holding his arm out to block her.

"I have to go to the ladies' room," Julia said.

"I'm sorry, but it's closed."

"Like hell it is. The store manager told me I could use the rest room."

"Sorry, lady. You ain't gettin' through."

"I'm about to wet my pants! It's an emergency!"

Julia started making not-so-subtle jiggling motions, as if she couldn't hold it another moment.

Branson appeared to weaken for a moment, but Mobley gave his partner a look that told him it was definitely not okay.

"Jesus Christ," Del muttered under his breath.

Should he step out of hiding to stop her? What was going on?

At that instant—before he could make a decision—he heard Julia's voice again. This time she was screaming: *"She's wired! Get out! She's wired!"*

The next ten seconds were a blur.

Paula heard the woman screaming in the hallway outside. Russ's eyes flared at Paula, and he hesitated a second, deciding whether to go or stay.

Then he left the way he had come in—through the high window over the entrance to the first toilet stall. With one powerful athletic jump he grabbed onto water pipes hanging from the ceiling, then swung himself out over the open window.

Julia was trapped between the door and the two Secret Service agents, who were drawing their SigSauer 9mm semiautomatic handguns and radioing for backup.

"Get down!" Branson yelled at Julia. "On the floor! *Now!*"

Julia dropped to the ground.

"Judge Candler," Branson called out, "you okay in there?"

Paula emerged from the rest room appearing perfectly composed. She looked shocked at what was going on.

"Cover her," shouted Mobley to his partner. Branson kept his gun trained on Julia as his partner stepped over the woman on the floor and pulled Paula down the hallway.

Just then a loud alarm went off.

Julia lifted her head and saw Del Owens peering over a stack of books. In the other direction, she saw the man who had been following her the other night in Georgetown throwing down a poetry book, then scrambling out the emergency exit.

Outside, in back of the bookstore, Scott was running as hard as he could.

He had followed Russ to M Street. Watched as Russ had climbed in through the small rest room window. Scott had gone into the bookstore, picked up a slim volume of poetry to look through as he watched everything happening from his strategic vantage in the café upstairs overlooking the rest of the store. It was from there that he had seen the President's wife come into the store and head down the hallway to where Russ was waiting. Scott had seen it all.

What was Judge Candler doing meeting with Remalli's lawyer in a women's rest room? The question blew him away.

Scott darted around the corner of the building in the direction of his car. He pumped his legs and arms hard.

Then suddenly hit something solid and reeled backward, collapsing with a loud thud against a Dumpster.

Under bright security lights Scott recognized the face of the man lying on the ground in front of him, the man he had just collided with. Don Russ was shaking his head even as he climbed to his feet. He gave Scott a quick look, then ran off into the darkness of the nearby alley and was gone.

Scott picked himself up and ran like hell in the opposite direction.

"I don't know who she is," Paula said. "Let's just go." Mobley nodded to Branson.

"Okay," Branson told Julia as he holstered his gun.

"Sorry," Mobley said to Julia. "Our mistake."

Branson helped Julia up off the ground. She swore something at them in Spanish.

"If you don't mind," Branson started, "we'd like to ask you some questions—"

Before he could finish the sentence, the woman had bolted out of the store and disappeared into the night.

The Secret Service agents held Paula by the elbows and all but carried her outside and pushed her into the backseat of the car.

Del waited until he saw the taillights of the Crown Victoria and Suburbans speeding away before emerging from the art section of the bookstore.

The bookstore staff were still standing around in a daze over what had happened. Del thought no one would question a customer having to relieve himself after all that excitement. He rushed toward the the rest rooms.

"Hey, you!" a voice called out after him. It was the store manager.

Del rushed into the women's rest room. He popped open the paper towel dispenser and removed the diminutive 8mm camcorder from inside, yanked free the optical wires and special fish-eye lens attachment. He stuffed everything into his coat pockets.

The manager banged opened the rest room door. Del was loudly pissing into a toilet.

"Hey!"

"Yeah?"

"This is the women's room."

"Sorry, I hadn't noticed."

Del finished and zipped. Under the suspicious eye of the manager, he washed his hands. With the paper towel dispenser open and empty, Del wiped his hands on his trousers as he passed the manager on the way out.

"You really need to keep those things filled, you know."

A half dozen anxious Secret Service agents crowded around Paula in her East Wing office. She had insisted on going there rather than the main part of the White House so as not to alarm her husband or children with all the commotion.

"I just can't figure out what she was talking about," Paula said, shaking her head.

"And you've never seen her before?" Mobley asked.

"Never."

"Strange," Branson said. "Maybe she was calling out to someone else she thought was in the rest room."

"Or maybe to that guy who ran out the emergency exit," offered Mobley. "I called the bookstore and the manager said there'd been a couple of times when someone tried walking out that back way without paying for a book, and it set the alarms off. He figured the guy was trying to make off with a book of poetry during all the confusion. You wouldn't figure someone interested in poetry would try stealing a book, would you?"

"Well, whoever that woman was, she wasn't talking to me," Paula said. "I know that for sure."

"I'm never sorry when we respond like that," Mobley said. "In hindsight, it may seem like overreacting, but you never know when there's a legitimate threat. We did the right thing. You sure you're going to be okay?"

"I'm fine now. It's just that I was so surprised when I came out of the rest room and found you with your guns drawn on that woman."

There was a knock on the door. The President came in with his own Secret Service escort.

"I just heard there was an incident on your way home from Tanya Pickering's dinner party. What's going on?" he demanded brusquely.

Paula took control before anyone else could reply. "A false alarm, Jim. We made a stop and the agents thought I was in danger. They had to draw guns, but everything's okay."

"What were you doing stopping at this time of night?" Jim asked.

Paula looked sheepish. "I had to go pee," she said meekly.

Jim Candler checked the nodding faces of Paula's Secret Service escort.

"You sure you're all right now?" he asked her.

"Fine, really. I just want to take a look at some things here before I come back over to the residence. I won't be a few minutes, okay?"

The President looked doubtful about the whole affair, but expressed his relief, then left.

A minute later there was another knock on the door. Del was ushered in.

"S'happenin', guys?" he asked.

"Just a little excitement on our way back from dinner," Mobley said. "Everything's under control."

Del hefted his briefcase. "I know it's late, but I've got a couple of things to go over with Judge Candler before tomorrow."

"Right," Mobley said. "Let's go."

The Secret Service agents filed out, leaving Paula and Del alone.

"Holy shit," Del said. He opened his briefcase, pulled out the camcorder and a radio receiver connected by wires to a microcassette player. He threw everything onto the small conference table in the corner.

"That was a disaster," he said. "And on top of everything, we got nothing of any use. Julia Menendez yelled out her warning before Russ had a chance to say anything incriminating. All we've captured on film is the two of you doing a verbal do-si-do in a women's rest room. Ditto on the wire you were wearing."

Paula went limp, completely drained. She had used every ounce of energy she had to confront Don Russ and then to maintain the façade with the Secret Service and her husband.

"I was so close," Paula said. "He was about to lay out the blackmail scheme. We would have had it all on tape."

Del was still shaking his head in disbelief. "It could have been a lot worse if the Secret Service had caught you and Russ alone together in the ladies' room."

"You were watching from the store. What happened?"

"I don't know. First, Julia Menendez forces her way into the store; then she's yelling at Ted and Richard to let her into the rest room. Next thing I know she's screaming about you being wired."

"How would she know that?"

In addition to having Del install the camcorder and pinhole fish-eye lens in the hand-towel dispenser, Paula had strapped on a body wire as a backup in case the camcorder failed to work properly. A specially tuned radio receiver in the trunk of Del's car was supposed to record their conversation.

"I haven't a clue," Del said. "Then some guy who'd been sipping cappuccino and reading a book of poetry at the upstairs café decides he wants to bolt out the back door, setting the alarms off. He wore a cap pulled down low and I never was able to see his face very well, but something about him seemed kind of familiar."

Paula rose from her chair, feeling exhausted. "Excuse me a moment."

She stepped into the bathroom off her office and un-buttoned her blouse, revealing a small microphone taped to her chest, the wires running to the back of her skirt, where there was a miniature transmitter and battery pack. She stripped herself of the apparatus, then got dressed again.

"Here," she said, throwing the tangle of wires onto the pile of Del's video equipment. "Get rid of this. All of it. I don't want any evidence left of what we just attempted." Paula slumped into a chair. "Del, I haven't been able to get my mind off something that happened earlier today. Someone phoned Helen and left a message on her answering machine that was a recording of me with the children. I think it was some kind of veiled threat. If they touch the children—"

"It won't happen. The Secret Service would never let them close enough."

"But if they did . . . it would be the last straw. I want you to double the number of agents on them until this trial's over."

"No problem. I'll take care of it first thing in the morning. But I think you'd better focus on the bigger threat. You know there's gonna be hell to pay tomorrow. Russ is going to be in fine form in court."

Paula thought about what it would be like sitting on the bench, looking Russ in the eye, both knowing what had happened the previous night. She had expected to be doing it from a position of power, knowing that she had the lawyer's blackmail attempt on tape. She had hoped that once Del played the tapes for Russ, he would be overcome by the acute embarrassment of seeing himself caught in the act, and fear would replace his smugness.

But she had failed. Russ would never trust her to get close enough again to try to trap him. Instead, he would be returning to court with new vigor. She had already begun mentally preparing herself. If she expected the worst, whatever he did would seem tame.

"What else can he do that he hasn't already done?" Paula said.

Julia pressed the cold washcloth to the massive bruise on Don Russ's face. He flinched.

"That sore?" she asked. "What'd you do? Run into a wall?"

They were sitting on the threadbare couch in the room at the Patriot's Inn, a rendezvous point they had agreed on before Russ's meeting at the bookstore.

"I ran into someone as I was leaving through the rest room window."

"Kinda tall? Short brown hair? Wearing a Georgetown sweatshirt?"

"Yeah, that's the guy. How'd you know?"

"He's the one who set off the alarm. I saw him leaving through the back door right after I yelled out. It's the same guy who was following me the other night after we met in Schwango's."

"You figure it's one of Del Owens's people?"

"Who else?"

"I don't know. He looked kind of familiar, but I just couldn't place him. Maybe it'll come to me later."

Julia dabbed at the bruise again.

"Hey," Russ said, "take it easy."

He took the washcloth away from her and held it to his face himself.

"I thought you were done for," Julia said, "when those two Secret Service agents had me pinned down with their guns. I thought you were next."

"I wouldn't have agreed to meet in that rest room if you hadn't checked the place over already and found there was more than one way out. The whole thing was a setup. Paula Candler never intended to cut a deal. You'd think you could trust a federal judge. The only thing she wanted out of that meeting was something to blackmail us with. By the way, all the way over here I was trying to figure out: how on earth did you know she was wired?"

Julia pulled a scanner out of her handbag and put it on the table. "I was scanning police frequencies in case it was a trap and some law enforcement was lurking about. When I heard you talking on two different frequencies, I knew there was something wrong. I thought at first it was some kind of freaky radio-wave harmonics. Then I realized that she had a wire on her, too."

"Ah," Russ said knowingly. He started unbuttoning his shirt. The farther down the front of his shirt he went, the bigger Julia's eyes got. He stood up and reached behind his back and yanked out a radio transmitter and battery pack.

"Here, I'll help," Julia said. Remaining seated, she gently pulled the taped wires off his chest, working her way around his flank and to his backside. She lingered at the small of his back, stood up, traced her finger up his spine, then ran her fingers through his hair. Their faces were only inches apart.

"Julia," Russ warned.

The severity of his rebuke broke the tension of the moment. She sighed and withdrew her hands.

"If our plan had worked," Julia said, "we would have been in an even better position. Having Judge Candler admitting on tape to killing the kid would have given us just one thing more to hold over her head."

"I'll give credit where credit is due," Russ said. "You had a good idea. Too bad they had to go screw it up by trying to tape us themselves."

Russ threw the washcloth into the kitchen. Julia grabbed his chin and tilted his head to get a better look in the light.

"You're going to have one helluva shiner by tomorrow morning. Not very photogenic." She dug into her handbag again, pulled out a bottle of makeup. "Better use some of this."

"Gimme a break."

"The whole world's watching you. You don't want them distracted from what you're saying."

Russ looked at the bottle, seriously considered it for a moment.

"No, thanks," he said. "I don't mind if everyone's distracted in court tomorrow. That's not where the real action's going to be taking place anyway."

"Really? You have something else in mind?"

Russ dug into his wallet, pulled out a slip of paper. "Find a fax machine first thing in the morning." Russ handed Julia a file folder. "It's time to make Paula Candler understand exactly how serious I am."

Julia looked at the name and number on the piece of paper, peeked inside the file. "Oh, Don. You don't really want to do *this*, do you?"

Chapter 26

The worst part of Lloyd Chapman's questioning was trying to avoid looking at Don Russ for two and a half hours. Only once, when Scott was certain the attorney had his head turned to talk to Remalli, did Scott sneak a quick look at him. One side of Russ's face was red and swollen, the result of their clash. It looked as if talking was painful.

As Scott was sworn in as the Government's next witness, he saw in his peripheral vision Russ leaning forward in his seat to get a better look at him. At the instant of recognition, Russ sat back in his seat hard and hit the top of the table with the flats of his hands. For a moment the clerk who was swearing Scott in stopped mid-sentence and turned along with everyone else in court to see what the source of the noise was. Even without looking directly at him, Scott could feel the heat from Russ's glare.

He knows. He knows I saw him with Paula Candler. And now he knows I'm an FBI agent.

Scott averted his eyes, glanced out toward the people sitting in the gallery.

Oh, shit. Now this.

At the back of the room, peering between the mass of faces, were the unmistakable sad, unblinking, menacing eyes of the mobster who had threatened him a few nights before.

Scott sat up, clenched his jaw, and tried to clear his

mind of everything except the task of answering Lloyd Chapman's questions. If anything, after the mobster's threat and seeing Russ with Judge Candler, Scott was even more determined to deliver the blow from the stand that would put Remalli away.

During his time on the stand with Chapman, Scott thought the U.S. Attorney did a masterful job of demonstrating his competence as an FBI black-bag specialist, having Scott recite his expert training and his previous work on other cases. Chapman then introduced into evidence portions of almost two dozen tapes, each including some allusion to the murder of Judge Ellen Goldsworthy. Every time a new tape was introduced, Scott had to vouch for its origin and authenticity, and attest to the accuracy of the transcription. Chapman passed out copies of the transcripts, which had been laboriously prepared by Scott himself.

Everyone knew that Scott's testimony was critical to the Remalli case, since the only direct evidence of the murder the Government had was Remalli's own words on the tapes.

Chapman saved for last the playing of the crucial tape with Remalli's bragging about the killing. It was the same tape that had been used by the Government in Remalli's detention hearing to deny him bond. The courtroom was perfectly quiet. The mobster's words were chilling as they boomed around the room.

CERUTTI: You popped her good.

REMALLI: I whacked her good. . . .

REMALLI: She got it where she deserved it—inna fuckin' mouth! Sometimes I get carried away like that when it's personal. . . .

After playing the tape, Chapman paused dramatically to allow the impact of what had been heard to sink in. It was gruesome listening. Everyone in the courtroom knew Scott had delivered the coup de grâce in the Government's case.

Over the course of the next half hour, Scott methodically summarized the evidence on the tapes, explaining that, taken as a whole, the secretly recorded conversations were unambiguous, incontrovertible proof of Remalli's role in the murder.

Chapman, obviously pleased with how his testimony had gone, gave Scott a rare genuine smile before he returned to his table.

Scott's stomach started churning, knowing that shortly Russ would be tearing him apart on the stand.

But Scott had already mentally prepared himself to do battle with the famous mob lawyer.

I can beat this guy, he assured himself. *I've got right on my side. I'm gonna win.*

"Cross-examine, Mr. Russ."

Don Russ strode to a position halfway between the bench and the witness stand. The side of his face was bruised and swollen, something Paula hadn't noticed when they met the previous night in the bookstore.

He still had not looked directly at her. It unnerved her that he had not yet made eye contact, although they were almost finished with the morning session.

Then, without warning, Russ smiled broadly at Paula and said in a cheery voice, "Thank you, Your Honor."

Russ took a few moments longer to scrutinize the witness before beginning his cross-examination. "Mr. Betts, how long have you been a special agent with the FBI?"

"I graduated from the Academy four years ago."

"You've testified that you received specialized training in electronic surveillance. Did this training include breaking into the premises of a suspect for the purpose of installing surveillance equipment?"

"Actually, they're separate specialties within the Bureau, but—yes—I received training in both."

"How many times have you carried out an installation?"

The witness thought a moment. "About a half dozen times."

"By yourself?"

"No, with someone else."

"Who were the people you were making the installations with?"

"Other FBI agents."

"Does the FBI certify agents in electronic surveillance?"

"Yes."

"Had you been certified at the time you participated in these other installations?"

"No."

"So what exactly was your status?"

"I was a graduate of the Academy; I had completed a couple of years in the field; then I enrolled in a program of specialized training."

"Would it be fair to say that these other installations were part of your training?"

"Yes."

"So, Mr. Betts, your first time to install equipment by yourself was in this case?"

"Yes, but—"

"It would, then, be fair to say that you are not very experienced in installing hidden listening devices."

The witness tensed. "I received the finest training in the world by the FBI. But in terms of actual experience I hadn't done any on my own."

"Fine. In the last tape Mr. Chapman played, this recording was made from a listening device that you yourself installed on Mr. Remalli's business premises?"

"Yes."

"Could you explain, please, where the device was installed and why it was installed where it was?"

Paula looked to the back of the courtroom. A lot of new faces among the spectators. After word about the previous session's fireworks got out, demand by the media and the public to view the Remalli trial increased dramatically. To accommodate all the requests for the limited seating, Paula had been forced to issue revised instructions for press rotation, and had reduced to thirty minutes from an hour the amount of time any individual observer was allowed to sit in on the case.

"There were actually three listening devices," the witness answered. "One in the reception area, one in the back storage room, and one in the hallway leading from the reception area to the offices."

"Were there any other areas which you had targeted for installation?"

The FBI agent hesitated a moment. "Yes."

"Where might that be?"

"Mr. Remalli's office."

"Why didn't you install one there?"

"Our plan was to install a device in the office, but we had to terminate the operation when Mr. Remalli returned to the premises unexpectedly before we were finished."

"I see. So tell me, Mr. Betts, why did you want to install a device in Mr. Remalli's office?"

The witness hesitated again, shifted his eyes to the U.S. attorney's table. Paula interpreted this hesitation as Russ's having found a weakness in the Government's case.

"Because we figured that this would be the place in the business where Mr. Remalli would be most likely to carry on conversations where he discussed criminal activities."

"But you did not have a listening device there."

"No."

"Well, now I'm confused. Didn't you previously testify that the conversations on the last tape were of Mr. Remalli speaking in his office?"

"Yes."

"But you just said that you had no listening device in the back office."

"The conversation was recorded from the listening device in the hallway."

"Ahh," Russ said, as if this were some great revelation. "You could pick up conversations in the office from a device in the hallway."

"Yes."

"But wouldn't this device, being outside the office, result in poorer-quality recordings?"

"The quality of the recordings would have been better had we been able to place a listening device directly into Mr. Remalli's office."

"Yes." Russ held up a copy of the transcript. "If I can call your attention to the transcript you prepared of this last taped conversation Mr. Chapman played, page thirty-four."

"Okay."

"You personally transcribed the tapes?"

"Yes."

"Would you mind reading, please, line ten, starting with what you have listed as 'Mr. Remalli.' "

Scott Betts found the line and began to read:

"CERUTTI: She ain't got no more brains to think with. Look, Tony . . . it's dark, but can you see little bits of her brain all over the wall?

"REMALLI: I see it. I see it. Man . . .

"CERUTTI: You popped her good.

"REMALLI: I whacked her good—"

Russ cut in: "Okay, Mr. Betts, you can stop there. Now let me ask that those same lines be played for the court. And I'll ask you to listen closely to the words."

Scott twisted in his seat and leaned in toward the speakers. Russ's assistant played the portion of the tape Scott had just read.

"Now, Mr. Betts, could you tell me, after the person you've identified as Mr. Cerutti says, 'You popped her good,' the other man says what?"

"He says, 'I whacked her good.' "

Russ seemed startled. "Really? That's not what I heard. I heard something completely different. Is it possible that the person you've identified as Mr. Remalli said, 'I *smacked* her good'?"

I see where this is going, Scott thought. "That's not what *I* heard," he said defiantly. "I suppose that's possible. But within the context—"

Russ jumped on Scott's words: "Now, wait just a second, Mr. Betts. I didn't ask you anything other than if it was *possible* that what the voice on the tape said was 'smacked' rather than 'whacked.' Yes or no?"

"Yes," Scott said through clenched teeth.

"I'm sorry, I'm not sure everyone heard what you said."

Scott cleared his throat, spoke louder. "I said yes."

"Thank you. So perhaps we should change the official transcript to reflect this change?"

"That's not what I would do."

"I'm sure you wouldn't. But what if we change the transcript to reflect that the word used was *either* 'smacked' or 'whacked.' You have to agree that they could mean very different things, don't you?"

"I'm not sure I could say."

"And that's exactly my point. You, being the Government's star witness, are not sure about your own testimony. Which begs another very important question. Is the error due to your interpretation error—what you may or may not have heard—or is the error due to your not being able to hear the exact words on the tape clearly?"

Scott did not immediately answer. Russ paced with his arms folded.

"Mr. Betts?" Russ said.

"The error could have been due to either."

"Or both."

"Yes," Scott admitted with great reluctance.

Russ smiled, turned in profile so everyone else in court could see how pleased he was with how the cross-examination was going. "I would like to note that the witness has just agreed with me that there actually was an error."

"Actually, what I meant to convey—" Scott tried to interject.

"What? You're not certain you said that? Would you like us to have the court reporter read back your own words?"

"That won't be necessary, thank you very much."

Don Russ struck a pose of scrappy confidence. He knew he was scoring points.

I'm not letting you get away with this! Scott thought. *Before I get off this stand*—

"Mr. Betts, in preparing transcripts such as these, what do you do when you hear words that are ambiguous or you can't hear clearly?"

"Make an educated guess based on the context of the conversation. If the word is truly unintelligible, that will be noted as such in the transcript."

Russ seemed flabbergasted. "So you're making words up? Putting words into the mouths of the people you're secretly recording?"

"I didn't say that."

"You just did. You said you make a guess as to what they're saying. Either that, or you mark the words as unintelligible. But, Mr. Betts, having closely read the entirety of the transcripts presented by the U.S. attorney, I can tell you that I have seen extremely few instances where words are marked as unintelligible. Which would lead me to believe that most of the words you were not able to understand, you simply made up."

Scott needed to stop him from going down that path: "No—"

"So," continued Russ, "if we take this one small example of an error, how many more are there in these transcripts?"

Scott didn't answer.

"One? A dozen? Hundreds? Thousands? Last night I took the time to estimate the word count in the transcripts submitted as evidence. Nearly half a million words. Specifically, how many were guessed at?"

"I wouldn't know specifically. I'd have to take a look."

Russ stormed over to the defense table and picked up the huge pile of tape transcripts.

"Permission to approach the witness?"

Russ must have seen Judge Candler's nod in the corner of his eye, because he didn't bother looking up at the bench. He took the pile of transcripts and dropped them heavily directly in front of Scott.

"Well, by all means, Mr. Betts, take a look."

Russ stood with hand on hip and waited. Scott saw Tony Remalli crane his neck to the back of the courtroom and scowl at his associate.

Scott refused to touch the transcripts. *I know what he's trying to do*, he thought. *And I'm not going to cooperate with his courtroom theatrics just so he can try to embarrass me.*

Chapman rose to be recognized. "Your Honor . . ."

*   *   *

Paula saw that Russ wasn't going to let go of the FBI witness until he had chewed him up and spit him out.

"Mr. Russ—" she started.

But the attorney was unrelenting. "But you're the Government's witness. A supposed expert in electronic surveillance. Why can you not give me an estimate as to how many other words were made up?"

Paula said sternly, "Mr. Russ, I believe you've made your point. Please move on."

Russ still did not acknowledge her presence.

He took a couple of steps back away from the witness. "Finally, Mr. Betts, does the name Ellen Goldsworthy, or Goldsworthy, or Ellen, or any variation of any of these words, appear anywhere in the transcripts of tapes entered into evidence?"

"Not specifically."

"No?"

"I said no."

"Does the person speaking on the tapes ever use the word 'murder'?"

"Not that I recall."

"Does the person speaking on the tapes ever use the word 'kill'?"

"I don't believe so."

" 'Kill'?"

"No."

" 'Die'?"

Scott was getting irritated. "I'd really have to go back and look."

"One final question: how do you know that the person that you claim to be speaking on the tapes is my client?"

The witness looked to the Government's desk again. "Well, I just do. We knew when his place of business was empty; then we saw him go in and he started talking. Sometimes this was when he was alone, talking on the phone, so it couldn't have been anyone else. Over time we learned what his voice sounded like."

Russ kept hammering away. "The FBI had someone watching Mr. Remalli's office?"

"Yes."

"Every day?"

"Most days."

"Most days? You mean the FBI did not have Mr. Remalli's office under visual surveillance every minute of every day throughout the period when these tapes were made?"

"No."

"And on the date in question on which the tapes were made where this person is talking about seeing a photograph in the newspaper?"

"I'm not exactly sure. There were hundreds of stakeouts."

"Try to recall. It is important. A man's life is at stake here."

The agent thought for a moment. "I'm sorry, I just couldn't say positively one way or the other."

Russ smiled. "Well, let me suggest to you, Agent Betts, that if the FBI had had visual surveillance of Mr. Remalli's office on the day the tapes in question were made, they would have already presented evidence to that effect. Are you aware of any evidence the FBI has that could corroborate Mr. Remalli actually being in his office?"

"I'm not, no."

"So you cannot be absolutely certain that Mr. Remalli was even in his office at the time the tapes were made?"

The witness defiantly leaned forward in his chair, almost lifting himself off the seat. He was seething. "I know what you're trying to do, Mr. Russ," he said, his voice rising. "No matter what you try to make me say, everyone in the courtroom knows that your client—"

Paula gaveled for order, but the witness wouldn't stop talking.

"—your client was caught on tape confessing to the killing of Judge Goldsworthy!"

"Agent Betts!" Paula said, still gaveling. Finally the witness sat back in his seat. Russ had an almost bemused expression on his face. "Please refrain from any more outbursts of that kind. It does nothing to further the business of the court. Do you understand?"

"Yes, ma'am."

"Mr. Russ, please continue."

"Thank you, Your Honor." Russ approached the witness, rested a hand on the partition in front of him. Paula was about to ask the defense attorney to move away, since he had not asked permission to approach the witness. Then with his back turned so no one except Paula could see him, Russ mouthed something to the witness. The FBI agent's eyes flared, and Russ stepped away.

What was that? Paula wondered. *Did Russ just say something to the witness?* She checked the court reporter's transcript on her laptop, but saw no record of anything being said.

"Agent Betts," Russ said. "I'll repeat the question for your benefit. Can you be absolutely certain that Mr. Remalli was even in his office at the time the tapes were made?"

"I'm not in a position to testify to that."

"So this person speaking on the tape could be anyone, couldn't he?"

The FBI agent didn't answer. He just sat glaring at Russ.

"Thank you, Mr. Betts. You've been *very* helpful."

The young agent's cheeks were burning as he climbed down from the witness box.

"Your Honor . . ." At last Russ looked Paula in the eye.

And smiled. The kindest, friendliest smile anyone had given Paula in a very long time. "I have no further questions at this time."

"Mr. Chapman, this was your final witness, was it not?"

"Yes, it was," the U.S. attorney answered sullenly.

"Mr. Russ, do you still anticipate needing a week for your proof?"

Paula caught Russ's quick glance to the Government's table to see if Chapman was watching. "No, actually, I don't. We had our witnesses all lined up waiting here ready to go, but I feel confident that we've raised enough doubt in our cross-examination of the Government's own witnesses, so we don't need to offer any proof."

Paula had had defense attorneys try this tactic in her court before, but never in a nonjury trial and never in a capital murder case.

The look on Chapman's face said it all. He must have assumed since Russ had not requested discovery or the Government's witness list that Russ was planning an ambush with surprise witnesses. The bigger surprise turned out to be the fact that Russ was putting on no proof at all.

"Well, then, I suppose we're all ready for closing arguments. Mr. Chapman, can the Government be prepared for its summation by tomorrow?"

Chapman was still suffering from acute disorientation. He still hadn't figured out what had just transpired. "Yes, if that's what Your Honor wishes."

"Mr. Russ?"

"We're ready, Your Honor." He smiled pleasantly at her in an overly familiar way. Then he did the unbelievable. He mouthed, "You're screwed."

It threw her. Badly. On top of everything else. She could not fathom what was going on.

She shuffled papers to buy a few moments to collect her thoughts. She, too, had been caught off guard by how quickly the end of the trial had come. She had been counting on having at least another week to figure out how to thwart the blackmail attempt. Now it looked as if she had only a matter of days. Or hours.

"Lunch?" her case manager reminded her softly.

Paula snapped out of it. "Yes. We'll be in recess until tomorrow morning. Nine-thirty sharp."

Paula stood and everyone else in the courtroom rose. She took a final glimpse from the bench before she darted to the door leading to her chambers.

Russ was positively beaming at her.

Nothing he could have done would have been more disconcerting.

Chapter 27

Scott was already flying down the steps—three, four at a time—even before Judge Candler had gaveled the morning session into recess.

A door burst open somewhere in the stairwell above him. "Betts!" a rough voice called out. "Scott Betts!"

Scott moved faster down the steps, knowing who it was. He had seen the mobster in the back of the courtroom leave just as he was finishing up on the witness stand. Tony Remalli's enforcer had figured out that Scott was making his escape from the building by way of the stairs rather than the elevator.

"Goddammit!" he bellowed. "Get back here!"

Scott pushed himself even harder, trying to put more distance between himself and his pursuers. He counted at least three pairs of feet following him down the stairs.

Scott passed the sign for the third floor, then hurtled down the next flight of steps. He stumbled on the second-floor landing, picked himself up, then pushed through the door leading back into the heart of the building.

Scott's advantage was that he knew the building. And he had planned his getaway even before stepping into court. Finally reaching the other side of the building, Scott yanked open a door, leading to another set of steps. Down two more floors, hoisting himself up and over a rail, dropping to the ground; then he shoved open an emergency exit door to the outside.

He took a breath and wiped the sweat from his eyes. On the street, parked illegally fifty yards away, was a car. A turbo-charged Saab. The new rental car he had acquired on his way to the courthouse to make it harder for the mobsters to trail him.

Cautiously at first, looking back and forth to make sure no one had seen him, he began a slow jog toward the car. He was in the clear, a full run now, the Mafia hit man still wandering lost through the courthouse building.

Scott sprinted the last ten yards, jumped behind the wheel, and laid rubber for half a block in front of the courthouse.

"*Son of a bitch!*" he shouted, punching the roof of the car.

Russ thinks he got away with twisting the facts of my testimony? No way. No way in hell. Not as long as I've got a breath left in my body.

Scott stomped down on the accelerator and felt the car surge like the adrenaline pumping through his veins.

Paula grabbed the stack of messages off her secretary's desk before she rushed into her office. The phone rang as she was entering her door.

"Get that, Marla," Paula ordered brusquely. She was in no mood for niceties.

Paula quickly scanned the messages. The chairman of the local Chamber of Commerce asking her to speak. Shelby Trimble, bless his soul, wanting to know if the new office arrangements for her Secret Service escort were to her liking and if there was anything else he could do to make them more comfortable. There was also a message to return a call from Peter Lambuth at the *Washington Post*. He had been one of the many after her for an interview. He had called three times already.

Marla answered the phone and put the person on hold. "It's Mr. Lambuth again from the *Post*," she called into Paula's office.

Lambuth was the best known and most respected of the Washington investigative reporters. He and Paula had often joked during the campaign about how Jim Candler would be the dullest president since Jimmy Carter and put Lambuth out of business. Lambuth and the other investigators in the media had spent months trying to dig up dirt on her husband. They found nothing. No dirt, no juicy columns. How would he continue to justify his fat salary? she once asked him.

If they hadn't been such good friends, she would have had Helen handle the call.

"I'll take it in here," Paula said. She shut the door and picked up the phone. "Hello."

"Paula, I didn't know you had such an extensive criminal record."

The statement so flustered Paula it took her a moment to gather her thoughts.

"Peter . . . How are you? What did you just say?"

"Oddest thing. Someone faxed me a printout of your police record early this morning. I must say I am very disappointed to learn what a scofflaw our new First Lady is. Failure to come to a complete stop at an intersection? Kind of makes me wonder about all the other things you *didn't* get caught doing."

Paula was relieved it was nothing more. She half laughed, which primed Lambuth, who roared over the phone. He was clearly amused.

"Why would someone send this to me?" he asked.

"I don't know. Practical joke. Some crank."

"Well, if this is the worst you've ever done, you've lived a pretty boring life. You should see my record."

"I probably shouldn't. It might lower my opinion of you even more than it is."

"Is that possible?"

They laughed.

"Hey, I wouldn't be doing my job if I didn't follow up on hot tips like this."

"You're not going to press with this, are you?" Paula said jokingly.

"What? Miss out on an exclusive like this? Actually, I'm running it through the shredder as we speak. Hear that?"

"Thanks. I feel safer knowing that you're the keeper of my deepest, darkest secrets."

"By the way, about that interview . . ."

"As soon as I get caught up on work. I promise you'll have the first one."

Paula said good-bye and hit the speed-dial button for Del's mobile telephone number.

"Yo," he answered.

"It's begun," Paula said. "They sent an anonymous copy of my traffic violation from college to Lambuth at the *Post*. I was wondering all day why Russ was going overboard to be so nice to me in court."

"They want you to panic. Don't give in. Lambuth's not going to run with some crazy shit like that. Even if he does, it just humanizes you."

"But what about the next time? And the next? What other clues will they feed him? Are they just going to keep dribbling out information like this, slowly, agonizingly, to heighten my anxiety? How long will it take Lambuth or someone like him to put all the pieces together?"

Del was silent.

"They did this to remind us of the power they have over us," Paula said. "Eventually they'll involve Jim in this. Aggressive reporters like Lambuth aren't going to walk away from a story smelling of scandal involving a new president. They'll keep hammering away, following the trail until—"

"Don't worry about Lambuth," Del said. "If I have to, I'll call and tell him it was some nutter. I've always shot straight with those media guys—never had a reason not to."

"Until now. Del, I have this horrible vision of Jim having to answer questions about the whole affair at some news conference."

"Russ knows you're most sensitive about how your situation affects Jim. They're still bluffing. Jim's squeaky clean and the media know it."

"That's what people have said about almost every president in the last twenty years. I don't need to give you a history lesson on how the mighty have fallen. Lambuth knows every president is human, and humans have faults. Every one of them."

Del carefully asked, "And Jim's fault is?"

Of the hundreds of hours she had spent agonizing over her dilemma, the question Del asked had never before broken through her conscience.

"Me," she said quietly.

Del gave her a moment for the thought to sink in.

"Paula, you have to tough this out. For your sake and Jim's. I'm involved in this just as much as you are, and if I can do it, so can you. We're in this together. This has come down to a contest of wills. A battle of grit and determination and sheer staying power. We can win this thing. I told you I'm staying with you until it's over."

"I'm not sure when it's ever going to be over. I can't bear the thought of Jim finding out. Or the kids. It would just kill me. They're the most precious things in the world to me."

"Don't let them shake you up. If Russ didn't already expose what you did after you betrayed him last night, my feeling is he's not going to do anything. Plus, I heard he was the perfect gentleman in court this morning."

"And you're not going to try to change my mind about not cooperating?"

"Never."

"I desperately need your help. You're sure?"

"Without any doubt whatsoever."

Paula trusted Del's instincts. His reassurances gave her hope. She felt ready to do battle.

"I was just on my way out to lunch," Del said. "I can swing by the courthouse afterward if you'd like to talk things through."

"That would be great. I'll be waiting." she said.

Inside the Baptist Bookstore, an expansive modern one-story building only a half mile from the federal courthouse, a woman in a modest knee-length dress wearing dark sunglasses thumbed a paperback copy of the Spanish-language edition of a Bible, then returned it to the shelf.

"Can I help you with anything?" a clerk asked eagerly. He was in his early twenties, close-shaven, with an all-American haircut.

"No, thanks," she said. "Just browsing."

The clerk went back to stocking books on the other side of the store.

The woman made her way slowly around the perimeter of the room, finally ending up next to a well-dressed man looking at book titles in the Men's Issues section of the store.

"Thought I'd find you over here," she said, nodding to the sign.

Julia Menendez peeked over the top of her sunglasses at Don Russ.

"This is the last place anyone would ever expect to see either you or me," Russ said.

"Even less likely than a rockabilly bar."

The same nosy clerk circled behind them. Julia picked up a pamphlet on a table, handed it to Russ.

"Here, you could use this," she said.

The title of the pamphlet was *Yes, Real Men Really Do Cry*.

The clerk quickly peered over Russ's shoulder, then, apparently satisfied with Russ's selection, left them alone.

"Sorry, I'm not feeling particularly sensitive at the moment," Russ said. "Especially after finding out that the FBI not only raided my Chicago office, but are spying on me even as the trial is under way."

"It blew me away. I saw that guy on TV coming out of the courthouse. Special Agent Scott Betts. The same one who was shadowing me in Georgetown. He must have followed you the other night to Schwango's, then decided to tail me."

"That's why this is our last face-to-face meeting until this trial is over. I think I put the fear of God into that agent on the stand this morning"— Russ looked around the store—"if you'll pardon the expression. I kept a respectable distance from the witness stand when I was cross-examining the kid—he looked like he was going to blow chow he was so nervous. He knew I had seen him last night. Even if he hadn't been terrified about whether I was going to ask him why the FBI spies on defense attorneys, I still would have slaughtered him. The way the Government witnesses are folding under cross-examination, it's possible I could still win this case on its merits. My one big concern, though, is, did that FBI agent see who I was meeting with? The last thing we need is for the Government to find out we've got something going with Paula Candler. As long as we're the only ones with the knowledge of what she did to that boy two years ago, we make the rules."

"You're dumping me from the case, aren't you?"

"Not as such. I still need you in town. It's just too dangerous for us to keep meeting one-on-one."

"You're seeing someone else, aren't you?" Julia deadpanned.

"I believe that's a personal question."

"I saw a funny T-shirt in a shop on the beach a couple of weeks ago in Miami. I almost bought it for you."

"I'll bite. What did it say?"

Julia took her sunglasses off and looked Russ directly in the eye. " 'My Wife Thinks I'm at Promise Keepers.' "

"You can leave my wife out of this, thank you very much."

"Go to hell."

Julia's voice carried around the nearly empty store. The clerk looked up from his work and frowned at them.

Julia turned and headed toward the front door. Russ grabbed her arm roughly and stopped her.

"Do this without me," Julia said loudly. "I never did like the idea of following the President's kids around and taping them. That sucks, Don. It's going too far. I don't get off on threatening people with their children's safety."

"Keep your voice down," Russ said.

Julia spun on her heels. "Keep your manhood in your pants," she shot back.

"What's got into you?"

"I've had time by myself to do a lot of thinking over the past few days. Did your wife know about me when she asked you for a divorce?"

"What's that got to do with anything?"

"I just want to know."

"Jesus, Julia—at a time like this! Do we have to go over all that again?"

"You told me you were going to tell your wife about us. Next thing I know, there's a message on my answering machine telling me you weren't going to be able to call me again, but you'd like to keep me on retainer with the firm for a thousand a month. Was that check you wrote every month supposed to make you feel better about how you dumped me?"

"We're not having this discussion, Julia. Shouldn't the fact that I called you to come help me here in Washington say something to you?"

"Yeah, it does. It says that you had a case you knew you couldn't win without my help again. That's the only reason you called me. Don't try to con me with some bullshit about wanting to see me for any reason other than your own selfish needs."

Julia waited for Russ to try to make some form of human contact with her—gently touch her arm, stroke her cheek, hug her—but it was impossible for him.

"You told me you loved me," she said. "And I believed you. So much so that even after you dumped me, I even considered keeping your baby."

Russ's face hardened. Other than a flash of the eyes, he showed no reaction to what she had just implied.

"And now you're asking me to go along with this blackmail," Julia said. "You push too hard, Don. I've given you your case, made you a winner. But did you stop to ask yourself why the hell I would drop everything and jet up here when you called, even after all the crap you put me through?"

"Julia—"

"You know my phone number. I'm leaving town first thing tomorrow. Don't bother coming by unless you want to talk about something other than a professional relationship. If you can't do that, I don't ever want to see you again."

Julia walked fast out the door and disappeared around the corner. The store clerk stood with one hand on his hip, scowling.

"Julia!" Russ called through gritted teeth, but it was too late.

Russ jammed his hands into his coat pockets.

"Jesus Christ," he swore.

The clerk looked as if he were going to blow a gasket.

Russ felt a piece of paper in his pocket. Pulling it out, he remembered he had kept the copy of the marshal's phone log of Remalli's outgoing calls.

His eyes scanned the page, finally resting on the telephone number of his client's business associate running the Snap-on Tools franchise.

Chapter 28

Del had acquired the daily habit of stretching his legs before lunch by walking several blocks away from the White House over to Constitution Avenue. It felt good to be outside on the pavement, anonymous, jostled by faceless bureaucrats and lobbyists on their way to lunch, just another cog in the great wheel of the federal government he helped run.

Walking helped clear his head. He thought about the Remalli situation. So far the Government's case had been bungled badly enough that there was already talk among the media and legal observers that Paula might reasonably find Tony Remalli not guilty of Eleanor Goldsworthy's murder. The problem was that Don Russ was pushing Paula for an answer now, not later. The lawyer wanted to know the outcome of the trial before the verdict was read in open court.

Del started looking for a taxi once he got to The Mall in front of the Labor Department Building. The usual queues of taxis were gone due to the lunchtime rush. He stood on the corner and looked up the street, waved at a few taxis, but none stopped.

Finally, a vacant taxi pulled to the curb and Del climbed into the back.

"Where to?" the driver said.

"That sushi place over by the Capitol Yacht Club?"

"Don't know. Don't eat fish bait."

"Just get me to the club, and I'll give you directions from there."

The driver, a large man with an olive complexion and bushy hair disappearing down the back of his neck, looked Del over carefully in the rearview mirror as he pulled away from the curb. He spoke quietly into his radio. Then he pushed the electric button to lock the back doors. Del was separated from the driver by scratched plastic safety glass.

The taxi turned down Seventh Street, the usual turn heading south. They cruised past the Department of Transportation Building, then left onto the interstate.

"Listen, sport," Del said. "You can drive around the city a dozen times and I'm still only paying you five bucks. Let's get us turned around the other way, how 'bout it?"

At first Del thought the driver hadn't heard what he said. Then the taxi accelerated for the length of the Southwest Freeway, made another turn south onto Capitol Street.

"Hey," Del said irritably, "I may be new to town, but I know for damned sure I don't want to be going this way."

"A shortcut," the driver mumbled.

"The hell it is. Stop the car."

The driver ignored him and pushed the accelerator down, slamming Del's head against the back of the seat.

They were crossing the Frederick Douglass Bridge, heading into Anacostia, one of the toughest Washington neighborhoods. They exited the highway and entered a severely depressed area. Menacing faces peered into the taxi as they merely slowed for a stoplight to see if traffic was coming, then shot through the intersection.

Del tried opening the backseat doors, but neither would unlock. "Shit!"

He was being kidnapped.

Then Del remembered. His cellular phone. He discreetly pulled it out of his pocket and punched in 911 low behind the seat with the sound turned off so the driver couldn't see what he was doing. Just as the operator answered, the brakes slammed on hard and the car skidded to a stop. Del hit his head hard on the safety glass and went sprawling off the seat, the phone knocked from his hand.

The back door opened. Del was still trying to recover from the bang on the head as someone reached inside and grabbed the phone from the seat, dropped it to the ground outside, and crushed it under his heel.

The man forced his way into the backseat beside Del.

Del stared into a face that was strangely both melancholy and menacing at the same time. He held the semiautomatic handgun against Del's side with a steady hand.

"Here, use mine," the man said in a rough New York accent as he pulled out his own cellular phone from inside his suit vest. "Someone's waiting to talk to you."

"We've been watching your comings and goings for several days," Don Russ said over the cellular phone. "We noticed you like to walk a few blocks before catching a cab to lunch. We're glad you decided to patronize the taxi we acquired for your convenience."

"Damned nice of you."

"I'll be brief. Closing arguments in the Remalli case begin tomorrow. Either you're going to cooperate or I make sure that Peter Lambuth at the *Post* gets the whole story on how Paula Candler killed that kid and how you helped her cover it up. I'm just as happy with a mistrial and a new judge at this point. Either way, we win."

Del experienced the same disbelief Paula had. How

could a high-profile lawyer make these kinds of threats to the top aide to the President of the United States?

"You must be pretty desperate to be talking to me yourself," Del said. "Where's Julia Menendez?"

"Miss Menendez is no longer involved. You'll be dealing directly with me from now on."

"Well, I'll tell you the same thing I told her. Paula Candler makes up her own mind. She's the judge. She's not going to be swayed by whatever I have to say on the subject."

"Come on, Owens. You're not kidding anybody. You're involved in this just as much as she is. You're the only person she can turn to for help and advice. She's certainly not going to her husband, is she?"

"I wish I could tell you what you wanted to hear. It's really out of my hands. Now, how about telling your goons here to drop me off at the restaurant?"

"This is my final, personal appeal, Mr. Owens, as politely as I know how. I'm not going to ask anymore. You'll have to come to me."

"Fuck you," Del said. "I take my orders from the President of the United States. I'm not caving in to some sleazeball mob lawyer."

"Have it your way," Russ said. "Please hand the phone back to the nice man sitting next to you."

The man with the gun listened silently to what Russ had to say, then raised the hand holding the phone as if giving a signal. At that instant a truck pulled up behind the taxi.

The mobster shrugged, lifted his eyebrows to the pair of eyes watching him in the rearview mirror. The driver shot open the door locks and Del's door flew open. A large man in a suit stood outside, the bulk of his massive shoulders blocking the sun. He bent down into Del's face.

"Who the hell are you?" Del asked.

"The friendly Snap-on Tool man," he answered humorlessly.

Del turned in his seat to see the Snap-on Tools logo on the truck behind them.

The man with the gun handed Del a piece of paper.

"That's Mr. Russ's cell phone number," he said. "He said he'd expect to hear from you tonight. But first he's asked me and my associate here from New York to kindly clarify some of the finer points of the deal."

The gunman nodded to his partner, who grabbed Del's arm and yanked him outside the taxi, then shoved him toward the truck.

"Into the back," he said as two more men emerged from the rear truck door. "We wanna show you some tools we're real proud of."

Paula pushed aside the remnants of a soggy BLT that the White House steward had delivered over two hours earlier to her East Wing office. At just before eleven o'clock at night, CNN droned in the background. A legal pad lay before her on the dining room table, blank except for the neat concentric doodles she had repeatedly drawn. She wrote out the name Del, circled it, underlined it, put a question mark by it, then in a frenzy scribbled it out. She ripped the page off the pad and crumpled it up.

Where's Del? He hadn't shown up after lunch as he'd promised. No calls, nothing. What was going on?

She had come back to her White House office suite to wait for him, praying he would show up. The children were asleep over in the residence. Jim was still in a meeting.

She saw the news segment beginning on the television again and turned up the volume. She had watched it every half hour all evening since returning to the

White House. For five hours she had studied the same excerpts from her husband's press conference she had missed earlier in the day while she was in court.

The reporters asked questions about the crisis in the Middle East. Jim looked somber, weary, eyes red, his voice hoarse. His sentences were thoughtful, measured, meant to convey the stability of the new administration.

At the end of the session, Jim called on an older female correspondent, a former legal editor for a major city newspaper, who had been a pain in the rear end to half a dozen Presidents.

"Mr. President, in light of the strange goings-on in the Eastern District of Virginia Federal District Court, doesn't it seem in hindsight that your wife should have recused herself from the Remalli case?"

Paula saw for the tenth time the same tight camera shot of Jim's eyes flashing. He didn't miss a beat, though.

"As you well know, as the President, it would not be appropriate for me to comment on the actions of the federal judiciary, especially on an ongoing case. Let me say this, though. I have the utmost confidence in my wife's abilities as a judge, and I'm sure the law will be applied to the defendant in that case without regard to me or my position, just as she's done for many years."

Jim broke out into his famous disarming smile.

"Of course, that's just when she's in her courtroom. When she's home, she's the executive and I have to do what she says, even if it's against my better judgment."

The reporters and staffers lining the wall laughed at the President's self-deprecating humor.

Paula turned off the television.

She looked again at yet another message from Peter Lambuth at the *Post*. This time he was urgently requesting her to return his call before the newspaper's copy deadline at midnight for the first edition in the morning.

If Del had been there, she would have had him return the reporter's call on her behalf. What confused her was that Lambuth had said the information about her minor driving offenses was of no interest to him. Why was he calling back, and what was so urgent? If she called him herself, at least she would find out what she would be facing in the morning so she could give the White House some warning.

She had picked up the phone to dial Lambuth's number when there was a knock at the door. "Yes?" she said. The Secret Service let Del in.

He looked dazed, a vacant expression she had never seen on his face before.

"What happened to you?" she asked. She put the phone down.

Del didn't answer. He sat with obvious physical discomfort next to her at the table. His face was ashen.

"I've been doing some thinking about things," he said.

Del's speech was slightly slurred and his eyes unfocused. He took shallow breaths, almost pants.

"Have you been drinking?" Paula asked.

The way Del shook his head had a dreamlike quality to it. "Must be the medication," he said.

"What medication?"

"The painkillers."

"What's wrong?"

Del smiled faintly. "Doesn't matter. We need to reconsider our position," he said. "Come to a definite resolution tonight."

He was making no sense. "What are you talking about?"

"We've been fooling ourselves," he said slowly. "You killed a kid, I helped you cover it up. Don Russ has all the proof he needs to pull you and me and Jim down.

I've finally concluded there's no way out of this. Tonight . . . before I leave this room . . . you're going to tell me that Remalli's getting a not guilty verdict."

Paula had been waiting hours to speak to Del, but this was not what she wanted to hear.

"What's happened since this morning that would make you do a complete about-face?"

Del pulled his shirt out of his trousers, lifted it up to show her the bruises and taped ribs.

Paula gasped.

"I just spent the last two hours in the emergency room. I spent an hour having the shit beat out of me by a couple of mobster friends of Tony Remalli. Then they dumped me in Anacostia. Can you even begin to imagine what it's like to be wandering around lost at night in one of the worst neighborhoods in D.C.?"

Paula had to look away from Del's injuries. "I'm sorry," she said.

"Don't be sorry. Just tell me Remalli's going to walk."

Paula turned back to Del, his face screwed up in a grimace. "I can't do that, Del."

"Why the hell not? This whole thing's about to come crashing down. You have the power to stop it."

"The trial's still not over. I haven't heard the concluding remarks."

"The hell with that! You've heard the evidence. Can you not tell me that Russ has given you at least some small basis to acquit?"

"I honestly haven't made up my mind."

"Well, make it up now!" he said, pounding the table for emphasis. "You don't have any choice. They've started tipping off Lambuth. He's going to be hot on the story if they feed him any more information he can go on."

Paula held up her message from the reporter. "It's already happening."

"See? They're doing exactly what they said they'd do. You won't make a commitment, so now they're going public with the story. But they haven't given anyone in the media anything really incriminating yet. It's not too late to turn this thing around."

Paula was up, pacing the length of the room.

"Think about Jim," Del said. "And the kids."

Paula spun around and pointed a finger at Del. "What the hell do you think I've been doing every waking hour since I found out about this? What do you think fills my dreams at night? If I could see some way out of this which wouldn't involve Jim and the kids without—"

"What? Sacrificing your principles? Get off it. You compromised those two years ago when you drove away from the scene of the accident and left that kid dying by the side of the road."

"That's not how it happened."

"Maybe not. But that's how it's going to be spun. When it comes out that you ran down the Tisdale boy, all that talk about bad weather and a lousy road and some cock-and-bull story about hitting a dog isn't going to amount to shit in front of a jury."

"It's not just my principles," Paula said. "It's the fact that they can blackmail us again and again. When will it ever end? Russ knows, that Menendez woman knows. Who else?"

Del didn't answer.

"How can we trust these people?"

"How can we not?"

Paula picked up the message from the reporter. "He's looking for some comment before copy deadline tonight. Would you please call him back for me?" She handed him the message.

"Will you promise me Remalli goes free?" Del shot back.

Paula slowly shook her head.

Del crumpled the note, tossed it onto the table.

"You're not going to help me?" Paula asked.

"Maybe you need to sweat it out by yourself, get a taste of what it's going to feel like if you don't make the right decision."

Paula walked to the door, hesitated before opening it. "This was never about helping me, was it? It was always for Jim."

"At this point, my time's better spent in the West Wing."

Paula yanked open the door. "Then get the hell out," she said.

Del left without saying anything. Paula slammed the door behind him as hard as she could.

At fifteen minutes before midnight, Don Russ was sitting alone at a table in the empty bar at the Ritz-Carlton Pentagon City. He was making notes for the next day's final arguments when the call came in on his mobile phone.

"Yeah," he answered.

"Russ?"

"This is Don Russ. Who is this?"

"It's me, goddammit."

Russ didn't immediately recognize Del Owens's voice. There was a halting unevenness to it, a hard edge lost, even with the profanity. It was the voice of the once powerful laying down the sword in surrender.

"She's not cooperating," Del said. "But I am."

Russ twisted in his seat to make sure there was no one in hearing range. He was alone in the bar except for a cocktail waitress clearing tables on the other side of the room.

"That wasn't the deal," Russ said. "You were supposed to call me after you'd got her agreement."

"I'm calling to let you know I did everything possible. I got thrown out."

"That doesn't portend very well, does it? You were supposed to reason with her, not antagonize her."

"I've told you guys from the beginning, she doesn't respond well to pressure. Plus, she still thinks she has the high moral ground and figures somehow justice will prevail in the end."

"Oh, it will," Russ said. "When she's being booked into the Richmond city jail on homicide charges. Has she talked to the reporter from the *Post* yet?"

"Not as of when I left her place."

"She's just one more phone call away from complete ruin. She and her husband both."

"And *me. Me*, Russ. That's why I'm calling. Not for her or the President, but for myself. I've got other plans. I'm going to make sure she gives you the ruling you want. In return, I want you to promise no more leaks to the media that might give them enough information to dig up the rest of the story about what happened that night. Can't you see I'm trying to be cooperative?"

"What kind of other plans?" Russ asked.

"It's better I not say. But you have my promise— Paula Candler will *definitely* give you what you're after."

"You sound pretty certain of yourself."

"Certain enough for you to stop talking to any more reporters," Del said.

"I don't know why I should trust you—other than the fact that you know you'll end up in the back of a tool truck again if you're lying—but consider it delayed. No more calls to the media. I'm afraid it's too late to stop Lambuth following up on the information we just gave him tonight, though. Nothing I can do about that."

"I'll just have to believe you," Del said. "There is one other important matter."

"What's that?".

"I've got the same concern Paula does about too many people knowing too many details. I can't justify doing what I'm about to do if this gets held over my head again."

"Only two people know: Julia Menendez and myself. The secret's safe. And it won't come back to haunt you. I give you my word."

"Sorry if I'm not convinced. Coming from an extortionist that doesn't mean a whole helluva lot to me. Especially since you told me Julia isn't involved with this anymore. How do I know she won't go off on her own and try to blackmail me herself, or try selling her story to the press?"

Russ thought for a moment.

"Hello?" Del said.

"Just thinking. . . . I'll take care of Ms. Menendez. On that, you'll just have to take my word."

"It's gonna take more than your word, Russ."

"Check out the local news in the paper. Under the heading 'Violent Deaths.' That ought to answer your question."

"I think I get it."

"You do your part, I'll do mine."

The speaker went dead; the call was over. Scott punched the button to lock in Don Russ's cell phone frequency on his scanner.

Scott sat in a car in the parking lot of the Ritz-Carlton Pentagon City. He had heard the entire conversation between Russ and his caller, someone Scott couldn't identify by his voice. But it was clear Russ was plotting something highly illegal. And it looked as if Judge Candler was still involved.

Scott turned off the Record button on the microcassette player attached to the scanner.

Ever since evading Tony Remalli's goons at the courthouse after his testimony earlier in the day, Scott had been stalking Russ. Not letting the mob lawyer out of his sight. Listening in and recording every conversation he had had on his cellular phone. And now it looked as if Scott's persistence had paid off.

Even someone as smart and careful as Don Russ will eventually screw up, he kept telling himself.

Before he had a moment to think through all the implications of what Russ had just said, a loud dial tone blared from the scanner speaker. Russ was about to call out again. Scott slid the Record button back on. The microcassette player recorded the tones of the number Russ was punching in.

"Hello?" a woman answered.

"Julia," Russ said smoothly.

"Oh, hi." The woman sounded surprised but subdued.

Scott figured it was the same Julia Menendez that Russ and the man had just talked about. He also recognized her as the woman who had zapped him with the laser pointer.

"What are you doing?" Russ said.

"Well, I'm sure as hell not sittin' around here waiting for you to call me. I was just about to go out."

"Not much open this late on a weeknight. This isn't South Beach."

"Yeah, well, you've got a real firm grasp on the obvious. It just so happens that I was stepping out to a little joint someone told me about today which plays jazz late."

"So you've got plans?"

"Depends. What'd you have in mind?"

"I called to apologize. I'm sorry about what happened earlier today. I'd like to make it up to you."

"Unh-uh. Like I told you, I'm catching a plane out of

this hick town first thing tomorrow morning. You want to apologize, fly down to Miami. I won't hold my breath, though."

"I have a better idea. Why don't you let me pick up a nice bottle of wine and come on over to your place now?"

"Don't you have closing arguments in the morning?"

"Just finished my notes. Look, Julia, I've been thinking. Before this case, we hadn't seen each other for a long time. There are obviously some issues we left unresolved. We can talk—"

"*You* usually end up doing all the talking."

"Okay, you talk and I'll listen. I'd like us to work things out. You know, on a personal level. I don't want you mad at me. I think a lot of you."

"Yeah, sure." She was skeptical.

"Meet me at the front door of your place so I don't have to wake up that manager, will you? It'll only take me half an hour to find some decent vino and scoot on over there."

"This isn't like you. Since when did you get a conscience about anything you've done to me or any other woman?"

"Julia . . ." he scolded lightly.

"Okay, okay."

"Hey, just a question: you've got that key to the Crown Victoria's storage unit in a safe place, don't you?"

"It's here. In a safe place."

"Good. All right, I'm really looking forward to it. A chance for us to get back on track."

"Really?" she said hopefully.

"Sure. And who knows what could happen? See ya, babe."

Russ hung up, but Scott let the recorder run. His instincts told him that Russ wasn't through making calls.

Scott was right. A few seconds later, a dial tone, then numbers being punched in.

"Yep," a man answered.

"This is Don Russ. I'll require your assistance tonight."

"Tony told me you might be calling sometime." The man had a distinctive New York accent. "I need to bring some help?"

"No, just you. You've got hardware?"

"Never leave home without it."

"I'll pick you up in fifteen minutes."

"Got it. Later."

Scott stopped the recording. He rewound the tape to the portion where the phone numbers were being punched in to the woman named Julia. As he was plugging in his telephone tone decoder with one hand, he dialed the FBI's number tracing center with the other.

Scott gave the numbers Russ had called to an agent manning the night desk, started up the car, and waited. Two minutes later, the agent gave Scott the Patriot's Inn address nearby in Alexandria.

Scott threw the car into gear and flew out of the parking lot.

There wasn't a moment to spare.

Chapter 29

"Thanks for returning my call, Paula. I hate to be bothering you this late at night. But there's something I need to ask you about."

She'd given herself ten minutes to cool down after throwing Del out, then decided to call Peter Lambuth. There was a noticeable lack of humor in his tone of voice compared to the last time he had called about Paula's traffic violations.

"Yes, Peter. What is it?"

Paula held her breath. Even before Lambuth told her, she sensed the inevitable.

"I got an anonymous call less than an hour ago. A man, I think, although he was obviously using one of those voice synthesizer gadgets. He said he was the one responsible for sending me the fax on your driving tickets."

"Yes?"

"You understand, this is a bit difficult. I like you and Jim."

Paula had lost the power of speech.

"It was a tip of sorts. He said I might be interested in—I'm just reading from my notes—an 'unsavory episode' involving you and Jim while he was governor. Those were *his* words. He suggested I might want to start by taking a look at the state troopers' records in the basement of the governor's residence to see who was coming and going on the night of October twenty-seventh two years ago. He told me he had more information and that he'd call me again. Then he hung up."

Paula felt as if the floor had fallen out from under her feet. Her worst fears had just become a reality. The blackmailers had reached out and touched Jim.

Paula forced herself to laugh, although she was afraid it wasn't very convincing.

"Peter, you're not going to waste your time chasing some bogus story about Jim, are you? It's just not credible."

"Something specific comes in like this, I've got to ask the questions."

"I told you before. Some crank. A disgruntled Virginia state employee."

"It sounds a bit more serious than rolling through a stop sign. Obviously this person knows something. He has access to information."

"So why are you calling me?"

"A comment. Reaction. Before I start to follow up on this tip tomorrow. I'm driving over to Richmond first thing in the morning."

Paula's mind was racing. Russ had made good on his promise to involve Jim if she didn't cooperate.

"You still want that exclusive interview?"

"Of course."

"Meet me in my chambers after my morning court session. Just one condition."

"What's that?"

"You hold off your investigation until after we talk."

"And what do I get in exchange?"

The blackmailers were only one step away from revealing everything. She had made up her mind not to give them that satisfaction. It's what she knew was right. And it's what would make Jim most proud if he knew her situation. He promised he would support her—*no matter what*. He had always told her that she was more important than anything else in the world—any political office, even the presidency. She knew her actions would be the ultimate test of their love for each other.

She had decided that if the damning information was going to come out, she wanted to control it. She would beat them to it. She'd never give them that satisfaction.

"The story of the year," Paula said. "No, the story of a lifetime. Everything. Nothing held back."

Lambuth sounded both confused and excited. "I can't very well refuse that offer. So we'll talk again tomorrow." Then, as an afterthought before hanging up, he said, "I'm sorry."

"For what?"

"I'm not sure. For whatever."

"I am, too, Peter. Good night."

Julia scrounged for munchies in the kitchen: a half-eaten bag of tortilla chips, dried-out carrot sticks, and a jar of black olives were all she could find. She arranged the food as artfully as she could on a chipped plate and set it on the coffee table.

She looked around the room with disgust. Even though it was where Don Russ himself had ordered her to stay, she was still embarrassed to be entertaining him among the scratched and threadbare furniture. She turned the lights off. She went back into the kitchen and got a candle stub she had found earlier under the sink cabinet, set it in a saucer, lit it, and took it back into the living room. It did help take the edge off the room a bit.

She sniffed the air: it smelled of old shag carpet and twenty years of cigarette smoke. She got a bottle of cologne from her purse and sprayed the air twice, waving her hands around to disperse the aroma.

She surveyed the room once more and frowned. It was still a dump. So much for romantic atmosphere.

Julia had only fifteen minutes left before she had to be downstairs at the front door to meet Russ. Now that she had done all she could do in the short time to prepare the proper mood for the evening, she raced into the bedroom to change clothes. She had, of course, lied to Russ about having plans to go out.

She looked at herself in the mirror, trying to decide what to wear. Don liked his women dressed up when they were out on the town, but her experience with him during the weekend they had spent holed up together in the New York hotel told her that he was also turned on by a softer, more casual look. She decided to leave on the oversize sweat shirt and dancer's leggings she was wearing.

She rushed into the bathroom to brush out her hair. It took her a little longer than usual to apply her makeup and lipstick because of the crummy lighting, but finally she achieved the sex-kitten look she was aiming for.

She checked the kitchen cupboards to see if she even had any decent glasses for the wine Russ was bringing, then stopped suddenly as she passed her bedroom.

She backed up and looked inside.

Could she even consider the possibility they would make it that far?

She set the bedside radio on low volume to the classical music station, which was playing a Chopin piano sonata for its late-night listeners. She turned back the bed covers, plumped the pillows, and dared to dream.

Julia quietly shut the front door behind Don Russ.

"You look nice," he said as soon as he was inside.

"You don't look too shabby yourself."

He gave her a brown bag. She peeked inside and saw the bottle of wine.

"Ooh," she cooed. "Something bubbly."

"Already chilled. We need to get it back onto ice."

He squeezed her shoulders tenderly and gave her a kiss on the top of her head. She looked up into his eyes; then he kissed her. A long, full-mouthed kiss of the kind he knew she hadn't expected.

Her free arm went around his neck. He felt her body pressing against his. She leaned into him, pushing him back against the front door.

"That's every bit as good as I remember it," he said.

She smiled wickedly. "What else do you remember?"

"Everything. Every little detail, right down to that cute freckle inside your upper thigh."

He kissed her again. She was totally engrossed in his attentions.

At the same time, with his other hand, he reached behind him and pushed the button on the door latch so that the door could be opened from outside without a key.

"The champagne's getting warm," he said.

"That's not the only thing."

She pulled away from him and, with a look of mischief, led him to her room.

They sat with their knees touching on the faded brown couch, the candle stub burning perilously low. He had been listening to her talk for over an hour. The Remalli trial wasn't mentioned even once except for when Russ thanked her for the great job she had done.

She talked about her escapades as a private eye in Miami. She entertained him with hair-raising stories from the mean streets: heartbreaking tales of runaway kids, some never found, others already turned to prostitution; the sneaky ways of cheating husbands and wives; a sleazy drug runner who threatened to sell Julia into white slavery after finding out she had spied on him.

He actually kept his mouth shut and listened to her for the first time.

Russ nodded and smiled and even laughed a couple of times. He kept their glasses filled with wine. He agreeably nibbled the food she had put out.

She talked around it, discussing everything except what really mattered: the future of their relationship.

Julia was just about to broach the subject when the candle sputtered and finally went out. The only light was from the bedroom down the hallway.

Julia put her hand on his chest, felt the hard muscles beneath his shirt. "Still working out?"

"Every day."

She let her hand slide down to the top of his belt. She playfully tugged at his shirt, loosened a button, and slipped her hand inside. "Nice abs." Then she let her fingers reach even lower, below the top of his trousers. Her eyes widened. "And a rock-hard, wrist-thick, throbbing—"

Russ hushed her with a finger upon her lips. He stood and took her hand, pulling her to her feet.

"Julia," he said, looking deeper into her eyes than he had ever done before.

"Yes?"

"I want to love you for the rest of your life."

She threw her arms around him, kissed him passionately, then led him to her bedroom.

He was even more perfect than she had remembered.

Other lovers rushed the preliminaries; Don Russ made it seem like the main event.

Beneath the covers of her bed in the small dark room,

Russ found a hundred different ways to pleasure her. He explored her with his hands, his mouth. She let him take control. Wherever he led, she would follow.

They touched each other, rediscovered places too long forgotten.

She heated up, felt his hardness. She thought he was about to enter her. A shiver ran up her spine. She was ready for him. She had been waiting for this moment for two years.

He gently drew away. "I'll be right back," he whispered.

"Anything wrong?"

"Everything's just perfect," he said, kissing her hair.

"Don't make me wait too long," Julia said as he left the room.

She lolled on the sheets. The slit of light from the hallway illuminated the simple furniture, the tacky framed print of a unicorn above the bed. The contrast to the opulence of the New York hotel where they had made love could not have been any greater. Yet this was grittier, sexier.

Don Russ could have any woman he wanted, wherever he wanted her, she thought. But tonight he had chosen to spend with her. In this shabby little room in Alexandria, Virginia.

She heard the toilet flush. The loud sound all but covered a strange noise in her bedroom.

"Don?" She strained to see through the dark.

Someone was over her before she could utter another word. Covering her mouth and lifting her naked body out of the bed as she squirmed and thrashed like a gator in a Florida swamp, then carrying her inside the closet and shutting the slatted door.

"I'll *kill* you if you make a noise," the man hissed.

"Oh—"

He clamped a hand over her mouth. Only a moment later, she heard footsteps enter the room, hesitate a moment. Without warning, there was the sound of six shots fired quickly from a silenced semiautomatic handgun, the bullets tearing into the bed.

Julia flinched with each shot. She fought the urge to scream.

"Shhh," the man holding her warned.

"Come on!" she heard Russ whisper harshly from outside the room.

"All right," another man's voice answered. Then another three shots were fired.

"Let's go," Russ said.

"Okay, okay."

The man who had fired the gun left the room. In another few moments Julia heard the front door to her suite close.

The man holding her in the closet kept his hand over her mouth.

"Listen!" he whispered into her ear.

They both listened. The sound of the hotel's front door closing. Two pairs of footsteps walking briskly on the sidewalk. A car engine turning over, then driving away.

And then nothing but the sound of two hearts pounding hard and fast inside the closet.

Chapter 30

Paula met up with Chief Judge Malcolm Crane inside the courthouse elevator. He held down the Open button as Paula arrived with her Secret Service escort.

"Malcolm!" she said. He had been away for two days to La Jolla, California, for a national meeting of federal chief judges. "How was California?"

"You'll notice the nice, even tan I've acquired," he said drolly.

The Secret Service agents couldn't restrain a snicker.

As they rode up Malcolm said, "You're just about to wrap up the Remalli case?"

"Yes. I hear closing arguments today. Have you got a few minutes before court?"

"Absolutely. As much time as you want."

Malcolm nodded like royalty to people he knew as they walked down the corridor to his office. They chatted about the weather out west and how much Malcolm hated airports and how good it was to be back in Virginia among "real" people. "Those people out there are kooks," he said.

The Secret Service agents parked themselves in the chief judge's reception area as Paula and Malcolm went inside his private office.

Malcolm sat on the couch and started his pipe-lighting routine. He didn't look at her as she settled across from him. "Yes?" he said.

"Malcolm . . ." Even after being confirmed a federal judge she still felt uncomfortable calling her old law school mentor by his first name. "Have you ever had a case where you felt a decision you made was on the tail end of the curve, just within the absolute limits of what could be considered to be reasonable?" Malcolm didn't answer. He was still concentrating on getting his pipe lit. "Did you ever find some way to rationalize allowing a man whom you knew was guilty of a serious crime to walk free, just because of some personal considerations you had?"

"What is this?" he chuckled. "A seminar class in legal ethics?" But then he assumed a grave look. "Those are two distinct questions, each with distinct answers."

The pipe finally aglow, Malcolm leaned back into the couch.

Paula had said as much as she dared. Delving any deeper would cross the line of what she knew Malcolm would think appropriate. As long as they were talking in generalities, Malcolm was comfortable. But she knew he understood she was talking about the Remalli case; he just didn't know how burdensome those "personal considerations" really were.

"Yes," he said, "I've made decisions that were in the extreme tail end of the curve of reasonableness. And it was always in favor of the defendant. That's not because I'm a judge with a liberal bent, as I've heard it said about me, but because that's what the law says we must do to protect the rights of the innocent. And, no, to answer your second question, I have never knowingly allowed a defendant to walk free because of my own personal considerations. But then, I've never had a case quite like yours." He raised an eyebrow at Paula.

Paula stared at her hands in her lap. She was waiting for more. Some small word that would tell her what to do.

"I've sat as finder of fact on many cases, mostly civil, but a few criminal," he said. "It's an awesome responsibility. Usually we can just sit up on the bench and pontificate about this or that and grunt orders and abuse the lawyers and not even pay close attention to the case, because we know it's not we who are going to decide the fate of someone, but a jury. But when you're a finder of fact, everything comes down to you. And in a capital murder case like yours, a man could live or die based on your decision.

"I've also never had the close media scrutiny you've undergone," he continued. "Not only have you been accorded celebrity status because your husband is the President, but this is a high-profile murder case with both attorneys coming into court each day thinking they're about to do battle at Armageddon."

Paula looked thoughtfully into Malcolm's face. Could he sense how close to the brink of disaster she had come?

"You're a judge," Malcolm said, "and a damned good one. You've been deemed worthy enough to sit on the federal district court bench and empowered to make important decisions. This is your job. I can't tell you what to do. No one can. You can listen to me, the lawyers, the media, and your law clerk. But the only voice that matters is the one inside your own head."

Paula smiled weakly. Malcolm must have been able to see that she was still struggling. He reached across to his desk and picked up a book.

"Looked at one of these lately?" he asked.

It was an old Bible, its black leather cover cracked, pages yellow and brittle with age. It must have been on his desk all the other times she was in there, but she had not taken any notice of it before.

"This book has been in my family for over a hundred

and fifty years. It was the Bible owned by the Crane who was freed as a slave from a farm only ten miles from where we're sitting. My grandmother gave this to me on the day I was sworn in. You were there, too, so you'd know. You remember how she stood beside my wife and held her hand under the Good Book? I'll never forget the look on her face, or what she told me afterward. She was so proud. She said, 'Malcolm, you have an awesome responsibility. Before, you were helping people learn the law, and a teacher is a respectable job. But now you are surely doing the Lord's work.' "

Paula smiled. She and Jim had sat with Malcolm and his family at her funeral the previous year.

Malcolm flipped through the pages of the book, placing his finger in the text. He read: " 'For with the judgment you pronounce you will be judged, and the measure you give will be the measure you get.' "

Paula felt herself blush, but Malcolm didn't see it.

"I know you've got one of these around somewhere," Malcolm said, "because I held it when I swore *you* in a few years back. I don't mean to get all preachy on you, but if you're still looking for answers, you might consider this." He thumped the book.

"I'm afraid I'm not much of a Bible reader, Malcolm."

He shrugged. "All the same, there's great wisdom in those pages, whether you're a regular Sunday go-to-meetin' person or not. Something to think about."

Paula was slightly embarrassed with all the church talk. She glanced at her watch, then stood. "I've got final arguments today," she said.

"I understand."

Malcolm walked her to the door.

"Thanks, Malcolm."

Paula looked at his face, wondered what his expression would be after all hell broke loose and he learned she was a child killer. At least for her final case as a federal judge he would know she had listened to him and had not caved in to all the personal pressures.

"I have no doubt you'll do the right thing," he said.

In the solitude of her office, Paula opened a drawer at the bottom of her desk, reached into the back, and pulled out the small Bible that her children had given her to be used for her swearing-in ceremony three years earlier.

Inside was an inscription, in the shaky handwriting of a child: "To Mom—We know you'll be just as good a judge as you are a mother. Love, Chip and Missy." There was a heart drawn by her daughter and a stick-figure picture of a judge behind the bench with an oversize gavel drawn by her son.

Tears came to her eyes.

She leafed through the pages of the book. She didn't even know where to begin. It had been years since she had read it, back when she was a girl in Sunday school in a small town in western Virginia. Back then she had to memorize Bible verses every week. She used to be able to recite the names of all the books of the Bible in order, but no more. She had forgotten everything, and there wasn't time to relearn what had been lost over so many years. She was due to hear Lloyd Chapman's summary arguments in the Remalli case in less than five minutes.

The Bible hadn't been cracked since the swearing-in ceremony.

Except once.

She turned to a bookmark near the back, a photocopy of a newspaper clipping Del had given her when he first told her about the blackmail—the obituary for Billy Tisdale.

She didn't have to read it again. She had read it enough times over the past two weeks so that the details of the boy's life and the funeral arrangements were forever etched into her memory.

The contrast with the death notice and the life-affirming inscription from her own children was heartbreaking.

"I know what I must do," she said out loud.

She closed her eyes and said the closest thing to a real prayer she had said in thirty years: "Please help me."

The intercom buzzed, breaking her trance.

"Mr. Owens is on hold," Marla said.

Paula thought for a moment. "Thank you, I'll take it."

She took a deep breath, picked up the phone. "Yes?" she said in a monotone.

"One last chance," Del said. "The moment of decision. You've got to tell me right now. What's it going to be?"

Paula looked at the newspaper clipping inside the Bible. "I'll decide in accordance with the facts of the case," she said evenly. "When the lawyers are both finished talking."

"I take that as a no."

"Take it however you'd like."

"What is this bullshit? Do I need to remind you that drastic measures will be taken?"

The fact that Del himself—the Candlers' oldest and closest friend and adviser—was now threatening her shook her for a moment, but then she remembered Malcolm's words and regained her composure. "I'm going to do the right thing. Now, if you'll excuse me, I have a courtroom waiting for me."

Del had already hung up before she had finished her sentence.

* * *

Paula sat serenely on the bench, the only cool head in the courtroom.

Reporters elbowed each other irritably in the seats, even more crowded by members of the public, who were now only being allowed fifteen minutes at a time inside for what was to be the last day of the Remalli case. The two opposing lawyers stared at legal pads covered with bulleted points and heavily underlined phrases.

Paula's usual Secret Service escort were more visible—Richard Mobley standing on one side of the bench, Ted Branson on the other. With their clenched jaws, and bulging suit coats, they were far more imposing than any criminal defendant she had ever had in her courtroom. Branson had enlisted the help of six additional Secret Service agents. They were sitting surreptitiously among the spectators, just in case the unexpected happened.

Branson had also requested that additional U.S. marshals be brought in to control the crowds outside, and to prevent any possible disruptions inside. Two extra marshals were posted at each of the exits, and an additional pair were seated behind Remalli.

The defendant's eyes were cast mournfully up over her head to the seal of the Federal District Court. Antonio "Rimshot" Remalli, who had steadfastly maintained a minimal physical presence throughout the trial, seemed even less a key player today, almost incidental to what was taking place.

Paula waited until absolute quiet engulfed the room. Then she waited another few seconds as the marshals outside silenced the people in the hallway.

"Mr. Chapman," she pronounced in a clear, loud voice.

Lloyd Chapman rose to his feet, instinctively made a

step in the direction of the jury box, then righted his feet toward the bench. It wasn't often he got to give one of his closing statements directly to a judge.

"Your Honor . . ."

Uncharacteristically, Chapman proceeded to stumble and stutter for a quarter of an hour as he recounted the murder charge against Remalli, offered in graphic detail a scenario of what had happened that afternoon in Judge Goldsworthy's stables, and began logically linking Tony Remalli to the crime.

His concentration was failing him. He stopped at one point in his reading of the transcript from the FBI's hidden listening device where Remalli discussed killing the judge, and looked up at Paula, his eyes almost pleading. The blank face looking down at him from the bench must have been what was unnerving him.

Chapman's timing continued to be off for another few minutes as he discussed Remalli's motivations for murdering the judge. There were embarrassed coughs from the assistant U.S. attorneys at the Government's table. It was evident that Chapman couldn't find his rhythm. Without a jury to play to, he seemed lost. He needed an audience for whom to perform, but Paula was giving him no satisfaction, no reaction one way or the other.

Then Chapman turned to his desk for a glass of water and saw the crowd: the local media, the wire services, the national network reporters. A face was pressed against the glass of the rear door—one of *his* public— trying to get a look at the great drama being played out. Now Chapman had found his true audience.

He quickly threw away his script, walked away from the lectern and left his legal pad behind. He began speaking in easy-to-report sound bites.

"I'll not dwell any further on the evidence that the

Government has already presented. I'm sure the court remembers well the facts of the case."

Chapman paused, sucked in his lower lip, dropped his head, and turned so the media could get a good look at his brooding profile.

"Everyone here has heard the tapes," he started off quietly. "No *reasonable* person," he emphasized, "could dispute that those are the words of a vicious killer.

"Mr. Remalli has been portrayed as an asset to his newly adopted community. A successful small business-man, an *entrepreneur*." Chapman spoke the word sar-castically. "Well, *his* kind of business we don't need in this town."

Chapman had regained his stride. He was facing Paula but playing to the audience behind him.

"Opposing counsel has tried to ridicule the Govern-ment for wanting to keep people like him out of this community, off the streets." Chapman shook his head in disgust. "The public knows what Mr. Remalli is. And I have no doubt whatsoever that the court also knows what Mr. Remalli is: a cold-blooded killer who resorts to murdering a distinguished jurist exercising the duties of her office, then bragging about this heinous act as he's merrily looking at the newspaper report of her death. I am sickened."

Chapman paused, put a finger to his lips as if physi-cally nauseated. He swallowed hard.

"This is the man seated at that table, Your Honor, whose attorney has tried to dress him up in a Brooks Brothers suit and a hundred-dollar haircut and present him as a candidate for Rotary's Citizen of the Year."

Paula kept her eyes on Chapman, but in her periph-eral vision she saw Remalli stiffen.

Chapman spread his hands on his chest. "I do not apologize for that characterization. Indeed, I challenge anyone of intelligence to offer any proof to the contrary. In fact, the defense had the opportunity to rebut that characterization and refused to do so. The best defense counsel could do was to spend day after day insulting fine public servants. I take it that the court's intelligence will not be equally insulted by the façade of respectability presented by his attorney."

Chapman was gathering strength.

"Throughout this trial, I've heard it said that I have taken on too much. Picked the wrong battle, challenged the wrong opponent. No, I will gladly carry that burden. If I am known for nothing else in my life other than being the man who kept a monster like Antonio Remalli off the streets, I will consider myself to have accomplished much, and will go to my grave a fulfilled man."

Chapman paused again thoughtfully. "Why do we do it?" he asked. He swung his arm wide, encompassing the entire courtroom. "For the brave men and women in the FBI and the police departments who risk their lives fighting crime on the streets. For my colleagues at the Government table and the others behind the scenes who have toiled endlessly to pull this case together under the most arduous of circumstances. For the people sitting in the back of the room, who will leave here today and tell the whole country that we're not going to allow vicious criminals to rule the streets anymore. And mostly, Your Honor, for the men and women and children outside that door." He pointed at the back of the courtroom without turning away from Paula.

"But, Your Honor, if you truly feel—after listening to those tapes—that this man is not the murderer of Judge Eleanor Goldsworthy . . . then set him free. In fact, our system of justice *insists* that he go free. But I . . . I would not want that on my conscience."

Chapman shook his head slowly. He smiled to himself and said carefully, "No . . . I would not want to be the person"—he swung suddenly and pointed at Remalli—"who let this killer loose in our community. To walk freely among our husbands and wives and children." Chapman assumed a reflective attitude. "If I may be frank, I myself would not want to live in the same community as this man. To chance running into him, knowing what he had done to Judge Goldsworthy. And, with all due respect, Your Honor, I doubt that after hearing those tapes, you yourself would want to run into him either."

Chapman looked to Paula, who still had shown no response. But it did not seem to bother him, now that the evidence had been presented and his summation had been redirected to the larger community, a jury who was judging *him*.

Beneath the calm surface which everyone saw in the courtroom, every nerve of Paula's body seemed to be firing at once. Out of sight behind her desk she was repeatedly capping and uncapping a fountain pen. Then she realized what she was doing, remembered that the pen had been a gift from Del Owens upon her being sworn in as a judge. She threw the pen into the trash.

Chapman picked up a copy of the Federal Statutes and held it high. "Quite simply, Your Honor, the federal statute on murder was written specifically for cold-blooded killers like this. You are the conscience of the community. I," he said with an almost imperceptible bow, "I am merely a public servant, whose job it is to bring before the courts of justice those who are unable to follow the rules that society has given us all to live by. My duty today is to ensure that this community remains safe from vicious killers like Antonio Remalli. It's now time for you to do your duty—for us, the people. Keep us safe from

this man. Convict him of the murder of Judge Eleanor
Goldsworthy. I fear that to do otherwise would be to
make the people lose faith in the courts."

Chapman allowed himself a congratulatory nod of
appreciation for all that he had just done. "That's all,
Your Honor."

Not a single person took a breath.

It was a daring, unambiguous challenge to Paula—an
overtly political threat, another form of blackmail: rule
in favor of the prosecution or your career is over. Nobody is going to support you for elevation to the court of
appeals if you blow this one. You face becoming a political pariah, ostracized for failing to convict a man whom
everybody else has already determined to be guilty.

In Paula's mind, Chapman's ham-fisted attempt at
political blackmail was totally unnecessary.

"Thank you, Mr Chapman."

Not even a whisper. It was then that Paula realized
she had not looked at Don Russ since coming into
court. Now she turned her attention to him.

He was oddly agitated, working his jaws. His eyes
were questioning. He still did not know how she would
rule. And he hated it.

Had he finally realized that he had made a miscalcu-
lation of tremendous proportions by asking for a nonjury trial? Because, like Lloyd Chapman, he had no jury
whose sympathies he could arouse with a final, impas-
sioned speech?

"Mr. Russ, I'll hear your summation after lunch,"
Paula said curtly. "We'll be in recess until one-thirty."

The Secret Service closed ranks and ushered her
swiftly out the door.

Chief Judge Malcolm Crane was hunched over his
cluttered desk, trying to solve a mystery.

He puffed on his pipe, his sentimental favorite, a cheap Dr. Graybo his children had pooled their money to buy at the local drugstore before they were even in their teens. Its smoke draw was harsher than his other pipes', but that fit his mood perfectly at the moment.

Malcolm turned the last page of the Remalli transcript after a final careful reading. What bugged him most was that the government had surmised Remalli had somehow discovered Judge Goldsworthy had signed the T-3 application for the telephone tap, yet could offer no explanation as to how this was possible. The applications had been in the presence of the judge and the FBI agents in the privacy of Eleanor Goldsworthy's office, then placed under lock and key in her chambers.

Malcolm had worked through all the possibilities and arrived at the only feasible explanation.

He rose from his desk, took with him the docket book, walked through his empty outer office and quietly down the hall. He took the stairs to the floor below so that the chime of the arriving elevator would not warn anyone of his coming. The only judge who had an office on that floor was Thomas Harding, the judge on senior status who was out for the rest of the week.

Malcolm tested the doorknob to the outer office. Finding it locked, he used one of the master keys to get inside. The lights were on over the secretary's desk, but she was gone.

Malcolm stepped into the middle of the room and stood perfectly still. He held his breath and listened. Behind the door leading to Harding's inner office was the sound of shuffling papers. As silently as he could, Malcolm opened the door, peered around the corner.

A short man with a black suit was going through a drawer of the filing cabinet next to Judge Harding's credenza.

Malcolm's voice boomed. "What do you think you're doing?"

The man's shoulders tensed slightly. He did not turn around, but resumed looking through the file folders. "Just doing some filing, Judge."

Shelby Trimble, clerk of court and the most trusted person in the courthouse, was riffling through a file drawer labeled in large block letters that Malcolm could see even from across the room as CONFIDENTIAL.

"You're an inveterate snoop."

"Oh, no, Judge," he said in his tiny voice. "Not me."

Malcolm strode across the room to the filing cabinet and slammed the drawer shut with a loud thud.

"Those are confidential files," Malcolm said. "Only judges are supposed to see those."

"I'm not sure what you're talking about, Your Honor."

"May I see your key ring, please?"

"Sure, Judge." Shelby pushed his suitcoat aside and took the massive set of keys off his belt, handed them to Malcolm.

Malcolm shook his head. "Shelby, I didn't realize you hated Eleanor Goldsworthy so much."

"What do you mean, Judge?"

"Come with me."

Malcolm led Shelby to the elevators. Silence for one floor up. Down the hallway to Eleanor Goldsworthy's office.

Malcolm let himself in. Shelby followed him into the chambers office, where there was an identical filing cabinet to that in Judge Harding's office.

"Which one is it?" Malcolm asked, holding out the keys.

Without hesitation Shelby showed him. Malcolm unlocked the cabinet, yanked out the drawer labeled CONFIDENTIAL.

Malcolm ran his fingers along the tabs, mainly folders marked as SEALED INDICTMENTS. Near the back of the drawer was a tab marked T-3 APPLICATIONS. Inside the hanging folder was a file marked REMALLI.

"I thought so."

Shelby reached out to touch the filing cabinet, and Malcolm grabbed his arm.

"Please don't touch it. I'm sure the FBI will want to dust it for fingerprints."

Shelby's shoulders drooped. He looked even smaller than he was.

"The only reason I could think of for why you'd tipped off Tony Remalli that Goldsworthy had signed off on a wiretap was that you must have known what could happen to her. You knew the mob would try to get revenge on her and stop her from authorizing the FBI to bug them."

Shelby was silent. He removed his glasses and wiped the lenses with his tie.

"I know it's not politically correct to ask, but how old are you now, Shelby?"

"Sixty-two. Why?"

"I figure you'll be well over a hundred before they let you out of jail."

Shelby's face fell; the game was up.

"Just sit there while I make a call," Malcolm told him.

"Certainly, Judge."

Malcolm picked up the phone, dialed the number of the U.S. Marshal's Office. He spoke quietly into the phone, keeping an eye on Shelby, who was staring at his shoes.

They waited in silence for three minutes before a single U.S. marshal appeared. He looked at Shelby with disbelief.

"Everyone's at lunch, Judge," the marshal said. "I'm really not supposed to move him through the building without another marshal. Security procedures, you know."

Malcolm settled into the desk chair of the late Eleanore Goldsworthy. He exhaled loudly. "So we wait."

The marshal moved to a position near the door, folded his arms across his chest.

In a small voice that made the diminutive clerk sound like a little boy, Shelby said, "I have to go to the bathroom."

The marshal looked to Malcolm, who nodded. "In there." Malcolm pointed with his head toward the door to the judge's private lavatory.

The marshal escorted Shelby into the rest room. Malcolm put his hand into his coat pocket, felt for the smooth burl wood of the pipe bowl, but realized he had left it back on his own desk. He was thinking how much he wanted to light up back in his own chambers when the concussion from a tremendously loud popping noise bounced the framed law student diploma off the wall near his head, crashing to the floor.

"What the devil . . ."

Malcolm rushed across the room. As soon as he opened the lavatory, smoke billowed out and the smell of gunpowder filled his nostrils. The marshal came reeling out, patting himself down as if to make sure all his parts were still there.

"What happened?" Malcolm shouted. "Where's Shelby?"

The marshal was holding his ears in pain, unable to understand anything Malcolm was trying to say.

Malcolm looked inside. Shelby Trimble lay still on the floor, bleeding profusely from a ghastly wound to the side of his head. He was still clutching the marshal's semiautomatic handgun.

"Damn," Malcolm said. "God help us all."

*   *   *

Paula was on hold in her chambers office, the White House operator scrambling to catch her husband before he went into another meeting.

Paula had prepared for this moment by imagining the worst case scenario: back at the White House, seated between her children on the couch in the family living quarters, slowly explaining how she had killed a boy about their age. She would tell them it was an accident, but good people with a conscience must take responsibility for their actions. She would try to prepare them for the shameful stares of their classmates.

The thought of the immeasurable pain she would cause Jim still induced an almost paralyzing sensation of dread.

As the minutes passed by, she couldn't believe the thought that ran through her head: *It still isn't too late to change my mind.*

Then he was suddenly on the line. "Paula." There was tension in his voice.

"Jim."

"They said it was urgent."

"It is."

An awkward moment of silence as Paula tried·to figure out where to begin.

"I know this is a bad time," she said.

"Paula, I hate to cut you short, but I've got a room full of people waiting for me. We've got to make some important decisions immediately. Things are escalating here very rapidly. If maybe we could talk later today, I could—"

"This isn't something we can cut short," Paula insisted. "I need two minutes of your uninterrupted attention. Just listen to me. Tomorrow's too late."

She heard Jim take a deep breath on the other end. "Okay, I'm sorry," he said. "It's just that everything's crashing down around us over here. You're all wrapped up in that mobster case, and I'm spending almost every waking moment trying to figure out how not to get us into a war—"

"Jim, listen—"

"I'm sorry. What were you saying?"

"I didn't see you this morning before I left for work. I just wanted to thank you for what you said yesterday in the news conference. It meant a lot to me. You can't know. For you to be so supportive in such a public forum. But, Jim, I've got to tell you—"

"Oh, before I forget. Helen told me. The kids are out today for a teacher's in-service meeting. Thank God for Del, though."

"What do you mean?" Paula barely disguised the panic in her voice.

"He volunteered to take Missy and Chip up to Camp David for the day with him. He was meeting with a couple of big union contributors up there anyway and thought the children would enjoy the trip up to the mountains. That Del. Always thinking of us."

"Camp David? You're sure?"

"They should be there by now."

"Did their Secret Service escort go with them?"

"I'm sure they did."

"Find out," she said emphatically.

"What?"

Paula raised her voice. "I want you to find out if their Secret Service escort went with them."

"Why?"

"I want to know!"

"Hang on a sec."

Paula bit her lip, waiting for Jim to come back on. She heard him asking someone to find out where the children's escort was.

"The Secret Service went on the helicopter with them, as they usually do. What's going on?"

"Who are those union people Del's meeting with?"

"Lobbyists, contributors. Del said they were some people who helped us in the campaign. He thought it would be a good way to thank them for all the money they raised and the endorsements. I was grateful for his suggestion to go to Camp David: start to pay back some of our political debts while keeping the kids occupied. Kills two birds with one stone. Why are you asking all these questions?"

"Whose words were those?"

"What words?"

" 'Kill two birds with one stone'?"

"I don't know, Paula. I guess that's what Del said."

"Did Helen go, too?"

"Helen? No, why would she? I just saw her a few minutes ago in the hall."

Paula said under her breath, "Oh, my God."

"What's going on? What was all this business about it being urgent we talk right away?"

Paula nearly jumped out of her chair when the intercom buzzed.

"Judge Candler," Marla said.

Paula punched the speaker button. "What is it?" she said angrily. "I'm on the phone with my husband."

"I'm sorry, I didn't know. It's Mr. Owens. He said you'd want to take his call right away."

"Tell him to hold," Paula ordered.

"Jim—"

"I'm confused," Jim Candler said. "But listen, after you're done with the trial and I'm done with this Mideast situation, let's clear our calendars and make a date, how 'bout it? Dinner? Just the two of us? I'm sorry, I've really got to go. I'll see you back over here later, okay?"

"Sure," Paula said softly. "When I'm done."

* * *

Paula stared at the flashing light on her phone for a moment, forcing herself to remain calm for the sake of Chip and Missy. She punched the button on the phone.

"What are you doing with my children?" she said with barely controlled rage.

"Paula . . . Glad I could catch you before your afternoon session."

Paula could no longer contain her anger. "What are you doing with my children?" she exploded.

"They're fine . . . for now. Listen. . . ."

Paula heard her children's voices in the background. "Damn you," she spat. "The children, Del? Why did you have to bring the children into this?"

"It started out about a kid and it's ending with kids. It was the only way to get your attention."

"You're their godfather."

"Yeah, kind of ironic, isn't it?"

Paula's only thought was of her children's safety. "I want to talk with them."

"I'm sorry, Paula, but they're busy right now. They're outside. I can see them through the window. They're talking to the other guests who've come to stay with me for the day."

Paula felt her heart lurch. "The union reps?" she asked.

"In a manner of speaking. Some friends of a friend of Tony Remalli. When were you planning to deliver your verdict?"

Paula could barely speak.

"Paula? You still there?"

"Tomorrow morning."

"Unh-uh. *Today*. After Russ concludes his summation. No use putting it off. I don't think you want to drag this out any longer than necessary. We've got CNN on here. They said they're going to cut into their programming as soon as the verdict is announced. As soon as I see that Remalli's been acquitted, I'll bring the kids back to Washington; then we can forget any of this ever happened."

"And if he's not acquitted?"

"Well . . . you know, even in a place as peaceful and secure as Camp David, accidents do happen. Even with the Secret Service hovering. Hell, look what happened to Kennedy, Reagan. A nasty fall. A bump on the head. Someone forgets to properly set the emergency brake on a car. Electrical shock in the bathroom. All sorts of misadventures. You just can't be too careful. Anything could happen."

Paula opened her mouth to make a noise, but nothing came out.

"I haven't the slightest doubt that you'll do what needs to be done," Del said. "I'll let you go. I'm sure you need to get back into court."

Del hesitated before hanging up, giving Paula a chance to hear the sounds of Chip and Missy again.

Then there was dead silence.

Chapter 31

The lawyers, clerks, security men, media and court observers all seemed to rise in slow motion as Paula entered the courtroom. The muffled din of papers shuffling, chairs scraping back, and throats being cleared roared in her ears. The cool fluorescent light was curiously disorienting.

She sat in her chair, gazed listlessly at the defense table. Feeling as if her mouth had been deadened with a shot of Novocain, she said with great effort, "Mr. Russ."

"Your Honor," he said, moving to the lectern. He briefly consulted his notes.

As soon as he began to speak, Paula's brain shut down. There was no question about what she would do now. Anything Russ had to say was irrelevant.

The lawyer launched into his closing arguments, but she wasn't listening. At that moment, her only thoughts were of getting her children back.

Nothing else in the world mattered but her precious Chip and Missy.

President Candler stood over the conference table in the Situation Room to take a closer look at the enlarged satellite photo that had just been laid before him by the chairman of the Joint Chiefs of Staff.

"They've now got less than an hour to respond to our deadline," the general said. "The bombers have been deployed from the base in Saudi Arabia, just as you've ordered. We can strike at any moment after the deadline."

"And we're absolutely certain that the missiles are armed with biological weapons?"

The Defense secretary spoke: "Our intelligence, both technical and human, is unambiguous, Mr. President."

"And the missiles are definitely targeted at Israel," added the secretary of defense. "It's pure provocation. He knows *we* know what he's doing."

The President sat back down, templed his fingers.

"We can effectively wipe out their strategic offensive capabilities and deter them from a large-scale war," said the secretary of state.

"What if they launch before the deadline?" the President asked. He was waiting for an answer when his principal Secret Service agent entered the room.

"Mr. President," he announced, "I'm afraid something requires your urgent attention."

All heads turned to see the agent's somber expression.

"What is it?" Jim Candler said.

"Could you follow me to the Oval Office, sir?"

Jim Candler clearly did not want to leave the Situation Room at such a critical point.

"Go on, Mr. President," said the general. "We'll let you know as soon as anything happens."

The Secret Service agent held the door open as a bewildered President Candler hurried upstairs to the Oval Office.

"This had better be pretty goddamned important," he said.

Standing in the Oval Office when he arrived were the FBI director and the attorney general.

"Mr. President, I'm sorry to have to interrupt you like

this," the FBI director said. "But there's someone you need to listen to."

"Well, who the hell is it?" Candler said in exasperation. "We're about to drop bombs and you've invited yourselves over here for coffee?"

The FBI director nodded toward the door, a signal to the Secret Service agent who was monitoring them from the outside. The door opened and a woman came in, clearly nervous, escorted by two Secret Service men.

"Mr. President, this is Julia Menendez. She came to us this morning with information concerning your wife. We have thoroughly debriefed her. It's vital you listen to her. *Now*, sir, if you don't mind. Time is of the utmost importance."

Don Russ droned on in the packed courtroom, methodically ticking off all the weaknesses in the Government's case, widening the holes even further in the logic of how they had attempted to link the defendant to the murder of Eleanor Goldsworthy.

But, of course, Remalli was guilty. Paula was convinced of that by the facts of the case.

She was equally convinced of the necessity to acquit him. He would be walking free within the hour.

Paula busied herself sorting through a pile of correspondence. She kept her eyes down, unwilling to give Russ the opportunity to smirk at her again.

Something moved in the corner of her eye. A note being passed to her by her clerk.

What now? she thought.

She read the message. Susan was calling her attention to the fact that for the first time since the trial had begun, Judge Goldsworthy's family was seated in court.

Paula looked up, searched the faces of the crowd until she found the dead judge's husband, himself a prominent local attorney. Then she saw two women who looked very much like the judge. They must be her sisters. Seated on either side of her husband were Goldsworthy's two teenage sons, not much older than the Tisdale boy.

Paula reread the last line of the note: *They've come to hear the verdict.*

Ordinarily, Paula would have felt a great deal of sympathy for the victim's family, but in this situation she was gripped by an even greater debilitating sense of sorrow: for what the Goldsworthy family would be feeling in the next few hours, for the sense of injustice and betrayal by the system, and, most likely, for the hatred they would feel toward her.

The presence of the Goldsworthys was unexpected added pressure, which only made it harder for her to carry out what she had already decided to do.

Suddenly, something Russ said registered in her subconscious. *What was it he just said?*

She glanced at the court reporter's screen on her desk. She scrolled back, read the words: *"Kill two birds with one stone."*

The phrase sent a chill down her spine, shook her from her trance. Instinctively she looked up. Russ was watching her expectantly, as if waiting to gauge her reaction. Once he was certain he had her complete attention, he resumed his arguments.

They were the same words Del had used with her husband. It was a signal, Russ's way of confirming that the two of them were now collaborating in the blackmail.

In the Oval Office there was pandemonium. Julia Menendez, after she had recounted all she knew, had been swept away by FBI agents. The President was seething, shouting in staccato fashion to Secret Service agents and White House aides, who scrambled to execute his orders.

"Find out what the status is of the trial in Alexandria. Are we too late? Get in touch with the children's Secret Service escorts at Camp David and surreptitiously alert them to what's about to happen. Do *not*—I repeat—do *not* do anything that will endanger the children. No one up there except the Secret Service is to know what's going on. Is that understood?"

"Yes, Mr. President," a chorus of frantic aides replied.

"Call the press secretary and tell him to get ready to make a statement in fifteen minutes. I'm drafting it myself."

The President bounded toward the door.

"I'll be in the Signal Office," he said. "They say they're good; let's just see."

"Sir?" an aide in the office of the White House counsel said. "I hate to mention this, but have you considered the legal implications here? Separation of powers? There might be an issue of your getting over involved in the judiciary—"

The President stopped, turned, and pointed a finger at the man. "Whoever you are, you're fired. I'm taking direct control of this situation. I'm now personally responsible."

On his way out of the office, Jim Candler slammed his fist into the door.

"I'm going to personally kill the son of a bitch!"

Don Russ continued with the defense's closing arguments for another half hour, pitching his theory that Judge Goldsworthy had killed herself. "This is a joke," he laughed. "The FBI is called in to investigate a suicide?"

Then he did it again. "You just can't be too careful," he was saying. "I'd like to think that it wasn't a suicide, although that seems a very plausible explanation. Perhaps it was simply just death by . . . misadventure. A nasty fall. A bump on the head. Even an accidental discharge of a firearm. Accidents do happen, even under the most careful circumstances."

Russ must have known that she had finally given in—there was nothing a mother wouldn't do to save the lives of her own children. So what was the purpose of mercilessly hammering the point again and again?

Before she could answer her own question, he was concluding his remarks.

"So, Your Honor, I know I don't need to remind the court that it is not my responsibility to prove Mr. Remalli's innocence. I do feel, though, that the public would benefit from the briefest of civics lessons by way of reminding everyone here today that it is the Government's responsibility to prove my client's guilt beyond a reasonable doubt, and this they have emphatically failed to do. When you have taken into consideration all the relevant issues of this case, I am confident that the court will make the right decision—for *everyone* involved. Thank you, Your Honor."

Chapman rose and proceeded to rebut Russ's closing arguments point for point; then Paula was startled by how suddenly the case had been concluded. The lawyers were finished, the evidence presented, the witnesses brought forward and cross-examined, and now the spotlight was on her.

Paula spoke. "If everyone will please be available to reconvene sometime later this afternoon, I think we can conclude this matter then. I expect to be able to return a verdict at that time."

"All rise," the clerk called out.

Paula quickly and unsteadily made her way to the door leading to her chambers. She felt as if she were going to be ill again.

A Secret Service agent opened the door for her. She was so distracted that she almost walked into the semi-circle of a half-dozen stern-faced but anxious men in dark suits blocking the hallway.

"Judge Candler," the man in front of her started somewhat nervously. He presented his identification card. "I'm Special Agent Tom Kennedy with the FBI's headquarters division. I have instructions to have you accompany me immediately to the office for questioning."

"For what possible reason?" Paula said indignantly.

"We are investigating possible obstruction of justice in the matter of the case of *The United States* versus *Antonio Remalli*."

Paula looked helplessly at her Secret Service agents.

"What is all this?" Richard Mobley demanded.

"The director personally has requested Judge Candler's assistance," answered Special Agent Kennedy.

"I have a case. There's a trial under way," Paula said.

"Okay, okay," Kennedy said. "Let's just not make this any more difficult than it already is." He appealed to Paula again. "I'm sorry, ma'am. My orders are to escort you directly back to headquarters—without delay."

"She's not moving one goddamned inch without her Secret Service protection," Mobley warned.

"That's fine," Kennedy said. "We've got no problems with that." He turned and addressed Paula. "Perhaps you should take off your robe before we go?"

All the color had drained from Paula's face. *The children*, she was thinking. She had to regain control of the situation.

Agent Mobley began arguing with the FBI again over procedures for moving her out of the building.

Paula summoned every remaining ounce of willpower: "Hold it!" she shouted. "Just wait!"

Her Secret Service escort and the FBI stopped squabbling.

Paula spoke forcefully. "I am a federal judge. This is my court, and I must go back in there to deliver my verdict."

The FBI man stood his ground, shaking his head.

"Am I under arrest?" Paula demanded.

"No, ma'am."

"Have I been indicted for any crime? As of this moment?"

"No, but—"

"Then you will kindly remove yourself from my offices."

Agent Mobley pressed his finger to his earpiece. "Hold on," he said.

"What is it, Richard?" Paula said.

"The President would like to have a word with you before you go back into court."

Paula looked at the FBI agents. "He knows?" she said.

Agent Kennedy nodded, and Paula felt the floor fall out from under her.

Do I really want to hear what Jim has to say? What difference will it make at this point?

She would tell him exactly what she had just told the FBI agents. She was going back into court to finish the job.

Paula's clerk ran down the hall toward them. "The President is on the phone, Judge. You want to take it in the privacy of your office?"

Paula wasn't about to budge. She didn't want to leave her position next to the door leading back into the courtroom, in case she needed to flee back in there for sanctuary. To gavel the court back into session and deliver a speedy verdict.

"Bring a phone to me," Paula said. "And start rounding up everyone so we can reconvene the trial. Make sure the media knows we're about to start up again. Do it now!"

Marla scurried off.

"At least listen to the President, ma'am," pleaded Agent Kennedy.

He was talking to a deaf woman.

Marla returned with a phone, plugged it in to a nearby wall jack, and handed it over to Paula.

"Jim," Paula said stoically, "I'm sorry I can't talk. I'm just going back into court."

She cracked the door to the courtroom. Court observers were still in the aisles. Through the back door opening and closing she saw the media people in the hallway all abuzz.

"Okay, Jim. I'll give you one minute. That's all."

Chapter 32

At the mountaintop presidential retreat, Del Owens sat in the rustic comfort of the main lodge's living room. He sat low in an overstuffed armchair, staring zombie-like at the television, watching CNN. He had sent the "union officials" off to one of the nearby guest lodges to await further instructions. Outside, he heard the sounds of the Candler children.

Suddenly he was jolted out of his slouch. Without warning, he was looking at the familiar interior of the White House press room. A news presenter hurriedly announced in a voice-over that they were breaking into regular programming for an unscheduled announcement. Del turned the sound up on the television.

Stepping up to the podium in front of the White House logo was Kevin Hadley, the President's press secretary. He shuffled notes, adjusted the microphone, and began reading.

"The President has asked me to convey a few brief thoughts on his behalf concerning the verdict just handed down in the Remalli case. . . ."

Del leaned in toward the television.

"The case has been very closely followed by this administration. When U.S. District Court Judge Eleanor Goldsworthy was brutally murdered in her home last year, the full weight of the federal authorities was brought to bear to find and prosecute her killer. The not-guilty verdict just delivered is a great disappointment, as the Department of Justice was certain that it had built a case to convict the defendant beyond a reasonable doubt. . . ."

Del leapt up. "Bingo!"

"Normally, the President would not be commenting on a legal matter such as this, but due to the intense media coverage of the case, and the fact that the judge sitting on the case was Judge Paula Candler, the President's wife, he felt he owed it to the public to acknowledge these facts and make a statement. Although he—like many others—is very disappointed, the President wants to remind everyone that he is certain the case was decided fairly on its merits. This was a matter for the judiciary, and the court has spoken. There will undoubtedly be analysis of the case, and some people may wonder why the Government did one thing or another, but the fact is that none of this matters now, because there is no reversing the court's decision."

"Yes!" Del said triumphantly out loud.

"The President would like to thank all members of the Department of Justice, the U.S. Attorney's Office, and the FBI for their hard work on the case. He also wants to assure the public that this administration will do everything in its power to continue to pursue the killer of Judge Goldsworthy and bring the murderer to justice. Thank you. There will be no questions at this time."

A voice-over announced that they were returning to their regularly scheduled programming.

Del shouted toward the front door to the Secret Service agents outside, "Tell them to get the helicopters ready. We're going back."

*　　*　　*

The President sat back in the swivel chair in the White House Signal Office and nodded slowly at the television screen.

"Was that okay, sir?" asked the Marine Corps major who was running the office.

"Excellent, Major," President Candler answered. "Now, then, your people have only five more minutes to finish setting up everything over in my wife's East Wing office before she returns."

"Finished two minutes ago, sir."

"Good."

A Secret Service agent stepped in. "Mr. President, Judge Candler has arrived at the White House. She's waiting in her office."

The President jumped up and left the room, heading toward the East Wing, his Secret Service detail in tow.

"Mr. President," an agent said, almost having to run to keep up with his charge.

"Yes?"

"I'm getting a request from the group waiting in the Situation Room for you to return there immediately."

Jim Candler didn't slow down. "My approval to bomb a missile battery can wait for five minutes while I talk to my wife."

"Yes, sir. I'll let them know."

"Has everyone left Camp David?"

"Yes, sir," the agent answered. "Mr. Owens is flying in the lead helicopter ahead of DRUMBEAT and DIVA."

The President shot him a hard, disapproving look.

"I mean the children, sir. Chip and Missy. They're in the second one, just as you ordered. Mr. Owens should arrive within the next ten minutes. Our regular snipers on top of the Old Executive Office Building and on Treasury are on special alert . . . just in case there's any kind of trouble."

"There's not going to be a 'just in case.' All right. Tell Helen van Zandt to meet the children when they arrive and take them to the family quarters and wait for Paula and me. And under no circumstances are you to allow Del Owens access to his staff, either in person or by any other means."

"We've already taken care of that, sir. He'll be incommunicado when he gets back to the White House."

Jim Candler reached his wife's office door. He took a moment to collect his thoughts, then pushed through, leaving all the Secret Service escorts outside.

Paula was alone, perfectly poised on a couch as if to receive some dignitary's wife for coffee. Except for her contorted face. It was obvious she had been through hell.

"I'm so sorry, Jim."

"Hush. Just come here."

Paula stood up but didn't seem to have the energy to move. Her husband crossed the room and embraced her.

"I just wanted you to know I love you," he said. "Nothing in the world would ever change that."

"It was the children, Jim. I would never have considered doing it except for the children."

"I know now, honey. You don't have to say anything more."

What started as a faint whir became louder, though still muffled by the thick bulletproof windows. A helicopter was landing on the South Lawn.

"That'll be Del," the President said. "I've got to go. I just had to see you first."

There was a knock on the door; then a Secret Service agent looked inside. "Mr. President, I'm sorry to interrupt, but if we don't leave right now we won't make it back in time."

Jim Candler gave Paula a final hug.

Then she was left alone again.

Del poured himself a double bourbon from the cabinet in Paula's office.

"Another crisis averted . . . thanks to me," he said. "Oh, sorry, I should have asked. Care to join me in a celebratory drink?"

Paula shook her head.

"Look, Paula, I apologize about the kids, okay? It's just that you pushed me to the limit and I had no choice. You understand that now. Anyway, they're on their way back to see their mama. No harm done. Hell, I think they enjoyed their little field trip today. Gives 'em something to talk about at school."

Paula resisted the urge to grab the vase off the side table and throw it at his head.

"Well, Paula," Del said, raising his glass, "here's to ya, babe. For doing the right thing." He took a large sip and swallowed.

"What choice did I have?" Paula said.

"None. And we both knew it. I just wish you hadn't dragged the thing out like you did."

Del put his feet up on the coffee table and eased down into his chair. He exhaled loudly. "Jesus, I'm beat. Now that it's over and done with, I'm sure you must be relieved. Hell, I know I am."

"Actually, I'm not feeling much of anything at the moment."

"Yeah, well, you'll get over it."

"What really happened that night, Del?"

He held the crystal tumbler up to the sun, slowly turned it, watching the way the light refracted. He narrowed his gaze and let out a low grunt. "What really happened is that I saved your ass and that of your husband."

"You seem awfully proud of that fact."

"I did what I did out of necessity."

"You didn't do anything, Del. You just left a dead child to lie rotting in the open. It was a cowardly thing."

Del smiled to himself. "Hmm. It wasn't as simple as all that."

"No?"

"No." Another swallow of the bourbon. "Why do you want to know? To make yourself feel better about what you yourself did that night? About what you did today in court?"

"I didn't even know about the boy until two weeks ago. If I had known back then, I would have called for help immediately. Regardless of the circumstances. All I want to know is the truth."

"Oh, yeah, I forgot. You're a judge. Truth is your business. Okay, Paula, I'll tell you what really happened that night. The night you hit that Tisdale boy . . ."

Paula couldn't bear to watch him as he talked. She loathed him, detested the sight of him. She found a comfortable place to look, outside the window at the manicured White House lawn.

"We both knew you had hit *something*," Del said. "Neither of us saw anything as you went around that sharp curve. You stopped the car immediately and asked me to take a look. Fair enough."

"You told me you thought it must have been a dog or some small animal that had been hit and run off. Were you lying then?"

"No. I saw nothing when you stopped the car. I went back later on a hunch. It wasn't until then that I found the boy."

"Dead. And you did nothing. I cannot believe you could just leave him. There was always a chance, Del. What if you were wrong? What if he could have been revived?"

"Well . . . I didn't just leave him there, Paula. Maybe you're right. Maybe he could have lived, if you really want to pursue the point. I take real exception to your calling me a coward, Paula. Not after what I did for you and Jim."

Paula steeled herself for whatever new bombshell he was about to drop. Even though part of him was reluctant, Paula could tell Del wanted to talk. To justify his own actions, to let Paula know exactly how much she and Jim owed him. "What do you mean?" she asked bitterly.

"Let's just say I made sure he wouldn't be able to tell anyone about the car that hit him."

Paula was frozen. "What did you do?"

"He was coming round when I got back out there and found him. He was banged up and a mess, but he would've made it. Except that he had the misfortune to be lying in a deep puddle of water."

"What?"

"And for some reason that goddamned idiot of a kid just rolled over facedown into the water and drowned. He couldn't seem to get his breath. It was as if something were holding his head down."

The horror of what Del was saying struck Paula with a crippling blow. "You held him facedown in the water until he drowned?"

"Something like that."

Paula was on the edge of her seat. "You killed that child?" she whispered harshly. Then louder, "You drowned that boy?"

"We couldn't survive a scandal like that, Paula. Not even an accident. You just can't have a presidential candidate's spouse going around running fourteen-year-olds down with her car."

Paula tore at her hair.

"You're telling me it wasn't worth it, Paula?" Del's voice was rising. "You damned hypocrite. Look who just threw the trial of a murderer! You let go someone who killed a fellow judge. A premeditated act of cold-blooded murder." Del turned bitterly ironic. "And now who's still sittin' pretty on the bench as a rising star in the federal judiciary, married to the goddamned President of the United States?"

Paula was furious. "You let me think I killed that boy! I've been going through hell for the last two weeks thinking it was my fault he was dead! How could you do that?"

"It was your fault for hitting that boy in the first place," Del said. "What difference does it make now anyway?"

Paula buried her head in her hands. "Just go."

Del was already up out of his seat. "I was already going." He called to the Secret Service man outside the door to come in. "Where's the President?"

"He's in the Oval Office."

"Fine. We bombed anyone yet?"

"I wouldn't know about that, sir."

"Why is it nobody seems to know anything around here? Guess I'll have to go find out myself."

Del turned in the doorway to Paula. "By the way, you're welcome," he said.

Chapter 33

The Secret Service agent assigned to Del Owens spoke discreetly into his two-way radio. "HAMMER is on his way to Oval Office."

By the time he arrived in the West Wing, Del was high-fiving perplexed junior aides he passed in the hallway. He was free again. Free of the tyranny of the blackmailers. Free to help Jim Candler run the country. He had taken a chance with leveraging the Candler children and got away with it. Paula Candler was pissed, but in time she'd get over it.

"Hot damn," he said to himself as he approached the Oval Office, pleased with how he had saved the day once again. "I'm a fuckin' genius."

Coming from the opposite direction was Peter Lambuth, the investigative reporter from the *Post.* Del hated the bastard but gave him a friendly wink anyway. "Sorry you boys weren't able to ask Hadley any follow-ups in the press room earlier today," Del said as they passed. "Come see me for an off-the-record chat if you'd like."

Lambuth looked confused. "Sorry? What are you talking about?"

Jim sat behind the great desk *Resolute,* rubbing his hands on the freshly waxed oak. At that moment, the mind of the most powerful man in the world was filled not with weighty matters of state, but only with thoughts of his family. The main thing was that they were all safe.

He looked out the window as another helicopter touched down on the South Lawn. The Secret Service agents were unable to keep Helen van Zandt from dashing out to meet it even before the rotors had stopped turning.

He breathed a sigh of relief when he saw the children emerge. "Thank God," he said to himself.

He turned upon hearing the voice of a Secret Service agent. "Mr. Owens is here, sir," he said.

"Wait outside."

"But, sir . . ."

"Wait outside," he ordered sternly.

The President stood and escorted the agent to the door.

Jim Candler buttoned his suit coat and straightened himself as if he were receiving a foreign dignitary. The door opened again, and Del Owens strode in, the door closing quietly behind him.

"Mr. President—" Del started to say, extending his arm for a handshake.

Jim Candler put everything he had into the punch to Del's face. The force of the blow sent his chief of staff reeling backward into the door.

"That's for my wife," Jim Candler said through gritted teeth. He took hold of Del Owens's shoulders, righted his stunned friend, then swung hard into Del's midsection. "And that's for my kids."

The door flew open, and in ran three Secret Service agents. "Mr. President!" one of them shouted as he got between the President and Del while the other two took hold of his dazed chief of staff.

Jim Candler pushed the agent aside and landed another punch to Del's face before the agents could stop him. "And that's for me, you traitorous bastard!"

The President smoothed his hair back into place and returned to his chair behind the desk. The Secret Service agents helped Del to remain standing.

"Get Hadley in here," the President ordered.

The press secretary was quickly ushered into the room. Del looked at him through the blood of a cut eye.

"You forgot I was a drama major at Yale," Hadley told Del. " 'Excellent preparation for the job of press secretary,' isn't that what you always said?"

"You idiot," the President said to Del. "Hadley never made any statement to the press about the Remalli case earlier today. The Signal Office rigged the satellite feed to Camp David showing Hadley speaking to an empty press room. It was all to get you to free my kids."

Hadley nodded in agreement.

The Secret Service outside the Oval Office were trying to stop anyone else from getting through, but the President saw who it was. "Let him in," he commanded.

The Marine officer from the Signal Office was shown into the room. He handed the President a cassette tape recorder and nodded.

The President placed the recorder on the desk and pushed the button. The room filled with the sound of Del speaking with Paula in her East Wing office, explaining how he had killed the Tisdale boy.

"Nice work," Jim Candler told the officer.

The President let the soundtrack run another few moments until he was sure that Del understood the implications of his taped confession.

"Richmond city detectives are already on the way with a warrant for your arrest on murder charges relating to Billy Tisdale," the President said. "And the U.S. attorney is drawing up a long list of federal charges, starting with obstruction of justice in the Remalli trial."

Del was shaking his head, thoroughly confused. "Paula?" he managed to croak. "The trial?"

Paula Candler's voice was heard outside the door. She pushed her way into the room and stood by her husband.

She looked at Del with a mixture of pity and disgust. "After I talked with Jim, I never went back into the courtroom after my morning recess," she said. "The trial isn't over, but I'm done with it. I've got other important matters to attend to with my husband. Up on the second floor of the residence. With my children."

Jim Candler took his wife's hand and led her out of the room.

As soon as they had left, a team of FBI agents entered the Oval Office. Del Owens was handcuffed as one of the agents read from a card: "Mr. Owens, you have the right to remain silent. Anything you say may be used against you. You have the right to counsel. . . ."

Chapter 34

Twenty minutes after six o'clock that same evening, a U.S. marshal stuck his head into the small office where Don Russ and Mike Fein had been awaiting word all afternoon that court was being reconvened.

"You're up, man," he told Russ.

"Jesus," Russ said. "What the hell could have taken so long?"

"Maybe it had something to do with that clerk of court who killed himself," Fein said.

Russ ignored him, grabbed his briefcase, and pushed his way through the crowd clogging the hallway. It looked like Mardi Gras in New Orleans, with just as many police and weirdos. The only thing missing was the girls flashing their breasts for beads.

Television reporters who had staked out positions preened and tested their equipment with their cameramen and sound technicians. Paid runners inside the courtroom would rush out as soon as the verdict was announced, and the reporters would go live with the news.

The marshals blocking the courtroom doors recognized Russ and Fein and waved them through. Once the two were inside, all heads turned and followed them to their seats at the defense table.

As soon as the marshal by the side door saw Russ sit down, he disappeared outside.

Fein was fidgeting. Russ put a hand on his associate's

back and leaned over to him. "We win this, it's because of your hard work and legal strategies. I couldn't have done it without you."

"And if we lose?"

"No way we're losing. Trust me. I've been down this road before, and I know what I'm talking about."

Remalli was brought out from the side door and his handcuffs removed. He was escorted to his seat next to Russ.

"I'm dyin' for a fuckin' mint," Remalli said.

"I'm out," Russ said. "You can walk with me through those doors in a few minutes and buy your own damned mints."

Remalli grinned broadly and slapped Russ hard on the back, then patted Fein's face.

"You owe me big time," Russ said. "*Big* time."

"Yeah, yeah. Just send me your fuckin' bill."

The court reporter came out and took his seat, adjusted his machine. That was the first signal. Next came marshals taking up positions near the doors and lining the walls, many more than usual.

"Whadda they think?" Remalli said. "The judge don't make the right decision, some of my boys gonna cause trouble?"

The door to the judge's chambers opened. Judge Candler's clerk stepped out, a clue that she was about to appear. The air crackled with tension.

"All rise," she said.

En masse, everyone stood up.

For a moment, Paula Candler did not appear. The Secret Service would have to come out first and take up their usual positions. Then a flutter of black robe just on the back side of her chambers door.

Russ clenched his fists to his sides in anticipation of triumph. "Yes," he said under his breath.

Then the judge came in.

Judge Malcolm Crane.

There were gasps, and a low murmur set in.

Judge Crane settled into the chair, surveyed the courtroom over his glasses. "Sit down, please," he said.

The courtroom became quiet again.

The blood in Russ's veins had turned to ice. *What's this?* he was thinking. *What the hell is this?*

Malcolm Crane was distracted. He cleared papers from the desk in front of him, adjusted the computer monitor and microphone. He seemed ill at ease on another judge's bench.

Remalli leaned over and whispered, "What the fuck's goin' on?"

"Shut up and listen," Russ snapped.

"Thank you all for coming," Crane's voice boomed over the speakers. "I apologize for the delay. Obviously, Judge Candler will not be sitting this session. As chief judge for the Eastern District of Virginia, I am temporarily assuming judicial responsibility for the administration of the case of *The United States* versus *Antonio Remalli.*"

He paused and looked first at the Government's lawyers, then directly at Russ. Then he looked around the perimeter of the room.

"The U.S. marshals will not allow anyone in or out of the courtroom until I say," he ordered.

At that, people began squirming in their seats and a buzz grew.

Russ looked over at Lloyd Chapman, who seemed just as confused as he was.

"Please," said Crane. "I expect we'll be finished here in just a few minutes."

Crane nodded to one of the marshals guarding the door leading to the judge's chambers. He pulled out a cart bearing a television, then wheeled it into the corner of the room so everyone could see. The marshal plugged it in to the electrical outlet while another screwed in the coaxial cable into the back of the set connecting it with the satellite dish on the roof. He turned the television on, stood to the side, and adjusted the volume as soon as the sound emerged from the speakers.

Judge Crane looked up at the clock on the wall. Russ checked his watch. It was 6:29.

"I would ask you all to direct your attention to the television," Judge Crane said.

The picture finally snapped into focus on the television screen: an obnoxious salesman in shirtsleeves hawking appliances for a local discount appliances store.

The marshal winced. "Channel Five okay, Judge?" he asked.

"Doesn't matter. Channel Five is fine."

The commercial faded out. The theme music to one of the national news shows blared and the network's anchor appeared and introduced himself.

"We're standing by for a hastily called news conference at the White House," the anchor said. He spoke to an image of a reporter standing in the White House drive. "Any word yet on what this is all about?"

"No," the reporter answered. "The President's press secretary hasn't given any indication as to the subject of the press conference, although speculation is that it must pertain to the crisis brewing in the Middle East, which has consumed much of this young administration's time over the past two weeks. Even the usual reliable sources—"

"I'm sorry," the anchor cut in. "We're going inside the White House, where the President is about to address the nation."

The camera shot was of President Jim Candler striding down the corridor leading to the podium set up in the East Room. Beside him walked Judge Paula Candler. They were holding hands. The President's features were taut, his eyes fixed on the lectern.

The President stepped up onto the podium, Paula Candler by his side. The President pulled a note card from inside his suit pocket. He surveyed the room, looking directly at several of the reporters who had traveled with him those many months on the campaign trail.

"I have a brief prepared statement," he started. "A little over two years ago while I was serving as governor of Virginia, a young boy named William Tisdale died after being struck by a car while he was walking home from school at night. Despite the best efforts of the local law enforcement officials at the time, the driver of the car was never found. At the time it was believed that the boy was killed by a hit-and-run driver. Today I have learned the identity of the person who hit the boy. It is with profound sadness"—the President paused, took a deep breath—"that I inform you that my wife was involved in this terrible tragedy."

In the courtroom in Alexandria, as well as in the White House, there were gasps. On the bench, Judge Malcolm Crane slowly shook his head. Don Russ gripped the arms of his chair and stared disbelievingly at the television.

In the East Room, the cameras clicked and whirred as the President drew another breath.

"I have learned just today of the facts of that evening, how my wife accidentally injured the boy walking in the road as she was driving home. She did not know at the time that it was in fact a child she had hit. She herself did not know of her role in the accident until very recently.

"In her defense—as has been pointed out to me by

the appropriate legal authorities within the last hour—
are substantial extenuating circumstances, which clearly
underscore the fact that, as horrible as this tragedy was,
it was unambiguously an accident, for which my wife is
in no way to blame.

"Only moments before coming out here, both my wife
and I telephoned the parents of Billy Tisdale and in-
formed them in detail of what I am now telling you. We
told them how terribly, terribly sorry we are. Nothing, of
course, we can ever say or do can bring this boy back to
his family and friends. As a mother of two children, my
wife's sorrow knows no bounds for the Tisdales. The
boy's family—themselves now fully aware of all the circumstances leading up to their son's death—have gra-
ciously granted my wife's plea for understanding and
forgiveness. Out of respect for their privacy, I ask you,
the American people and the media, not to intrude into
their lives and compound their grief by pressing too hard
for answers that will eventually be forthcoming, but to
have faith in the judicial system and let those who are ultimately responsible for the boy's death be brought to
justice."

The television camera was on Paula Candler now.
Her eyes were moist, yet she stood tall beside her husband.

The President continued in a somber voice. "The facts
of this matter came to light in the context of a most sinister attempt at perverting justice. As you know, my wife
is a federal district judge in Virginia. She has been presiding over a highly unusual case during which she has
been subjected to the most extraordinary pressure . . .
not of a lawful nature."

Don Russ felt a stab of adrenaline.

Remalli leaned over. "What's he talkin' about?"

Russ ignored him.

"Since this case is still under way, I cannot comment on many of the specifics, except to say a member of my staff has been arrested, charged with the murder of the Tisdale boy."

There was a stunned silence among the White House press corps. The shocked faces of the White House staffers lining the walls indicated their complete surprise.

In the Alexandria courtroom, Don Russ was beginning to look panicked.

The President looked out at the reporters gathered in the room. He was no longer reading from his carefully worded statement but speaking from the heart.

"Those of you who have followed me for the many months of the campaign will know that, even more than a President, I am a father and husband. I care for my family more than anything else in the world. I love my children. I love my wife."

The President paused and looked at Paula Candler, who bravely returned his smile and squeezed his hand.

"My duty is also to you, the American people. You have my solemn word that no one who is proved to be a part of this conspiracy to undermine our judicial system will go unpunished."

The President read again from his cards. "I also know that you have been closely following the events of recent days in the Middle East. That crisis is still upon us. We are working to avert war, but we will not shirk our duty there. I ask you, the American people, to pull together as we have always done in times of crisis. Criminals both foreign and domestic must be ruthlessly crushed."

The President paused a moment for his pronouncement to sink in.

"The press office will distribute copies of my statement after I leave. There will be no questions at this time. Thank you."

The President and Paula Candler stepped down from the podium. Despite Jim Candler's announcement, the press shouted questions after them as he took Paula's hand and led her back down the corridor.

"All right, folks," said Judge Crane in the courtroom. "Would you please turn off the TV? I think we've seen enough."

The room was immediately filled with people talking as Malcolm Crane pulled some papers from a file folder. He gaveled repeatedly for order.

Russ heard footsteps behind him and turned around in his seat. Six marshals had moved forward and were standing directly behind him and Remalli.

"I have," said Judge Crane, "at the request of the FBI, just signed a warrant for the arrest of Don Russ on various charges related to extortion, obstruction of justice, attempted murder, and conspiracy."

Russ felt a powerful grip on his shoulder.

"In light of the affidavits presented to me, I am also removing Mr. Russ as attorney from this case and declaring the matter of *The United States* versus *Antonio Remalli* to be a mistrial. New trial date to be set at a later time."

The judge handed the arrest warrants to a marshal, who carried them over to Craig McNary, who was now standing beside Don Russ. Remalli glared at his ex-lawyer.

Malcolm Crane shook his head. "It's a sorry state we've gotten ourselves into."

He stood up quickly.

"All rise," the clerk called out.

McNary had already snapped the handcuffs on Russ before the judge had made his way out of the courtroom. The media climbed all over each other to get to the phones.

Mike Fein, Russ's legal associate, was stoic, digging through his briefcase. He presented Russ with a newly minted business card, embossed with THE MICHAEL FEIN FIRM, P.C.

"You were already planning to leave?" Russ asked.

"I took to heart what you said about my being ready to do what you do when I was big enough to quit your firm and strike out on my own. You're going to need a good lawyer. Give me a call."

The marshal jerked Russ by the shoulders. "Come on," he said. "We've got to get you fitted out for a new suit. Something in orange."

Chapter 35

As safe houses went, it wasn't bad, she was told. In fact, it was the nicest place Julia Menendez had ever stayed, not including the weekend she had spent with Don Russ in New York at the Helmsley Plaza.

A four-bedroom home at the end of a cul-de-sac in a new development in Prince William County, Virginia. Lots of finishing work to be done on the inside to provide cover for all the U.S. marshals and FBI agents coming and going disguised in blue jeans, work boots, and flannel shirts.

Over the past twelve hours since she had been taken to the secret government hideaway, she had come to know the place pretty well. Two floors of the best wall-to-wall carpeting, custom kitchen, faux-marble fireplace mantel, and brass-plated chandeliers that a hefty mortgage could buy.

It was all temporary. The FBI had told her that as soon as Don Russ's trial was over, she'd be moved. A decent-sized city with an "ethnic" population so her Latino bloodline wouldn't be so noticeable. Miami was definitely out—too many connections, too many people to recognize the woman who'd almost brought down the President and his wife. She'd have to find another city to have a wild time in.

Or not.

She wasn't dressed for a wild time. She wore blue

jeans and a heavy sweatshirt, a new pair of Nike running shoes that were still blindingly white. Women hiding out in suburbia weren't supposed to look as if they were about to step out onto the dance floor in South Beach.

Word on the street in Chicago and New York was that there was a million-dollar price on her head. When the FBI agent had told her that, he suggested she might seriously consider changing the way she looked. She had been looking up information on cosmetic surgery on the Internet and had been mulling over exactly how blond she would be dying her hair.

Julia had barely slept a wink since her narrow escape from the Mafia hit man in her bedroom at the Patriot's Inn two days earlier. All morning that next day she had been debriefed by a team of FBI agents who methodically pulled out every bit of information she had: everything she knew about Don Russ's dealings with the mob, the evidence linking Paula Candler with the Tisdale boy's death, Del Owens's role in the cover-up, the blackmail attempt. Thanks to Julia, they were able to stop Judge Candler just in time from returning an irreversible verdict of not guilty for Tony Remalli.

Voices from the outside, someone being let in through the side door. "She's in there," she heard one of the marshals say.

A tallish, good-looking guy dressed in construction clothes like all the others came into the kitchen, where she was staring out at a couple of hunks nailing shingles on the house two doors down. He put away the identity card he had used to get in.

At first she thought he was just another one of the U.S. marshals. Then she realized it was the man who had saved her life.

"I've never seen you in the light of day," Julia said. "You're a pretty handsome guy." She checked out his ring finger and frowned. "And married, too, I see."

"Last time I saw *you*, you were naked." He stuck out his hand. "We never did get properly introduced," he said. "My name's Scott Betts."

"How about satellite?" Julia said, taking the boiling kettle off the stove top.

"You'll be long gone by the time the house is connected," Scott said."

Julia stirred hot water into a mug of instant coffee, handed it to Scott, who was leaning against the kitchen counter.

"I'm going to go stark, raving mad if I have to stay cooped up in here," she said.

"I'll stop by on my way out and drop off some paperbacks. What do you like to read?"

"Anything with a cover picture of a woman being rescued or ravished by a man. The trashier the better. And I'm going to need some other things."

"Like what?"

"Like stuff you find in the feminie hygiene aisle at the supermarket."

"Oh." Scott blushed. "You'd better talk to the marshals about that."

He sipped the coffee, casually strolled around the room, and peeked through the doors to make sure no one was within hearing range.

"What did you tell them about me?" he asked quietly.

"Nothing, just like we agreed. I said I got scared after Don tried to have me killed. I said I had got out of bed just before the hit man pumped it full of lead. I fled the apartment, then the next morning I decided to go to the FBI and tell them everything I knew in exchange for leniency."

"If they give you a polygraph?"

"I'll refuse to take it. They're not going to chance pissing me off by doing something like that. Plus, they believe me. I've delivered the goods on Don Russ."

Scott shook his head. "You're a brave woman."

"You had a big role in it too, you know. If you hadn't broken into my hotel room and hidden in my bedroom closet while I was primping in the bathroom before Don arrived, I'd be dead. And everything would have turned out differently."

"Well, let's just keep that our little secret, okay?"

"No problemo."

"Thanks."

"I'm worried about something else, though. I heard some of Tony's men threatened to kill you if you testified."

"We mopped up his Washington organization this morning. I identified the men who roughed me up. I'll be okay now."

"I also heard rumors that Owens is singing, trying to cut a deal for himself," Julia said. "I don't think he's going to get much of a break, though, considering he basically kidnapped the President's children."

"No. The FBI and U.S. attorneys will string him along to get as much information as they can out of him. But he's going to be doing plenty of time. By the way, someone told me that he had agreed to help Russ if Russ made sure you were out of the way. Had you heard that?"

Julia still felt as if someone had stomped on her. The thought of what she had done for Don and how he had taken advantage of her affections for him sickened her.

"I figured it out on my own," she said. "Don is getting everything he deserves. Looks like he'll get to be spending a lot of time alone with the one person he cares about—himself."

"You sound bitter."

"I sure as hell am. But I'll get over it. I always do."
She brightened.

One of the marshals knocked and stuck his head into
the kitchen. "Julia, we need to go over some things," he
said.

"Be just a minute," she said.

Scott checked his watch. Almost eight o'clock.
"Which reminds me. I need to make a call. Where's the
phone?"

Julia pointed to the living room. "I'll say good-bye
now."

"Okay . . ."

They stood awkwardly, not knowing whether to shake
hands or hug.

"Julia!" the marshal called out.

"All *right*! Good luck," she said as she left the room.

"You, too."

Scott picked the phone up off the floor and dialed a
number. A woman answered.

"Hi, honey," he said enthusiastically.

"I think you want Tammy. Hold on, Scott."

Tammy's mother sounded just like her. He heard his
mother-in-law call for his wife, then footsteps across the
linoelum floor.

"Scott?"

"How soon can you be packed?"

"What do you mean?"

"I'm driving to your mother's house tomorrow morning. Picking you and the twins up, then we're heading
home."

"I'll believe it when I see you coming down the driveway."

"You must have seen it on the news—a mistrial. It'll
be another month at least before a new date is set.

Rumor is that he's going to plea-bargain anyway to get life rather than risk the death penalty."

"What about the incident report you were so worried about?"

"Everything's going to be okay. Suddenly I'm a hero again. Maybe even a promotion at the end of this thing. McNary was forced to revise his version of what happened during the raid. He's taking a paid leave of absence. Frankly, after the internal investigation is finished, I don't think he'll be coming back. Anyway, they've given me the rest of the week off. Now go tell your mother to help you get packed."

Julia had sneaked back into the room. She placed a loud kiss on Scott's cheek while he was still talking on the phone, then tiptoed away.

"What was that?" Tammy said.

"Oh, just some gorgeous woman I've been hanging out with, giving me a good-bye kiss."

Jim Candler sat in the Situation Room surrounded by military and civilian staffers watching an eerily silent video feed on the blitzkrieg destruction of defensive missile batteries around a desert city. Each bombing ended with a blinding flash of light.

Simultaneously, the President's advisers told him, covert military operations to disarm the biological weapons and take control of the delivery systems had been successfully executed.

"There will be no war, Mr. President," said the secretary of state. "This time, opposition forces have successfully overthrown the dictator and his supporters."

"He's dead," the national security adviser added. "We have positive confirmation. If you'd care to see the photos . . ."

"No," the President said. "That won't be necessary.

I'm just thankful that no American lives were lost in the operation. And that a threat to stability in the region has finally been removed."

"It's been a tremendous success, Mr. President. You were right to respond as you did so quickly and forcefully."

Jim Candler acknowledged the compliment with a thoughtful nod. "Thank you all. Let me know as soon as anything else develops. Simon, could you stick around a second?"

Everyone filed out of the meeting, exchanging congratulatory pats on the back, except a man with steel-rimmed glasses about the President's age. He clutched a manila file folder tightly to his chest. After everyone else had gone, he slid it across the conference table.

"The official letter from the Richmond Commonwealth Attorney's Office," he told the President. "Although they were able to give us their verbal commitment before you went on television yesterday, it was important we have it in writing. I wanted you to take a look before we released it to the press."

Jim Candler read the letter inside the folder.

"No charges will be brought against Paula," his lawyer said. "She's totally in the clear. I also spoke to the police detectives this morning. They had made a decision two years ago at the time of the accident to withhold that vital piece of information from the public concerning the boy. They were more interested in finding out about the circumstances of the accident than shifting blame to the victim. Would have been unseemly."

The President looked again at the folder and shook his head.

"Isn't there some other way we can do this? The Tisdale family's already been put through enough hell."

"I'm sorry, Mr. President, I wish there were. We need to get the complete, truthful story of what really happened that night out—*fast*. The public needs to know that there was nothing Paula could have done. The media is going to get their hands on this eventually anyway. Better we control it than people read about it first in some tabloid. Plus, the Tisdales understand. I talked to them again just before coming in here. They're willing to go on TV and say whatever to support us."

The President shook his head. "Damn," he said under his breath. "Have you still got that other file?"

The lawyer dug into his attaché and pulled another folder out, handed it to the President.

Jim Candler's eyes narrowed as he looked at its contents: copies of the Richmond medical examiner's autopsy photos of the Tisdale child. "What the hell was that boy thinking? Bright kid like that? Near the top of his class? A gifted athlete? You know, we've since found out that he played baseball against Chip in summer league. Brings it kind of close to home. Hell, that could very easily have been *my* son."

"Yes, sir."

"I don't like to think myself naive, Simon, but why the hell would anyone intentionally spray paint into a plastic bag and then breathe the fumes in? Does that make any sense to you?"

"No, sir, it doesn't. The police interviewed the friend he had been with that night. Said they were just experimenting in the garage. Paint huffing evidently has made it into even the better schools and neighborhoods. And apparently there's some status associated with huffing gold spray paint."

"Hence the gold under the boy's chin the medical examiner found."

"The police know right away what the kids have been

up to when they see that telltale clue. Mr. President, the detectives told me it screwed the Tisdale boy up in the head. Bad. He was in no way fit to be walking home along that road or any other road, daytime or nighttime. He would have been totally incoherent, weaving all over the roadside. The police speculate he probably just stepped out right in front Paula, maybe even leapt in front of her. Under circumstances like that, the driver of the car can't be held liable. It wasn't her fault. She was driving safely, well under the speed limit. She's not even contributorily negligent here."

"Damned waste of life," Jim Candler said bitterly. "And look how many other people were affected."

"Yes, sir, I know."

The President slid the folders back across the table and stood. "Okay, Simon, let's get this letter out. I want my wife's name cleared today so we can start putting our lives back together and move ahead with the nation's business. But go talk to Paula first. She's still over in the residence with the kids. She's had a great shock, just learning about the boy's death a couple of weeks ago. Tell her everything you've told me, in as forceful and lawyerly manner as you can. If I try telling her myself, she'll think I'm just trying to make her feel better."

"I understand, sir."

"One other thing. No need to show her those photos. Lie if you have to. Say you never saw them. My wife's been through enough."

"Yes, Mr. President."

"Then let me know as soon as you're done. With this Middle East crisis effectively behind us, I need to spend some more time with her and the children. The healing process begins this moment. By Executive Order of the President of the United States."

Chapter 36

The President found his wife shoeless in their daughter's room.

Paula was sitting cross-legged on the bed, with Missy sitting in front of her having her hair braided. Chip was sprawled out on the floor, flipping through an issue of *Sports Illustrated* with one hand as he flexed his fingers around a football with the other. A boom box was softly playing a CD by the latest girl group.

Jim Candler stood in the doorway absorbing the absolute normalcy of the moment. He reckoned the same scene was being played out in houses across the country. He took off his suit coat, then loosened his tie before entering the room.

"Hi," he said.

Jefferson, the yellow Lab, raised an eyebrow and thumped his tail a couple of times before falling back to sleep.

"Hi, Dad," Missy said.

Chip tossed him the ball, and he flipped it back.

Jim sat next to his wife. She turned without moving her eyes off her work and kissed her husband.

"Just like it was even before we moved into the governor's mansion," he said. "We've got this enormous house, but everyone still ends up in the same room together."

Paula smiled at that.

Missy was lost in the music, Chip in his sports pages.

"You okay on everything now?"

End over end, Paula worked her way down Missy's hair. "Intellectually, I understand it wasn't my fault. There will be no charges. But it's not something I can just forget about, Jim. I'm still grieving for that boy."

Jim put his arm on her back. "And you will. But you know you didn't kill him."

"I know. It will just take time, that's all. Simon also told me about Shelby Trimble. Frankly, I'm still pretty upset about that as well. Is it really true he killed himself?"

"I'm afraid so. Malcolm called and explained everything."

Paula finished plaiting her daughter's hair, put in a barrette to hold it in place. Missy was oblivious to everything except the words of the song she was lip-syncing.

"By the way," Jim said, "Malcolm has suggested that you might want to take some time off."

"Oh, no. I'm returning to the bench bright and early Monday morning. Just like you'll be back in the Oval Office and the kids will be back in school. To do otherwise would be to give in to those who would love to see us fail. I'm not going to make it any easier for them by playing the victim."

Jim Candler loved his wife's combativeness. It reminded him of their first political campaign for state representative, when the votes were won door to door and the battles fought in the trenches. They were both at their best when they were working toward something as a team, each supporting the other.

"Yes," he said. "The whole world is watching us. They will be looking to see how we are going to cope with what we've just been through. We're going to set the example of how to survive a catastrophe."

"Admittedly with a new perspective," Paula said. "Life is so fragile. I take nothing for granted anymore. Certainly not you or the kids . . ." He thought she was going to choke up. Paula looked around the room, at the walls of the White House they occupied. "And not any of this. I'm grateful for every moment we have together in this wonderful life."

"I love you," he whispered to her.

"I love you, too, Jim. I couldn't have got through these past few weeks without you."

It was then that Jim Candler noticed something. He scrutinized his daughter's ears more closely. "Hey, what's this?"

Missy fingered the gold studs in her earlobes and beamed.

Jim Candler raised an eyebrow at Paula. "Isn't she a little young?"

"Dad!"

"I said it was okay," Paula said. "Helen had a woman from the jewelry store come in and pierce her ears this afternoon."

"Just promise me you're not getting your navel or eyebrows pierced," Jim said.

"How about her tongue, Dad?" Chip piped in. "Mike Carrera's girlfriend just got her tongue pierced."

Jim Candler started to react until he realized his son was pulling his leg. "You really know how to get to me, don't you?"

Chip threw the football hard to him and he caught it.

"Not too bad," Chip said, breaking out into a wide smile. "For an old man."

Missy cocked her head to the side in thought. "Then how about . . . a small tattoo?" she said. "A butterfly on my shoulder? Or maybe a unicorn on my backside? The girls at school tell me there's a place in Georgetown they all go to. They swear the needles are clean."

"Don't push your luck, young lady," Jim warned.

Paula finally had to laugh. "She's just kidding, dear."

Jim Candler tweaked his daughter's cheek. "I knew that. Really I did."